Jo Walton won the John W. Campbell Award for Best New Writer in 2002, and the Hugo and Nebula Awards for Best Novel in 2012. Her novel *Ha'penny* was a co-winner of the 2008 Prometheus Award. A native of Wales, she lives with her son and husband in Montreal, Quebec.

# FARTHING

In a world where England has agreed a peace with Nazi Germany, one small change can carry a huge cost . . . Eight years after they overthrew Churchill and led Britain into a separate peace with Hitler, the upper-crust families of the 'Farthing set' gather for a weekend retreat. But idyll becomes nightmare when Sir James Thirkie is found murdered, a yellow Star of David pinned to his chest. When her Jewish husband is framed for the crime, estranged Farthing scion Lucy soon finds herself plunged into a fraught and perilous world in this all-too-believable and dark alternative history.

Books by Jo Walton
Published by The House of Ulverscroft:

HA'PENNY
HALF A CROWN

JO WALTON

# FARTHING

*Complete and Unabridged*

# CHARNWOOD
Leicester

First published in Great Britain in 2014 by
Constable & Robinson Ltd.
London

First Charnwood Edition
published 2015
by arrangement with
Constable & Robinson Ltd.
London

A catalogue record for this book is available
from the British Library.

ISBN 978–1–4448–2244–1


Published by
F. A. Thorpe (Publishing)
Anstey, Leicestershire

Set by Words & Graphics Ltd.
Anstey, Leicestershire
Printed and bound in Great Britain by
T. J. International Ltd., Padstow, Cornwall

This book is printed on acid-free paper

This novel is for everyone who has ever studied any monstrosity of history, with the serene satisfaction of being horrified while knowing exactly what was going to happen, rather like studying a dragon anatomized upon a table, and then turning around to find the dragon's present-day relations standing close by, alive and ready to bite.

# Acknowledgments

I must acknowledge here my debt to the dead writers of English mysteries, especially Josephine Tey and Dorothy L. Sayers, and to the master of living ones, Peter Dickinson.

This story arose largely out of my thoughts on various political situations, and out of wondering what date Josephine Tey could have imagined *Brat Farrar* to be set. Sarah Monette's fascinating and illuminating essays on Sayers, and Micole Sudberg's comments on homosexuality and revelation in Dickinson's *Some Deaths Before Dying* and Sumner Locke Elliott's *The Man Who Got Away,* helped to crystallize various things for me.

I'd like to thank Patrick Nielsen Hayden for wanting to read this book, Emmet O'Brien and Mary Lace for useful comments while it was in progress, and Sarah Monette, Rivka Wald, Tom Womack, Laura Tennenhouse, Kate Nepveu, Jennifer Arnott, David Dyer-Bennet, Janet Kegg, Alison Scott, David Goldfarb, and Chad Orzel for useful comments after it was done.

Every farthing of the cost,
All the dreaded cards foretell,
Shall be paid, but from this night.
Not a whisper, not a thought,
Not a kiss nor look be lost.

— W. H. Auden,
  'Lullaby (Lay Your Sleeping Head, My Love)'
  (1937)

All the brass instruments and big drums in the world cannot turn 'God Save the King' into a good tune, but on the very rare occasions when it is sung in full it does spring to life in the two lines:

> Confound their politics,
> Frustrate their knavish tricks!

And, in fact, I had always imagined that this second verse is habitually left out because of a vague suspicion on the part of the Tories that these lines refer to themselves.

— George Orwell,
  'As I Please' (December 31, 1943)

# 1

It started when David came in from the lawn absolutely furious. We were down at Farthing for one of Mummy's ghastly political squeezes. If we could have found any way out of it we would have been somewhere else, but Mummy was inexorable so there we were, in my old girlhood bedroom that I'd left behind so happily when I'd married David, him in a morning suit and me in a little knee-length beige Chanel thing.

He burst in, already drawing breath to speak. 'Lady Thirkie thinks you should sack me, Lucy!'

I didn't see at first that he was spitting mad, because I was busy trying to get my hair to stay on top of my head without disarranging my pearls. In fact, if my hair had been less recalcitrant about that sort of thing probably it would never have happened, because I'd have been on the lawn with David, and then Angela would never have been so dim. In any case, at first the whole thing struck me as funny, and I absolutely gurgled with laughter. 'Darling, you can't sack a husband, can you? It would have to be divorce. Whatever have you been doing that Angela Thirkie thinks is enough for me to divorce you?'

'Lady Thirkie appears to have mistaken me for the hired help,' David said, coming around behind me so I could see him in the mirror, and of course, when I saw him, I realized at once that he wasn't the slightest bit amused by it, and that I shouldn't have laughed, and in fact that laughing was probably the worst thing I could have done in the circumstances, at least without bringing David around to seeing the funny side of things first.

'Angela Thirkie is a complete nincompoop. We've all been laughing at her for years,' I said, which was completely true but didn't help even a shred, because David, of course, hadn't been laughing at her for years, hadn't been there for years to laugh at her, so it was another thing pointing up the difference between me and him and just at the time when he'd had the difference rather shoved down his throat in the first place because of Angela's idiocy.

He looked rather grim in my mirror, so I turned around to see if he looked any better the right way around. I kept my hands up in my hair because I nearly had it right at last. 'She thought I shouldn't be helping myself to cocktails and she said she'd tell your mother and recommend she sack me,' he said, smiling but in a way that meant he didn't find it even the least bit funny. 'I suppose I do look rather like a waiter in this getup.'

'Oh darling, you don't; you look delicious,' I said, automatically soothing, although it was true. 'Angela's a nitwit, truly. Hasn't she been introduced to you?'

'Oh yes, at one of the engagement parties, and then again at the wedding,' David said, his smile becoming even more brittle. 'But no doubt we all look the same to her.'

2

'Oh darling!' I said, and let my hands go out towards him, abandoning my hair for the time being, because there was nothing I could say — he was right and we both knew he was. 'I'll come back out with you now and we can give her such a snub.'

'I shouldn't mind it,' David said, taking my hands and looking down at me. 'Except that it reflects on you. You'd have been much more comfortable marrying someone of your own kind.'

And this was true of course, there *is* a sort of comfort in being with people who think exactly as you do because they've been brought up exactly the same way and share all the same jokes. It's a feeble kind of comfort and doesn't last beyond seeing that you've nothing truly in common except that kind of upbringing and background. 'People don't marry in order to be comfortable,' I said. Then, as usual with people I trust, I let my train of thought go haring off out of control. 'Unless maybe Mummy did. That would explain a lot about her marriage.' I put my hand to my mouth to cover a horrified laugh, and also to try to catch back the train of thought that had got away from me. My old governess, Abby, taught me to think of it that way and to do that. It helps for the blunders, at least if I do it in time, but it does mean that Mummy has reproved me on several occasions for keeping my hand up to my mouth more than a lady ought!

'Then are you sure you didn't marry me for the opposite reason?' David asked, ignoring the diversion. 'Especially so you could use me to

3

enjoy snubbing people like Lady Thirkie?'

'That's absurd,' I said, and turned back to the mirror, and this time I caught up my hair and the pearls all in one swirl and managed to get it just right where all my careful trying before had failed. I smiled at my reflection, and at David where he was standing behind me.

There was a certain grain of truth in what he said, but a very distant grain that wouldn't be good for either of us or for our marriage if we spent time dwelling on it. Daddy had made me face all that on the night he'd agreed to the marriage going ahead. David had imagined that Daddy would make endless difficulties, but in fact he just gave me that one really hard talk and then buckled down and accepted David as one of the family. If was Mummy who made the difficulties, as I'd known it would be.

Daddy had called me into his office in London and told all the secretaries and everyone not to let anybody in. I'd felt simultaneously rather important, and as if I were ten years old and on the carpet for not doing my homework. I had to keep reminding myself I was the thoroughly grown-up and almost-on-the-shelf young lady I really was. I sat in the leather chair he keeps for visitors, clutching my purse on my knee, and he sat down behind his big eighteenth-century desk and just looked at me for a moment. He didn't beat about the bush at all, no nonsense with drinks and cigarettes and getting comfortable. 'I'm sure you know what I want to talk to you about, Luce,' he started.

I nodded. 'David,' I said. 'I love him, Daddy,

4

and I want to marry him.'

'David Kahn,' Daddy had said, as if the words left a bad taste in his mouth.

I started to say something feeble in David's defense, but Daddy held up a hand. 'I already know what you're going to say, so save your breath. He was born in England, he's a war hero, his family are very wealthy. I could counter with the fact that he was educated on the Continent, he's a Jew, and not one of us.'

'I was just going to say we love each other,' I said, with as much dignity as I could manage. Unlike Mummy, who could only make a nuisance of herself, Daddy really could have scuppered the whole thing at that point. Although I was twenty-three and, since Hugh died, heir to pretty much everything except Farthing and the title, I didn't have any money of my own beyond what Daddy let me have, and neither did David. His family were wealthy enough, but he himself hardly had a bean, certainly not enough for the two of us to live on. His family, which surprised me at first though it made sense afterwards, didn't approve of me one whit more than mine approved of him. So it could have been a real Romeo and Juliet affair if not for Daddy seeing sense and coming over to my side.

'Having seen you together and talked to young David, I don't doubt that, funnily enough,' Daddy said. 'But what I want to know is whether that's enough. Love's a wonderful thing, but it can be a fragile flower when the winds blow cold against it, and I can see a lot of cold winds

5

poised to howl down on the pair of you.'

'Just so long as you're not one of those winds, Daddy,' I said, pressing my knees together and sitting up straight, to look as mature and sensible as I could.

Daddy laughed. 'I've seen you sitting like that when you want to impress me since you were five years old,' he said. Then he suddenly leaned forward and turned really serious. 'Have you thought what it's going to mean being Mrs. Kahn? We share a name that we didn't do anything personally to earn but which we inherited from our Eversley ancestors, who did. It is a name that opens doors for us. You're talking about giving that up to become Mrs. Kahn — '

'Kahn means that David's ancestors were priests in Israel when ours were painting themselves blue with woad,' I said, quoting — or probably misquoting — Disraeli.

Daddy smiled. 'All the same, what it means to people now and in England will close a lot of doors in your face.'

'Not doors I want to go through,' I said.

Daddy raised an eyebrow at that.

'No, really, I have thought this through,' I said, and I had, or thought I had. 'You remember when Billy Cheriton was taking me about everywhere?' Billy had been one of Mummy's worst ideas, the younger son of the Duke of Hampshire, who's Mummy's cousin and who happened to be married to one of her best friends. We'd known each other all our lives, gone to the same nursery parties, and then the

6

same young-people parties, and Mummy's idea had been what a natural match it would have been.

Daddy nodded. He didn't think much of Billy.

'Once we were down at Cheltenham for the racing because Tibs had a horse running and Billy was showing the family flag. We were in a crowd of nice people just like us, and the horse lost, of course.'

'Tibs Cheriton has never had an eye for horseflesh,' Daddy said. 'Sorry. Go on.'

'So we were drowning our sorrows in Pimms, and I was bored, suddenly, bored to screaming point, not just with Cheltenham and that crowd but with the whole thing, the whole ritual. Tibs and one of the other boys were talking about horse breeding, and I thought that it was just the same with us, the fillies and the stallions, the young English gentry, breeding the next generation of English gentry, and I couldn't think of anything more excruciatingly boring than to be married to Billy, or Tibs, or any of that cackling crowd.' Not that I'd have married Tibs if he were the last man in the world, because I was pretty sure he was Athenian, and I think Mummy knew it too, otherwise it would have been Tibs she'd have been pushing me into going around with, not Billy. 'I don't want that. I've been presented and done all the deb stuff and even before I met David I knew it wasn't what I wanted.'

That was when Daddy said it. 'Are you sure you're not marrying David just to escape from that?' he asked. 'To shock Billy and all the Billies by doing something they can't countenance? Because if you are, it isn't kind to David, and that'll stop being fun too, much sooner than you think.'

I thought about it, and I could see the smallest grain of that in me, the desire to give it all up and rub their faces in it with someone totally unacceptable by their own ridiculous standards. I'm afraid Mummy had rather done her bit to encourage that part of my feelings, while intending the opposite, of course. 'I do think there might be the tiniest bit of that, Daddy,' I admitted. 'But really I love David, and he and I have so much in common in ways that aren't to do with upbringing and education and that count for a lot more with me.'

'He assured me he didn't intend to pressure you to convert,' Daddy said.

'He's not very religious himself,' I said.

'He told me he has no intention of giving up his religion.' Daddy frowned.

'Why should he?' I asked. 'It's not just a religion, it's a culture. He's not very religious, but he's not ashamed of his culture, his background, and converting would be like saying he was. It wouldn't make any difference to anything anyway — people who hate the Jews hate converts just as much. He says Jewish children take the religion of the mother, so that's all right.'

'In the same way it would make no difference, people will always talk of you as 'that Mrs. Kahn, Lucy Eversley that was.'' He made his voice into a cruel imitation of a society woman, of Mummy

8

at her absolute bitchiest really.

I can't say that didn't hurt a bit, but even as it hurt, the tiny sting of it made me realize how unimportant it really was, compared to the way I loved David. I shook my head. 'Better that than not marrying David,' I said.

'You know, in Germany — ' Daddy began.

'But we're not in Germany. We fought a war — you and David both fought a war — to ensure that the border of the Third Reich stops at the Channel. It always will. Germany doesn't have anything to do with anything.'

'Even in England you'll come in for a lot of trouble, which your young man is used to but you won't be,' Daddy said. 'Little things like not being allowed into clubs, big things like not being allowed to buy land. And that will come to your children. When your daughters come out, they might not be allowed to be debs and be presented, with the name Kahn.'

'So much the better for them,' I said, though that did shake me a little.

'There might be stings and insults you don't expect,' Daddy added.

But although he was right, I generally found I didn't mind them, or thought them funny, whereas poor David wasn't used to them at all, like this thing now with idiotic Angela Thirkie and her stupid assumption that anyone with a face and coloring like David's had to be a servant. Maybe he was better able to deal with an outright snub than this kind of casual disregard.

I let my hair go, cautiously, and when it stayed

9

up, I turned back to David. 'I wanted to marry you because of you, and I've never given a damn about those people one way or the other and you should know that.'

For a moment he kept on looking pained. Then he smiled and hugged me, and for the time being everything was all right again.

He took my hand and we walked out into the garden, where Mummy's ghastly bash was now in full swing.

What I was thinking as we walked out there was that David and I really did have a tremendous amount in common, books and music and ways of thinking about things. I don't mean usual ways of thinking, because I'm scatterbrained and not really very bright while David is tremendously clever, of course. But time after time we'll come to the same conclusions about whether something is sound, starting from different places and using different methods of logic. David never bores me and he never gives me the feeling that other tremendously brainy people I've known have given me of leaving me streets behind. We can talk about anything, except perhaps some of the trickier bits of our own relationship. There are some things best left to the subconscious, after all, as David himself says.

I gave his hand an extra squeeze just because I loved him, and he looked down at me, for once not picking up what I meant but thinking I wanted something. So I put my face up to be kissed, and that was how we snubbed stupid insensitive Angela Thirkie, who was married to the most boring man in England, who everyone knows didn't even want her, he wanted her sister, by kissing like newly-weds on the lawn when in fact we'd been married eight whole months and really ought to be settling down to life as old respectable married people.

But anyway, when I heard that Sir James Thirkie had been murdered, that's the first thing I thought of, Angela Thirkie being mean to David the afternoon before, and I'm afraid the first thing to go through my mind, although fortunately I managed to catch the train before it got out of the tunnel that time so I didn't say so, was that it well and truly served her right.

# 2

Inspector Peter Anthony Carmichael had been vaguely aware that Farthing was a country house in Hampshire; but before the murder he had only really heard of it in a political context. 'The Farthing Set,' the newspapers would say, meaning a group of loosely connected movers and shakers, politicians, soldiers, socialites, financiers: the people who had brought peace to England. By peace was meant not Chamberlain's precarious 'peace in our time' but the lasting 'Peace with Honour' after we'd fought Hitler to a standstill. The Inspector included himself in that 'we' — as a young lieutenant he'd been one of the last to get away from Dunkirk. He'd cautiously welcomed the peace when it came, although at that point he'd had a sneaking fondness for crazy old Churchill's fighting rhetoric and been afraid Hitler couldn't be trusted. 'This Farthing Peace isn't worth a farthing,' Churchill had wheezed, and the newspapers had shown him holding up a farthing mockingly.

But time had shown that the Farthing Set were right. The Continent was the Continent and England was England, and old Adolf admired England and had no territorial ambitions across the Channel. Eight years had been enough to test the terms of the Farthing Peace and show that England and the Reich could be

12

good friends. The Farthing Set had been vindicated and stayed at the centers of power. And now there had been a murder in Farthing House, so Farthing changed its meaning for him again and Inspector Carmichael found himself being driven through a green, peaceful, and very beautiful England on a Sunday morning early in May.

Carmichael came from Lancashire: not the industrial southern Lancashire of cotton mills and unemployment, but the bleak northern uplands of moorland and fell. His father lived in a crumbling house not much better than the farmhouses of his tenants and struggled to send his sons to minor public schools. Carmichael's had been so minor it had since perished, with no loss to anyone, especially Carmichael. If he ever had sons, which he increasingly doubted, he'd certainly not have chosen to send them to that hellhole to be starved and beaten. Still, that, with the Dunkirk experience, had been good enough for Scotland Yard, and he was a full inspector now at twenty-nine, with good pay and excellent prospects for advancement. Many hadn't done as well in the lean post-war years. His older brother, Matthew, whose public school had been better, if still minor, was living in the North helping his father with the sheep. He didn't see civilization more than once a month when he went into Lancaster to the bank and the solicitor and maybe a stop for lunch at the King's Head and a quick hour at the pictures in the afternoon. It wasn't much, and Carmichael sometimes paused in his enjoyment of the good things in life to consider the pitiful lot of his distant brother.

All the same, there was enough of the Northerner left in him to distrust the Hampshire countryside that was doing its best to beguile him. The trees, so much more frequent and so much broader here than on his native moor, were in fullest leaf and cast a delightful shade. Beneath them spread as solid a carpet of bluebells as he had ever seen, sending their scent drifting into the car as he was driven on past them. The sun was shining from a deep blue sky, as it rarely shone on Lancashire, the fields were ploughed and planted, the hay was already high, the grass was a verdant green, and the birds were singing. As if this wasn't enough, every few miles the road wound its way through a little village with a church, a pub, a post office, thatched cottages, and just sufficient individuality to tell it from the last one. One might boast a manor house, a second a duck pond, a third a village green, or a mighty oak with two old men sitting beneath it as if they were about to hand down the wisdom of the elders. Carmichael sighed.

'What's wrong, sir?' Sergeant Royston, at the wheel of the police Bentley, spared a quick glance for his superior. 'Didn't fancy Sunday duty?'

'Not especially,' Carmichael said. 'Though I hadn't anything special to do today, and I might as well work now if the Yard needs me and have a free day in the week when the shops are open. It's just this countryside depresses me somehow.'

They swept into another little village. This one

had a pretty girl feeding white Aylesbury ducks outside one of the cottages. 'It is lacking a bit of life compared to town,' Royston said as he rounded the curve back into the endless fields and spinneys.

'It's not that,' Carmichael said, as it suddenly came to him what it was. 'It's all so fat and complacent somehow, as if it's had too long living on its rich soils and warm summers. It's fallen asleep in the sunshine. It could do with something to give it a shake and wake it up, like a famine, or a plague, or an invasion or something.'

Royston slowed as they came into yet another village. Just past the church was an unpleasant reminder of the invasion that had nearly happened, an Anderson shelter, with children playing, running in and out of it. Royston said nothing, but Carmichael felt the red tide of embarrassment burning on his cheeks. He hadn't meant the Germans, nothing had been farther from his mind, he'd been centuries away imagining Vikings or pirates descending on these smug sleepy peasants.

'I don't much care for bluebells myself,' Royston said. 'If we had to drive down this way, I'd have preferred to do it a few weeks ago in primrose season. Primroses are a beautiful color, very cheering.'

'I find them a bit on the soft side myself,' Carmichael said. 'Bluebells, now, we do have them in the North. I wouldn't have thought you cared for flowers at all, sergeant. I thought you were a strictly town man.'

'Well, I was born and bred in London myself, but my mother's family lived in the countryside.'

'Round here?' Carmichael asked.

'Kent. I have an aunt who still lives there; some of the family go down to see her at Easter and for the hop picking. Easter's when we used to see the primroses, when I was a boy. It's a good way east of here, but I suppose from the perspective of Lancashire it would count as these parts.'

Carmichael laughed. 'All these years, and I'd never have suspected you of having a Kentish aunt, Royston. You hide it very well.'

There was a fork in the road ahead. Royston slowed to a halt to check the arms of the little signpost. 'Would we want Farthing Green, Upper Farthing, or Farthing St. Mary?' he asked.

'Castle Farthing.' Carmichael checked his notes and his map without effect. There was an area on the map labeled unhelpfully THE FARTHINGS. 'Head for Farthing St. Mary,' he said, decisively.

'Yes, sir,' Royston said.

Carmichael knew the first secret of command, which was making a decision, right or wrong, but going ahead without hesitating. He might have sent them off the wrong way and condemned them to an endless trek through the barely charted Hampshire countryside, but at least he had made a decision.

By pure luck he was right. The next sign offered CASTLE FARTHING on one of its branches, and the lane it led down, with its heavy hedgerows, came at last to an end with a loop around a village green. There was a church, larger than most, a pub, the Eversley Arms, a row of cottages, and a high wall containing a pair of wrought-iron gates with the word FARTHING scrolling indolently across them as if there were no other possible Farthing, as indeed, for anyone beyond this little corner of Hampshire where people no doubt knew one Farthing from the next, there was not. Beneath the name was the ubiquitous robin, the reverse of the farthing coin, the political symbol of the Farthing Set. With a start, Carmichael realized that considering the antiquity of the gates, a century if it was a day and probably more, this particular robin must pre-date the 'Set' and was doubtless the prototype for the whole thing.

Meanwhile, the gates were closed. Judging from the ruts in the gravel, this was an unusual state of affairs. 'Probably the local police shut them to close off the house from press and sightseers,' Carmichael said, indicating the ruts.

'Sightseers? Here?' Royston's London face dismissed the possibility. 'All the same, they should have left a bobby on the gates,' he said, his tone reproving the absent local constabulary. 'Shall I try if they're open, sir?'

'You do that, sergeant,' Carmichael said. As a young officer he'd have got out to try them himself, and lost all his subordinate's respect in the process. Now he sat back and watched Royston crunch across the gravel.

With the engine off, the bird-song seemed very loud. A nearby but invisible blackbird

17

chirruped, 'Look at me. Look at me. This is my territ'ry.' He was answered by other birds seeking mates, building nests, or defending their boundaries. They stilled to silence when they heard the clang of Royston shaking the gate, then started up again, for all the world as if they were gossiping about it. Royston started back towards the car, shaking his head.

Carmichael stuck his head out of the open window. 'Let's give them a quick blast and see what that roots out,' he said. Royston grinned. Carmichael leaned across the driver's seat and tapped out a quick salute on the horn: 'Pa pa pa paaaarp!'

The only immediate result was another avian hush, and Carmichael was about to try again when a middle-aged woman came hurrying from the nearest cottage, wiping her hands on her apron. 'You'll be the police,' she said. 'Excuse me not hearing you, but I was just getting dinner out.' As if to authenticate her statement, the church clock suddenly chimed through its sequence and then struck noon. It was so close that none of them could speak over the clamor.

'Isn't that a bit loud?' Royston asked, taking his hands down from his ears.

'Oh, we're used to it,' the woman said. 'It has to be that loud so they can hear it up at the house.' She nodded towards the gates.

'Are you the gatekeeper?' Carmichael asked.

She blinked. 'No . . . and I'm not rightly the gatekeeper's wife neither, because there hasn't been a gatekeeper since my father died. The gates stand open, mostly. I was saying to Jem this

18

morning that I don't know when we shut them last.'

This confirmed Carmichael's observation. He nodded. 'They're not closed even at night?' he asked.

'No, not for ever so long now,' she said. 'Not since my father died probably, the same year the old king died.'

It was as Carmichael had thought. Anyone could have driven up to the house. The fine gravel held tracks. The local police would have driven up it this morning, but it might be possible to find some evidence even so. He got out of the car and stood beside Royston. 'So, if you're not the gatekeeper, who are you?' he asked the woman.

'I'm Betty,' she said, 'Betty Jordan. My husband Jem is the mechanic up at the big house.'

'Mechanic?' Royston asked, surprised.

'He keeps their cars and that going,' she said.

'But you have a key to the gate?' Carmichael asked.

'Yes, and the policeman from Winchester said you'd be arriving and to let you in when you did,' she said, brandishing a large iron key inset with a robin to match the robin on the gates. 'You are the London police, aren't you?' She took their silence for assent and went on immediately. 'Isn't it terrible, anarchists murdering Sir James in his bed like that?'

'And to think it might have been prevented if they'd only locked the gates,' Carmichael said, taking the key from her unresisting hand. 'I'll be sure to lock them behind me now, and to see that this key is returned to you later. We'll also need to interview you and your family — does your husband sleep at home?'

'Jem?' she asked, as if he might mean some other husband. He smiled at the thought that a bigamist might ask that question that way. 'Yes, he does, he sleeps down here.'

'And did you see any signs of anarchists last night? Any unusual cars?'

'Well, yes,' she said, very flustered now and twisting her apron in her fingers. 'Any number of them. But they were having a party. People were to-ing and fro-ing all the time. Who's to say who any of them were? Half of them could have been terrorists and assassins and we wouldn't know.'

Carmichael's heart sank at the thought of the work involved. 'A party?' he repeated.

'Well, yes,' Betty said. 'A garden party in the afternoon, and then dinner and a dance in the evening, some weekend guests and some just coming in for the festivities. That's the usual way when Lady Margaret's entertaining.'

'How many people?' Carmichael asked.

Betty shook her head. 'I couldn't say. Maybe not so many as sometimes.'

'Did you hear cars arriving after you went to bed?' Royston asked. 'You might have seen lights on your bedroom ceiling.'

'Oh yes, ever so many,' Betty agreed promptly.

Carmichael was wiser in the ways of the country than Royston. 'What time did you go to bed?' he asked.

'A quarter after eight,' Betty said. 'There's one

good thing to be said for the big clock — it certainly keeps you straight about time.'

Carmichael couldn't help but agree. He and Royston exchanged a glance, and he shook his head a fraction. He couldn't see much purpose in interrogating Betty any longer. 'Well, we'll let you go back to your dinner,' he said.

She went, with a few looks back at them as Carmichael opened the gate. 'Walk or drive up, sir?' Royston asked.

'Before she mentioned the circus, I was thinking walk, to see if there might be tracks. Now, I suppose we might as well drive.'

'There still might be something to see,' Royston said.

'Got a hunch?' Carmichael asked. Royston was famous, or notorious, for his hunches. Sometimes they were useful. Often enough they were a waste of time.

'Perhaps I shouldn't, sir,' Royston said awkwardly, locking the car and pocketing the keys.

'You can say what you like about hunches, that they're good or bad, that you should follow them or shouldn't, but the one thing you can't say is that someone shouldn't have them.' Carmichael swung the iron gate open with an ear-splitting creak that set the crows rising out of an elm tree in the parkland beyond.

'Do you have them, sir?' Royston asked.

'Occasionally, sergeant,' Carmichael admitted. 'My rule with a hunch is that if it calls for more work, like right now, follow it. If it calls for less or something like skimping, then ignore it. If it's a case where there are sixteen leads and none more likely than any other and you might as well take them in alphabetical order, then a hunch might well be at the back of your mind drawing your attention to something the front of your mind missed.'

The gravel path swept up between two sloping tree-studded fields. There was no sign of the house yet. The tightly packed gravel revealed that Betty was right — there had been many cars driving over it, and recently. It was possible to pick out the tracks of this morning's Winchester police car as fresher; otherwise they were so overlain and mingled as to be almost indistinguishable. There were occasional indications of footprints, in both directions, including one very large pair heading both up and down. 'The Winchester bobby?' Carmichael hazarded as Royston measured the print.

'Not unless he buys his boots in Savile Row,' Royston said, straightening. 'Fourteen inches, and a very aristocratic pattern. Probably Lord Eversley himself. I don't see many of the guests strolling all this way down.'

'I've seen photographs, and I'm fairly sure Eversley's not a big man,' Carmichael said. 'The murdered man was though, Thirkie, great giant of a fellow.'

'Maybe they're his prints,' Royston said. 'Not much help to us then, because whoever made them was definitely alive at the time.'

'Awkward sort of business,' Carmichael said as they continued on up the drive. 'Aristocrats, politicians, that kind of thing.'

'That's why the locals had the sense to call us in,' Royston said. 'Do you think it was a whatsit, a political assassination then, terrorists like Mrs. I'm-not-the-gatekeeper down there said?'

Carmichael looked up at the house, which was just coming into view. If it had ever been a castle, it was no longer. It was a pleasant seventeenth-century manor house of warm red brick roofed in gray slate. It had an open welcoming look to it, perhaps because the rows of mullioned windows glinting in the sunlight gave it the look of a smile. 'No,' he said, answering Royston's question. 'Murders aren't political, or anarchist, not one time in a thousand. Murders are sordid affairs done between people who know each other, nine times out of ten for personal gain, and the tenth time because someone lost their temper at the wrong moment, the *crime passionel* as the French call it. I doubt we'll find that this one will be any different from all the others, except for the elevated surroundings.'

Royston was looking at the house as well, or at the row of half a dozen cars drawn up outside. 'Is that a hunch, sir?' he asked.

'No, sergeant, that's not a hunch, it's merely the voice of experience,' Carmichael said.

# 3

I've read through what I wrote and it's hopeless, isn't it? All over the place, just like me. Bursting out all over, like June, as Abby used to say, although physically I'm nothing like that at all, very buttoned down, and, well, deb-looking. But my brain bursts out. Maybe I should go back to the beginning and tell how I met David and what Daddy said all in chronological order and the proper place, because what Daddy said is part of it, and maybe I should have written everything he said, about how our children wouldn't be able to go to Eton and would take Jewish places at Marlborough and Winchester that real Jewish children could otherwise have used. It's typical of Daddy that he should have appealed to my non-existent children, whereas Mummy kept harping on about how we'd never be able to travel on the Continent, not that it didn't cause me a pang to think of never again seeing Paris, or the Riviera.

Anyway, I think what I'm going to do is just muddle on forward and write it all down as it comes and not look back, and then afterwards cut out huge swathes of it that turn out to be heading nowhere, or move them around if that seems to be the best plan. Because if I started in now about how I met David I don't think I'd ever get to the bits about the murder. And if I try to make myself very neat and disciplined the same thing will happen as used to happen with my diaries, which I began with lofty intentions and which never had a word written in them after January 2nd.

So, to return to that Sunday morning. I woke up in my girlhood bed with David crushed in beside me. The birds were making a frightful racket outside; one forgets about that in London. It was practically the crack of dawn, and the crack of dawn is terribly early in May, but I was wide awake and not likely to fall back asleep. I listened for a little while and I caught the chimes of the clock over the birds. It was a quarter to something, probably six, I guessed.

It was early, but I'd been to enough weekend houseparties at Farthing to know that there wouldn't be any hot water unless I was quick, so I jumped up and went down the hall to nab a bathroom and wash my hair. I always wash my hair on a Sunday morning — it isn't penance or anything, not any more than having hair like mine is a penance anyway, it's just that I need to do it every week and doing it on Sundays means that I don't forget. I came out of the bathroom swathed in towels — we have wonderful soft emerald-green towels that came as a wedding present from dear practical Aunt Millicent.

I was walking back to our room, to wake David and see if he wanted a bath before the hordes descended on the water, or possibly if he might like to make love (now that I'd got myself so beautifully clean since our delightful lovemaking of the night before), when who should I see but Mummy. I stopped dead with astonishment

25

and my mouth probably fell open. Now Mummy had absolutely no reason to be on our floor, because it's only nurseries and guest bedrooms, and apart from that it was only a little after the crack of dawn. If it had been a quarter to six when I went into the bathroom I doubt it was even seven yet. I can be a long time washing my hair, and other parts of me, but not really that long. Other people, other hostesses of large weekend houseparties, might well be up at seven and stalking about the guest floors. Mummy never was. She had Sukey to see to all that, and the housekeeper, Mrs. Simons, and if there's one thing Mummy believes in it's delegation. She never woke before ten and was never seen before noon. I don't think I'd ever seen her before eleven in my life before, not unless she'd been up all night to that point anyway.

'Good morning, Lucy,' she said, her chin in the air. She was dressed, and not dressed as she had been the night before. She was wearing quiet Sunday morning church-going clothes, pastels and pearls. But there was something strange about her make-up that made me wonder — in fact, for a moment there in the corridor I was absolutely sure that she was having an affair with one of our guests, right under Daddy's nose.

'Good morning, Mummy,' I said, and she swept past me and off down the corridor like an old-fashioned ship of the line going into battle.

The next thing of any significance was early breakfast, which David and I were a little late for. Mrs. Simons always lays on a special early breakfast on Sundays for those who want to go to church. David didn't want to go to church, of course, but he came down with me and nibbled at toast and tea. I left him there chatting away to Tibs Cheriton about geology. David was born with a wonderful ability to make even the most boring people become interesting in his presence. I think he does it by really taking an interest in them, in what interests them, and they shine by reflection. I've known Tibs all my life but I don't think I've ever exchanged three words with him that weren't entirely conventional platitudes, but David, who had never talked to him before that breakfast as far as I know, could zoom in and find the secret passion that would open him up like that.

Church-going at Farthing is obligatory, for Christians at least. But Tibs decided talking to David was more interesting than early communion, and said he'd go to Matins later. I was being crafty myself, because for one thing early communion only lasts half as long as Matins, for another because there aren't any hymns, and I detest hymn singing, and thirdly because I knew Mummy would go to Matins, because she always did. Of course I was wrong about that, because while I was putting my hat on in the hall she came downstairs with a prayer book in her hand, pulling on her gloves.

'Going to church, Mummy?' I said, my heart in my boots, because I'd been looking forward to the quiet little walk down into Clock Farthing, and now I'd have her company for that and for the service as well.

27

'Of course, darling,' she said. 'Isn't anybody else coming?'

'David's not, and Tibs is waiting for Matins,' I said.

'Isn't anybody else up?' she asked. 'What a lot of heathens we've invited. They might as well all cut the tops off their willies and turn Jew.'

'Honestly, Mummy!' I said, writhing, but she's impossible, she knows she is, she makes a profession out of being impossible and impervious. She did know she was hurting me and insulting David, there's no doubt about that. She isn't a fool. But she didn't say it to be insulting, the way somebody else might. She just said it because she wanted to say it and she didn't care if it hurt me — like the difference between someone aiming a gun at you and someone just shooting out of the window without looking. I've sometimes wondered if Mummy doesn't suffer from trains of thought getting loose the way I do, but I've never dared suggest as much to her.

Anyway, as I said that, Daddy came down, and just behind him, Angela Thirkie, and behind her Sir Thomas and Lady Manningham, who were almost strangers to me. The church bell began to ring. Hatchard, who had been there all the time, of course, listening to Mummy abuse the Jews in front of me, bowed and opened the front door for us.

Outside, one of the chauffeurs, a new one since I left home, a swarthy smiling man, was opening the door of the Bentley for Mrs. Richardson the cook, and two of the upstairs maids who were RC and driving over to mass in

28

St. Giles at Farthing Green. The other servants, except the Baptists like Hatchard, who would make do with an evening service in a blue barn called Bethel in Upper Farthing, were waiting to follow us down to church. If it had been an ordinary quiet weekend they'd have gone on their own, no doubt. I remember times when I was a child when Daddy and I went down to early communion and the servants slipped in later. Sometime during the war, which coincided with me going away to boarding school, so I missed the change, church-going became more formal. Before that, things were quieter, too, I think; afterwards it seemed that almost every weekend we were in Farthing at all we had guests.

The service was traditional and very English and very sweet, just the vicar and one server and the words people have been using to worship since King James, or Henry VIII, or whoever it was wrote the prayer book. (It must have been King James — surely a bad husband like Henry VIII could never have written all those lovely sonorous words?) It was a beautiful day, I don't think I mentioned that, and the windows were all open and there was a marvelous smell of bluebells, although the Altar Guild flowers on the altar were formal and dull. I remembered decorating the altar once when it was Mummy's turn and she was in St. Tropez, using armloads of tulips and daffodils, and it was such a pleasant memory that for once I didn't even mind the din of the clock, though I noticed Lady Manningham jump when it struck the three-quarter.

After church I felt in a mood to be charitable with all the world, even Mummy, even if she wasn't charitable to me. David said she couldn't forgive me for being a girl, especially now that poor Hugh was dead, but I think in fact that while she would have preferred a 'spare' male heir, she wouldn't have minded me being a girl so much if I'd been the right kind of girl — one who cared about the things she cared about. She always treated me as if I was a dress that had come from the shop with one sleeve too long and the other too short and completely the wrong kind of sash. She used to look at me as if to say, 'Now is this a complete waste or can I make something out of it?' At that point, the day of the murder, she much more often seemed to be thinking I was a complete waste. Yet I was only there at all that weekend because she'd absolutely insisted, pulling all the stops out. Otherwise David and I would have been in London having a much more pleasant weekend. I'd have popped out to church in St. Timothy's with Myra and come back to wake David as I had the week before.

I was so deep in this pleasant reverie of my own real everyday life that I'd walked almost halfway back to the house before I started to pay any attention at all to the others. Daddy was walking with Angela Thirkie, talking about the countryside. Mummy was walking with Sir Thomas, talking about servant problems. This left me with Lady Manningham, whom I barely knew. She was quite young, much younger than her husband, and she was looking at me timidly as if she would like to have a conversation but didn't know where to begin. 'Isn't it a glorious day,' I said, insipidly enough.

'Beautiful, yes, and such lovely countryside,' she said.

'The gardens were laid out by Nash,' I said, slipping easily into my old role as daughter-of-the-house. 'We have his plans for the gardens. There are also some very interesting sketches the young ladies of the family made of them soon after they were planted. The trees, of course, were saplings. It seems strange to me sometimes that we are seeing them as Nash meant them to be seen, when he himself could only imagine them in their full glory.'

'That is strange,' she said, struck by the observation. 'So much we do casts such long shadows. Do you plant more trees?'

'When one dies or is blown down my father always plants a new sapling,' I said. 'And when Hugh and I were children we used to plant acorns, hundreds of them every year. It was a project of ours, and we'd think of our descendants marveling at the oak forests.'

But Hugh was dead, and my putative descendants wouldn't be Eversleys or grow up here. That was just as true when I was a child and would have been true whoever I married. After Daddy dies the estate and the title will go to cousin Alfred, though I was due for most of the money and plenty of other bits of land that aren't entailed on a male Eversley heir.

'Tom and I live in quite a small house,' Lady Manningham confided. 'We don't have any family property like this. Tom's a bit of a self-made man.'

'One of the best kinds,' I said, entirely sincerely.

'He was made a baronet for services to industry,' she went on, encouraged. 'I thought it quite silly at first, being Lady instead of Mrs., but being here has made me see it in quite a different light. I mean people have always been ennobled for serving their country; it's just a matter of how and what, isn't it?'

'I think one of my ancestors was ennobled for doing something unspeakable for Henry VII,' I said, truthfully enough, and then repented of it when I saw how she was trying to cover up her look of horror. 'No, seriously, you plant some acorns for your descendants,' I said, and she put her hand on her stomach in that way that newly pregnant women always do, with that look. I raised my eyebrows, and she put her finger to her lips and nodded, so I just smiled. She was a much nicer person than Mummy usually invited along to her bashes, though I suppose it was Sir Thomas who had actually been invited, and Lady Manningham had just come along as his wife.

She looked away, clearly seeking for some different topic of conversation. I was glad enough, because however pleased I was, and I was, that she was knocked up, I couldn't help feeling envious, because it was what I was so longing for myself at that moment. It was all very well David saying it was nice to be on our own for the time being and that there was plenty of time, and he was right, of course, but I did so want to start a family right away, and couldn't help being cross sometimes that stupid nature wasn't cooperating.

'So, you still go to church,' Lady Manningham said.

'Yes,' I said. It was the only possible answer unless I wanted a long conversation about things that were none of her business, such as David's lack of particular religious feeling and my non-conversion to Judaism. If she'd known anything about the religion at all she'd have been able to tell I hadn't converted the day before when she was introduced to me and saw that I wasn't wearing a hat. I was wearing one that morning, of course, I'd just been to church, but I hadn't taken up covering my hair as Jewish women do. However, she clearly didn't know a thing. If anything, I go to church more often than I would if I hadn't married David. I'd always gone at Farthing, naturally, everyone goes to church in the country. But now I went regularly in London as well, which I'd let slip to some extent before. It somehow seemed more necessary to point up my Christian identity, which I hadn't even been aware of before meeting David, not in contrast to him, but to make it perfectly clear to other people.

I'd been pretty intent on this conversation, and hadn't been listening to the others — and if I had I'd only have heard Mummy on the servant problem, a theme of hers I knew very well indeed. But then Angela raised her voice and began to recite Browning's 'Oh to be in

33

England.' I know it has some different proper name, 'Thoughts of Home' or something, but that's what everybody calls it. She recited it with grace notes and quavers in the voice and dramatic pauses and everything Abby taught me to hate, and it took her all the rest of the way up to the house — and she hadn't finished when we got there. It didn't make it any easier that all the things Browning was rhapsodizing about were around us then, or that it was in fact May, which meant that Browning had got it wrong, though I suppose it's not all that surprising considering that he was doing it in Italy or Greece or wherever it was, and his wife missing her spaniel. Abby told me about them, eloping abroad, but somehow it was the spaniel that stuck in my mind. I can picture it now, very soulful eyes, rather like Angela Thirkie, but more forgivable in a spaniel somehow.

Mark was standing out on the terrace, looking awkward. He was smoking a cigarette, which seemed a strange thing to do on the terrace after breakfast. He raised a hand when he saw us coming, but Angela didn't stop reciting, so he stood and shuffled and looked awkward and tried to break in a few times without success. Mark Normanby was Angela's brother-in-law, married to her sister Daphne, so I suppose she thought she needn't take any notice of him, though he's something frightfully high up in the government, and incredibly clever, and incidentally terribly gorgeous, in a touch-me-not way. Mummy looked restless and I thought she was about to quote, 'Mary has delighted us long enough,' the way she always used to do with me when she was tired of my recitals, but thank goodness Angela wound down at last.

'Good morning, Mark,' Mummy said, and would have gone past him into the house, but he raised a hand to stop her.

'Something rather unpleasant has happened,' he said. 'I was waiting here to catch you on your way back from church.'

'Unpleasant?' Mummy's elegant eyebrows went up under her hair, and she pronounced the word as if it came in two distinct crisp sections, separating it like the segments of an orange.

'There's been an accident, well, an accident or something. It's rather awful,' Mark said.

'What's the matter?' Daddy asked. 'Who is it?' He'd guessed at once that it must be one of the guests, and so had I.

'It's James actually,' Mark said, looking at Angela.

'Is James ill?' she asked. It was a natural enough thing to say, I suppose, but her voice sounded very unnatural. It might have been the voice of someone who realizes that she's been making a fool of herself reciting 'Oh to be in England' when something Mark Normanby could describe as 'rather awful' has happened to her husband.

'Not ill, no . . . well, the thing is that he seems to be dead,' Mark said, and that's when I had my uncharitable thought and Angela fainted dead away and was caught very neatly by Daddy.

35

# 4

The door was opened by a very grand butler.

'Scotland Yard, I presume?' he asked, inclining his head a trifle.

Carmichael handed him his card. The butler inclined his head a fraction more over it.

'Mr. Yately asked to be informed when you arrived,' the butler said. In response to Carmichael's questioning look, he amplified. 'Mr. Yately is the police inspector they sent over from Winchester.'

'Very well, show us to Mr. Yately,' Carmichael said.

The butler opened the front door and let them into a splendid paneled hall. There were wooden doors leading off in all directions and a curving staircase leading upstairs. The brass of the door handles gleamed. There was one window immediately above the door, which allowed light to fall on an old portrait of a lady in a ruff, accompanied by a little dog, also in a ruff.

By some magical mechanism known only to servants, the butler had summoned a footman. 'Show these police gentlemen to the dressing room of the blue bedroom,' he instructed. Carmichael liked the ambiguity of 'police gentlemen.' Everything about Farthing subtly suggested wealth and privilege and class distinctions very carefully maintained. Then here he came, tramping in police boots to disturb the hierarchies as they were laid down by bringing in an entirely orthogonal power. In civilian circumstances, he would be recognized here as on the very lowest rank of gentry, and Royston would be sent to the servants' entrance, wherever that was — which he must find out; it might be important.

The minion bowed, took a step towards the stairs, and looked inquiringly at Carmichael. Carmichael, with a quick exchange of glances with Royston, followed obediently. The butler vanished through the door under the portrait, which Carmichael tentatively labeled as likely to lead to the servants' quarters. He must get hold of a floor plan, or have one drawn up. That would be a job the local police would probably be sufficiently competent to manage.

'So, where is everyone?' Royston asked the footman.

The footman looked outraged for a moment, then presumably remembered that he was talking to a policeman. 'Her ladyship is resting in her room.' Carmichael immediately placed him as a local. His accent was only a little smoother than Betty at the gate. 'His lordship is in the library with some of the guests. Most of the other guests are in the drawing room. Miss Lucy — Mrs. Kahn I should say — and Mrs. Normanby are looking after Lady Thirkie, who is having hysterics in Miss Dorset's room. Miss Dorset was in the kitchen talking to the staff when I left, sir.'

'And who is Miss Dorset?' Royston asked.

'Miss Dorset is her ladyship's cousin, and her

secretary-companion,' the footman said.

Poor relation, Carmichael mentally appended, but surely a secretary-companion shouldn't be talking to the servants, even if she was one of the family? Carmichael was more interested in Mrs. Kahn, anyway, who he remembered, now that he heard the name, from a minor fuss in the newspapers the previous autumn. 'English rose plucked by Jew,' the *Daily Express* had screamed, and even the *Telegraph* had asked more quietly, 'Should the daughters of our aristocracy be permitted to mingle their blood with the trash of European Jewry?' Lucy Eversley, yes, he remembered now — there had been photographs, nothing especially pretty, but very determined, which he supposed she'd have to be to come from this home and marry a Jew. Surprising that she was still invited down here for weekends.

'Is Mr. Kahn here?' he asked.

'Mr. Kahn is in the library,' the footman said.

Carmichael filed the fact for consideration. Certainly any Jew would have reason enough to hate old Thirkie. He ran his hand along the wooden wall as they went up the stairs. It was as smooth as silk; it must be polished regularly. The stairs were carpeted with a strip of dark blue drugget held down by irons.

'How many are there on staff?' he asked.

'I can't rightly say, sir,' the footman replied. They came to the top of the stairs, the bannister terminating in a carved acorn. 'There are those of us who belong to the house and those his lordship and her ladyship bring down with them from London, and just at the moment there are also the visiting staff.'

'How many on the permanent staff?' Royston asked.

'Twelve,' the footman said without hesitation, leading the way up a second flight of stairs. 'The new housekeeper, seven housemaids, Mrs. Smollett the cook — undercook presently, of course, being as Mrs. Richardson is here — two kitchenmaids, and myself.'

'So the butler and the cook come down from London?' Carmichael asked, intrigued by this glimpse of upper-class life.

'Yes, sir, they travel in advance of the family. And some of the kitchen staff too, as well as the family's personal attendants.'

'Another dozen then?' Royston asked.

'I'm not rightly sure who exactly is here this time,' the footman said, more confidingly. 'That's about the right figure, but it's been proper chaos downstairs the last two days. I haven't known if I've been coming or going myself.'

'Worse than a normal houseparty?' Carmichael asked.

'Much worse — well, normally we have more notice.'

Interesting, Carmichael thought, and possibly worth following up later.

'I'd have thought it would have taken more than seven maids with seven mops to keep a place like this in this condition,' Royston said as they reached another landing. This time they did not continue up; the footman led them down the corridor.

'They work very hard, sir, and of course we have girls from the village who come in to do the rough work as needed. I suppose I should also mention the stable staff and the garden staff, who do not live in. You don't think — I mean you don't suspect any of the staff, do you, sir?'

'We've only just got here, we don't suspect anyone yet,' said Carmichael, amused at the supernatural powers of detection attributed to Scotland Yard. 'We just want to get a feel for the situation.'

'I see, sir,' the footman said, as he paused before one of the doors.

'And your name?' Royston asked, taking out his notebook.

'Jeffrey, sir,' he replied.

Royston rolled his hand in the air. Jeffrey frowned, unsure of what was wanted. 'Would that be Something Jeffrey, like Judge Jeffrey, or would it be Jeffrey Someone?' he asked.

Carmichael almost laughed. Royston was constantly surprising him. Fancy him knowing anything at all about Judge Jeffrey, even the name!

'Jeffrey Bartholemew Pickens,' Jeffrey said, with a faint air of being put upon.

Royston wrote it down carefully. 'I'll remember that if I need you,' he said.

'Yes, sir,' Jeffrey said, and tapped gently on the door.

It was opened abruptly by a uniformed bobby. 'Two gentlemen from Scotland Yard,' Jeffrey announced, his voice now a clear imitation of the haughty butler below.

'Good, good, come in,' came a voice from inside the room. The footman and the bobby stepped out of the way and Carmichael and Royston stepped inside.

The corpse lay sprawled across a narrow bed at the far side of the little room. He had apparently been stabbed, for there was bright red blood all over his chest and the handle of a knife sticking out. Something didn't look right about him. Carmichael frowned, took a step towards him, and was intercepted by Yately, a tubby little Inspector from Winchester. He insisted on introducing the bobby, who rejoiced in the name of Izzard, and a thin police doctor called Green.

'This is a bad business,' Yately said. 'I haven't moved him or done anything, though they moved him a little before we got here, trying to determine whether he was dead, that sort of thing. I could see at once that it was a case for Scotland Yard and had you called right away. You've made very good time down from London. I'm glad you're here — once you've had a good look we can get on with things.'

'When did you get here?' Carmichael asked.

'The body was found just before nine,' Yately said. 'They telephoned for us immediately, and we arrived at nine-forty. I then telephoned Scotland Yard.'

'We left at ten and arrived at the gates at noon,' Royston said. They heard the chime of the clock, made tolerable and even pleasant by distance. 'It's quarter-past now.'

41

'What's the time of death?' Carmichael asked.

'It'll be easier to say when Green's had a proper look at him,' Yately said. 'At the moment, with all that stuff on him, it's very hard to tell.'

'The blood?' Royston asked.

'Ah, fooled you, did it? It almost fooled me as well. Look more closely. That's not blood, not real blood anyway.'

Carmichael strode across the room and stood over the corpse, not touching him at all but inspecting him closely. The deceased appeared to be a tall middle-aged man, clearly well cared for. He was clean-shaven and his face was very flushed. A choleric temperament, Carmichael would have said, if the man had been alive. His eyes were open, staring upwards and bulging with what appeared to be alarm. He was wearing an old-fashioned nightshirt made of heavy linen. His chest was smeared all over with the red substance, and in the center above his heart was a dagger, pinning a square of navy blue cloth on which was embroidered a six-pointed yellow star. The red substance smeared all over his chest was not blood, but it wasn't paint either. Carmichael sniffed at it, trying to separate the scent from the usual excretory smell of a recent corpse. He knew it was familiar but couldn't quite place it. There was no real blood around the wound, suggesting that it must have been made after he had been dead for some time. Interesting.

'It's lipstick,' Royston said in amazement. 'Not the kind in a tube, the kind you paint on.'

'Any suggestion for cause of death, Inspector?' Yately asked.

'Clearly strangulation,' Carmichael said in a bored tone. He didn't want to play this kind of game.

'Yes,' Yately said, sounding disappointed. 'Shall we let Green get on and do his thing?'

'Here?' Carmichael asked, surprised.

'No, not here. There's nothing really I can do. I'll take him back to Winchester for a proper workup,' Green said.

'Is this exactly how he was found?' Carmichael asked.

'We've looked at him the way you just did, and Green tested his arms and legs for rigor, but we've not moved him at all,' Yately said. 'I can't answer for before we got here.'

'Who found the body anyway? His wife?'

Yately turned pages in his notebook. 'His wife was in church, apparently. The body was found by his brother-in-law coming in to see if he was getting up for breakfast.'

'Not his servant?' Carmichael was surprised.

'It seems he didn't bring a personal servant down with him.'

'Every time, or just this time?' Carmichael asked.

Yately shrugged. 'I didn't ask. In any case, Mr. Normanby knew he didn't have a valet to wake him so he popped in on his way past.'

'The wife didn't sleep in here?' Carmichael asked. It was a formal question. There wasn't room. This was a dressing room, with only the one narrow bed. There was barely space for one man to sleep in here, and Carmichael was surprised that Thirkie had done so.

'In the connecting room,' Yately said. 'Sir James apparently came to bed later than Lady Thirkie and considerately slept in here rather than disturb her.'

'Who do you have this information from?' Carmichael asked.

'The brother-in-law, Normanby. He's the only one I've interviewed. He apparently accompanied Sir James upstairs and said good night at about one A.M. They had been playing billiards, he said.'

'Do you think he did it?'

'Did it?' Yately looked startled. 'Mr. Normanby? He's an MP.' There, Carmichael thought, in that attitude, lay the reason why the country needed Scotland Yard and could not rely on the local forces. They were good enough with ordinary criminals — with the criminal class if you like — but their ingrained and perfectly natural respect for those above them made them completely unimaginative in cases like this. 'Why would he do it? It's obvious some anarchist did it.'

'This does look like evidence of the crime being political, sir,' Royston said, touching the square with the yellow star.

'It looks as if someone wants us to think it's political,' Carmichael said. 'That doesn't mean it isn't political, but it might not be the kind of political it looks, or it might be personal. This' — he touched the material at the edge of the star as Royston had done — 'doesn't

44

rule anything either in or out. It is evidence, but not in the way you mean. I wonder how easy these are to get hold of.'

'They're issued to Jews on the Continent, sir,' the bobby said. 'They have to wear them all the time to keep them in their place, so that anyone can tell at a glance who they are.'

'I am aware of that,' Carmichael said. Yately spread his hands as if to say that he couldn't answer for the idiocy of his subordinates. 'But the Jews there need the ones they have, and we don't issue them in England, so I wonder how easy they are to come by here. Should we be looking for someone who's been to the Continent and come by one there, or are they in fact available for sale here? Is this in fact a genuine Continental star, or a copy? It's good material and professional looking, not like the lipstick, so my guess would be that it's genuine. If it's genuine it might be traceable. Royston, look into it.'

'Yes, sir,' Royston said, making a note.

'The dagger too. It's unusual and oriental. It should be fingerprinted, and identified if possible.'

'It's already been identified,' Yately said. 'It belongs to the deceased, Normanby said. He apparently used it as a kind of ornamental pocket knife. It had a kind of sheath, a scabbard I suppose.'

'And he brought it away with him?' Royston asked.

'He must have done,' Yately said, spreading his

hands again, this time at people's unaccountable ways.

It was time to take charge. Carmichael girded his mental loins and set to it. 'Green, get on with it. Take him to Winchester, and send a bobby back with the car. You, Izzard, take this key and go down to the gate — it's your job to let police in and out, note all comings and goings, and prevent all goings at present that aren't police.'

'Yes, sir,' Izzard said, stolidly, and stumped off.

'You only brought the one bobby?' Carmichael asked Yately.

'It was Sunday, sir,' Yately said.

Carmichael looked down his nose at him for a moment, then sighed. Sunday in the country did tend to mean that everything ground to a halt, and he didn't want to make Yately impossible to work with. 'Good thing you were able to bring a doctor, then,' he said. 'Good thinking.'

Yately smiled.

'But without more men, I'm afraid you'll have to do a little leg-work yourself, Inspector. I want you to get me a floor plan of the house. They may have one; if not, get the footman, Jeffrey, to take you around until you can draw me one. I also want a list of the guests and of the servants.'

'Just the overnight guests or everyone who was here yesterday?' Yately asked.

Carmichael thought of what Betty had said about all the cars coming and going. 'That will depend very much on the time of death,' he said. 'Get the overnight guests for now. We know Thirkie stayed up late; maybe he outstayed the others. Don't interview them, just get me a list,

46

I'll interview them later. For now, Royston and I are going to go over this room, and the connecting room, to see what we can find.'

'Yes, sir,' Yately said, and rang the bell to summon Jeffrey.

Carmichael looked down at the flushed and furious face of the corpse. 'I'll need his will, if any, to see who benefits. The Yard will be able to get a copy from his solicitor. I also need to know about his enemies,' he said.

'Political enemies, sir?' Royston asked, making a note.

'Those too,' Carmichael said. 'When I talk to the Yard, I'll ask them to send me a summary of his political career, with especial note of enemies. I'll also ask what Thirkie was doing at the moment, what legislation he was sponsoring and promoting, what might suffer from his absence. If it is political, there may be a reason why he was killed now, at this moment, rather than last year or next year.'

'I thought you didn't think it was political?' Yately interrupted, confusion plain on his face.

'That doesn't mean I intend to neglect the political angle,' Carmichael said. 'I also said it might not be the kind of political it was made to look and it might be some other kind of political.'

Yately's broad country face looked confused. Carmichael looked back to the corpse and wished, as he almost always wished in murder cases, that he could get the dead man to answer some of the most burning questions. 'In the midst of life we are in death,' the prayer book says, and lying here, in the heart of the country house which must have been as familiar to him as his own home, Thirkie had gone from what was by all accounts a dynamic and voluble life into the stricken, sullen, silence of death. Thirkie would never again answer a question, either in Parliament or in his bedroom, and any questions Carmichael had to ask him would have to be answered by others or go unanswered. Death, Carmichael thought, as he always thought at some point in surveying a corpse, was God's most egregious mistake.

# 5

Daddy carried Angela to Sukey's room. It was the obvious place, with her own room being out of commission, and easy to carry her to because there was only the one step down. I trailed in there behind him, though we lost Mummy and Mark and the Manninghams along the way.

I opened the door and Daddy put Angela down on the bed. Sukey's room was impeccable, as always, all the lace edgings on her dressing table neat, her prayer book and little gold cross laid out ready for Matins. I can mess up a room in thirty minutes flat, but Sukey had been living in this one, on and off, for thirty years without leaving so much as a dusting of talc or a scarf out of place.

Angela flopped onto the bed, about as unconscious as a person could be. There was no question of her faking it. Daddy looked down at her in irritation. 'Find Daphne,' he said to me.

'Good idea,' I said, and dashed off in search of her. I ran her to earth at last alone in the library, looking rather green about the gills and gulping tea with brandy in it. At least, the brandy bottle was open on the trolley beside her and she had a teacup in her hand. She had a cigarette in her other hand and was puffing on it between gulps.

'Angela's fainted,' I said. 'Do you think you could look after her a bit?'

'Me?' Daphne asked, as if I'd asked her to

climb the Eiffel Tower single-handed, rather than look after her own sister.

'You have heard about James?' I asked.

'Heard about him?' Daphne said, with an odd little laugh. 'My dear, I found him.'

'Where was he?' I asked. I took the teacup from Daphne, mainly because her hands were shaking so much I thought she was likely to drop it, and it was one of Mummy's precious Spode set that belonged to Great-grandmother Dorset and had been handed down mother to daughter ever since. Although Mummy had made it perfectly clear that I wasn't fit to inherit them, or the Ringhili, or any of her other mother-daughter stuff, I didn't want to go through the fuss that would ensue if I'd just stood by and seen one of them smashed on the library floor. I sniffed it as I set it down. I suppose there must have been some tea there at some point, or she'd never have got hold of a cup rather than a glass, but by now it seemed like almost pure brandy.

Daphne blew out smoke. 'In his dressing room. And he's been stabbed by some damned Jew and he's all over blood and cold and dead and you're telling me Angela's fainted and I ought to go and look after her because she's the grieving widow when she never really gave two pins for James except that he could make her Lady Thirkie, and he never cared about her except that she was the nearest he could get to me.'

'She is the grieving widow and you'd better pull yourself together if you're not going to let the side down and embarrass everyone with a lot of stuff and nonsense that can't be put on display,' I said. I might not have said it so rudely if she hadn't said 'some damned Jew,' but I'd have thought it and meant it just as much. It's funny, I despise a lot of things about Mummy and one of them is her hardness, but there I was in a crisis acting exactly like her, telling Daphne to pull herself together and cover what needed to be covered. 'Letting the side down' is purest Mummy and not something I'd normally think of myself as saying, but I'm absolutely positive I said it then. I mean most of what I'm putting down here is what I think I said and other people said, my impression of it, except for some frightfully significant things that I remember word for word. I'm probably more accurate recording what other people said, because I listened to that, whereas for what I said, I just remember the general gist. But I know I said 'letting the side down' to poor Daphne. I don't think I thought that at the time, that I was being like Mummy, I mean. I was so cross with Daphne for being such a fool. I also thought she was using 'Jew' the way she might say 'anarchist' or even 'murderer' or 'bastard' — I had no idea then about the star or anything.

'You're right,' she said, snatching up the cup again and swallowing all the brandy down in one go. 'She's the grieving widow, I'm her devoted sister, Mark is my devoted husband, none of the rest of it matters or shows. Sorry. Thank you.'

The strange thing about that was that she obviously meant it — she really was thanking me for being such a bitch to her. I'd never known

Daphne all that well. Angela was a few years older than me, but within my age cohort. Daphne was six or seven years older than her, probably ten years older than me, Hugh's age. She was old enough to have been one of 'the big ones' when we were children. Then she came out and got married when I was still at school. Angela was one of 'last year's debs' actually two years before, when I came out. The only thing I really knew about Daphne was that while both sisters looked very much alike, she was the one who Nature's lottery had handed all the brains meant for both girls, which meant that Angela looked like a student's copy of the masterpiece that was Daphne, because Daphne had the animation to go with her looks.

That morning, Daphne was wearing dove gray and ruby red, a gray skirt and jacket and a red sweater underneath, with no jewelry. She was carrying a red clasp-bag the exact color of her sweater, and now she stubbed out her cigarette in the ashtray, opened her bag, drew out a gold compact, powdered her face, squinted, frowned at her reflection, snapped the compact shut, and took a deep breath. 'Show me where to go to play devoted sister,' she said.

She followed me back to Sukey's room. Daddy looked terribly relieved to see us. Angela was still out cold.

'This is very good of you,' Daddy said to Daphne. 'She's had a terrible shock.'

'Poor Angela,' Daphne said, entirely in control of herself now, and to all appearances full of sororal concern.

52

'I'll leave you to see to her, loosen her stays or whatever,' Daddy said. I rolled my eyes at him. I'm sure he knew that stay loosening was pure Victorian bunk, but then I suppose that so is fainting like that, so maybe he was justified. 'Ring if you need anything,' Daddy said, and went off.

Then began an afternoon that remains unrivaled for sheer bloody ghastliness. Daphne soon did whatever stay loosening needed to be done. She spent her time sitting on the windowsill and smoking continuously, not using a holder, lighting one cigarette from the stub of the last, shedding ash all over Sukey's immaculate cushions. She barely spoke to me except to say when she saw a police car draw up outside, but when I tried to leave she begged me to stay.

I'm not sure what I felt myself, except embarrassment and irritation. Sir James didn't mean anything to me personally. I'd never known him well. He was always 'Sir' James in my mind, never just James the way a friend would be. Before I came out he was just one of Daddy's boring friends; after all, he must have been all of fifteen years older than me. I vaguely remember hearing about the scandal with Daphne when I was in school. She was a deb, seventeen or eighteen, and he was old enough to have made a good start on his political career. He was married to someone else, whose name was Olivia, and who I vaguely remember as one of those very political women with really formidable hats. She was one of Mummy's allies, but never really a friend. We didn't see quite as much of Sir James when she was alive as we did later. The scandal with Daphne was something deliciously wicked that people used to whisper about. I remember asking Hugh, who would have been perhaps sixteen then, whether it was true what Angela had told me, that Daphne was in love with him as well, and wasn't it like Romeo and Juliet. Dear Hugh poured cold water on my romantic imaginings and explained the word 'adultery' to me.

'They sometimes call it 'Paris' and try to make it seem very sophisticated and romantic,' Hugh said. 'But I think it's sordid and horrible, and it's like somewhere — like — like Bognor.' Bognor Regis was a horrible little town that thought very well of itself. It had once been a fashionable watering spot but was now impossibly vulgar. It was also known as somewhere people went for illicit weekends. Adultery was always 'Bognor' to us from then on.

In any case, Daphne was married off as fast as possible to the first possible contender, who was Mark Normanby, then a rising young politician, very bright, very handsome, but not really anybody yet. Then, during the war, Olivia Thirkie died in the Blitz, one of the very first casualties, and when I heard about it, true to form the first thing I thought was that it was too late for Sir James and Daphne, and I clapped my hand to my mouth to catch the train, of course, but people thought I was very cut up about it because I had known her. It even gave me a sort of cachet in school for a little while, to have known someone killed by a bomb, until it became so commonplace that the unusual thing was not to have had it happen. Several girls lost parents and brothers — both of Angela's parents were killed, her mother by a bomb and her father at Dunkirk. By the time Hugh died in the spring of 1941 it wasn't thought of as anything special for a brother to be killed, so, ironically, I was given rather more sympathy and consideration at the death of Olivia Thirkie, who I hardly knew, than at the death of Hugh, who I worshipped.

Then, after the war, Sir James became very close to Daddy and Mummy, especially Mummy. He was always here for houseparties, and very often overnight, which hadn't been the case when Olivia was alive. He was very involved in the peace accords, of course, and the whole Farthing Set thing, which seemed mostly humbug to me, because it was just people Daddy and Mummy knew, and sometimes the papers would say someone was one of the Set who I knew Mummy particularly disliked. All the same, insofar as there was a Farthing Set and they had a coherent policy in the early years of the peace, it was Mummy and Daddy and Sir James and Mark Normanby who were at the core of it, with other people like Uncle Dud and so on hanging on.

I wasn't around especially much in those years, because I was in school, and when I was at Farthing I used to mope about doing the things I'd done with Hugh and missing him and making myself thoroughly miserable. If I paid attention to any of them it was Mark, who I had a kind of crush on, and not Sir James, who always seemed very dull — in a good kind of way, I suppose, but he seemed to lack any kind of spark. Then, when I was seventeen I had a few months in Switzerland with Abby and then came out, and suddenly Sir James was one of my set, as well as one of Mummy's, and after waiting five years or so after the death of Olivia, he married Angela the minute she was twenty-one. He'd have married her before, she told everyone, except that her stuffy old guardian, who was a great-uncle or something of that nature, had refused permission because of that ancient scandal about Daphne.

The funny thing was that everyone had assumed that Sir James was marrying Angela because he couldn't have Daphne, and it had never crossed anyone's mind as far as I knew that he *was* having Daphne. I'd never heard a breath of scandal about Daphne since her marriage until she'd as much as admitted to me that morning that she was having an affair with him. I was shocked, although I didn't want to be. Hugh was right. Adultery was sordid, not in the least romantic. Bognor.

I tried to feel sorry about Sir James's death. I tried to recapture the feeling I'd had in church of loving the whole world. It wouldn't come back no matter how hard I tried. I couldn't think of a single time Sir James had been nice to me, or even especially taken notice of me, except to lecture me about the inadvisability of mixing my blood with that of a lesser race. I'd told him he had no right to talk to me, and really he didn't, not a shred. I'd listen to that sort of thing from

Mummy, but hearing it from her friends was the outside of enough. He said he'd make marriage between Jews and people like me illegal if he had his way, and I said it was a good thing he didn't have his way. Nobody could get a bill like that through Parliament in England, whatever happens on the Continent.

After at least an hour, which felt like one of those geological eras Lyell talks about, Angela started to stir. We naturally got up and went over to her. She woke, saw us, and began to scream. I rang for a pot of strong tea.

'Strong tea, madam?' Jeffrey asked, astonished, and allowing his astonishment to show as no proper London servant ever would.

I grinned at him. 'Very strong Indian tea, and plenty of milk and sugar.'

'Very good, madam,' Jeffrey said. 'Just the thing for shock.'

I nodded, and he bowed and hurried off to fetch it. He must have heard Angela carrying on but that was the only reference he made to it. There are some servants who remain strangers however long they stay with you and others who become members of the family. Jeffrey was definitely in the latter category.

I had learned to drink tea during the war when sugar was rationed and not to be wasted on young girls. By the time it became readily available again I had learned to like my tea weak, milkless, and unsweetened. This was a taste David and I shared; he said this was the usual way to drink flavored or China teas on the Continent. At home we drank vast quantities of

Lady Grey from the elegant white-on-white Shelley tea set we had chosen together. But for shock, and nobody could deny that Angela had suffered a shock, there was nothing like strong Indian tea.

When Jeffrey brought the tray, I saw that it had been exquisitely prepared. There was a silver teapot, a silver hot-water jug, and a smaller silver milk jug, a large silver sugar bowl, three china cups and saucers, not the Spode, just everyday Royal Albert, and the open bottle of brandy that had been in the library. I set it all down on Sukey's dressing table, moving the prayer book. 'Where is Miss Dorset?' I asked Jeffrey. 'Does she need her room?'

'She's with her ladyship,' Jeffrey said. 'She told me to tell you to make yourselves comfortable in here.'

'That's very kind of her,' I said, and Jeffrey bowed his way out.

I managed to get several cups of the tea into Angela. She refused the brandy. She kept crying and almost howling, and clinging to me. There was something quite excessive about the way she behaved. She wanted to go to her husband's body, which I didn't think advisable. Daphne, thank goodness, didn't let on that she had seen it. She drank some of the tea sitting ramrod straight on the edge of the bed.

'Are you sure you won't have some brandy?' I asked Angela as I poured her another cup of tea. 'It's very calming.'

To be honest, I had an ulterior motive with the brandy. I was hoping she might pass out again

58

and be someone else's problem when she woke up. I still didn't feel much in charity with her.

'It's not good for me in my condition,' Angela said, her hand on her stomach exactly like Lady Manningham earlier.

Again I felt a wave of envy, and for the first time some actual sympathy, for the poor baby. Bad enough for the poor little thing to be fatherless, but to be fatherless and to have a mother as idiotic as Angela Thirkie seemed very unjust.

'You're making it up,' Daphne said, standing up and taking a step away. She looked as if someone had unexpectedly punched her in the stomach.

I looked at her in surprise.

'Why should I be?' Angela said, rubbing her stomach. 'We've been trying for four years, after all. I'm going to have a baby in December, and the one thing that gives me comfort in this terrible situation is that James knew about it before he died.'

She said this in almost the same way she'd recited the Browning earlier, as if it was something she'd memorized. I didn't know what to say. I couldn't exactly congratulate her on her pregnancy in the circumstances. I glanced at Daphne, who was staring at her sister and looking suddenly old.

'Oh I know you're not pleased,' Angela said, sipping her tea and looking at Daphne over the rim of the cup. She had been clinging to me earlier — now she entirely ignored me, as if Daphne were the only person in the room. 'You always wanted James for yourself, and you've never had a baby. If you'd wanted a baby you should have married a man who could give you one, not a vicious nancy-boy like Mark.'

I clapped both hands to my mouth to hold back absolutely all the things that I was thinking, about sisters, Bognor, Macedonians, Sir James, Mark, and even pregnancy. It probably wouldn't have mattered. I think I was invisible to both of them. I looked from one of them to the other as they stared at each other. Angela looked triumphant and Daphne devastated, like a pair of goddesses done by some genius sculptor who wanted to show that Victory and Defeat have the same face.

# 6

The rooms didn't yield much of interest. They were a standard bedroom and dressing room, clearly furnished for guests. The bedroom was carpeted in the center of the floor with polished wood around the edges. It had a fireplace, with a fire laid but not lit, and a window that looked out over the same landscape the men had walked through. 'At the front of the house,' Royston said.

'Not that it means anything,' Carmichael said. 'I wonder where the bathroom is, and how many share it.'

'You'll have to ask Jeffrey that,' Royston said.

The dressing room had carpet that was fitted but of lesser quality. It also lacked a fireplace, having instead a small gas fire. 'Must get chilly in winter,' Royston said.

If the rooms had ever been blue, they were so no longer, except in the imagination of the household. The main bedroom was papered with lavender roses, and the dressing room painted cream.

Sir James and Lady Thirkie had apparently brought a selection of clothes, toiletries, and knickknacks appropriate for a country-house weekend and nothing more. After half an hour Royston raised his eyebrows at Carmichael and shook his head.

'Nothing significant,' he said.

'Did you think there would be?' Royston asked.

'Well, it's something to know that the separate bed business wasn't any matter of coming late to bed. His articles are laid out in here and hers in there. I wouldn't be surprised to learn they had separate bedrooms at home as well.'

'You'd hardly expect people of their class to share a hairbrush,' Royston said, putting down a splendid silver-backed instance of the same, monogrammed AT.

'No,' Carmichael said. 'I think I want to see Lady Thirkie first. Half the time in a murder it's the spouse who did it.'

'Enough to make you afraid of your nearest and dearest, isn't it?' Royston said, with a grin. 'I think you'll find that while that may be true in the East End, or in Lancashire, this one is the exception to all your rules, sir. It looks and smells political to me.'

'Lipstick smells political now?' Carmichael asked.

'I sniffed at three on Lady Thirkie's dressing table,' Royston said. 'They're all the stick kind, not the paint kind — one reddish, one pinkish, and one a very dark red. They didn't smell at all like the stuff on the corpse.'

'No, you recognized it at once, didn't you, meaning that it was a much more familiar smell,' Carmichael said, walking over to the dressing table and examining the lipsticks for himself. Two matched, monogrammed AT in gold and silver, and the third was dark blue with a gold line around it. 'Cheap lip paint, not expensive.

62

Woolworth's, rather than these, which are two Chanels and a Dior.'

'Bought especially, do you think?' Royston asked. 'By a man, who wouldn't know any better?'

'Or who wouldn't need any better for a gag. It wasn't meant to fool anyone it was blood; it was meant to suggest the red breast of the Farthing robin,' Carmichael said. 'I'm a bit surprised at that. It shows both some planning ahead and some improvisation, and usually you see one or the other. They must have planned ahead to get the idea and the star, and the lipstick. But they didn't bring anything to attach the star with. They attached it with the dead man's own pocketknife.'

'Maybe they brought something and then saw the knife and thought that would be better and took their something away with them again?' Royston suggested.

'That would fit the facts. So would the idea that they already had the things. Lip paint might be bought by anyone, but it also might already be owned by a lower-class woman. The star is more difficult — but I suppose any Jews who left the Continent might already have one. We'll have to check if any guests or staff are Jews.'

'Mr. Kahn,' Royston reminded him.

'We'll have to check him very thoroughly,' Carmichael agreed. 'But it almost seems too deliberately intended to point at him, unless he's a fool to do it and lay such a clear trail.'

'Who can say what Jews might do?' Royston

said. 'He might have been overcome with hate all of a sudden.'

'Anyone can lose their temper, but commit an elaborate and premeditated murder between one in the morning and breakfast time?' Carmichael rolled his eyes. He pulled off the dark blue cap and turned the bottom of the Dior tube and looked at the near-pristine finger of lipstick that extended. 'She doesn't use this one much. Odd shade, maybe it matched something in particular.' He examined the other two, which were older and much better used.

'The shade of the lipstick on the corpse was very close to blood red,' Royston said. 'That makes it seem more likely it was bought specially. We could try inquiring in chemists' shops.'

'And every Woolworths in the country,' Carmichael said, gloomily. 'It isn't an unusual shade like this Dior one. Half the women one sees have painted their lips blood red.'

'Do you think a woman could have done it?' Royston asked. 'I mean physically? Strangling isn't a woman's normal way to murder.'

'We'll know more after the autopsy,' Carmichael said. 'I'd say, maybe. If he was asleep, or if he trusted her to come up close. And in some ways it's more likely for a woman to walk into his bedroom than a man — whether his wife or any other woman. He was a big man, but he wasn't young, and he doesn't look as if he was very active or strong. There are plenty of women who could have got their hands around his neck. Whether it's psychologically something a woman could have done, I'm not so sure. It certainly isn't common.'

'If he'd been asleep, suffocating him would have been just as easy, or easier,' Royston said. 'There was a pillow.'

'I want to take a look at Lady Thirkie, see how big she is for one thing, and see what her attitude to her husband was for another.'

'The footman described her as having hysterics,' Royston reminded him.

'In Miss Dorset's room,' Carmichael remembered. 'I think I'll have Jeffrey take me along there to have a word with her while she's off her guard.'

'Shall I come too, sir?' Royston asked, with a hesitation that made Carmichael laugh.

'No, I'll let you off questioning the screaming woman this time. You get on the blower to the Yard and ask about those things you wrote down earlier. Then round up Yately and see where my list of guests has got to. Then, probably, you can start interviewing the servants, but get back to me before that in case I've thought of something else for you.'

'Yes, sir,' Royston said.

Miss Dorset's room turned out to be at the back of the house on the ground floor. Jeffrey announced him. 'Inspector Carmichael of Scotland Yard.'

Carmichael swept in hard on the heels of this, anxious to see the effect on the inhabitants of the room. There were three of them, all women, in an airless space that at first glance seemed to be composed entirely of lace and ribbons. He wondered if this was what was described as a boudoir, or if the absent Miss Dorset were merely very fond of embroidering frills. Two of the women were dark and one very fair. One of the dark ones was sitting on the frilled and ruffled bed and the other on a broad cushioned lace-edged window seat surrounded by lacy ruffled curtains. She was engaged in staring out of the window and smoking. Either of them could have been the widow or the sister. Both of them seemed to be sitting in indifference; neither of them appeared to be in hysterics at this moment. The one on the bed was wearing green, with lace, and the other something gray.

The fair woman was sitting in a little pink frilled basket chair. She was the one who reacted most immediately to the announcement. She jumped to her feet and spun to face Carmichael. She had very blue eyes, pink cheeks, pink lipstick, and an expression that said she welcomed any distraction. She was wearing rather plain clothing that implicitly rejected all attempts at lace and ruffles and which stood out in that room as almost masculine. Carmichael recognized her from newspaper photographs as Lucy Kahn but wondered, now he saw her in person, what could have led her to throw herself away on a Jew? A possibly murderous Jew, at that? Oh well, they said love was inexplicable.

'Mrs. Kahn?' he said. 'I'm sorry to intrude, but I was hoping to have a few words with Lady Thirkie.'

'Oh that's quite all right,' Mrs. Kahn said. 'This is Lady Thirkie, and this is Mrs.

66

Normanby.' She indicated first the woman on the bed, and then the woman at the window. Then she went over to the bed and touched the shoulder of the woman there. 'Angela? Here's a policeman to speak to you.' To Carmichael's surprise, he saw that Angela Thirkie was crying. How could his first glance have failed to notice the tears leaking out of her eyes and streaming down her cheeks? Or had she just begun to cry?

'Have you come to take me to my husband?' the weeping woman asked. 'I haven't seen him yet, you know.'

Carmichael swallowed hard. The corpse had never been a pretty sight, and it would be worse now that Green would have been poking about at it. Besides, it would be in Winchester by now. 'I don't think — ' he began.

Mrs. Kahn deftly intercepted the conversational ball. 'Are you sure it would be a good idea in your condition, Angela?' she asked. 'I have heard of children being marked when their mothers saw horrors when they were in the womb. You wouldn't want that to happen.'

'No.' Lady Thirkie seemed struck by this. 'No, you're right. But how will you identify him if I don't see him?'

'There's no question of the identity of the dead man,' Carmichael said, quietly filing the information that Lady Thirkie was expecting. 'His face has been known to the nation ever since 1941.'

'Of course,' Lady Thirkie said. 'I hadn't thought of that.'

'There's only a question of identifying a body

if it turns up somewhere unusual surely,' Mrs. Kahn said, unexpectedly, with a little laugh. 'I mean Sir James was in his own bed, there isn't any question . . . ' She trailed off, her hand over her mouth.

The woman by the window, the sister-in-law, turned to them for the first time. She was wearing some kind of red shirt with a flounce down the front. 'I shouldn't think there could be any doubt that it was James,' she said in a doleful tone.

'No, no doubt at all,' Carmichael said. 'In any case, formal identification has been done by Mr. Normanby, so there's no need to cause any of you ladies any anguish.'

'By Mark?' Mrs. Normanby snorted and turned again to the window.

'I believe Mr. Normanby found the body,' Carmichael said, feeling he was missing something in the crosscurrents of the room.

'But — ' Mrs. Kahn began, and put her hand to her mouth again. Carmichael waited patiently. 'I didn't know he'd found him,' she said, rather feebly, after a moment. 'He told us that Sir James was dead. I didn't realize he'd actually seen the body.'

'Seen and identified,' Mrs. Normanby said, grimly. 'Good for Mark; how kind of him to spare the weaker sex this burden.'

'Oh do be quiet, Daphne,' Mrs. Kahn said, with real irritation in her voice.

'Who killed him?' Lady Thirkie asked. She was still crying, Carmichael noticed.

'We don't know yet, but we intend to do our

best to find out,' Carmichael said, as he had said many times before in similar circumstances.

'And then they'll hang, won't they, whoever they are?' she said, with a strange kind of relish. Carmichael wondered if she was mad, not the kind of deranged people sometimes temporarily became through grief, but genuinely and long-term cuckoo. Possibly she and her sister were both mad, hereditary madness — though why would two rising politicians have married them if that were the case? They'd been heiresses, but a man wouldn't want to taint his children. Could she have killed him, if she were mad? He looked at her hands, which were big and broad. If she had ever been wearing any lipstick it had worn off.

'Do calm down, Angela,' Mrs. Kahn said.

'Where were you at the time of the murder?' Carmichael asked.

Lady Thirkie gave a little squeak. 'Me? But what was the time of the murder?'

'Sometime between one A.M. last night and nine this morning,' Carmichael said.

'Well, I was asleep . . . and then I got up and went to church, to Early Communion.'

'What time is Early Communion?' he asked.

'Eight-thirty,' Mrs. Kahn put in, seeing Lady Thirkie floundering.

'My maid woke me,' Lady Thirkie said. 'She woke me and told me it was time, so I got dressed and went down, and I met Lord Eversley on the stairs.'

'That would have been at about eight-fifteen,' Mrs. Kahn said. 'I was in the front hall with my

69

mother when Lady Thirkie and my father came down.'

'Did all the guests go to church?' Carmichael asked.

'Very few of them went to the early service,' Mrs. Kahn said. 'Most of them prefer Matins, at eleven-thirty.'

So the house hadn't been almost empty for that hour as he'd been imagining it. What a pity.

He turned back to Lady Thirkie. 'So from one A.M. until just before eight-fifteen, you were asleep in the blue room, and after that you were in church.'

'Yes . . . ' she said.

'You didn't hear anything unusual, either in the night or early this morning?'

It took a moment for the significance of this question to sink in. Carmichael could see her understanding it when, several moments after he finished speaking, she actually flinched. 'You mean it was there? In the dressing room? That's where it happened?' she asked, her voice rising. Where, Carmichael wondered, had she expected her husband to be in the small hours of the morning? 'You mean I was there when the murderer came in? I just lay there, sleeping, while the anarchist killed James? Why, he could have come in and murdered me too!' She began to sob noisily, almost wailing.

'I'm very sorry to have distressed you, Lady Thirkie, but please understand that any evidence I can find, anything at all, might make it easier for me to find out who killed your husband,' he said.

70

'I didn't hear anything,' she sobbed.

Mrs. Kahn put her arms around her, wearily. Mrs. Normanby, still by the window, turned and looked at Carmichael. 'I think you'd better go,' she said. 'You can ask any other questions another time. My sister is too upset to be any more help to you now.'

'Very well.' Carmichael wasn't sorry to leave the stifling atmosphere and the wails. He wanted to talk more to all three women, or he wanted to get more information from them, at least, but he didn't need to do it immediately. He withdrew to the corridor and stood there for a moment taking deep breaths. Where next? Two possibilities immediately suggested themselves: the stables, or the gunroom — male preserves both, where he could be reassuringly free of either feminine wails or feminine ruffles. Laughing at himself, Carmichael strode off in search of Royston.

# 7

Sukey came by at last and tapped hesitantly on her own door. The afternoon had been an interminable drag. The sisters had spent it alternately sniping at and ignoring each other. We'd had a visit from the rather nice, though probably Athenian, Inspector from Scotland Yard. Angela had shown almost as much distress that Sir James had been killed in the dressing room as that he was dead at all, though she didn't quite faint. I opened the door to Sukey with a great sense of relief. If nothing else, I was hungry enough to eat a horse, without even cooking and skinning it. I'd even have eaten the saddle.

Sukey stood there in one of her dresses that Hugh had once unkindly dubbed 'pincushion frocks,' velvet with lace trim. 'It's nearly time to dress for dinner,' she said, in an apologetic whisper. 'I was wondering if I could tiptoe in and get a few things. I won't disturb you.'

I stepped out into the corridor and closed the door. 'I want my dinner too,' I said.

'I had thought trays,' Sukey said. 'Angela can't possibly appear.'

'No, she can't, but I can't stay in there with her. I don't think Daphne should either. Honestly, Sukey, trust me. Daphne is absolutely the wrong person to be with her sister now.'

Sukey frowned and stroked the velvet of her

sleeve — I'm sure she does it without knowing she's doing it, because I once heard her complain about the nap being gone there and saying it was inexplicable. Sukey's rather like a cat in some ways, a slightly fussy cat like a Burmese or a Siamese, and that stroking always reminds me of a cat licking its fur. She likes to have everything in its place, she likes lace and velvet and bobbles, but she's a superb manager. She's absolutely devoted to Mummy, they're cousins, and they've been together since they were girls, and while Sukey's title is 'secretary-companion,' the 'companion' added to show she's a lady and not a hireling, she actually organizes a tremendous amount for Mummy, the house, and political things as well. She keeps Mummy pointed in the right direction. Sukey stays on top of everything that's going on and kind of briefs Mummy so Mummy can just sail through. They're like a swan: Mummy's the part on top of the water gliding along effortlessly and Sukey's the part below the water kicking frantically. I know Mummy couldn't do without her, and what's more, Mummy knows it too. She doesn't pay her a tenth of what she's worth, and she couldn't, no matter how much she paid. You can't buy devotion.

'Then who is there?' Sukey asked. 'I'd do it myself, but there's so much else that needs doing. Can't you stay?' This last she said imploringly, but I shook my head.

'I've been there all day, and I'm at screaming point,' I said. 'How about Lady Manningham?'

Sukey put her head on one side, just exactly

73

like a cat. 'I could ask her,' she said. 'Are you sure Daphne wouldn't . . .'

'They're tormenting each other about who Sir James loved better,' I said. There was no sense in keeping anything from Sukey at this point, even though that meant it would go straight to Mummy. 'It seems Daphne walked into his dressing room and found the body, which looks like a spot of Bognor to me.'

'Oh dear,' Sukey said, distressed. 'You're quite right. Run along and get dressed. I'll ask Kitty Manningham to sit with her. Perhaps we should call Doctor Graham to come and take a look at her.'

'That might be a good idea,' I said. 'She says she's going to have a baby in December and that Sir James knew.'

'My goodness,' Sukey murmured. 'The poor thing!' I knew at once that she meant the baby and almost laughed because that was so much my own reaction.

Sukey patted my arm and scuttled off in search of Lady Manningham. I walked as fast as I could to my room to change, knowing full well that not even a murder would be sufficient to get Mummy to consider sitting down to dinner in day clothes acceptable behavior.

David was in the room, dressed and waiting for me. I kissed him, almost threw off what I was wearing, scattering garments heedlessly about the floor, and dragged on the dress someone had taken the trouble to lay out for me. It happened to be the purple thing from the Worth collection. It's not really purple, it's lavender with a purple creeping-leaf design all over it, and I remembered after I had it on that it was floor-length, which meant my hair had to go up. I fixed it up just anyhow, sticking about ninety pins in it because I'd just washed it and it didn't want to lie quiet. When I was looking at it in the mirror I remembered about the day before, and looked at David over my shoulder again. He was watching me, and smiling, but under the smile I could tell he wasn't one bit happy.

I picked my amethyst chain out of my casket. It's a single amethyst on a gold chain, with amethyst ear-drops to match, and I love them because they're the first thing David gave me after we were engaged. It wasn't my birthday or anything, just an ordinary day in Grosvenor Square, with Mummy being bloody; and rain, hard London rain that's so much dirtier and wetter than rain in the country. I hadn't been expecting David, he just dropped by, and seeing him was like the sun coming out, and he gave me this little box, and I opened it not knowing what, and there they were. Every time I see them or touch them I remember that. I bought the Worth dress to go with them, if you really want to know.

'Will you do my clasp up?' I asked, and then when David had done the clasp and still had his hand on my neck I turned and hugged him.

'What's the matter?' I asked. I had no idea, because I hadn't seen him since early breakfast, having spent all day since church stuck in Sukey's room trying to deal with Angela and Daphne.

'Just the usual,' David said. 'Well, except that

your mother and several of the guests seem to think I'm guilty of this murder.' He said it quite casually and as if the whole thing was absurd, which of course it was, but he didn't really take it as lightly as just the words sound written down. He's actually super-sensitive to slights and so on, but he manages to hide it from most people most of the time by seeming to be very thick-skinned. Few people will be really blatant; although some will, of course, like Mummy, only too often. When this sort of thing happened, David cared enormously but he'd never say, because in some ways David always has to be more English than the English just because he's Jewish — he feels he has to be more stiff-upper-lipped and keep the side up better than anyone.

I did react, I know I did. It was fury, at Mummy, and at the rest of them, whoever they were, for being so stupid, so prejudiced, so unthinkingly vile as to think that just because David was Jewish he was likely to be a murderer. If I'd never known David I might have carried on thinking all these people were basically good people, with odd little quirks perhaps, but I'd never have understood how foul they were. David took the blinkers off for me, and I've never been sorry, because who would want to go around in a world that's like a very thin strip of pretty flower garden surrounded by fields and fields of stinking manure that stretch out as far as the eye can see? And it's not as if those people are the only people in the world, though they may imagine they are.

It might surprise you that I'd spent all day

with Angela and Daphne, talking almost entirely about the murder, with excursions to Bognor and Athens, excuse me, adultery and homosexuality, without really once wondering myself who had done it. I'd even heard Angela ask the Inspector in her histrionic way, without stopping to connect up the fact that if there had been a murder at Farthing then there must also be a murderer here. Everyone else was ahead of me, and I suppose it was in fact frightfully dim of me, but I'd thought about Sir James alive and Sir James dead, and Angela and Daphne, but not at all about who might have killed him or why.

'Did they come right out and say so?' I asked.

'They hinted around the edges of it in a terribly well-bred way,' David said. 'I could pretend to ignore it.' ('English hypocrisy,' David said once, after three bottles of wine, 'can be a wonderful thing. People who hate and despise you, and who in the Reich would put you in a slave labor camp or kill you, in England bother to pretend that they're not really sneering.' And he meant it, too — meant that it was wonderful, I mean.)

'Let's go home straight after dinner,' I said. We could, because we'd driven down, and we could just pop straight into our little two-seater Hilton and drive back to London without anybody or anything getting in our way. We could be home in our flat by midnight at the latest. The thought of it was a tremendous relief; not just the thought of being at home, but getting away from Farthing, from all of this. We didn't have to stay. I'd already done whatever duty to Mummy I needed to. I wouldn't have come at all, if it had been up to me. I'd have thrown her insistence back in her face. It was David who felt that if it was so tremendously important to Mummy that we be here, we'd do better to oblige her. I still didn't know why she wanted us. I think David had felt that it was in some way a peace offering, that she had invited us both so insistently, but I know Mummy better than that. In any case, if it was intended as an olive branch, then it was a very thin one with ragged leaves and no fruit at all.

'There's nothing I'd like better,' David said, with an extremely kissable wistful expression. 'But the police have asked that nobody leave for the time being. To ensure that nobody does, they've locked the gates and put a bobby on them.'

I kissed him quickly, then went to the window and stuck my head out. I couldn't see the gates, of course; that wasn't why I did it. It was just that I needed to get my head into the fresh air because all at once I felt totally trapped. I always felt that a little at Farthing. It isn't claustrophobia, not in the usual way anyway. It's partly Mummy, and the sort of bashes she organizes — feeling as if I'm back in her power. It's also partly the physical fact that Farthing is so deep in the country that it's hard to get away from, even though it's only two hours from London. That's why I'd insisted on driving down, when we could easily have gone by train to Farthing Junction and been picked up from there, the way most people did. Now, despite taking precautions, despite having the Hilton with us, we really were imprisoned here, unable to get away. I felt that terrible crushing feeling in my chest, as if I were fourteen again, with Hugh newly dead and Mummy and Daddy leaning everything on me as if it were all a huge stone that was going to grind me under it. I took deep breaths out the window for all I was worth, but even the sweet May air with the scent of bluebells and lilies of the valley didn't help very much.

The gong rang then, for dinner, and it's just as well that it did. It broke my mood. I gave David my arm and let him take me down, which made me feel much better. As long as my hand was on his arm I felt we were together, there were two of us, even if we were for the time being trapped and surrounded by the enemy.

Mummy and Sukey were standing in the hall. Sukey had somehow found time to get dressed for dinner; she was wearing one of her typical lace-edged dresses, and a cap. Sukey must be the last woman in England to wear a cap. What I thought was she must have got Daphne and Angela out of her room in time. 'I understand he's a gentleman,' Sukey was saying as we came down.

'Policemen are never gentlemen,' Mummy said, decisively.

'He's a police Inspector,' Sukey said. 'I'd have thought he'd be just the kind of man it would be useful to know.'

'Expedient, perhaps, in some ways, but I

wouldn't want to sit down to dinner even with a Chief Constable,' Mummy said, with a slight shudder.

'His father is a squire in Lancashire,' Sukey said. 'I looked him up in *Who's Who*.'

From the 'Lancashire' I guessed they were talking about Inspector Carmichael, who had just the faintest touch of a Northern accent in his voice every now and then. It would seem ordinary and smooth, like a mouthful of pebbles rounded in a stream, and then it would catch on something and roughen, and you could hear a pebble that hadn't been fully rounded down to conformity. I liked it, but I was quite sure Mummy would hate it.

I didn't say anything except 'Good evening,' and left them to their little conflab. Mummy must have won, as usual, because neither Carmichael nor any other policeman appeared at dinner. In fact, company was quite thin — there were only the overnight guests. Goodness knows what the other invited guests had been told, or whether they'd simply been turned away at the gates by the police.

It was a funny group of people. Sukey must have had nightmares seating us. No wonder she wanted to bring in the policeman. There were four married couples — the Normanbys, the Francises, Mummy and Daddy, David and me; then there was Uncle Dud, and Tibs, and Eddie, who were a widower, his son, and daughter; and there was Sir Thomas Manningham, without his wife, who was off with Angela. Sukey sat with us herself, which she didn't always do, only when it

80

helped to even up the numbers, but even so the arrangements worked out very awkwardly.

I was between Tibs and Mark, and David was almost at the other end of the table between Sukey and Eddie.

Of course nobody talked about anything but the murder, and the servants didn't even pretend not to listen. Daphne, on the other side of Tibs, was drinking hard but she didn't do anything to disgrace herself.

The first course was watercress soup, absolutely exquisite, with little hot malted brown rolls. I should have been talking to Tibs, but I didn't do more than grin at him and tuck in. He covered up for me though, or maybe he really wanted to talk. He seemed genuinely shocked at the loss of a man he'd regarded as one of the saviors of his country, and looked up to, politically at any rate. Tibs wasn't political really, any more than Uncle Dud was. I sometimes thought the two of them just let Mummy feed them their views. I could imagine Uncle Dud saying that she was the daughter of a Duke and the wife of a Viscount, she had to be right about rearmament, or peace with Hitler, or some other complicated policy. Tibs surprised me by having a good grasp of the things Sir James had done — not just the Peace, which anyone would have known, but things like the education bill he was sponsoring at the moment. He surprised me again when he said that he believed that the murder had been done by terrorists.

'How would they have got into the house?' I asked, swallowing the last of my soup.

'Probably earlier in the evening, disguised as guests, and then hidden themselves to wait. They're always disguising themselves, these anarchist fellows,' he said. 'Or, perhaps they came in through the window. In and out again. With ropes.' He looked quite enthusiastic at that idea. 'Hugh and I climbed in at Allingham once,' he said.

'Allingham is Gothic,' I said. 'It's covered with protrusions. It's eminently climbable. Farthing isn't.'

Tibs looked a little dashed. 'They might have used grappling hooks,' he said.

'Why would anarchists want to kill him anyway?' I asked. The servants were bringing in the fish course, and it would be my duty to talk to Mark, but they hadn't reached us yet.

'Anarchists always want to stir up trouble, and killing a prominent politician would do that. Why, some people were saying he'd lead the party and then the country at the next election. Or they might just like killing people. Have you heard of the Thugs in India?'

I had, but I didn't think them relevant. Jeffrey handed me my plate and so I was obliged to turn to Mark, who annoyed me for the entire fish course by telling me lies about how he found the body. I knew they were lies, and so did he, but I couldn't tell him that I knew, which made it very awkward. I tried to change the subject, without success. Usually I quite liked talking to Mark, who was amusing and made me laugh, but not this time. He described the body to me, which is how I came to learn that Sir James was stabbed through the heart, and that there had been a Jewish star of the Continental kind left on the body.

I looked over at David, who was quietly spearing his asparagus and talking to Sukey. I had thought Mummy's accusations wild and prejudiced, but I had not known about the star. It occurred to me for the first time that David might be seriously suspected of the murder, suspected perhaps by the police. He must have realized this before; he must have heard the details earlier. Yet he sat there calmly and, feeling my eyes on him, looked up and smiled across at me. I wanted to protect him, to fling my arms around him and keep him from being hurt, or to enclose him behind castle walls where nobody could reach him. Instead I had brought him here where he had to sit down and eat salmon in hollandaise sauce among his enemies.

Mummy was at the head of the table, as usual. She was entirely absorbed in talking to Sir Thomas Manningham. I wished suddenly that Tibs's imaginary terrorist murderer who had come among us to stab a prominent politician had chosen to kill her instead.

# 8

It was late evening before they could even think about getting away from Farthing. With Jeffrey's cooperation they had managed to be assigned a little room, usually one of Lord Eversley's offices. It had a telephone extension and a desk, and could be used for interviews. Carmichael had appropriated the very comfortable chair behind the desk. Between them, they had managed to have at least a preliminary interview with everyone. The servants had brought them a very passable dinner, and even taken something down to Izzard on the gate. When Yately came to report, Carmichael told him that he was about done for the day.

'Can you recommend somewhere to stay in Winchester?' Carmichael asked. 'There's no point in going to town and coming down again tomorrow.'

Yately smiled. 'The Eversley Arms in Castle Farthing is very convenient, and I'm told the food is good and the rooms clean.'

Royston shuddered. 'The locals call that village Clock Farthing,' he remarked.

Carmichael laughed. 'Winchester will be quieter, I think.'

'There's the George, or the King's Head,' Yately said. 'Or there's the Station Hotel at Farthing Junction. That's very much on the spot.'

'We'll try it,' Carmichael said. 'Royston, get directions to Farthing Junction from Jeffrey. Make sure they're clear. And when you've got them, bring the car up.' The railway line was marked on his map, but he didn't repose much trust in the map anymore, especially in the dark.

'I'll be sending a man out to relieve Izzard as soon as I get back,' Yately said.

'Very good. Make sure there's someone on the gates twenty-four hours a day.' Carmichael yawned and stretched. 'Six-hour shifts probably makes most sense.'

'It's going to be a bit difficult keeping everyone here,' Yately said. 'Some of them have already been asking me about leaving.'

'Who?' Carmichael asked.

'Mrs. Kahn, Sir Thomas Manningham, and the Duke of Hampshire,' Yately said. 'I told them all that everyone is to stay for the time being but that they might be able to go home tomorrow.'

'The Duke of Hampshire might, but I'm not so sure about Mrs. Kahn,' Carmichael said.

'Ah, you think Kahn did it?'

'That would be anticipating a great deal,' Carmichael said. 'At the moment, I don't think anybody did it; I try to keep my mind open to all the possibilities. If Kahn did it, his wife must have been in it. She's his alibi. I can't see any possible motivation for her to have been involved, but then women are inexplicable and she clearly loves Kahn. Kahn is very much a suspect at present, but I don't really see any overwhelming evidence in any direction.'

'Some people can go about at midnight in

country houses more easily than others,' Yately said.

'It was later than midnight — he was seen alive at one,' Carmichael said, idly. 'I'll be very interested in Green's report; please do your best to bring it with you tomorrow morning.'

'It should answer a number of questions,' Yately agreed. 'But even as it is, we know the timing is between one and nine.'

'I think we can be quite definite that nobody could have got in from outside after one,' Carmichael said.

Yately sighed, reluctant to let go of the figure of the mysterious cloaked anarchist. 'Sergeant Royston has checked that the bedroom window is inaccessible. The downstairs windows could have been broken into, but not without leaving evidence, and there is no evidence,' he said, dolefully.

Carmichael put his finger on a spot on the floor plan. 'The servants were up in the attics, and couldn't come down without passing either Mrs. Simons or Mr. Hatchard, whose rooms are on the ends of the female and male servants' quarters respectively. The doors were locked and they had the keys. That lets out the servants entirely unless the housekeeper or the butler are either involved or complicit. That leaves us with the family and the guests, and Miss Dorset, however we classify her.'

'Then it has to be Mr. Kahn,' Yately said. Outside, Carmichael heard the friendly purring of the police Bentley, and the sound of the tires on the gravel. 'Out of the fifteen people, he's the only one with a motive.'

'Not much of a motive,' Carmichael said. 'His motive amounts to the fact of his religion. He's Jewish — Thirkie hated Jews and helped to make peace with Hitler. Do you think he couldn't subdue his anger at that if he could bear to marry the daughter of Lord Eversley? And to kill this way, leaving the star, would be the act of a very stupid man, which Kahn isn't, unless I miss my guess. I've only had a few words with him, I'll interview him properly tomorrow, but I'm keeping my mind very much open.'

Royston came back in. 'I've got the directions, sir, and the car's ready to go,' he said.

'Well done,' Carmichael said, standing up.

'I'll go too,' Yately said, opening the door. 'I don't know about your open mind, mine's open too, but if Kahn's motive is thin then it seems that nobody else has a motive at all.'

'*Cui bono?*' Carmichael asked, going out of the door. 'We'll know that tomorrow when we have his will. I've also asked for profiles on the other guests, just anything the Yard might have, to see if there might be some motives there. Maybe it is the Duke of Hampshire after all.'

Yately didn't laugh. Indeed, he looked a little affronted. 'Everyone knows his Grace doesn't care about anything except hunting and horseflesh,' he said, as if it were a severe reproof. Carmichael laughed and clapped him on the back as he went by.

The butler, Hatchard, opened the front door. Lady Eversley drifted out of one of the rooms as he did so.

'Ah . . . ,' she said.

'The police gentlemen are just leaving, my lady,' the butler said.

'Will that be all, then, Inspector?' she asked Carmichael. 'Is the matter over with, and can I expect to be able to come and go normally tomorrow?'

'I'm afraid not, Lady Eversley,' he said. 'We're stopping for the night, but we'll be back in the morning, and we won't stop until we have caught the murderer.'

'Stopping for the night, my goodness,' she said. 'Well, tomorrow is all right, but I absolutely have to be in London on Tuesday.' She smiled, a smile that reminded Carmichael of an illustration he had seen in Anderson's *The Snow Queen* when he was a boy. He found himself wishing for the second time that day for an invasion, even the invasion of the Third Reich the Farthing Set had averted. He didn't like Hitler — in fact he suspected that he disliked Hitler considerably more than Lady Eversley did — but Hitler's storm troopers might have shaken her ladyship up a little and made her rethink her priorities.

'A man has been killed,' he said, giving her ice for ice. 'I can't yet say how long this will take.'

'We're all terribly distressed about Sir James,' she said, confidingly. 'I hope it isn't making me seem short-tempered and callous. But there's a very important vote on Tuesday, and Sir James himself certainly wouldn't have wanted my husband to have missed it.'

'I'll do what I can, but I can't make promises at this stage,' Carmichael said.

'Thank you,' she said, with a very sweet smile, then swept back through the door she had come through.

'Bitch,' Royston said under his breath as they came out onto the gravel.

'Not impressed with her attempt to charm?' Carmichael asked, closing the door of the Bentley. 'Me neither. She's a country-running bitch. A first-in-class, best-in-show, one-hundred-percent bitch, thoroughbred Southern English.'

'She doesn't seem as upset as I'd have thought she would be that her friend's been murdered,' Royston said as he drove off towards the gates. Yately was behind them, his lights blinding when Carmichael glanced back.

'If he was her friend,' Carmichael said.

'Why would she invite him to stay in her house if he wasn't her friend?' Royston asked.

'He might have thought she was his friend,' Carmichael said.

Royston digested that in silence as they passed Izzard on the gates and began to wind their way through the little Hampshire lanes. 'Do you really think she did it?' he asked after a few miles.

'I'm keeping an open mind,' Carmichael said primly.

The Station Hotel was probably best described as 'unpretentious.' Carmichael didn't really get a chance to see it until he woke up there the next morning. He lay awake for a little while luxuriating in his comfortable bed and contemplating the cross-stitch text on the opposite wall: 'Hold fast to that which is good.' He couldn't remember where that came in the Bible, which was surprising, what with all the verses he'd had to learn in school. It had been the usual punishment, learning Bible verses, and if it had been useless, at least it had furnished his mind with quotations. He'd missed out on that one, though.

Hold fast to that which is good — what the devil did it mean? Grab onto something you like and cling on as tight as you could? There's a creed for the Eversleys and Thirkies of this world. Carmichael admitted to himself that he didn't like the inside of Farthing one bit more than he'd liked the countryside that surrounded it. Lady Eversley was holding fast to what she had, all right, and condescending beautifully to make sure nobody else got their hands on any of it. He didn't really think she'd killed Thirkie. She had no reason to, and her hands were small and delicate. Green's report should rule her either in or out on that count. He wished she had done it, though, because it would have been a pleasure to be able to hang her. Did they hang Viscountesses? Or did they rate execution by the sword, like Anne Boleyn?

How would she act on the scaffold? She'd keep a stiff upper lip to the last, no doubt, holding fast to that which is good until it was quite gone. Was it James the First who had continued to talk after his head had been cut off? Hold fast — Carmichael sighed. The text could perhaps be read as an exhortation to uphold the good and true. That sounded a little more like something Jesus would have said.

Carmichael got up, washed in cold water, and went down to breakfast. To his surprise, the food was good — fresh eggs, scrambled with ham and cheese, on good thick toast. There was even *The Times*, no doubt fresh down from London on the milk train, with an account of the Thirkie murder as the lead story, and a second column header that Kursk had changed hands again. Carmichael wasn't sure, and didn't bother to check, if that meant the Nazis or the Soviets had seized control this time. No doubt the press would be all over Farthing this morning. It was a good thing they had a bobby at the gate.

Royston joined him, and the landlady put another plate in front of him. She came back with a pot of tea. Carmichael, who liked his tea weak, put the paper down and poured his immediately. 'Tea?' he asked.

'In a moment, sir, if you don't mind,' Royston said. 'Did you sleep well?'

'I did, but I woke up with a cynical eye on the world,' Carmichael said. 'Is there a text in your room?'

'A text?' Royston looked startled.

'An embroidered biblical text, on the wall?'

'Oh yes,' Royston said, taking the lid off the teapot and stirring it. 'In the most horrible blue and red wool. It says 'Thou, O Lord, seeest me,' except that there are three es and no apostrophe in 'see-est,' so it looks very peculiar, as if it's pronounced like a cyst. My sister-in-law had a cyst, once.' He poured the tea and added milk.

Carmichael laughed. '*The Times* says Scotland Yard is making progress and expects to

91

make an arrest soon.'

'On what?' Royston looked startled.

'This case,' Carmichael said.

'How did they get hold of that?'

'On a Sunday, too, very enterprising of them. I strongly suspect that somebody told them. It might have been Betty at the gate, though I don't actually suspect her of having the intelligence. It might have been someone at the house, possibly Lady Eversley herself. She likes publicity.'

They both knew it wouldn't have been the Yard.

'Well, we couldn't have kept the lid on it forever,' Royston said, philosophically. He put a piece of bacon into his mouth and began to chew.

Carmichael checked that the landlady was out of earshot. 'I think we want to get someone in London to search the Kahns' flat. I'm not really expecting to find very much, but it would be interesting to see what we did find. I think we're justified, at this point.'

'New evidence in the night?' Royston asked.

'No, sergeant, I just wanted to sleep on it. You telephone that through as soon as we get in.' Carmichael ate his last bite of toast and sipped his tea. In his own little London flat, his man, Jack, would undoubtedly be taking the opportunity to sleep in. Jack had once been Carmichael's batman, and anyone who has ever served in the army took advantage of any opportunity life offered for a late morning. If Carmichael had been home, Jack would have got up without complaint, at dawn if need be, made him

92

breakfast and served him a perfect cup of Yunnan tea in his Japanese teapot and tea bowl. As it was, Jack got to lie in and Carmichael got to drink Ceylon tea that only wasn't stewed because he had picked it up quickly enough. Ah well, he had chosen his profession and nobody said that life was supposed to be fair.

'Ready, sergeant?' he asked.

Royston gulped down the last of his tea and gave him a resentful glance. 'Just coming, sir,' he said.

The drive out to Farthing was uneventful. It wasn't such a perfect day as the day before; a few clouds dotted the expanse of blue sky. There was also more traffic on the road — a tractor, several farm carts, and the occasional motor car. Motor cars became more common as they approached Farthing itself, until when they turned up the lane leading to the village it was lined with cars.

Press, Carmichael surmised. It must be a slow day. Either that or people cared more about Thirkie than he would have imagined. The bobby on the gate frowned at him as they pulled up. 'Nobody whatsoever is permitted onto the property,' he said, with the air of one who has said it too many times this morning already.

The clock struck nine, and Carmichael waited for it to die away before saying, 'Scotland Yard,' and showing his card. The bobby examined it carefully, handed it back, and opened the gates. The press, seeing the gates opening, gathered round, calling questions, which Carmichael ignored, and flashing pictures.

'A press release will be issued later this

morning,' he told the bobby. 'You can tell them that.' It was a waste of time, but unavoidable in the circumstances. He'd make Yately write it, though he'd have to give it himself.

'Thank you, sir,' the bobby said.

'Is Inspector Yately here yet?' Carmichael asked.

'Not yet, sir, but I'm expecting him very soon.'

This one was more alert than poor Izzard, at least. 'Send him up as soon as he gets here,' Carmichael said. 'Keep up the good work, constable. I'm sorry it has to be quite so tedious. I'll see if we can get them to send refreshments down to you.'

'That would be very welcome, sir,' the bobby said, and saluted smartly as they drove through. Several cameras popped on the salute.

'Obviously a better class of bobby working in Winchester on Mondays,' Carmichael said as they swept up the drive.

'Poor bastard, and it wasn't even nine o'clock,' Royston said, parking neatly.

The butler opened the door for them. 'Good morning, Hatchard. Has there been any post for me?' Carmichael asked breezily.

'I believe your mail has been delivered to your office, sir,' the butler said, with the air of someone who has gone out of his way to pay attention to the comfort and convenience of underlings.

'Thank you,' Carmichael snarled.

When they were in the little office with the door shut, he turned to Royston. 'When Yately gets here, have him interview Hatchard first.'

94

'You don't really think he did it? I talked to him yesterday, and it was all routine.'

'Not for a second, but it's possible he could have, so Yately can go over his evidence again. He could do with being taken down a peg or two.'

Royston laughed. Carmichael picked up his mail, a substantial envelope postmarked London. The Yard had come through, again.

'You call to organize searching Kahn's flat, and I'll go through this,' Carmichael said, sitting down in the desk chair once again.

'You look like a kid with a Christmas stocking,' Royston said, drawing the phone towards himself. 'Well, let me know if there's anything interesting in that lot. What are you expecting?'

'Information,' Carmichael said, smiling. 'I don't know what yet, but at present this case is very lacking in hard facts. After you've made the call, interview the rest of the servants, the ones you didn't already do. We might as well be thorough, and even if they didn't do anything, they might have seen something.'

'Yes, sir,' Royston said, but Carmichael was already deep into his envelope.

# 9

David and I lay very close together that night with our arms around each other, but we didn't make love. We didn't feel like it, neither of us — that was one of the things where we always felt the same. I was frightened, and I think he was too, but we didn't talk about it, we just lay there and held each other deep into the night. It wasn't a thing for talking about in darkness.

I didn't get up so early the next day, Monday. The bloody birds did wake me, singing their little hearts out at dawn, but I put the pillow over my head and went back to sleep. I half woke again when David got out of bed. When I woke up properly he was up, he'd washed and shaved already, and he was getting dressed. Mummy says it's frightfully bourgeois to get dressed in the room with your wife. She says she supposes coal miners and people like that have to do it because their houses are so small. I love to watch David dressing and undressing; his body is so beautiful, I love it in all the states. That morning I lay there and watched him covering himself up with ordinary clothes. He saw that I was awake and sat down on the side of the bed to kiss me.

'Don't get up unless you want to,' he said. 'It's only eight. I'm getting up because I'm fairly sure the police will want to talk to me again.'

They'd talked to both of us the evening before, after dinner, first David, for ages, and then me, quite briefly. They asked me where I'd been between one and nine, and they asked me who I'd seen. I told them I'd been in bed with David, and yes, we shared a bed, and yes, I'd have known if he left the bed because I slept on the outside and it wasn't a very big bed. It was what they call a three-quarter bed, four feet wide, only big enough for two people if they love each other very much. When I said that, Inspector Carmichael got a look on his face the way people do when newlyweds say soppy things, but the other Inspector, Yately, the one from Winchester, looked quite affronted. I couldn't tell if he was strait-laced or hated Jews. I told them about getting up for my bath and seeing Mummy, but they didn't seem very interested. I didn't tell them how unusual it was that she was up at that hour, but I did tell them her bedroom was on the floor below. Then I told them about going to church and who came down when, which they wrote down, with times.

'Is there anything they didn't ask you about?' I asked, sitting up and reaching for my hairbrush.

'I don't suppose so,' David said, stroking the underneath of my arm almost absently, but in a way that made shivers go through me. 'After all, there's nothing to ask, really. In the time they're interested in I was asleep, and then eating breakfast with you and Tibs. Most of their questions were about another thing. I think they think I'm the most likely suspect. The star and so forth.'

'It's ridiculous,' I said, vehemently. 'But darling, are you in serious trouble, do you think?'

He smiled at me, and I could see he meant to reassure me, but I put my hand up to still his hand and let him know that I wanted a real answer. Our bodies were very good at talking to each other, better than our minds sometimes. 'I might be,' he said after a moment. 'I haven't done anything wrong, but it would be very hard to prove that. It looks as if someone meant to make it look to someone stupid as if I'd done it.'

'Do you think Mummy knew, and invited us down so you'd be a suspect?' I asked, almost whispering. I'd thought of this in the middle of the night before.

'That would mean she knew Sir James was going to be murdered,' David said, very reasonably. 'I know you attribute supernatural powers to your mother sometimes, but seriously, how could she have? Unless she did it herself — and I have difficulty imagining her stabbing a friend.'

'That's because you haven't known Mummy very long. Besides, Sir James was an ally, not a friend. But you're right — her usual style is stabbing them in the back.'

'English police are wonderful,' David quoted, but meaning it too. 'They'll probably find the real culprit soon enough and we'll laugh to think we were worried. I just hope they do it quickly before there's too much unpleasantness.'

'Yes, me too,' I said, fervently. I kissed him then, and dropped my hairbrush.

He picked it up and before he handed it back to me ran his fingers over the back. 'L, R, E,' he said, reading the monogram. The 'R' is my ghastly middle name, Rowena, which Daddy chose, and which he got from *Ivanhoe.* 'We ought to get you a new one.'

'That's the only thing I've kept with my old initials,' I said. My new initials, LRK, make me think I ought to put the 'u' of Lucy in, and make it LURK and have done with it. 'Hugh gave it to me.'

'In that case you ought to keep it,' he said, understanding at once.

'That's why I have kept it,' I said, taking it from him and brushing my hair again.

'Do you think Hugh would have stood for it?' he asked. 'I mean you and me? If he'd lived?'

'You were his best friend,' I said, surprised. I'd always known Hugh would have been on my side through all the family battles, not to mention that it wouldn't have mattered so much if he'd been alive to inherit everything.

'Yes, but . . . It's a cliché, isn't it. Letting one marry your sister. He never introduced me to the family.'

'He talked about you in his letters to me.' My hair was all untangled now, and brushed, but hanging loose around my face like a savage or the Lady of Shalott. I slid out of bed and reached for my pins on the dressing table. 'That's how I knew who you were when I met you. He told me you saved his life.'

'Not any more than he saved mine,' David said. 'Hundreds and hundreds of times, and then the last time I couldn't do anything for him but watch him come down, in a field near Salisbury. It was a different life. We all felt sure we'd die, but at the same time, curiously immortal. We were like brothers — differences like race and religion and even whether you hated someone didn't matter. There was one man there who I fought in training, said Jews shouldn't fly aeroplanes, said even that we'd all support Hitler if it wasn't for the fact that he was persecuting us. We went outside and pounded each other for forty minutes until neither of us could stand up any longer. You can tell by this that we were both Englishmen, incidentally. Continentals would have fought dirty and finished the thing in five minutes. But in the Battle of Britain, when the Heinkels were thick on his tail, I dived and strafed them to draw them off, knowing he'd do the same for me — and he did, on other occasions. We saved each other's lives so many times that we lost count, and we still didn't like each other. But the hate had gone. The hate was all for the enemy then, and in a way the hate had been replaced by a kind of love, but a strange kind, love without liking. The kind you get in families sometimes.'

I didn't say anything, even when he fell silent, because David almost never talked about the war and I wanted to hear and I was afraid that if I asked he'd clam up. I got my hair under control and started dressing.

'All I'm saying is that the way Hugh and I felt about each other in 1940 doesn't mean that he'd have wanted you to marry me,' he said.

'He did,' I said. 'Almost, anyway. He said that he wished, when I was old enough to marry, that I might find someone as reliable, as honorable, and as kind. I know it almost by heart, I've read it so many times. It's the last letter he sent me, before he died.'

David had tears in his eyes. 'Will you show it to me?' he asked.

'It's in London,' I said, but that wasn't any answer. I sat down on the bed and patted the spot beside me so that he'd sit too. The trouble was that what I had to say was something we'd understood without talking, and it was something that people by and large didn't talk about, though Hugh and I had. The rest of it was that Hugh and I had developed our own private language to talk about it, because the way other people did talk about it always seemed so horrid. Hugh was six and a half years older than I was, and for some brothers and sisters that's a huge gap and they're strangers. But we were always very close. The first thing I can remember is toddling into Hugh's hands, when I must have been about two and him about eight. We'd always talked about everything, from when I was too young to understand how much other people disapproved or didn't understand. I wasn't entirely sure whether David was going to approve of my knowing, which was why we hadn't talked about it before — well, and the subject hadn't come up before, not like this, not as emotionally. I put my arms around him.

'If you read that letter, darling, which you're welcome to, you'd see that Hugh and I talked about some things men don't usually talk about with their sisters,' I said.

101

David went absolutely rigid. 'You know that?' he said.

'I know, and it doesn't bother me at all,' I said, and decided that whatever it sounded like I was going to use our terms rather than the ugly ones. 'Hugh knew that you were like him, Macedonian rather than Athenian.'

Surprisingly, that made David laugh. 'I know that whenever you start burbling absolute nonsense that you're really saying something very profound, but what on earth does that mean?'

'Alexander the Great was Macedonian,' I said. 'He loved Hephaistion, but he also got married twice and had a son. Plato was Athenian, and he thought love could only possibly be between boys. Then there are Romans, who think it can only be between men and women and are sometimes very down on anything Greek at all. Hugh thought most men were Macedonians pretending to be Romans, and a few really were Romans and a few really were Athenians. If you'd been an Athenian you wouldn't have wanted me.'

'You're quite extraordinary,' David said. 'And you've known this all this time and never mentioned it?'

'People often don't like to talk about it,' I said. 'I once shocked Eddie Cheriton almost out of her wits by asking if Tibs was Athenian.'

'You can take it from me that Tibs is as Athenian as . . . as Pericles,' David said. He was looking at me in an absolutely bemused way. 'So you knew all along that Hugh and I were lovers and thought it didn't matter?'

'I knew it mattered a great deal,' I contradicted. 'I knew you were in love — I told you, Hugh wrote to me about it. He talked about what you just talked about, that kind of male love you get when you're saving each other's lives, and the terrific friendship there was in the Squadron, and the special love you two had for each other. I wrote back that it must be like the Sacred Band, but I don't think he ever got that letter.'

'He got it the morning he died,' David said, and now tears were spilling down his cheeks. 'It was in the pocket of his flying jacket when he burned up. We always used to get the post at breakfast in the Squadron, and he looked so pleased reading it that morning that some of the fellows were teasing him that it was from a girlfriend, and he said no, it was from his sister, and then there was a flap so he slipped it inside his jacket and we went out to the planes.'

I was crying now; we both were. It was eight years ago, but it felt as if it had just happened. I could picture poor old Hugh putting the letter inside his jacket and going off to fight, dying knowing I thought it was like the Sacred Band.

'But how could you marry me and not tell me you knew all this?' David asked, after a little while.

'You never mentioned it either,' I said. 'And Hugh was dead, a long time before I met you. If he'd still been alive it would have been different. I suppose I was a tiny bit jealous that you'd loved someone else before you loved me, but it helped that it was Hugh, whom I loved too, and that it wasn't a woman. I know I can believe you when you say that I'm the first woman you ever loved.'

'I wish Hugh had told me he told you,' David said. 'But then I suppose I'd have been afraid to talk to you.'

'That ghastly concert,' I said. We smiled at each other, remembering.

It was a charity concert to raise money for rebuilding London houses that had been flattened in the Blitz. I don't know why they'd suddenly thought of doing this in 1947 when they'd been flattened in 1940, or maybe they'd been doing it all along and I hadn't noticed. David was there with his mother because his father was a big donor and had been given tickets he didn't want to use, but his mother had wanted to go. I was there with Billy because Eddie was performing, playing the cello in the first half. Terrible screeching — I'd be amazed if it persuaded anyone to give anything. But she was also playing a duet in the second half so we couldn't leave at halftime, and there was a kind of bun fight, trestle tables set up and lemonade and cakes at only ten times the price you'd pay for them at a Joe Lyons, but all in a good cause. I was bored rigid, and also parched. I sent Billy into the fray to get me a drink, and he came back with the drink and also with David.

I was bored, bored, bored, and here was someone really different. I liked his looks. Yes, he was obviously Jewish, but he was also obviously gorgeous, in a dark handsome way. I knew at once when I heard the name. 'Would that be

104

Flight Lieutenant David Kahn?' I asked.

'Not any more,' David said, and smiled meltingly at me. 'But would you be Hugh Eversley's little sister?'

There and then we made a date, though we didn't call it that. I insisted he call on me to talk about Hugh, and when he said he couldn't call on a young lady, I invited him along to a party Mummy was having the next week. Billy was horrified. When David had gone off to take lemonade to his mother he started hissing in my ear. 'Can't you tell the fellow's Jewish? You can't possibly mean to know him, Lucy.'

'You seem to know him,' I said.

'I've had business dealing with him, as anyone might. I don't know him socially!'

'You introduced him to me — that's knowing him socially,' I said, nastily. 'Besides, he was in the RAF with Hugh. I think it's nonsensical to make social distinctions that exclude someone who risked his life for his country.'

I didn't persuade Billy, but I enjoyed shocking him. Daddy accused me of using David against my family, the world they made and forced me to live in. At the beginning, that was half of what I wanted; the other half was to talk about Hugh. I didn't fall in love with David until the party when we really did talk, though he says he fell in love with me that first minute at the concert, seeing me there among all the others.

'You do know it's illegal,' David said now, bringing me back to the present.

'What? Oh, being Macedonian? Yes, I know. It's a crazy law; they never prosecute.'

'They do sometimes. They do if they want to get someone for something else. They keep the laws on the books as a way of controlling people, making sure everyone does what society wants. So they'd never prosecute Tibs, though he all but openly sleeps with his stable-boys. Billy will marry, and Billy, or his son, will inherit the title. If there wasn't any Billy, if they had to force Tibs to marry and produce a son, they could use the laws to threaten him — we could put you in prison for this, they'd say.'

'I won't tell anyone,' I said, giving him the reassurance that all this was really asking for. 'I haven't told anyone all this time, after all.'

'It's something a man needs to keep very quiet if he has enemies,' David said. 'And all Jewish people have enemies.'

That reminded me of something. 'Would you say Mark Normanby is Macedonian or Athenian?' I asked.

'He's married,' David said. 'Macedonian.'

'But they don't have any children. I'd always assumed that too, because really I've always thought he's quite attractive. It's just something Angela said yesterday and Daphne's reaction.'

'Angela accused Mark of being Athenian?' David said, astonished. 'Is this the kind of thing women talk about when they're alone?'

'Not usually, but they were being really vile to each other,' I said. 'Probably just bitchiness.'

I was going to go on and explain what they'd said, but there was a knock on the door.

Jeffrey was there. 'If it isn't an interruption, madam, Inspector Yately would like to have another word with Mr. Kahn.'

'He'll be down presently,' I said.

I hugged David hard, straightened his tie, and sent him off to the police, which felt rather more like sending him off to the middle of the Colosseum with the lions than I would have liked.

# 10

On top was a note from Sergeant Stebbings, the phlegmatic desk man at the Yard.

'Aren't you playing in exalted company! This seems to be most of what you've asked for. We're missing reports on a couple of the less well-known guests, which we'll get later in the morning and send down to you. I thought it was better to let this catch the last post tonight. Let me know if we can do anything else for you.'

Carmichael sorted through the documents underneath. Enough to be getting on with, definitely enough to be getting on with. Before he had glanced at more than half the pile, he noticed the thick bond and unusual length of legal paper and dragged that one out.

'The Last Will and Testament of Sir James Martin Thirkie of Thirkie, Bart,' he read. 'Prepared by Gillibrand and Stubbs.' It was the solicitor's copy, probably their spare copy, knowing Gillibrand and Stubbs, a firm who behaved as if it were still 1810. He was surprised they'd deigned to draw up the will of a mere baronet.

The will was surprising. It had been drawn up just after Sir James's marriage, and was dated August 6, 1945. The ancestral home of Thirkie, in Yorkshire; Campion Hall, in Monmouthshire on the Welsh border; Thirkie House in Knightsbridge; some other property, named and listed; and all he died possessed but ten thousand pounds went to 'Captain Oliver Sinclair Thirkie, address care of Whites Club, St. James's Street.' Ten thousand pounds went to 'Angela, Lady Thirkie, unless she should provide an heir, as by the terms of our marriage settlement.' Should she provide an heir, he got everything, with Angela as sole guardian in his minority. The marriage settlement had been thoughtfully appended, so Carmichael was able to see that 'Angela, née Dittany' had given up control of her own property on marriage, that she would get it back, in addition to the ten thousand pounds, as a widow. If the marriage was dissolved in any other circumstances . . . He skimmed over the provisions — nothing at all for her if she were divorced, a big loss for him if he were. The usual stuff in fact, except for the stuff about the heir. Lady Thirkie must be hoping rather vehemently that the baby she was expecting was a boy, he thought. He wondered if she would smuggle in a boy if it happened to be a girl, as some Queen of France was said to have done.

That settled the question of who benefited by his death. She did if she had a boy; if not, she did to some extent and his cousin Captain Thirkie inherited. Carmichael scribbled a note to investigate Captain Thirkie. He wondered if Sir James would have changed the will had he lived. As it was, if the child was a daughter she would be portionless. Surely that would have occurred to one or the other of them now that Lady Thirkie was pregnant? 'If you die and it's a girl,

109

she'll have nothing,' Lady Thirkie might have said. What would he have answered? 'By Jove, yes, I'd better get onto the solicitor chappies.' Or would he never have spared it a thought? He wasn't an old man, or sick, to worry about dying.

Carmichael turned to a neatly typed sheet, Scotland Yard's report on Sir James Martin Thirkie, Baronet.

'Born, 19 June 1909, Thirkie, West Yorkshire.'

If he'd lived, he would have been forty in six weeks. Carmichael was surprised he was so young. He'd have guessed from five to ten years older, from the corpse, and from the man's standing in the country.

'Parents, Sir Robert Martin Thirkie, Bart, 1880–1917; Lady Letitia Harriet Thirkie, née Francis, 1885– .'

Father killed in the trenches, mother still alive, though she must be getting on. He did a quick calculation. Sixty-four. She'd have seen it in the papers, if nobody had thought to tell her. It would be a terrible shock.

'Siblings, one, decd., Matthew Thirkie, 1907–39.'

Older brother killed right at the start of the second war. No younger brothers. Presumably Captain Oliver Thirkie was a cousin.

'Married (1) 1932, Lady Olivia Jane Larkin, 1914–40. No issue.'

Nobody could call them a fortunate family.

'Married (2) 1945, Angela Mary Dittany, 1924–. No issue.'

She was ten years exactly younger than his first wife, and fifteen years younger than him. No

110

issue wasn't precisely right; issue pending, more like.

'Educated, St. Crispin Preparatory School, 1916–22, Eton 1922–28, Magdalene College, Cambridge, 1928–31.'

About what he'd have expected. Sent away to school at seven, poor blighter, and his father killed the year after.

'Degree: B.A., Second Class Honours in Mathematics, 1931. M.A., (Cantab), 1935. Rowing blue.'

Maths, eh? An unusual choice for someone of his background. A predisposition in that direction? But second class, not first. And he rowed?

'Elected Conservative MP for Monmouthshire, by-election 1932.'

Of course, while his brother lived he'd have been capable of being elected to the Commons.

'Re-elected in General Election of 1935. Served in Chamberlain's National Government as Junior Health Minister, and later as a deputy to the Foreign Secretary. In November 1939, on the death of his brother, he ascended to the Lords, where he became Foreign Spokesman for the Chamberlain and later the Churchill Governments. In May 1941, he dealt with the Hess Mission, and went back with Hess to Berlin, returning on June 1 with negotiated peace terms that ended the war. He became Foreign Secretary after the 1942 'Victory' election, in which capacity he served until the 1946 election. From 1946–47 during the Charlton government he was Shadow Foreign

Secretary. Since the 1947 election he has served as Minister for Education.'

Yes, yes. Carmichael skimmed over the paragraph. He knew all that.

'Closest political associates the 'Farthing Set,' Lord and Lady Eversley, the Duke of Hampshire, Mark Normanby MP. Political enemy: Sir Winston Churchill, who frequently abuses him in conversation, calling him a traitor. Thirkie's relations with Eden and other leading figures in his own party are occasionally stormy but generally amicable. Thirkie is widely respected for his noted personal integrity.'

Churchill couldn't have killed him. He wasn't here.

'Sir James Thirkie is also generally hated by the Jews and other refugees from Europe who dislike the peace they consider him responsible for.'

Yes, very well, and painting his chest red was an attack on the well-known Farthing robin, and there was the star. But why now?

'Current political program: Thirkie was sponsoring two bills in the House. One was the Higher Education Bill, expected to pass this session, limiting access to Higher Education to those educated in Preparatory and Public Schools. The second was the School-Leaving Age Bill, presently in committee in the Lords, lowering the school-leaving age to eleven in rural areas.'

Not the kind of thing that would encourage anarchists to climb into your bedroom window and kill you, those. Carmichael sighed.

'It is expected that in the coming government reshuffle, those of the Farthing Set, including Thirkie, would have been given more prominent positions. Thirkie was widely tipped for either the Home or the Foreign Secretaryship.'

Well, that might be something. Who might get the job if he didn't? Anyone here? Carmichael put the sheet down and rubbed his head. He noticed a cooling cup of coffee beside his left hand and took a gulp of the unpleasant substance.

Who next? Kahn? No, stick to politics for a little while. Mark Normanby was next. Foreign Minister, lots of travel, especially to Europe, also America in the last year. He'd been at Eton with Thirkie, and also gone on to Cambridge with him, though he'd been a Trinity man. He'd got his first in Law, and gone on to be called to the bar before going into politics at the 1935 election. He'd been a step behind Thirkie then, but he was overtaking him now. He was tipped to be Chancellor at the reshuffle, with the hope of becoming Prime Minister later. Thirkie couldn't have hoped for that, any more than Lord Eversley could. They might lead their party but not the country; they were in the Lords. The very highest offices, the Prime Minister and the Chancellor of the Exchequer, always went to men who had been elected. It was the one advantage England gave to the commoner.

If it had been the other way around, he could have believed Thirkie killing Normanby out of jealousy, even if he was his brother-in-law. By all accounts they were close though, going upstairs together and waking him in the morning. They'd married sisters. Might there be some sexual element in the friendship? Possibly. It would be a good idea to talk to Normanby himself and get a feeling for that. He had married 'the Hon. Daphne Alice Dittany' in 1936 when she'd been eighteen — Carmichael wondered when she'd taken to staring out of windows and smoking. No issue, in fourteen years. There could be something wrong there. But even if there was, it wasn't necessarily connected with the murder. Unless it was something Thirkie could use to blackmail Normanby, and then Normanby could have killed him to stop it. Half the murders that weren't spouses killing each other were blackmail victims killing blackmailers. Dangerous profession, blackmail.

There was no report on Daphne. The one on Angela was perfunctory, giving no real information. The one on Lord Eversley was four pages thick, and he was hesitating over it when the door opened, revealing Inspector Yately, in a neat and pressed uniform, looking very pleased with himself.

'I have the report,' he said.

'Any surprises?' Carmichael asked.

'Oh yes.' Yately's smile broadened. 'Strangulation, didn't you think?'

'You mean it wasn't?' He couldn't have been stabbed after all. His face was suffused, and there hadn't been any blood. It came to him at once. 'Carbon monoxide poisoning?'

Yately's smugness faded a trifle. 'Yes.'

'There was a gas fire in the room, but I doubt

114

the doors are air-tight.'

'There's a fitted carpet that goes underneath them.' Yately spread his hands suggestively.

'Maybe it was suicide all the time.'

'But the lipstick — the star!' Yately objected.

'He might have wanted to kill himself and frame his political enemies.'

'Why would he want to kill himself?' Yately looked perplexed.

'I don't know of any reason. And you forgot to mention the thing that really stops it being suicide — the knife. A man could conceivably dress up in a way that would embarrass his enemies, but he can't stab himself with his own dagger after he's already dead.'

'No . . . '

'Unless he had someone to help him with that.'

'Are you joking, sir?' Yately asked.

'I was keeping my mind open to the possibilities,' Carmichael said, gravely. 'Does Green's report give a time of death?'

'Early, he says.' Yately looked uncomfortable. 'In fact, if we didn't know he was alive at one, Green would have guessed even earlier than that, like ten or eleven. But in any case, sometime soon after he went to bed, definitely not in the morning when people were getting up and going to church.'

On the whole, Carmichael was pleased to hear this. It gave them a definite time and excluded a lot of possibilities. It almost made up for the gassing, which let back in all the women that strangling might have excluded. 'Get someone to check the room for draftiness,' he said. 'Check with Normanby as to whether there was a smell of gas — I can't see how he could have avoided mentioning it before if there was.'

'There wasn't even the slightest whiff of gas when we arrived,' Yately said. 'The window was open, but if there had been enough gas to kill a man, I'd have expected to smell something.'

'Check the fire, too. It might be possible to see when it was last used, or if it has been left on.'

'I suppose he could have been gassed somewhere else and moved back to his room.'

'He was a big man,' Carmichael said. 'Still, it's certainly possible. But they'd have been risking someone seeing, even in the small hours. And why would they do that, when they could have left him wherever he was?'

'Depends where he was.'

'Get someone to check all the gas fires in the house.' Carmichael made a note.

'That would be a job,' Yately said.

'It's your job — make sure it gets done.' Carmichael wasn't in any mood to let Yately do things his way. 'Also check all the cars.'

'The cars?'

'One of the commonest forms of carbon monoxide poisoning is sitting in a closed garage with the car engine running. People kill themselves like that all the time.'

'But that would be an accident,' Yately said. He was biting his lip and clearly only one step from rubbing his head.

'You mentioned moving the body. It's possible this may have been an accident, or suicide, which someone else then came along and took advantage of for their own purposes. Or murder even, for that matter.'

'You mean somebody might have killed him and then somebody else might have moved him and dressed him up like that?'

'It's possible,' Carmichael said. 'Check the cars. I expect it'll prove to be that he was gassed from the fire in his room, but it won't do any harm to check everything out.' Yately was about to go, when Carmichael remembered the other thing. 'We need to issue a press release,' he said. 'I'll have to go down and give it to them. They expect Scotland Yard in a case like this. But you can write it. Tell them what we know so far.'

'What we know? What, everything?'

'No, just what we want them to know. That Sir James was killed by a person or persons unknown and that we are investigating.' Carmichael sighed again. 'Never mind, I'll deal with it.'

'Thank you, sir,' Yately said, looking immensely relieved.

Carmichael turned back to the papers, then looked up again as Yately was leaving. 'You know, if they did move the body, whether it was the murderer who did it or an accomplice, it wipes out all the advantage we have of knowing the time of death. We still need to know movements up to the time of discovery.'

'Yes, sir,' Yately said, and scurried out, doubtless before Carmichael could load any more work onto him.

Carmichael considered throwing something at the door, but couldn't see anything suitable. He picked up the next sheet.

Manningham, Sir Thomas, turned out to be a self-made industrialist who had recently been made a baronet. He controlled business interests and owned factories in England, France, and Germany. He traveled on business fairly often. His wife, Catherine Barbara, was the daughter of a country clergyman. Carmichael wondered why they were here, and being given ringside seats by staying for the whole weekend. Being courted by the Farthing Set, he thought. Industrialists and magnates were part of the Set. They were a party within a party, not really a democratic organization at all. Sir Thomas Manningham didn't have any political power, but he had money, and there would be things he wanted that money couldn't buy — laws against strikes and trade unions, perhaps.

Dudley, Duke of Hampshire, was considered to be firmly one of the Set, but not a great originator of policy. He deferred to both Lord and Lady Eversley. He was Lady Eversley's first cousin. He was a widower with three grown but unmarried children, Lord Timothy and Lady Edwina, who were here, and Lord William, who was not. Lord Timothy bred racehorses. He had a seat in Parliament and apparently voted as his father told him. Lady Edwina had recently broken off an engagement to the heir of the Duke of Stirling. Carmichael was always seeing her picture in the papers, 'sharing a joke' as they put it. The Duke of Hampshire was very rich, most of the money in land or in coal, he didn't take much personal interest in it.

118

Even straining hard, Carmichael couldn't think of any reason why any of the three of them might have wanted Thirkie out of the way. He'd have to interview them to see if they'd seen or heard anything, but if they wanted to go home today they could. The same, he supposed, applied to Sir Thomas and Lady Manningham, though he'd ask them all to keep in touch with the police in case he wanted to speak to them again.

He picked up the thick file on Lord Eversley again, and put it down. He drew a clean sheet of paper towards him and took out his fountain pen. 'May 7, 1949: Press Release,' he headed it. He took another sip of his coffee, which was now stone cold, and began to write as clearly and concisely as he could.

# 11

The breakfast room was empty when I got there, though there were signs that several people had breakfasted. There was even a copy of *The Times* on the table. I don't know how it had got into the house — maybe the policemen had brought it. The headline was screaming about Sir James being dead, with a picture of Farthing and another of Sir James, which must have been a fairly recent studio portrait. They said the police were about to make an arrest, which made my blood run cold for a moment until I remembered that the papers flat out make things up. The things they said when I was engaged were beyond belief. I had to stop reading them when they said I was going to have a baby.

I rang the bell and called for tea and a boiled egg. Meanwhile, I flicked through the paper. There was an obituary inside, much calmer and more the kind of thing one would expect of *The Times*. I expect the *Telegraph* was even more adulatory. I skimmed this one, as it was in front of me. It lingered on his achievements, and what it called the 'miracle' of the peace:

In May of 1941, the war looked dark for Britain. We and our Empire stood alone, entirely without allies. The Luftwaffe and the RAF were fighting their deadly duel above our heads. Our allies France,

Belgium, Holland, Poland, and Denmark had been utterly conquered. Our ventures to defy the Reich in Norway and Greece had come to nothing. The USSR was allied to the Reich, and the increasingly isolationist USA was sending us only grudging aid. We feared and prepared for invasion. In this dark time, the Fuhrer extended a tentative offer to us. Hess flew to Britain with an offer of peace, each side to keep what they had. Churchill refused to consider it, but wiser heads prevailed and sent young Sir James Thirkie to negotiate in Berlin. He was the obvious choice, a rising man in politics, noted for his personal integrity. The country held its collective breath as the bombing stopped. Then Thirkie returned, proclaiming 'Peace with Honour.' Not only would we each keep what we had, but Hitler agreed to let us take control of the French colonies in North Africa, while he, his flank secure, could at last do what he was born to do, turn East to face his true enemy, the Bolshevik menace. It was Thirkie's greatest hour of triumph, and the joy of the country, reprieved after two years of war, was comparable to that at Trafalgar or Mafeking.

I could remember the rejoicing. I was in school, it was high summer, term was nearly over, and we were being examined on the year's work. I always hated exams. I was sitting in the exam room, writing an essay on the Armada, making most of it up as usual because I couldn't remember the details. A beam of sunlight was falling on my desk, so I was shading the paper with my hand. A bee had somehow come inside the room and was stuck at the high window, buzzing and buzzing but unable to find its way up to the top where the thing was propped open. The sound reminded me of a bomber's engine far off. In that drowsy warmth and buzzing, I heard another, shriller sound, and thought at first it was a fighter coming to take on the bomber, though the bomber was a bee, and there had been no siren so there wasn't a raid. I kept on writing, wondering if they'd make us carry our papers down to the shelter if there was a raid or if we'd get out of the exam until later. I was almost hoping for the disturbance a raid would cause, though there were hardly ever daytime raids. The noise came nearer, and at last I could make it out. It was cheering. The mistress invigilating got up to investigate, walked to the back of the room, and then stepped out for a moment to speak to someone in the corridor. She came back in and walked back to the front. I could still hear the cheering, and the girls were starting to look at one another.

The mistress was flushed pink and smiling. 'Girls,' she said. 'It's peace. Sir James Thirkie has done it. Victory. The war is over.'

We all cheered, and some of us threw our papers up in the air. That night we tore the blackout material off the windows and made a bonfire out of it. Nobody else's brother or mother or father would die. We sang. I was happy, except when I thought of Hugh. Then I wondered gloomily what the whole thing was for, what we had now that we hadn't had in September 1939, why we'd bothered to be in the war at all.

Lizzie brought my egg, with bread and butter, just the way I like it, and a pot of very weak tea. 'You spoil me,' I said.

'Mrs. Smollett knows what you like,' she said.

'Oh, so Mrs. Smollett is in charge this morning, that's why I'm in favor,' I said, and Lizzie laughed. The servants had taken sides in the debate over my engagement. Mrs. Smollett, whose real name was Szmolokiewitsz, or something like that, and who was a refugee, naturally took my side. Lizzie was another of my old friends; she supported me because she believed in love.

'Mrs. Richardson isn't up yet this morning,' she said. 'She leaves getting breakfast to the Farthing staff.'

'I'm very glad to hear it,' I said. There was longstanding rivalry between the 'London' staff who traveled down with Mummy, and the 'Farthing' staff who stayed in Hampshire whether the family were in residence or not. Mrs. Richardson, who was head cook at whatever establishment Mummy found herself, was one of the servants who very much disapproved of my marriage.

I sipped my tea and looked down at the grainy and much reproduced picture of Sir James stepping off the cutter waving his treaty. Daddy was just recognizable in the corner. I had been a child when I cheered an end to the fighting and

123

privations. They had been adults, had known what they were doing. All right, eight years after and Hitler was still bogged down fighting the Russians, and maybe it would have been the same for us, the war going on endlessly, wearing us down, making us grayer and poorer every year. Or maybe there would have been a Bolshevik revolution here. I know Daddy was very afraid of that — there were strikes and demands even during the war. But we might have won, have set all of Europe free, as we did at the end of the Napoleonic Wars, made a peace like Vienna, not a peace like Versailles — this was David talking. I'd never thought like that until I met him.

Daddy came in then. 'How are you this morning, Luce?' he asked, ringing the bell.

'Claustrophobic,' I replied.

Lizzie came in. 'Bring me toast and sausages, bacon, black pudding, and fried potatoes,' Daddy ordered.

'Yes, sir. Anything more for you, Mrs. Kahn?'

'Just some more hot water for the tea, please Lizzie.' It had got too strong.

'Is that all you're having?' Daddy asked disapprovingly. 'An egg and bread and butter? You'll never get strong on that. Bring Miss Lucy a rasher, Lizzie. You can eat one rasher, Lucy.'

'No, thank you, Lizzie, I don't want any bacon,' I said.

'Haven't given it up, have you?' Daddy asked. Lizzie bobbed a curtsey and went out, getting out of the line of fire.

'No, and as you'll have noticed at dinner last

night, both David and I happily ate the roast pork and applesauce. I just don't feel like bacon this morning.'

'All right. Sorry, Bunny,' Daddy said. 'Bunny' was his pet name for me since I was small. 'What's making you feel penned in? The police or the press?'

'What about the press?' I asked.

'Clock Farthing is apparently packed full of them. The police tell me that any of us would be likely to be mobbed if we try to leave.'

Lizzie came back in with a jug of hot water for me and Daddy's glass and chrome French coffeepot. She put them down where we could reach them and went out again.

'I saw *The Times*,' I said, indicating it. 'I suppose the press are a necessary evil.'

I made myself another cup of tea. Half an inch of tea and the rest of the cup hot water, blissful, almost like the real thing.

'We can gag them when we want to,' Daddy said. 'If it's a national security issue, for instance. We try not to do it too much. Something like this, well, it's obvious they'd have a field day.' He picked up the paper and read a few lines. '"Tragic waste of his genius." What twaddle. James wasn't a genius, though he was a sharp man, and good at seeing a job through.'

'He persuaded Hitler to make peace with us and attack Russia,' I said.

'Hitler was panting to attack Russia,' Daddy said, pushing down the plunger on his coffee. 'He might have done it even without patching up a peace with us first. Even *The Times* admits

125

that it was Hess who started the negotiation.'

Lizzie came back in, carrying a covered plate. 'I'm sorry your lordship, but there's no black puddings. Mrs. Smollett is out of them, and we're not allowed to go to the village.'

Daddy threw down the paper in irritation. 'Very well, very well,' he said. 'Give me what you have.'

'Mrs. Smollett has given you an extra sausage and two more rashers to make up,' Lizzie said, putting the plate down.

Mark and Daphne came in at that moment. Daphne was heavily made up. Mark looked handsome and untouchable, as always. 'Bacon and scrambled eggs, and coffee,' he said breezily to Lizzie.

'I'll have the same as Lord Eversley,' Daphne said, sitting down beside me. 'Is there tea?'

'I'll bring tea, madam,' Lizzie said, and rushed out.

'There's no bloody black pudding,' Daddy said.

'You sound more distressed about that than about poor James being dead,' Mark said.

'Poor James,' Daddy mocked. 'I can see he's our new martyr. Pity there isn't a General Election; we'd be sure to win on the sympathy vote. And what the devil were you doing going into his bedroom anyway, Mark? Not up to your tricks again?'

Mark glanced at Daphne, who was staring at the rather frightful picture on the opposite wall. It's said to be early Dutch and from the school of someone or other, but it's a terribly dark picture of lots of very dead silvery fish on a slab. Mummy hated it, and as she never ate breakfast she put it in here to intimidate everyone else. I was used to it, but I've seen visitors change their minds about eating after seeing it. Then Mark looked at me, and back at Daddy, who had speared a piece of sausage as if it were an enemy.

If Mark didn't trust me, I didn't like to say that I already knew it was Daphne who had found the body. I had finished eating in any case, so I stood up.

'Going, Luce?' Daddy asked, looking up from his plate. 'How would you fancy a ride in an hour? We'd better not go off the property, but we could go up to the woods and around the lake, get some exercise. No point in keeping the horses down here eating their heads off for nothing.'

It was a wonderful idea, and it brightened the day immediately. I hadn't ridden in months — riding in London was no fun, going up and down the Row with everyone watching, more like showing a horse than riding one properly. Daddy was like that. He'd seem gruff and selfish, and then he'd see the right thing to do and suggest it.

'I'd absolutely love to,' I said, and Daddy smiled at me in a pleased kind of way. I went up to my room to change.

I hadn't brought riding clothes down with me. But I knew I had an old pair of black jodhpurs in the back of my closet unless Mrs. Simons had turned it out. She hadn't. They were hanging there among the other bits and pieces I hadn't bothered to take with me when I married, the lilac jacket with the stain on the pocket, the ghastly gold lamé dress Mummy insisted I wear to be presented, the brown leather jacket, much too big for me, that I used to use as a dressing gown when scuttling to the bathroom in the winter. I pulled on the jodhpurs, struggling to do them up. I'd put weight on in London. I added a cream pullover and the jacket of my heather tweeds. I'd brought the tweeds because tweeds are always correct in the country, and I really didn't have any idea what Mummy intended.

I went down to the stables and got Harry to saddle Manzikert and Trafalgar. I spent a little while saying hello to the horses, who were mostly old friends. There was one new little brood mare Daddy had picked up somewhere, called Clover, and a new colt out in the paddock, by Issus out of Valley Forge. Harry said they were calling him Dunkirk.

'I haven't had much time for the horses this year,' Daddy said as he came up. 'I miss your help in the stables.'

'I miss the horses,' I admitted.

'You could take Manny,' he said. Harry led the horses out and I swung myself up onto Manny's broad back. 'She's yours by any measure — you've ridden her for years.'

I patted her neck. 'I'm tempted, but I don't have anywhere to keep her and she'd hate to be kept in a hacking stable. Anyway, you know I never ride in London.'

'When you and David get yourself a country place,' Daddy said, 'you could start a stud.'

128

'One day,' I said, though I knew that David loved London and loved his work. David had a kind of bank, funded partly by his family money and partly by my money that I'd brought with me when I married him, and the bank loaned money in tiny amounts to poor people who wanted to start up in business or expand the businesses they had. Many of his customers are Jews and many of them are women, and there are little corner shops and traveling plumbers and building firms all over the country that are thriving now where otherwise people might be on the dole, all because David believed in his scheme and made it work. He hated to leave it even for a few days. I didn't think he'd ever want to live in the country.

Harry asked Daddy if he wanted his shotgun. 'Not while the birds are out of bounds,' he said. 'I could pot a rabbit or a hare, but where's the sport in that? Besides, Mrs. Richardson wouldn't deign to put it on the table, hey?' We all laughed at that.

'I'm very partial to jugged hare,' Harry said.

'So am I,' Daddy said. 'And hare with raspberry sauce.'

'Mrs. Smollett does a lovely jugged hare,' Harry said.

Daddy took the shotgun and slung it across the saddle. 'Just for you,' he said.

We walked the horses until we were up on the turf. Then we brought them to a trot, into a canter, and at last a good gallop. Manny definitely needed the exercise, she was raring to go, and Trafalgar gave her a good race. If we'd

129

gone on we'd have been on land that was part of Adams's farm, so Daddy pulled up and turned onto the track through the woods, where we had to walk them. The horses were happy enough to walk, having had a little run, and it did mean we could talk.

'Can the police really make us stay on our own land?' I asked.

'Yes and no,' Daddy grunted. 'They can ask us to, and we will, of course, because we don't want to pervert the course of justice. If we really wanted to go, they couldn't stop us without arresting us. Your mother says if they don't let us go tomorrow she's going to drive down to the gates and dare them to arrest her in front of the press and the whole world. They wouldn't do it, of course.'

No, they wouldn't arrest Mummy, or Mark Normanby, even though pretending he'd found the body when Daphne had was actually coming much closer to perverting the course of justice than I'd like to go. They might arrest David, though, if we tried to leave. It would give them an excuse. Nobody would protest, least of all the press, who were always stirring up hatred against Jews. I hoped they'd find the real murderer soon.

The woods were beautiful, bluebells every-where, and the trees in just their best leaf, all the green looking newly washed. The sun kept going in and out of the clouds, and every time it came out the landscape lit up again, so you never got tired of it. There were lots of ferns just uncurling under the trees — I kept feeling that I might catch one in the act. There was also a terrific amount of very vibrant moss anywhere it was shaded and the slightest bit damp, which Daddy shook his head at but which I privately thought very beautiful. We came out of the woods by the lake, where we could trot a little. We saw a few hares, too far and too fast to shoot, and plenty of whirring wood pigeons making, as Hugh once said, their insistent demands for a return to the one style of architecture that really suited them: 'Ro-coo-co! Ro-coo-co!'

We talked a little as we rode.

'Normanby's a donkey, and his wife's worse,' Daddy said. 'Know anything about that?'

'I'm not sure their marriage will last,' I said, looking at the bluebells and the woods and not at Daddy. If he was feeling me out to see if I knew about Daphne finding the body, I didn't want to play.

'It'll last if the silly ass wants to be Prime Minister,' Daddy said, and snorted. 'Divorce is a dirty word in politics. It's important to be seen to be doing the right thing.'

'They could live apart, though,' I suggested.

'Oh yes, they could live apart.'

We rode on, not talking about anything important, and then we came back around the woods, having made a circle, to where we could gallop back downhill towards home.

Manny sensed something before I did. Maybe it was something that showed more clearly to horse sense than humans. She put up her head and whickered. I turned to Daddy to say something about her being spooked, then something whizzed between us, stinging me hard on the cheek. I could swear I didn't hear a sound until afterwards. 'Dammit, he's hit you,' Daddy said, and then he yelled, 'Go, Lucy!' and in case I didn't, he slapped Manny's flank and she took off downhill as if it were the home stretch of the Derby. I tried to look back, but I couldn't see anything. There was something trickling down my cheek.

'Daddy!' I shouted. I heard another whizzing sound, and then the familiar bang of a shotgun.

I managed to get control of Manny and turn her back up the slope, which might have been crazy of me. David said it was. He also said it was the kind of thing people did in combat, so that was all right. I didn't think about it — there was no time to think about anything, really. Trafalgar came down towards us. Daddy was slumped over on her back, riding like a sack of turnips. 'Are you all right, Bunny?' he called.

'Me?' I was surprised he asked. 'I'm fine. How about you?'

'He winged me. I've a bullet in my arm. But I got him. Now we'll find out what's going on.'

'You got him?' I echoed.

One of the police constables came up and caught at Manny's head. 'What's happening?' he asked.

'My daughter and I were attacked by a terrorist,' Daddy said. 'I defended myself with my shotgun.'

'A terrorist?' I asked.

'Are you sure you got him?' the policeman asked.

'Oh yes, I got him,' Daddy said. 'He's dead.'

# 12

Royston interrupted Carmichael just as he was finishing with Lord Eversley's report.

'A couple of things, sir,' Royston said.

Carmichael set his report down, knowing Royston, unlike Yately, wouldn't interrupt him frivolously.

'Report on shoe sizes,' Royston began. 'The big feet going up and down the drive are definitely Kahn's. I asked him point blank and he said he had walked down to the village on Saturday morning. When asked what he'd done there, he said he'd looked around. When asked why he'd gone, he said he'd wanted a breath of air.'

Carmichael laughed.

'What's funny?' Royston asked.

'I expect he wanted to get away from his in-laws, that's all,' Carmichael said. 'Anything else of note on boots?'

'Nothing,' Royston said.

'Oh well, we thought it was probably nothing. What else?'

'I had to call the Yard twice about Kahn's flat. The first time I couldn't get hold of anyone who could authorize it. Too early.'

'Shocking,' Carmichael said, pulling a face.

'The second time, I arranged for that to be done, and I spoke to Blayne, who had been working on the star.'

Carmichael sat up. 'Yes?'

'You can get hold of them in this country, from refugees, but they'd usually be in a used and tattered condition, unlike the one we found. Otherwise it must have come from the Continent. In the Reich, they are mass produced, and sold, not individually issued as such. However, they have serial numbers, and the Jews purchasing them must use ration coupons to do so.' Royston grinned.

'You think that's funny, sergeant?'

'Making them use their ration-coupons to buy their stars? Yes, sir. You don't?'

Carmichael shook his head. 'I think it must be a very black kind of humor.'

'Well, it's lucky for us that they do, because we'll be able to trace the purchase and find out exactly where this one came from. In any case, from the serial number, our expert was able to tell that this one was sold in France within the last year — so it'll be the Milice we need to ask, not the Gestapo.'

Sir Thomas had been to France, so had Normanby, and so had the dead man. It was his dagger — could it have been his star? But for what conceivable purpose would he have bought one? As a souvenir? A prototype?

'Tell them to keep digging,' Carmichael said. 'Use my authority to make contact with the Milice.'

'Yes, sir,' Royston said.

'It wouldn't have to be a Jew who bought it, would it?' Carmichael asked. 'I mean they have identity papers — would they have to show them

134

to buy one, as well as handing over the money and the ration coupon?'

'I'll inquire,' Royston said. 'Though I can't see who else would want one; anyone seeing you with it would think you were a Jew. They have to wear them, sir, all the time. If they're caught without them they're in trouble.'

'Spies,' Carmichael suggested. 'Or people wanting souvenirs. Somebody bought that one for something, and someone pinned it onto Sir James. It needn't be the same person, necessarily, but finding out who bought it might be very informative.'

'I'll get back to you on that, sir,' Royston said.

'Oh, and has anyone informed the dowager Lady Thirkie of her son's death?'

'Surely the family will have done,' Royston said.

'Lady Thirkie was prostrate yesterday,' Carmichael said. 'How is she today, by the way?'

'She hasn't been down to breakfast,' Royston said.

'Find out how she is and let me know. And find out if Thirkie's mother has been told. I know it isn't our job, but someone has to do it.'

'It's been my job more often than I'd like,' Royston said. 'I'll inquire. Though if she reads *The Times* she'll have heard this morning.'

'Poor woman, that's no way to hear of your son's death,' Carmichael said.

'Yes, sir.' Royston put his hand on the door handle.

'And get them to send in more tea,' Carmichael said.

He picked up the Eversley report again. Lord Eversley had been in politics for so long, had been in and out of power so often, that reading his file was like reading a political history of the last thirty years. Politics had never been Carmichael's favorite subject. The facts served to confirm the general impression that the Farthing Set as a group within the Conservative Party had been out of power during the war, come back into power triumphantly with Thirkie's return with peace terms, been a little eclipsed in the last few years under Eden, edged out, and were hoping to return to power. What the devil any of it had to do with Thirkie's death, Carmichael couldn't say.

He read quickly through the reports on Richard Francis, MP, and his wife. He'd met them the night before. Clarinda Francis, née Darlington, was almost as much a bitch as Lady Eversley. Francis himself was charming. Carmichael had liked him immediately. They were part of the Farthing Set, he'd held positions in government — Carmichael skimmed faster and faster. He was expected to move up in the coming reshuffle. He was also noted as being ambitious and good with people. Ambitious, yes, very likely. What politician wasn't?

None of them had anything to gain by killing Thirkie, so far as he could make out. In fact, they lost, all of them, lost prestige that Thirkie, with his reputation as the man who-made peace and his 'noted personal integrity,' brought to them. He tossed the Francises onto the 'cleared' pile on top of the Hampshires.

There was a knock on the door, and a maid came in with a tea tray. Carmichael surveyed it with displeasure. 'Could you bring a jug of hot water?' he asked.

'Would you prefer a China tea, sir?' the maid asked.

'Yes, in fact I would, thank you very much,' Carmichael said. 'What's your name?'

'Lizzie, sir. It's just that Miss Lucy, I mean Mrs. Kahn, and Mr. Kahn too, they both like China tea, with extra hot water, so we have it in the kitchen if you'd like it. The other policeman should have said that's what you wanted. Mrs. Smollett thought policemen always liked strong Ceylon tea, with plenty of sugar and milk.'

'In general they do, Lizzie, but I am an exception.' Carmichael smiled at her. Poor girl, running to and fro with trays all day, beset by Lady Eversley, and taking time to consider her employers' preferences in tea. 'Why don't you take this tray to Inspector Yately, who will doubtless be delighted with it, and bring me a fresh tray of China tea when you have a moment.'

Lizzie gave a quick bob and vanished with the tray. The Eversleys certainly had excellent staff. Carmichael spared one thought for Jack, languishing in London, and picked up the next report, a single sheet.

'Eversley, Lady Margaret Violet Elizabeth, née Dorset, born November 4, 1900, Wessex House, London, parents, the Ninth Duke and Duchess of Dorset, both decd.'

If she was the daughter of a Duke, shouldn't

she be Lady Margaret, rather than Lady Eversley? Dukes outranked Viscounts, surely? Not that it mattered — they were both courtesy titles.

'Siblings, Peter Alan, 1904–, Tenth Duke of Dorset. Millicent Florence, 1906–. Married, 1918, Lord Charles Caspian Eversley, MC. Children, Hugh Caspian, 1919–40, Lucy Rowena, 1926–. Educated privately.'

Carmichael turned the paper over, but that really was all there was of it. Lady Eversley's political career had not been a thing of statistics, of positions held and relinquished, elections lost and won, but of influence, through her husband, her brother, her friends, her money. All officialdom recorded of Lady Eversley is that she was born, married, and had two children.

The door opened again, and Carmichael looked up, expecting Lizzie with his tea, and was surprised by Yately in a state of high excitement.

'You're right,' he said, without preliminaries. 'The gas in the blue dressing room hasn't been turned on since January, as best we can tell. The taps are very stiff. But his car — it's a closed car, and there was a hose in the boot that could have been fitted to the exhaust pipe to bring it inside the car.'

'That doesn't sound like an accident,' Carmichael said.

'No, not in the least,' Yately said.

'How would you induce a big healthy man to sit in a car to be gassed?' Carmichael asked.

'Could he have been knocked out first?' Yately hazarded.

'You'll have him killed three times, then? Knocked out, gassed, and then stabbed.'

'The stabbing wouldn't have fooled a child on close examination,' Yately said, defensively.

'Is there any evidence that he might have been knocked out before being gassed?' Carmichael asked.

'No,' Yately said. 'Though Dr. Green wouldn't have been looking for that.'

Carmichael did not snap that he should have been looking for anything unusual. 'Get him to have another look,' he suggested, mildly. 'Meanwhile, I want to talk to Normanby.'

'I've interviewed Mr. Normanby,' Yately said.

Carmichael raised an eyebrow and said nothing, a technique a master at school had used to quell disruption. Carmichael had practiced it in front of the mirror and always found it very effective.

'Here?' Yately asked, reduced to meekness.

'Is he up yet?'

'He's finishing his breakfast,' Yately said.

'Yes, send him in here then,' Carmichael said. Lizzie came back as Yately left. He held the door for her with old-fashioned courtesy.

'Sorry about the delay, only we had a rush with breakfasts and we needed to boil the water fresh,' Lizzie said. She set the tray down before him. There was a saucer with lemon slices, and a plate containing butterfly cakes.

'Thank you, Lizzie,' he said, in deep appreciation. 'Who's having breakfast now?'

'Mrs. Francis, the Earl of Hampshire, Lady

139

Thirkie, and Miss Dorset,' she said, after a moment's thought.

'Has Lady Eversley breakfasted yet?'

'Oh no, but she never does, she never touches breakfast, she says that's what keeps her slim!' She grinned at him, and left.

The cup was large and flowered. It matched the pot, the milk jug, the sugar bowl, and the saucer with the lemon slices. It still amazed Carmichael sometimes that this kind of luxury should exist, side by side with the world he usually saw where most people barely had enough to eat. His own Japanese teapot had cost him nearly a month's wages. He put a slice of lemon into his cup and poured out the tea slowly. Before he had finished, Jeffrey knocked at the door.

'Mr. Normanby, Inspector,' he announced.

'Thank you, Jeffrey.'

Mark Normanby came into the room with the air of a man used to taking command of a situation. He looked slightly smaller than Carmichael had expected from photographs. Also, in his presence, almost as soon as he was properly in the room, Carmichael had no doubt whatsoever as to Normanby's sexual orientation. Normanby was queer all right. That didn't mean that he and Thirkie had been up to anything, but it made more sense of why he had been in the room. Ah well. Carmichael began to have a little more sympathy for the wife who stared out of the window.

'Good morning, Mr. Normanby.' They shook hands. Carmichael stood until Normanby was seated. 'Can I offer you some tea? I could ring for another cup.'

'No thank you, Inspector, I've just had my breakfast,' Normanby said, with a charming smile. 'I have already spoken to Inspector Yately.'

'I'm afraid there's always some necessary duplication in a business of this sort,' Carmichael said.

Normanby nodded ruefully. 'I don't envy you your job, Inspector. Very well, what do you want to know?'

'I understand it was you who found the body?'

'Yes. I went in to see if James was ready for breakfast. I knew he didn't have his man with him, he'd mentioned it the night before, so I looked in on him.'

'Didn't you knock?' Carmichael asked.

'I knocked, but there wasn't an answer, so I opened the door to see whether he was inside.'

Carmichael didn't believe a word of it. It was all too pat, and not because he'd had to tell the story too many times. It was a lie, he was sure of it. Was Normanby the murderer? Could he be? Why? Or were he and the dead man lovers, was it a tryst, and was he entirely innocent? He couldn't tell.

'So you went inside, and what did you see?'

'James, on the bed, blood all over his chest, and a dagger sticking out of him.'

It wasn't the kind of distress a man would feel on discovering his lover dead, Carmichael thought. There was something too offhand about it, almost as if he was rehearsing events that hadn't happened. Who could he be covering up for? Or could he have done it? He was likeable, friendly, queer, but that didn't mean he wasn't a murderer.

'Did you see that from the doorway, or had you advanced into the room?' Carmichael asked.

Normanby had to stop to think. 'I saw the body and the blood from the doorway; then I went closer and saw the dagger,' he said.

'Did you see anything else?'

'I saw the damned Jew star, if that's what you mean, stuck on him like a bloody calling card.'

That seemed genuine, Carmichael thought. He had been in the room at least.

They went through it again as Carmichael drank his tea. 'To go back to the night before,' he said. 'Are you absolutely sure what time it was you escorted Sir James Thirkie to bed?'

'Not absolutely, no,' Normanby said, frowning a little. 'It was after midnight. I remember hearing the clock down in the village striking midnight while we were still in the billiard room.'

'Was anybody else with you?'

'No, we went up alone.'

'I meant in the billiard room, anyone who might have noticed exactly what time you left.'

'I don't remember,' Normanby said, almost peevishly.

Carmichael was astonished. 'You don't remember?'

'People were in and out. I don't recall if anyone was still there.'

'How long were you playing?'

'I don't know. An hour, longer probably. What does this have to do with anything?' Normanby seemed very uncomfortable now.

'It's just that the doctor has established the time of death as not long after you left Sir James Thirkie, so if we can find out when that was exactly, we might be able to be closer to pinning the murderer down.'

Normanby shrugged. 'I'm sorry, I can't help you there,' he said. 'Sometime around one, I think.'

'That's all for now then,' Carmichael said. 'I may have more questions for you later.'

'I'll do my best to help,' Normanby said, standing. He shook hands with Carmichael again, then looked down deliberately at the teacup. 'I see you drink it with lemon, rather than milk,' he said, smiling.

'Yes.' Carmichael smiled back.

'At Eton, we always used to call that the girls' way,' Normanby said, still smiling.

'I wasn't at Eton,' Carmichael said, holding onto his smile grimly.

'Oh, I know that, Inspector,' Normanby said. 'It's just a silly thing people used to say, and that I remembered because I always take tea that way myself.' He smiled again, deliberately charmingly, and left.

So, Carmichael thought, sitting down again, you know something about me and I know something about you, but does it get me any closer to knowing whether what you've told me is lies and what is truth? Was that intended as intimidation or seduction? He shook his head and made several notes on his pad. 'Check billiard room, ask all guests about billiards.

143

Determine all bedtimes.' He looked at these a moment, then added: 'Ask Lizzie about Normanby's tea.' She'd know.

He was just picking up the last of his papers when he heard the shots outside.

# 13

The thing itself was over in minutes; the fussing afterwards took forever. I wanted to go back up right away and see the dead anarchist, but of course they wouldn't let me, and my being wounded gave them an excuse. The bullet had whizzed past my cheek and torn it open. The wet stuff on my face was blood, of course. Head wounds bleed a lot, even when they're not very serious — I remembered Abby telling me that.

'Get her inside,' Daddy said, peremptorily. The sergeant from Scotland Yard put his hand up to help me dismount. Daddy, on Trafalgar, and all the other policemen, on foot, went tearing back up the hill. I slid down from Manny's back, although it was nonsense — really it would have been far quicker for me to have ridden back to the house. We were just the other side of the ha-ha. I let Manny loose to graze with her reins on her neck; once Trafalgar had gone, she wasn't likely to wander far. My legs were shaking a bit. I'd have been far better to stay up.

The sergeant drew an extremely clean white handkerchief out of his pocket, a real snowy white, I almost didn't like to mess it up. 'Stand still, miss,' he said.

He dabbed at my cheek, getting some of the blood off, and making it sting rather worse than it had done before. I don't know when I started feeling it. I know I hadn't felt it at all at first. I could feel it before the sergeant started doing his stuff, though. Even then it wasn't all that painful, similar to, but nothing like as bad as, being stung by a bee.

'It's just a scratch,' the sergeant said after a moment, and I laughed, because that's what manly heroes in stories always say about the most terrible things that they're making light of. A scratch, or a flesh wound, and I supposed it was a flesh wound as well — a cheek is definitely flesh. He looked at me for a moment as if I was mad, then he got it and laughed too. 'Just a scrape, then, a graze,' he amended. 'You were very lucky. Rifle wound, that is. A couple of inches and it would have been through your head.'

'Or Daddy's,' I said, sobered. 'I suppose it was Daddy they were shooting at. Nobody would want to shoot me.'

'I wouldn't know about that,' the sergeant said. 'Better not to worry about that side of it yet, the why and wherefores of it, not until after you've seen to the practical side. You'll want to wash that now, and get a doctor to look at it to see if they can do something to stop you scarring, and then you can start worrying about what he wanted and who he was aiming at. If you want to worry about it at all, that is, because by then it might be better to put it behind you if you want to sleep at night.'

'I suppose it might,' I said. 'Just at present I'm fearfully curious though.'

'Right now you've got things to see to and no time to be thinking about it,' he said. 'Wash the wound. See the doctor when he gets here. You don't want a scar, pretty face like you've got.'

The scarring didn't matter, but washing it was a good idea. I didn't want it to get infected. He handed me the handkerchief, which I'd already made rather a mess of. 'I could tell people it was a dueling scar,' I said, wadding it up and holding it pressed to my cheek.

'Young ladies don't duel, miss,' he said, and looked at me consideringly. 'Anyway, that's not a place a rapier would get you. Knife, maybe, not that young ladies knife fight either. Going to tell them you were a lady pirate?'

'Anne Bonney was a woman and she was a pirate,' I said. 'And there was another one too, Mary . . . Mary someone. They were pirates in the Spanish Main, not pirates' wives, pirates themselves. Anne Bonney was a pirate captain.'

The sergeant looked at me in frank scepticism, but it's absolutely cross my heart and hope to die true, and you can look it up for yourself if you don't believe me. Abby gave me a book about them for my birthday when I was ten. 'Catch your horse, now,' was all the sergeant said.

I caught Manny, who hadn't gone far, but didn't want to come. She was eating clover, which was terribly bad for her and likely to blow her out if she got too much. I had to drag her away from it. I've always wondered why horses have so little sense of self-preservation. It's amazing really that they lasted long enough to be domesticated and looked after by people. Still, if they had more self-preservation I don't suppose they could be ridden into battle, not that anyone does that anymore, not since that time the poor Poles tried it in '39 and got mowed down by tanks. But Manny had cavalry horses in her ancestry — she's a direct descendant of Great-grandfather's mare Agincourt, whom he rode into battle in the Indian Mutiny and the conquest of Sind. Perhaps horses who are descended from more peaceful ancestors have more sense.

'I'll take him back to the stable for you if you like, miss,' the sergeant said, dubiously, looking up at Manny as if she were an elephant.

'Her,' I said. 'And I'll take her, she knows me, and I get the feeling you're not all that happy with horses.'

He laughed. 'Not so many of them where I come from, miss.'

'Where do you come from?' I asked. We were walking along now, me leading Manny.

'Camden Town, in London,' he said.

'No, there wouldn't be many there,' I said. I knew Camden Town, at least I'd been through it. It was one of the poor areas that suffered a lot in the bombing. Just a few weeks before, David had told me about lending money to a family there to rebuild a shop they used to have. I couldn't tell the sergeant about that, of course. It was business, and David had told me in confidence. I'd have liked to have told him though, if I could.

'The police would have taught me to ride if I'd wanted to, but I never did. I don't care much for horses, great huge things that would step on you as soon as look at you. They're obsolete now, to

148

my way of looking at it, so I learned to drive instead.'

I laughed. 'Cars are nice too, and you're right, horses are mostly just for fun these days. But Manny's very gentle. I don't know about police horses — they use them for crowd control, don't they? So I don't suppose they can be gentle.'

'I never did any of that. I went straight into the Yard after being a runner, miss,' he said.

'My name's Lucy,' I said, because I didn't want him calling me 'miss' when we were being so friendly; it didn't feel right. Anyway, 'miss' is wrong; now I'm married it ought to be 'madam.'

'I'm Sergeant Royston, Mrs. Kahn,' he said, confusing me, and making everything revert to stuffy formality where we had been having such a nice conversation. It disconcerted me that he knew that, knew my name, knew who I was, and kept on calling me 'miss.' Some of the servants who had known me for years still called me 'miss' and 'Miss Lucy,' but there it was a case of finding it difficult to break a habit. There wasn't any habit with Sergeant Royston, and still he didn't treat me as if I was really married. That made all his friendliness before when we were talking about pirates and horses seem like a sham.

'Come along,' he said, after I'd just stood there for a moment, one hand on the handkerchief and the other in Manny's reins. 'You really ought to get inside, Mrs. Kahn. We don't know that the terrorist your father shot was alone.'

I hadn't thought of that before, but he was

149

right, the woods could have been crawling with assassins. I walked on thinking about that, which made my back feel sort of super-sensitive. I kept feeling I needed to keep my spine very straight just in case. I was relieved when I came around the corner of the house to the stable yard.

I took Manny in. Harry came rushing up right away and took her from me with lots of clucking about how terrible these murderers were and what a blessing Daddy took the gun. It was, too, so I started thinking about that. How strange to be alive because of Harry wanting jugged hare!

Sergeant Royston went off somewhere, probably back up the hill to look at the dead terrorist, where he'd doubtless been dying to be all this while he'd been wasting time looking after me. I went into the house.

Everyone was gathered round in the hall as if to hail the conquering hero, which made me want to laugh. I suppose I was feeling a bit hysterical. Mummy wasn't there, but I think everyone else was, even Angela, and a lot of the servants. David came up at once and hugged me. He seemed far more shaken at the scrape than I was. He was terribly pale. 'You could have been killed,' he kept saying. 'Oh Lucy, my darling, you could have been killed!'

I think I did go into shock then, which I hadn't before. Maybe it was David saying that or maybe it was knowing I was safe inside again. We went into the library, just the two of us, and Jeffrey brought us tea, which we both drank gratefully. I didn't even notice whether it was

China or Indian. After I'd had it, Sukey took me to the downstairs bathroom. That was the first time I got to see my face in the mirror, and it looked perfectly frightful. Fortunately, most of it was dried-on blood, which came off as soon as Sukey attacked it with warm water and cotton wool. Once that was off, I just had a row of cuts, a scrape, really. I did look like a pirate or maybe a gangster's moll. Sukey dabbed Dettol over the scrape, which made it burn and hurt worse than it ever had. She fussed over me dreadfully. I resisted all her efforts to make me go upstairs to lie down. I couldn't see what good it would do. She had already called the doctor, to look at Daddy's arm, and insisted that he'd see me as well, over my protests. It wasn't the kind of thing where stitches would help. She fastened a strip of gauze across it, held on by sticking plaster.

Then the police came back, which I'd known they would, which was why I'd resisted going up. I knew they'd want to talk to me. The doctor came at the same time and took Daddy off upstairs to patch him up. A police van was also there, which I suppose was for the corpse.

I was just hanging around, waiting for the police to want me and letting David fuss over me, when Mummy came into the library. She was wearing ordinary clothes, country tweeds, but she still managed to look like a dreadnought sweeping into some foreign harbor to claim it for the British Crown. She sat down under the bust of Portia and arranged her skirts as carefully as if they had swept the floor.

'Mr. Kahn,' she said, 'I'd appreciate it if you'd

let me speak to my daughter alone.'

I immediately grabbed David's hand. 'Anything you want to say to me, Mummy, my husband can also hear.'

'Do you have to be so tiresome, Lucy?' she asked, as if I were twelve years old.

David would have left us to it, but I clung onto him and wouldn't let go. As it was, I think he only stayed because I was wounded. I wanted him there not just for comfort but because she wouldn't be so savage in front of a witness. David said once he thought I was too afraid of Mummy and that gave her power, that if I stood up to her she'd back down — though when I did stand up to her, about marrying David, she didn't back down an inch, ever. Daddy forced her to come to the wedding, and she was threatening right up to half an hour before to go in mourning clothes.

'I don't want to intrude on your privacy, Lady Eversley, but Lucy wants me to stay,' David said.

'Oh very well, what does it matter anyway,' she said. 'While you're here, Mr. Kahn, I'll take the opportunity of asking you if you'd speak at a subscription dinner we're having in London on June sixteenth. It's a dinner for managers and businessmen, and the idea is to put across the case against the menace of trade unionism and Bolshevism. I wondered if you'd like to give the financial angle.'

'I'd be happy to give the financial angle against Bolshevism, if you mean against the USSR,' David said, giving a little bow. 'That is, I

152

can tell them that collectivized economies and human nature don't work well together, and even explain some financial details of that. But I'm afraid I see nothing very much wrong with trade unions, financially, there's no reason the workers can't combine to get a better deal for all of their labor, any more than would be true of a steel manufacturers group doing the same with their steel. Labor is the worker's capital, Lady Eversley.'

'But they have no right to withdraw their labor and paralyze industry,' she said.

'By the same argument you could say that a factory owner has no right to close his factory and throw thousands out of work,' David said.

Mummy frowned, clearly without an answer to David's lucid reasoning. 'Well maybe you'll keep to the Bolshevik side of things and leave the unions out,' she suggested.

'I'd be delighted, Lady Eversley,' David said, giving me a look that said: See, I told you your mother would become reconciled to the marriage eventually! I gritted my teeth.

'And Lucy,' she said, turning to me. 'When you speak to the police about this assassin, this double-murderer, who is, I hear' — she turned to David — 'actually a card-carrying Bolshevik, the next thing to a fifth columnist. In any case, Lucy, make sure you tell them your father shot him in self-defense. We need to put up a united front here. If there's any suspicion that your father needn't have shot him, it could become difficult. The police are, of necessity, not really gentlemen, and they

153

sometimes like to feel they have power over a person who is a gentleman. I don't suppose for a moment that any jury would bring in a verdict against your father, but let us make sure there is no possibility that it will need to come to that.'

'I really didn't see what happened,' I said. 'I know he shot first.' I put my hand up to my check. 'And he shot Daddy too. I can't imagine anyone would question it was self-defense.'

'Yes, that's the right line to take,' Mummy said. 'I think Mr. Carmichael will want to see you soon; Doctor Chivers is still digging the bullet out of your father's arm.'

She smiled at me with a wintry approval that was still the most I had won from her for several years, and swept out of the library again.

I thought about what Daddy had been saying earlier about perverting the course of justice. It really was self-defense, but Mummy didn't care about that at all. She wouldn't even care if Daddy had just murdered some innocent farm worker; she just cared that there wasn't a messy trial just at a time when there was a chance of Daddy getting a better government position.

'A Bolshevik assassin,' David said, looking almost pleased. 'That should stop the police from being so suspicious of me. And see, your mother is starting to find it useful to have a banker in the family. I knew she would.'

Before I could say anything the door opened, revealing Jeffrey. 'Inspector Carmichael would like to see you in the little office now, if you have

154

time, Mrs. Kahn,' he said.

I hugged David and went off to give my evidence, much less happily than if Mummy hadn't come to make sure I was going to tell them the right thing.

# 14

The whole incident of the rifleman infuriated Carmichael. It didn't make sense; it didn't form part of the picture he'd been carefully constructing at all. If he had a rifle, why gas Thirkie? And how could he have had access to the house — did he have an accomplice inside? None of it made sense. It was as if the jigsaw pieces he had been assembling had been shaken up so that what he had thought was a piece of sky turned out to be part of the eye of a whale. This always happened in a complex case, but there was something wrong about this, Carmichael felt, something he couldn't put his finger on, that made him feel the whole business was a clever conjuring trick.

Lord Eversley sat on his horse, looking down over the hedge at the dead man. Yately bent over the body, examining it. Carmichael stood to the side, where he could watch Yately and spot anything he missed. Izzard leaned over, breathing heavily from the uphill run, blocking everyone else's vision.

Royston came up just as Yately drew out the bloodstained card from the corpse's pocket. A hammer and sickle leered up at them and the name Michael Patrick Guerin, 1769830. 'Looks like you got it wrong this time,' Royston murmured in Carmichael's ear.

Carmichael looked sideways at him and he

subsided. He didn't mind being chafed. It *did* look as if he'd had it wrong. It just didn't feel as if this was right either.

'A Bolshevik, by God,' Lord Eversley said, craning forward to look at the card. 'Haven't potted one of them before.'

The word 'potted' grated on Carmichael. It put the dead man in the class of game shot for sport. Carmichael had often dealt with policemen and householders who had shot miscreants in self-defense. He had noted that they usually had a sense of being appalled by what they had done, which sometimes they demonstrated by shocked silence, but more often led them to put up a defensive bluster about it. Lord Eversley, despite being slightly wounded, sat imperturbably on his horse seeming merely pleased and curious.

The dead man was young, in his early twenties insofar as Carmichael could judge when most of his head was missing. He was splayed across the dark earth and the green sprouting wheat, where he had fallen back when the blast hit him. It had taken him in the side of the head, so he must have been running sideways, under the cover of the hedge. His rifle lay where it had fallen near his outstretched hand. Dead, whatever he was, and all his secrets dead with him.

'Izzard,' Carmichael said. 'Follow the hedge for ten minutes and see what you find.'

'Yes, sir,' Izzard said, and set off downhill.

'It runs down between my land and Adams's farm until it comes to the road,' Lord Eversley said.

157

'Thank you,' Carmichael said curtly.

Lord Eversley looked down at Royston. 'How's my daughter?'

'Mrs. Kahn's safely in the house,' he said.

'Good. Not badly hurt?' Lord Eversley asked.

'It's just a scrape,' Royston said, smiling about something. 'They're going to call the doctor to look at it, and at you too, sir.'

Lord Eversley merely grunted again. Carmichael had to admire his physical courage. He wasn't sure he'd have sat calmly on a horse chatting about a corpse with a rifle wound in him. The newspapers used to characterize the British as 'the bulldog race,' and there was something very like a bulldog about Lord Eversley, ugly and unappealing, but unquestionably brave and tenacious.

'Irish.' Yately tapped the card.

Maybe, Carmichael thought, looking back to the body, but more likely London or Liverpool Irish than bog Irish. His clothes, clean but scruffy, were town clothes, and his shoes were definitely English. While you found individual Irishmen anywhere in the world when there was a scrap going, the Comintern got short shrift in the Republic these days.

Yately checked another pocket and drew out an identity card. 'This is made out in the name of Alan Brown,' he said.

'So, he operated under a pseudonym!' Lord Eversley said.

'If he was Irish, and a Communist, he'd have had trouble doing much in this country without good false papers,' Yately said.

158

'Is that a good false paper?' Carmichael asked. He took the card and turned it to the light. Brown's year of birth was given as 1925, which would have made him twenty-four. His place of birth was Runcorn, which Carmichael knew to be a hellhole of an industrial town very near Liverpool. It might be worth inquiring with the police there. It gave a current address in Bethnal Green, one of London's East End slums. He would have judged the card genuine, which might mean it had been officially issued to someone who already had his false identity established. The address would certainly be worth checking in any case.

'Photograph with it,' Yately said, handing that up. Lord Eversley craned to see, so Carmichael glanced at it once and handed it over. It was an ordinary snap by a seaside photographer of a young woman, tolerably pretty, a servant or perhaps a shopworker, Carmichael would have guessed from her clothes and hair. Lord Eversley handed it back with a grunt and Carmichael turned it over to read the name of the photographer's studio, which was printed in florid typescript: Burton and Sons, The Promenade, Leigh-on-Sea. Leigh was the smart part of Southend, near enough to London to do in a day on the railway.

'What's this?' Yately said, in sudden excitement, pulling something from the outside pocket of the corpse's coat. Carmichael almost laughed when it proved to be a handful of shells for the rifle and half a bar of Fry's chocolate. The other pocket contained a piece of string, two pound

159

notes, and about five shillings in change, much more than Carmichael would have thought a man dressed like that would be carrying around. Carmichael took one of the coins, a bright copper farthing, and turned it in his hand, looking at the robin on the back. That was the other side of the British character: if the aristocracy were bulldogs, the poor were robins, hopping about cheerfully in hope of finding something good, never fleeing the winter but putting a good face on it, dowdy brown with one flash of bright color. Yet it was used as the symbol of this group of upper-class politicians — from the house, of course.

'Did this house give its name to the coin or the other way around?' he asked Lord Eversley, putting the coin into his pocket.

'Eh? The other way,' he said, taking the unexpected question in his stride. 'One of my ancestors lent a devil of a lot of money to Henry VII, and in return he handed out this manor — this whole area they call the Farthings — for a farthing rent a year to the crown. We still keep up the payment. Wouldn't like to get behind on a thing like that!' He wheezed with laughter. 'A farthing wasn't worth very much more then than it is now. It was still only a quarter of a penny. Maybe Henry VII could have bought a loaf of bread with it, while I doubt George VI can get more than a slice!'

Izzard came back, red-faced and gesticulating. 'I've found a motorcycle!' he said, when he was near enough to hail them. 'Under the hedge down there, by the road!'

Guerin/Brown could have run back to it in a couple of minutes, and been off and away before any search for him could have begun.

'The press are down there too, sir,' Izzard finished. 'On the road, like.'

'It's a public road,' Lord Eversley said, in evident annoyance.

Carmichael turned and saw a black closed Bentley that had to belong to a doctor crawling up the drive, following the same police van that had taken Thirkie's body away. He picked up the rifle, carefully, checking it was unloaded.

'Royston, you take care of the bike, and tell the assembled gentlemen of the press that we'll be making a statement — Scotland Yard, tell them, in two hours, at the front gate. Izzard, help Inspector Yately with the corpse. When you've finished checking it here, it wants to go back to Winchester for an autopsy. Lord Eversley, the doctor's here, we should go back to the house. I'll want to talk to you when he's had a chance to patch you up a bit.'

'He fired at me, I fired at him, I was lucky, he wasn't, that's all there is to it,' Lord Eversley said.

Carmichael was horribly sure that he'd stick to just that, without detail. Yet bluff and bulldog-like as he seemed, he wasn't a fool. No fool could run several companies and help run the country the way Eversley did. Carmichael watched him riding down towards the stables as he followed him down towards the house. Not a fool, though his exterior made you think he was. What a pity he'd killed the rifleman.

A motorcycle, he thought, was the perfect escape vehicle for these little country roads; it could go much faster than any car. Guerin/ Brown had been intending to shoot and get away fast. How would he have hidden the rifle? How did he, when he came here in the first place? Better ask for anybody who might have seen him. That would be something concrete to ask the press to do, and it might lead to something.

Back in the room he was already thinking of as his office, he immediately put a call through to the Yard. It rang through immediately. Police priority combined with a quiet time of day let him speak to London for once as easily as he might speak to someone on the same exchange. 'We've had another death,' he said.

'That's too bad,' Sergeant Stebbings said. 'Who was it?'

'It was a man with a rifle who was shooting at Lord Eversley and Mrs. Kahn.'

'Good gracious,' Sergeant Stebbings said, his tone betraying no surprise whatsoever.

'Lord Eversley shot him.'

'Clearly self-defense?' Stebbings asked.

'About as clear as it could be — the man had a rifle, Lord Eversley and Mrs. Kahn are both wounded, and Lord Eversley killed him with a shotgun. I don't think there's any need for anything like an inquiry into it.'

'And the man?'

'I want you to check two names for me. One is Michael Patrick Guerin, who has some kind of Bolshevik identity card with the number 1769830. The other is Alan Brown, of number

23 Sisal Villas, Bethnal Green. Brown's driving license claims he was born in Runcorn in 1925; perhaps you could check with the police up there too. There's also a snap of a young woman, which it might be possible to identify, and which I'll have sent up to you.'

'I'll get onto that straight away and get back to you,' Stebbings said, reassuringly. 'G-U-E-R-I-N?'

'That's it,' Carmichael said.

'Should we check with the Garda?'

'It might be worth asking them, but I don't expect anything to come of it,' Carmichael said. 'There's also a rifle. Can you check with the Mets whether Brown has a license for one — or anyone else of that address.'

'What kind of rifle is it?' Stebbings asked.

'Perfectly ordinary Lee-Enfield,' Carmichael said, glancing at it where he had leaned it in the corner behind the desk. He noticed something anomalous and picked it up to check. 'Hold on — no it isn't, by God, it looks like one, but actually it's a .22.'

'A popgun?' Stebbings sounded a little taken aback. 'You can kill someone with a .22, I suppose, but you don't need a license for one.'

'No,' Carmichael said, putting the rifle down again. 'It's still self-defense — when someone's shooting at you, you don't stop to ask the caliber of the weapon. But it's a funny thing to choose.'

'Perhaps it's all he could get hold of,' Stebbings suggested. 'You can buy one of those anywhere. Kids use them.'

'Ones that look like a real rifle?'

163

'Anywhere. They're rather popular with villains, actually, people who want to intimidate with a gun but don't want the extra time they'll serve for having one. But mostly it's kids who want a rifle just like a real one.'

'It still seems like a funny choice for an assassin. Not much stopping power. You can buy a shotgun anywhere as well,' Carmichael said, and sighed. 'Well, check into all of that. They'll be sending you down the corpse's fingerprints from Winchester.' He made a note to remind Yately about that. 'Have you got anything else for me while I'm on?'

'We're still working on things. We're not going to be able to do Kahn's flat before tonight.'

'Probably not important now anyway,' Carmichael said.

'You think the Bolshie gunman killed Thirkie too?'

Carmichael hesitated, and the line to London hummed in his ear as the wind blew through the wires connecting them. 'No,' he said. 'Maybe, though if he did I don't know how, or why he used the method he did. It doesn't fit. There's something that isn't right about all of this.'

'Well, one other thing,' Stebbings said. 'It's very small, but you never know. You asked if any of the people on your list had criminal records, and we said they don't. That's true as far as it goes, but one of them would have, except that he got it erased. I happen to remember it because I was involved. Mark Normanby, MP — he was one of those arrested and brought in when the Metropolitan force did that big sweep in Charing

Cross Underground that time, remember?'

'Oh yes.' Carmichael did remember. Charing Cross Underground station was a notorious haunt of men looking for youths, and of youths from the slums who were prepared to go with a man for money, or perhaps beat him up and steal his valuables if they saw their way clear to doing that. The victims in those cases would not complain. They could not afford to say why they had invited someone of that nature into their home. The police raided the Underground station frequently, without making much of a dent in the traffic that went on. Then, two years ago, the Mets had gone in in force, at all entrances, and arrested hundreds of people. For several weeks, the station returned to respectability. Then of course, they started to come back, those desperate enough to risk it at first, and then more and more as they started to feel safe again.

He especially remembered the raid because it had led to a quarrel with Jack, who had seen it as a sign the laws against homosexuality were about to be enforced. Carmichael had argued that these men who preyed on youths were no brothers of his. The youths might not even be queer. Some of the men, he had heard, preferred it if they were not, if they hated what they were doing. He said it was more in the way of a crackdown on prostitution. He said there was no purpose in feeling solidarity with men who exploited others that way. They had made it up at last, but not before Jack had called him a policeman, which of course he was.

'Normanby was one of those caught in flagrante, in the bathroom, with his pecker in the mouth of a boy no more than fifteen. The boy's in prison now, but Normanby pulled strings and insisted the evidence against him disappear — he's down in the records as an innocent bystander. I was the one who had to destroy the Yard's copy of the file. So in case it makes any difference to anything, you can take it as absolutely proven that he's a sodomite.' Stebbings's tone did not vary as he said all this.

'A powerful sodomite who can pull strings,' Carmichael said.

'That's just it,' Stebbings said. 'I don't like seeing justice made a fool of that way.'

'One law for the rich and another for the poor,' Carmichael said, sourly.

'The boy's guilty of no more than being poor enough to agree to do something disgusting, and he pulled five years hard labor,' Stebbings said.

Carmichael wondered if Normanby was one who preferred boys who didn't want to do what they were doing. He could easily imagine the man being like that, the power being as much of a thrill for him as the sex. It made him feel queasy. 'Thank you for telling me, sergeant,' he said.

'Not that it probably means anything to your case,' Stebbings said. 'Not now you have a Bolshevik gunman tangled up in things.'

'Then why didn't he shoot Thirkie as well?' Carmichael wondered aloud. 'There's something about all of this I don't like at all. I don't like the smell of it.'

'Would that be a hunch, sir?' Stebbings asked.

'No it would not,' Carmichael said, grumpily. 'I'd appreciate it if you'd get me any information from the files as soon as possible, Guerin or Brown. And please send someone down to Bethnal Green to check out Brown and any associates, right away. Also get someone digging on the Bolsheviks in London and why they might be wanting to kill off the Farthing Set. Oh, and whether there's been any stir among the Bolsheviks recently, or at the Russian consulate or anything like that.'

'What are you going to tell the press?' Stebbings asked. 'They've been ringing up.'

'I've announced a press release in two hours, which will give me time to talk to Mrs. Kahn and Lord Eversley,' Carmichael said. 'I'm going to have to tell them the truth, so far as Guerin/Brown goes, anyway. Some of them seem to have heard the shots, and it's possible that someone might have seen him on his motorcycle with the rifle.'

'Good luck,' Stebbings said. 'Don't get yourself shot by any Bolsheviks.'

'I won't, thank you, sergeant.'

Carmichael put the heavy black receiver down carefully and rang the bell.

'Tea. China tea,' he said to Jeffrey when he came. 'And ask Mrs. Kahn if she has the time to speak with me.'

# 15

Inspector Carmichael opened the door to me and ushered me into Daddy's little back office, which he'd quite taken over. He had papers all over the desk, which Daddy never would; Daddy's terribly tidy and always uses folders and clips for everything and puts them away as soon as he's done. The Inspector had them in little piles, and he had notes everywhere too.

He rang for Lizzie, and when she came, asked her for a tray of China tea. 'You needn't, just for me,' I said, though I was touched and surprised. 'I don't mind Indian for once.'

'The Inspector prefers China too, madam,' Lizzie said.

'Really?' I asked, surprised. He didn't look one bit like a man who'd care about his tea.

'Is it such an unusual taste?' Inspector Carmichael asked. He turned to Lizzie. 'Are we really the only ones in all of Farthing who prefer it?'

'Yes, sir, at least, there's Mr. Kahn as well, but otherwise everyone wants their tea strong, or they prefer coffee.'

'Barbarians,' the Inspector said, but he was frowning. He made a tick against something on one of his piles of notes.

'I wanted to say, madam, from me and the rest of the staff, that we're very glad indeed that you're all right,' Lizzie said.

'That's very kind of you, and really, I'm fine. I was more shaken up by the whole thing than hurt. It's just a . . . a graze really.'

Lizzie went off to fetch the tea. I could see I'd be swimming in it by the end of the day, but it was all meant very kindly.

'So tell me exactly what happened, Mrs. Kahn,' Inspector Carmichael said.

'I don't know. I didn't see anything. My horse did.'

'Unfortunately, we can't question her,' he said, with a funny little smile. 'How do you know she did?'

'She checked her stride, and whickered, as if she heard something. Then the next thing I knew the bullet passed between us.'

'You were riding close together?'

'Quite close, yes, perhaps six feet apart, maybe closer. I'm not exactly sure. After the bullet, or maybe there were two, because I thought I heard the sound after it hit me.' I stopped. 'I'm sorry, I'm not being very clear. Did Daddy show you where it happened?'

'Lord Eversley was kind enough to show me, yes. I could also see the prints of the horses quite clearly. You checked, you heard at least one shot, one certainly scored your cheek, and then you galloped down towards the house?' When he said 'Eversley' he sounded very Lancastrian all of a sudden.

'Daddy told me to run, and I didn't do anything, but he gave Manny a great wallop that sent her charging off downhill,' I said.

'Manny's your horse?' he asked.

'Short for Manzikert,' I said, laughing a little. 'It's a battle, but don't ask me who fought in it or what year it was. Practically all our horses are called after battles. I learned to ride on a pony called Hastings.'

'Manzikert was 1050, in Anatolia, Greeks versus Turks,' he said, surprisingly, because I wouldn't have thought he was the kind of man to know about battles either. He was a surprising sort of man altogether. 'I'm sorry. Your father cuffed your horse, and she ran away with you. What did he do then?'

'Didn't he tell you?' I asked.

'He told me — now I want to know what you saw.' The Inspector was watching me very carefully.

Of course, this was where Mummy wanted me to be very clear and lie if necessary to get Daddy off any hook he might be on for having killed the terrorist. I decided I was going to tell the complete truth and not a word beyond that. 'I didn't see anything,' I said. 'I'm sorry. Manny took off, and I was trying to get control of her. Daddy was behind me. I didn't see him or anything he did until I turned around again, and by then he was coming down towards me, with a bullet in his arm.'

'Did you hear any more shots?' Again he looked at me with that wary look.

'I heard the shotgun, definitely. I think I may have heard more rifle shots.'

'You were aware it was a rifle?' He pounced on that.

'Not at the time, no. Your sergeant told me afterwards.'

Carmichael looked a little irritated. 'So how many rifle shots would you say were fired?'

There was a knock and Lizzie came back in and set the tea things down. I poured, asking the Inspector about milk and lemon, and there was all the paraphernalia of cups and saucers — she'd brought the best china, Mummy's Spode. Mummy would have a fit if she knew it was being wasted on a policeman, even such an unusual one as Inspector Carmichael. Not that Mummy would have appreciated his unusual qualities — knowing about battles and drinking China tea wouldn't have cut any ice with her; indeed, it would probably have made the ice deeper, if I know Mummy.

We settled back down, with our tea, and he asked me again: 'How many rifle shots, Mrs. Kahn?'

'I definitely heard one, after the bullet scraped my cheek,' I said. 'Then I'm fairly sure I heard another as I was going down the slope, just before the shotgun blast. That's all I could swear to.'

'But there might have been more, before, and when you were going downhill?'

'There might have been the whole Battle of Mons up there,' I said, in a shaky kind of way. 'I couldn't see, and I couldn't get Manny turned around. I thought they'd killed Daddy.'

'That was a very reasonable thing to think, because the intruder had a rifle, and your father only had a shotgun. A rifle has a much longer range, as you know.'

'I know. It's quite incredible really that Daddy managed to pot him.'

The Inspector just looked at me for a moment. Maybe he was adding something up in his head. 'Well, he was very lucky,' he said. 'Does your father generally carry a shotgun on rides around the property?'

'It depends on the time of year,' I said. 'In the autumn, practically always. In winter too. But at the moment all the birds are out of season. All there is to shoot is a hare or a rabbit, which isn't much sport. He only took the gun today because Harry insisted.'

'Harry insisted,' Carmichael said, making a note.

'Harry in the stables,' I expanded.

'I know who Harry is, Mrs. Kahn,' he said. 'So you and your father were very very lucky indeed. You probably owe your lives to Harry insisting.'

'I was thinking about that earlier,' I said. 'It's one of those horseshoe nail things, isn't it?'

'I suppose it is,' he said, getting the reference at once, as I'd known he would. It's a poem about a whole battle being lost for the want of a horseshoe nail. Hugh used to love it and recite it. He knew the whole thing by heart when he was quite a little boy and I wasn't much more than a baby. 'Who suggested that you go riding this morning?'

'Daddy,' I said. 'I'd mentioned feeling restless and cooped up, you know, because we have to stay here and can't go home, and he suggested that we could take the horses out. He said it would be all right if we didn't go off the property. We didn't — we kept very carefully to Farthing land.'

'He couldn't have known you'd be there, then,' the Inspector said. 'The assassin, I mean. It wasn't something you planned and told the servants about so that anyone might have got to know about it?'

'No, it was pretty much spur of the moment,' I said. 'Daddy suggested it as I was finishing my breakfast. I went up and changed and then met him in the stables. It was hardly an hour.'

'Who else was at breakfast when you discussed it?'

'The Normanbys,' I said. He made a note, his pen strokes very hard.

'Were any servants in the room?' he asked.

'No . . . Lizzie was in and out, but I'm almost certain she wasn't there just then.'

'There isn't time for it to have been a conspiracy,' Carmichael said, almost to himself. 'They couldn't have conjured him up in that time; he had to have been waiting.'

'Waiting in case anyone happened to come along, I suppose,' I said. 'Only it isn't all that likely, is it?'

'Nobody went up there yesterday,' the Inspector said. 'He could have been there then. He could have been prepared to wait until he found someone.'

'Have you found out yet about the — you called him the intruder?' I asked. 'If you don't mind me asking. Who was he?'

'We'd know a lot more if he was alive to

question,' he said. He frowned again and tapped his fingers together. 'From what he had on him, and without more inquiries, he appears to be a Bolshevik agent.'

'A Russian agent?' It seemed incredible, like something from the tuppenny papers, like the sergeant saying my wound was 'just a scratch.' It seemed absurd, although I supposed that the Russians had no reason to like Sir James, after he'd got Hitler to attack them, or Daddy either for egging him on.

'Either that or someone who wanted to make us think he was one.' Inspector Carmichael's face was unreadable. 'It could be a masquerade. Though the mystery there would be who it's aimed at and how they persuaded him to be involved.'

'And is this Bolshevik the one who killed Sir James as well?' I asked.

'I don't believe it for a minute.' Inspector Carmichael's face was a picture. He wasn't looking at me at all. He could have posed for a bronze statue of 'Determination' to set on the Embankment.

'Then why did it happen now — isn't it an awful coincidence?'

'It would be, if it were a coincidence. But once Sir James was killed and it was in the papers, I suppose the Russians might have thought it was open season on the Farthing Set.'

I shuddered at the image.

The Inspector seemed to remember that he was talking to someone. 'I'm sorry, Mrs. Kahn, I really didn't mean to distress you. It's just that this business doesn't make any sense. You mentioned horseshoe nails, and finding the horseshoe nails is part of my job, and following them on to the horseshoe and the horse and the soldier, if you see what I mean, fitting the pattern together. But this time I have the pieces, and there's a very obvious pattern they could fit into, but it all smells wrong. It's like one of those conjuring tricks, sawing the lady in half, now you see it, now you don't. There's a whiff of sawn lady about all this, and I feel I'm being led by the nose to come to certain conclusions, which just don't fit.'

'But who would be leading you by the nose?' I asked, thinking all the while that it must be Mummy, that world-class expert in nose leading. I wondered what she would have said to me if David hadn't been there. I finished my tea and put the empty cup down on the desk.

'If I knew that I'd know who killed Sir James,' he said, which left me feeling just a little taken aback.

'You think it's David, in league with the Bolsheviks,' I said, then put my hand to my mouth too late; I'd already blurted it out.

'I don't,' he said. 'I'm Scotland Yard. I'm not interested in politics. I'm keeping an open mind. I haven't ruled out the possibility that it might be your husband, but at present it seems to me far more likely that someone wants me to think it is.'

'I know he didn't do it,' I said. 'I know you won't believe me, but he was with me all night, from considerably earlier than one o'clock, and I know you think I'd say that anyway, but it does

175

happen to be true, Inspector, and I wish you'd believe me.'

He just looked at me. I'd jumped to my feet somewhere in that, for no good reason, but I'd have felt even more of a fool to sit down again, so I stayed standing, holding on to what little dignity I had left.

'I do believe you, Mrs. Kahn,' he said. 'I believe you believe you're speaking the truth in any case, not trying to shield your husband or anything of that nature. That doesn't mean that what you're telling me is true, but I believe you're speaking the truth. And while we're on the subject, just to reassure you, on the whole I'm not inclined to believe that Mr. Kahn is involved. What did he have to gain? Revenge, because Sir James Thirkie got us out of the Jewish war? Maybe in the penny dreadfuls people who are certain to be caught kill for that kind of motive, but not in life.' He hesitated, and I sat down again. 'Do you ever watch the cartoons?' he asked.

I nodded. 'Mickey Mouse and Donald Duck and so on? I've seen them at the movies.'

'Yes . . . well, it seems to me that someone wants me to find a simple cartoon story, the kind that would make sense for a cartoon but doesn't in real life, where people aren't drawings of mice and rabbits who can squash each other with anvils and after being squashed flat walk away blowing themselves up again. And what worries me is who would do that and what would they expect to get out of it, and how many innocent people might get squashed flat along the way.'

Mummy, I thought again; she'd steamroller David and me anytime without even a qualm. Then I remembered the gunman, and I knew that was nonsense. Mummy wouldn't be involved with anything like that.

'You're forgetting the Bolshevik gunman,' I said. 'He's real, not something from a brightly colored cartoon.'

'He's real and he's dead and he raises an awful lot more questions than he answers,' the Inspector said. 'Thank you, Mrs. Kahn, you've been very helpful.'

# 16

Carmichael sat alone in the office, staring out of the window at a huge blue hydrangea bush. His mother would have loved that bush. Her hydrangeas would only ever grow a muddy pink, and these were splendidly, brilliantly, blue. Probably some secret the aristocracy conspired to keep from people like his mother, who merely aspired. How Lady Eversley would have condescended to her if they had ever met. He shook his head. The hydrangea had nothing to do with the case and neither did his mother, poor woman. He had been cooped up in here too long, they all had. He should go for a walk — and risk being shot at by more snipers? He should collect Royston and take him back to the Station Hotel for dinner. Or perhaps they should even go back to London. Anything to be discovered about Guerin/Brown would be done there, not here. There wasn't anything left here. Farthing would keep its well-bred secrets. He had already told the papers about the Bolshevik assassin Lord Eversley had shot, and seen them all but licking their lips over the sensation. There could be little doubt that he was Thirkie's murderer. He should let everyone go, let air back into the house. Yately had even suggested it when he went back to Winchester for the day. But Carmichael kept on sitting there, stubbornly, because it didn't feel right. If it was a hunch, it

178

was the kind to follow through.

Royston tapped on the door and came in without waiting for an answer. 'We've found the lip paint, sir,' he said.

'Specially imported from Russia, I suppose, sergeant?' Carmichael asked.

Royston checked and frowned. 'Sir?' he asked.

'I'm fine, sergeant, just making a joke.'

Royston gave him a sideways look. 'It belonged to the housemaid, Molly,' he said. 'That'll be Mary Cameron on your list, sir. She says it was stolen from her room on Friday night. She noticed it missing on Saturday morning, and mentioned it to one or two of the other servants then, and afterwards she forgot about it with all the fuss. She remembered it today. It seems that this is her evening off, and she wanted to go off to the bright lights of Farthing Green looking her best. She mentioned the theft to Lizzie when asking to borrow some of her lipstick, and Lizzie had the sense to bring her to me.'

'Good girl, that Lizzie,' Carmichael said, touching his empty tea cup reminiscently. It was very thin china, white with a tracery of gold flowers painted around the bowl. 'Had you talked to Molly, before this?'

'Inspector Yately had,' Royston said, expressionlessly.

'Ah,' Carmichael said, noncommittally. 'And the lip paint was right?'

'"Woolworth's in Winchester; price sixpence; red of a shade called Carmine; lip paint to be applied with a brush,"' Royston read from his notes. 'This is the brush.' He held up a little

179

make-up brush, green-handled, the bristles stained blood red of a shade that matched Carmichael's memory of the front of Thirkie's nightshirt. He took it from Royston and turned it in the light.

'That's it, all right,' he said. 'Well done, sergeant. Very well done. She's sure it was Friday she missed it, not Saturday or Sunday?'

'Absolutely sure, and more to the purpose, so is Lizzie.'

'Then as that is progress, it calls for celebration,' Carmichael said. 'We'll go back to the Station Hotel for the night. There's not much chance of the Yard having anything more for us before morning.'

'Yes, sir,' Royston said. 'Can't say I'll be sorry to get out of here for a bit.'

'You wouldn't think it was a place people usually angle for invitations to,' Carmichael said, ungrammatically. 'But maybe it's the gloom of the deaths and it's usually very jolly.'

No Lady Eversley intercepted them on their way out tonight. The family and guests were at dinner. Carmichael informed the butler that they were leaving and would return early in the morning. 'Very good, sir,' he replied, in sepulchral tones, opening the door.

It was dusk; the sky was almost purple and the air was cool. Royston opened the car. 'Do you think it might rain, sir?' he asked, seeing Carmichael taking deep breaths.

'Why would they steal lip paint from a servant?' Carmichael asked, rhetorically, unable to remove his mind from the scene as easily as he could remove his body.

'Why did they do any of that rigmarole?' Royston countered, as they both sat down.

'Yes, that is the question. They could have shot him easily enough. They could have got away with it too; nobody would have been expecting it. So why did they gas him and dress him up and all of that?' The engine purred to life and the Bentley puttered down the long drive in moments. The avenue of elms reached above them like great open arches, dark against the darkening sky. Venus was just visible in the west.

'They must have wanted to make a point,' Royston said, drawing to a halt for the bobby to open the gate for them.

'What point?' Carmichael felt his hands bunching into fists; he unclenched them. 'There is no point. It's pointless.'

'Good night, sir,' the bobby called. There were still two lone journalists slouching around the village, Carmichael noticed. He wondered which papers they represented, and whether they were foolish or optimistic. They looked up as the police car passed but made no attempt to intercept them.

'Maybe it's pointless,' Royston said, as they sped through the village. 'Maybe they wanted to make the point that they were here and powerful and we should be afraid of them. Just shooting him wouldn't do that, but showing they could get into someone's house and make a mockery of them, painting them up like a robin, and leaving their calling card, maybe they thought that would make people afraid.'

Carmichael considered it for a moment as they passed through a dark spinney and came out into wheat fields. 'Would it make you afraid, sergeant?'

'It might if it was somebody I knew,' Royston said.

'Then who could it be meant to intimidate? Lord Eversley? Normanby?'

Royston shook his head. 'I don't know. Being shot at is frightening, but not in the same way, if you know what I mean.'

'Yes, it's cleaner somehow. More manly. Strange, really, dead is dead.' They passed through a village, one of the Farthings. The inn doorway shed golden light into the street as a fat pretty woman came out, pausing a moment in the doorway to say something to her friends inside. Something witty, from the look on her face, Carmichael thought, envying her companions their cheerful evening.

'Murdered in your own bed has a very different feel from shot out riding,' Royston said.

Carmichael's mind, never far from the case, came straight back to it. 'But if it was the Bolsheviks killed Thirkie, how could they have done it? We already established that they couldn't get into the house.'

'They must have had an accomplice on the inside,' Royston said.

'And who would your bet be on that?' Carmichael said.

'Kahn, maybe?' Royston suggested. Carmichael frowned. 'Or there's a cook who's Jewish, a refugee years back, changed her name to Smollett from the heathenish thing it was before. She's one of the permanent staff. She could easily have stolen the lip paint. She might have got past Mrs. Simons somehow, or Mrs. Simons might be in collusion with her.'

The car bumped over the railway lines of the level crossing and drew up outside the Station Hotel. Carmichael barely noticed. 'You think she'd have opened the door for the Bolsheviks? Where's Mr. Smollett? Perhaps still in Russia? Maybe they said they'd hurt him if his wife didn't do what they said, or that they'd let him out to England if she did.'

'I'm not sure there ever was a Mr. Smollett,' Royston objected, opening his door. 'Female upper servants get called Mrs. as a courtesy.'

'But she might have left family behind her in any case.' Carmichael liked the idea. He stepped outside, and looked up. There were more stars now, more stars than you ever saw in London. Country stars, the same here as they were in Lancashire, though the landscape and the people were so different.

'Any family would do for blackmailing her into helping them,' Royston said.

'But it doesn't solve the problem of how anyone could have killed him by sitting him in his car and putting the exhaust in through the window,' Carmichael said, locking the door of the car and checking at the tightly wound window with London caution.

'So say he killed himself,' Royston suggested, as they walked up the hotel steps. 'Say he killed himself, in the car, and she found him, and thought, here's this bastard, this man who stopped Britain from freeing the Jews of Europe before Hitler had his way with them, and he's dead. Why don't I humiliate him now, put my own star — no, it can't be. Put some star I have from somewhere on him, paint his breast red, arrange him back in his own bed.'

The landlady came up to them as soon as they stepped inside, smiling with professional cheer. 'Dinner, is it, gentlemen?'

'What do you have?' Carmichael asked.

'How about some nice steak and eggs?' she asked.

'Sounds good to me, sir,' Royston said.

'Two, in the dining room,' Carmichael agreed. 'And bring us a couple of pints of your best bitter.'

They went into the room where they had breakfasted and sat down at the same table. It felt almost like home. There was one man sitting in the corner, eating sausages and reading a book; otherwise they had the place to themselves.

Carmichael spoke quietly, so the stranger wouldn't overhear. 'That's a nice scenario, but what you're forgetting is that she'd have had to have stolen the lip paint the night before, which argues an unlikely degree of premeditation. And could she have carried him up two flights of stairs? No Bolsheviks there to help this time. How old is she, anyway?'

'About fifty, but very hale.' Royston screwed up his face. 'I bet she could. She's a cook — she

184

carries sacks of potatoes and things around all the time. And the beauty of it is, if she was caught doing it, then she was outside because she went to get a drink of water or whatever, a breath of air, and she found him and was bringing him in. As she wasn't caught, she could go ahead with her scheme.'

'That one would work with anybody finding his corpse after he'd killed himself,' Carmichael said. A barmaid brought their beer, two brimming pints with foaming heads, in old-fashioned pink china tankards. 'Anybody who had reason to humiliate him, anyway.' Kahn, he thought. He couldn't imagine Kahn murdering him, but would he have done that? He sipped his beer.

'But why would Thirkie kill himself?' Royston asked. 'And if he did, why would just the wrong person come along first to play games with the corpse? And why would the Bolsheviks come around the day after with their little rifle?' He took a draught of his beer, and smacked his lips.

'What would make a man like Thirkie kill himself?' Carmichael asked. 'A man with a national reputation, a career that looked to be getting itself back on track, a pretty-enough wife, a baby on the way, and a much praised air of personal integrity.'

'Exposure,' Royston said, instantly. 'Some scandal that was going to get out and lose him everything. Better a dead lion than a live jackal.'

'Yes,' Carmichael said, putting his beer down. 'That would do it. But what disgrace?'

Homosexuality? Could Normanby have threatened to expose him, perhaps as part of some power game? Say Thirkie wasn't queer, say he'd had a passage with Normanby between his marriages, an experiment, one that Normanby wanted to continue but he didn't, not now he was happily married and had a kid on the way. Then if Normanby threatened to expose him unless it went on, said he'd come to his dressing room the next morning and expect to find him ready — yes, that might be enough to drive a man to choose death with his reputation unstained.

The landlady came bustling in with two plates of steak, fried potatoes, fried eggs, mushrooms, and onions. A concession to nambypamby ideas of healthy eating could be found at the side of each plate, where a single lettuce leaf, one thin slice of cucumber, and a quarter of a tomato wilted, topped with a few strands of mustard and cress.

'Do you think anybody ever ate one of these salads?' Carmichael asked, poking at his.

'I've never eaten one,' Royston admitted, his mouth full of steak and potato.

'Neither have I, and I doubt one man in a hundred does. Yet the cooks keep carefully arranging them on plates in inns all over England, and just as carefully scraping them off again into the dustbin afterwards. Yet they must imagine, somehow, that people want them. I've been served this same pathetic excuse for a side salad from Bodmin to Skegness.'

Royston shook his head. 'No accounting for

women, sir,' he said.

The steak was good, overcooked by Carmichael's standards, but he knew from experience that he might as well take the well-done steak the kitchen knew how to prepare rather than try to educate them into the mysteries of what was meant by medium-rare.

'If he killed himself,' Carmichael said, speaking quietly once more, 'if he'd gone out in the night to his car and killed himself, who would be the most likely choices to find the body, any time between one and — let's say eight, when the Catholic servants set off for church?'

'Hold on, sir, what about rigor? Wouldn't that make him hard to move, for someone who found him at the wrong time?'

'Good thought, sergeant. Pity rigor's such a tricky thing to time. Let's say right after he died then, before it set in, or in the morning, after it had passed off. Who might stumble across him?'

'Most likely would mean in the morning rather than late at night,' Royston said. 'I mean, anyone could have been up just after one, but the house was locked up.'

'He got out to kill himself.' Carmichael speared a mushroom. 'He could have left the doors open behind himself.'

'Then our joker would have had to lock them up afterwards, because Hatchard found them locked as usual in the morning.'

'What time was that?' Carmichael asked.

Royston pulled his notebook out of his pocket and turned pages, pausing to take another bite of steak, then turning more. Carmichael ate without tasting his food while he waited. 'Six-fifteen,' Royston said, at last.

'So after the door was opened at six-fifteen, who might have gone out and strolled among the cars?'

Royston looked dubious. 'Anyone might have, but it wouldn't have been a very natural thing for someone to do.'

'We have a record of everyone's movements for that time?'

'Yes, but most of them were in bed until much later.' Royston turned pages again. 'Lord Timothy Cheriton was up early, Mr. and Mrs. Kahn, and practically all the servants got up sometime between six and seven.'

'How about Normanby?'

'He got up just before he found the body,' Royston said. 'His testimony and his wife's corroboration.'

'They share a bedroom?' Carmichael asked, surprised.

'They say they do,' Royston said. 'They have two connecting rooms, much the same as the Thirkies.'

'I think I want to talk to Mrs. Normanby tomorrow,' Carmichael said, taking another draught of his beer. 'Do you think she'd cover up for her husband?'

'I don't think there's all that much love lost there, sir, but I don't doubt she'd do that if she thought it necessary.' Royston swallowed. 'They probably all would — they'd stick together, like, cover up for each other. Not the servants; the nobs. That's very much the feeling I've got — not so much that they are covering up anything, but that they would if they felt they needed to. The way they look at me — none of them cooperate the way you'd expect. They treat me as if I'm their servant — not the public's servant, answering to the people, but their own personal servant doing a job under their own personal orders.'

'Lord Eversley was certainly like that this afternoon,' Carmichael said.

'Lord Eversley, Lord Hampshire, Mr. Normanby, Lady Eversley, the whole pack of them. Even Lady Thirkie.'

'And Kahn?'

'Not quite in the same way, but I don't think he's telling me everything.'

'I like Mrs. Kahn,' Carmichael said. Royston looked inquiring, but Carmichael shook his head. 'I don't know. Do you think they're all covering something up? Something we ought to know?'

'I don't know,' Royston said, unhappily. 'I can't tell. I suppose it's a hunch, really, just that they would if they wanted to.'

'Well that's very interesting, sergeant, and thank you very much for telling me,' Carmichael said. 'I know how difficult it can be to pin down that sort of impression, and yet it's something that might be very useful indeed.'

'But now any scenario we make has to include the Bolshevik, doesn't it, sir, and I can't imagine any of them having anything to do with a Bolshevik.'

'I know very little about the Bolsheviks myself,' Carmichael said. 'They'll send a report down from the Yard tomorrow. Until then, we're probably best enjoying our dinner and sleeping on what facts we have.'

# 17

Dinner that night, the Monday, was even more bloody than it had been the night before. I'd hardly been able to look at myself in the mirror beforehand. It wasn't the scrape, it was my body. I'd always been able to say before that I had the usual debby kind of looks, and it was true enough of my face, which looked just like the portrait of our Eversley ancestor who got out of being burned at the stake under Queen Elizabeth because it rained that day. The rest of the family gave up Catholicism when it went out of fashion, but she stuck it out in the Tower. There's a portrait of her in the gun room, and the top part of her face is really extraordinarily like mine. Hugh used to call me Heretic sometimes, and Mummy, once, when she was very cross with me about wanting to marry David, said that I was just following her terrible example. But my body isn't like hers at all, as far as one can tell — she's wearing one of those Elizabethan dresses that don't show the figure very much. My body went straight from puppy fat to middle-aged spread, and my life is a constant struggle not to become a hippopotamus, like my Grandmother Dorset. It's most unfair that those genes skipped Mummy, who is as thin as a stick, and went directly to me. My hips are a constant trial to me.

That day, dressing for dinner, without the

consolation of being able to say that my face was all right at least, I had to wrestle with my hair and my body, and I knew I looked awful. David usually said I was delightfully curved and as thin as any healthy woman could hope to be, and when he said it that cheered me up even if I was having a fit of despairing over my bottom, but that night he was sunk in gloom himself and didn't even notice. He was sure the police suspected him of being in league with the assassin, and he felt guilty for not having somehow magically protected me from the bullet. He seemed to think that had he not been Jewish and therefore under suspicion and talking to the police, he'd have been with me and able to throw himself between me and it. It was completely pointless to tell him that he'd have got himself killed to save me from a flesh wound. He wanted to make that kind of gesture, or at least the poor dear felt he did.

I put on my beige Chanel sack again, which I'd worn to the party on Saturday, but I didn't have anything with me I hadn't worn; we'd expected to go home on Sunday. I'd had to give some underclothes to Molly to have washed for us or we wouldn't have had them either. We went down to dinner with David looking very smart and elegant, but unmistakably Jewish, as he always did, and me looking awful. There had been a picture of us like that in the *Herald* once, without the wound, of course, but me looking beastly and him looking wonderful, and they had titled the article with it: 'Is he marrying her for her position?' I'm quite sure that nobody looking at it who didn't know David could have doubted it for a moment. I swore then I'd eat less and lose weight, and I do manage to lose a pound or two from time to time, and David swears I'm as flat as a board and as thin as Mummy. Then the pounds creep back on somehow when I'm not looking. It seems beastly unfair, but there isn't any way around it.

It struck me as we sat around the dining table, all dressed for dinner, jewels glinting in the candlelight, how simply absurd the whole thing was. Here we were gathered to eat, but not just to eat, to eat specific courses in a prescribed order. Mummy would probably have been more horrified to have meat before fish, or a savory before the soup in the French way, than she was by a terrorist shooting at Daddy and me. We sat in a prescribed order, we ate and talked as the conventions dictated, and the whole thing was as artificial as one of those elaborate plaster wedding cakes confectioners keep in their windows. I'd have much rather had a big bowl of soup and half a loaf of bread in my room.

I was seated between Uncle Dud and Sir Thomas, neither of them the world's greatest conversationalists. Sir Thomas tried to tell me about the economics of copper production. I sat in silence much of the time, or eavesdropped on the general conversation.

Angela had come down to dinner, with that very smug and serene look women sometimes get early in pregnancy. She was wearing a black dress she must have had with her, though black wasn't usually her color, and she wore with it the

193

famous Thirkie Fall, a Victorian diamond necklace. It was a family heirloom, of course. I remembered seeing Olivia wearing it years ago but I didn't think I'd ever seen it on Angela before. It was the first time most people had seen her since the morning before, and she accepted condolences quite gracefully. She was sitting across from me, between David and Daddy, so I could hear it all quite well.

Daddy's arm was in a sling, the only evidence that the shooting had happened, apart from the piece of fresh gauze the doctor had stuck across my cheek. He looked a little tired, which might have been from pain or it might have been from something the doctor gave him for the pain. He wasn't drinking his Moselle — I noticed the glass was still almost full when Jeffrey took it away to replace it with claret. Looking across the table at him, I found myself wondering exactly how old he was. He'd fought in the Great War, and then again in the Second War, so he had to be nearly sixty. He had always seemed younger.

Daphne was on the other side of Daddy. She looked terrible, as if she'd been crying all day, which she might have been — I hadn't seen her since breakfast. It struck me, as people were telling Angela how sorry they were and how much they'd miss Sir James, that Daphne was the only one who would really miss him, and probably the only one who was really sorry too. Angela would have the baby, and she'd probably remarry; she was young, and pretty. Besides, I wasn't sure she'd ever really liked her husband. Daphne had definitely been in love with him. I

194

saw Mark looking at Daphne, too, and smiling to himself, as if he was enjoying her being upset, which was beastly of him, even if she was his wife and Sir James her lover.

'It's not that I don't enjoy your hospitality,' Uncle Dud said, across the table to Daddy. 'But I really would like to get home to my roses.'

'To London,' Mummy put in, from his other side. 'There's the important vote coming up tomorrow.'

'The arrangement was that I was going to go to London with you today, vote tomorrow, and be back at home tomorrow night.' Uncle Dud looked peevish.

'We can all go up to London tomorrow and vote, and if you don't mind the long journey you can be back among your roses before bedtime,' Daddy said. 'I've spoken to the Chief Constable in Winchester, and to Penn-Barkis at Scotland Yard. No matter what Inspector Carmichael says, we're all free to go after ten o'clock tomorrow. It's possible that Carmichael will want to have a last word with some of us immediately after breakfast, but then we can get away.'

The atmosphere around the table lifted immediately. Only Daphne remained sunk in gloom. I looked at David, who smiled across at me. I could tell he was thinking just the same as I was, how glorious it would be to be home! To be back in our own dear little flat with our own things and our own servants! To be out of gloom-sunk Farthing and away from Mummy!

'Well done, Charles,' Uncle Dud said.

'And you'll come up to London to vote?' Mummy inquired.

'Of course I will,' Uncle Dud said. 'And Tibs will too.'

Tibs, on the far side of Daphne, and trying valiantly to engage her in conversation, looked up when his name was mentioned. 'I will what?' he asked.

'You'll come up to London to vote in the House tomorrow,' Mummy said.

'Oh, rather,' Tibs said. 'It's the important vote, isn't it, the new leader of the party thing? I wouldn't miss it for the world, Aunt Margaret, even if I didn't hope for a better job in the reshuffle, because I know you'd never forgive me if I didn't.'

Mummy merely smiled one of her glacier smiles.

I was so pleased that we were going home that I forgot all about my new resolution to lose weight and ate up every bite of Mrs. Richardson's wonderful jam roly-poly and custard.

After dinner, people started doing the usual country weekend thing of making up fours for bridge in the drawing room. Tibs and David disappeared to the billiard room. I refused to admit to any interest in bridge and said I was going to bed, but Eddie Cheriton buttonholed me. 'I need something to read,' she said. 'Billy always said you know about books; come on, find me something.' She almost dragged me into the library.

It isn't true that I know about books, though I

196

know more than Billy Cheriton. What Billy probably meant was that he'd seen me reading on occasion. Even Georgette Heyer and Dorothy Sayers would count as high literature to Billy. Anyway, I've always loved the library at Farthing. I learned to read there. Hugh taught me, from a huge old leather volume with pictures of fairies. It's a wonderful place, what with the smell of the books and the look of their leather bindings, the way the matched sets and the classics are mixed up with things Daddy picked up in Waterloo to read on the train, so you might find absolutely anything next to anything else. David once found James Burnham's *The Managerial Revolution* between Machiavelli's *The Prince* and the collected poems of Lord Byron! 'What sort of thing are you looking for?' I asked Eddie. As far as I knew she'd never read anything before but cello music.

'I don't really want a book, silly,' she said, lighting a cigarette and putting it into her holder. 'I wanted to ask you if you have any idea whose baby it is that Angela Thirkie's having.'

'She told me and Daphne that it was Sir James's,' I said, absolutely shocked in a terribly Victorian way. It always struck me as the very worst form to have a Bognor baby.

'Well she'll get away with that now,' Eddie said, running her finger down Shakespeare's nose. 'But she was asking Marion Stepney a fortnight ago if she knew who to go to when you wanted to bring a baby off, and that isn't the sort of thing she'd want to do if it was her husband's baby. Marion told me that Angela told her they

197

had separate bedrooms and she wouldn't get away with it.'

'Marion was probably romancing,' I said, though I didn't believe it. Marion was a silly woman, but she did have a reputation for sailing close to the wind and being a little racy. She was exactly the person Angela would go to if she wanted to find out about abortions.

'She wasn't, though she told me in strictest confidence and I haven't told a soul. I assumed you'd know, after spending absolutely all day closeted with her yesterday.' She tapped ash off her cigarette into the ashtray on the piano.

'She didn't say a word to make me doubt her,' I said. 'And you'd better not go spreading that story.'

'Oh, it was obviously that Bolshevik who killed him, not Angela,' Eddie said. 'I can't picture Angela stabbing him, can you? Not really her style at all.' She sighed and twisted a curl of her hair around her finger. 'I felt sure you'd know. I can't ask her, and Daphne's worse than useless, going about like Ophelia.'

'Poor Daphne,' I said.

'Yes, she'll have to find herself another lover now,' Eddie said, callously.

'Has she been involved with Sir James all this time?' I asked.

'Since she was barely out,' Eddie said, blowing out smoke. 'I'm surprised you know about that; you'd hardly have been out of the cradle. They married her off to Mark, and gave him a safe seat into the bargain. Now if he'd died when Sir James was free to marry, that would have made me suspicious! But he didn't, and however much he looked the other way about the Daphne thing, he wasn't going to give her a divorce. No politician would. So Sir James married Angela. Every politician wants a wife to do their entertaining, never mind who they sleep with. That's why I broke up with Rex — I could see he didn't want me, he wanted a political hostess. And if I want to be a political hostess, I can be one for Daddy, who will, frankly, do better in politics than poor Rex ever will. I'll marry for love, or for considerably better advantage than Rex would bring me.'

'I knew about Daphne and Sir James long ago, but I didn't know it went on,' I said. 'How well known is it?'

'Not as well known as all that,' Eddie said, consideringly, lighting another cigarette. 'I believe there was a time when it was off, when he first married Angela, but then it was on again. They kept it pretty dark, and Daphne's never been a particular friend of mine. Not as dark as Angela's affair, though. I do wonder who it could have been?'

'If I hear anything, I'll let you know,' I said, though I didn't mean it. There was no malice in Eddie Cheriton, but precious little good either. She was one of the parasites and time-wasters I wanted nothing to do with, and her tongue was hinged in the middle and flapped at both ends.

'Well, I'd better take a book or people might wonder,' she said, picking up something at random from a shelf and blowing dust off it. *Gods and Fighting Men* by Lady Gregory.

199

Whatever is it? Oh, is it some of that Ossian stuff?'

'Something like that,' I said. 'I don't know why you expect me to have read every book in the house.'

'Are you saying Billy isn't to be trusted?' she asked, laughing and tucking the book under her arm. 'You were quite right not to marry him anyway, he's an idiot, and the nobility is quite sufficiently inbred as it is. Although you needn't have taken eugenics quite as far in the opposite direction!' She laughed again, and went out.

I stood in the library grinding my teeth for a little while, then I went off to the billiards room, where I found Mark leaning against a pillar looking elegant while watching David and Tibs finishing their game. I looked at him covertly. Was he really Athenian, and quite happy for his wife to have spent the last fifteen years or so having an affair with someone else? Or did he resent her affair? He seemed glad to see her unhappy. And if he'd resented it, might he have hated Thirkie and allied himself with Bolsheviks to arrange his death? He laughed at one of Tibs's feeble jokes, and I couldn't quite believe it, but I couldn't quite put it out of my mind either. I'd always rather liked him.

I watched David knocking balls about and joking in that very male, English way, which I knew wasn't natural to him but which he could put on so well when he was with people like that. He thought it would make them accept him, and I couldn't tell him that nothing he did would make the slightest difference to that. We had real friends, I thought; we shouldn't waste our time with these people. Tibs won, barely, and began a game with Mark. David and I went up to bed, and all the way I was thinking triumphantly: Tomorrow we're going home, we're escaping, we're getting out of here and going back to our own life, and I'll never think about any of this again if I can help it.

We made love. And as David exploded, and I did, I knew. In the still small place that was the center of all that lovely shuddery excitement, in a place deep inside me that I visualized as being like the heart of a red flower, with big shivery pink petals whose lips reached all the way out, two seeds found each other, and started to grow into a baby. I kept very still, hugging David, loving him more than ever, though I all at once understood what it is that pregnant women always look so smug about.

# 18

Carmichael woke early beneath the embroidered exhortation, 'Hold fast to that which is good.' Fresh eggs did imply a rooster, but did it have to be a demented rooster bound on waking the whole world? It was joined by the whistle of the 6:35 from London to Southampton. Carmichael gave it a judicious ten minutes, then rang the bell and asked the sleepy maid for tea, hot water, and today's papers if they had arrived yet. She brought them up while Carmichael was shaving. He poured himself an indifferent cup of tea and got back into bed to survey the delights of the London press.

The Times led with the Bolshevik attack on Lord Eversley and Mrs. Kahn, almost in the words of Carmichael's own press release. It suggested that more money for the Navy would prevent similar occurrences. The front page also mentioned that Foreign News, on page 4, would inform readers about starvation and cannibalism among the defenders of Stalingrad, and another Japanese massacre of insurgents in Shanghai. Carmichael was mildly astonished there was anyone left to starve in Stalingrad or to massacre in China, or that The Times could believe that anyone in England could care about them on a beautiful May morning. He tossed the paper down dismissively.

The Telegraph talked about the Bolshevik

menace, and seemed to take it for granted that the same man who had attacked Lord Eversley had killed Sir James Thirkie. 'Englishmen will not allow our policy to be set by armed anarchists in the pay of Soviet Russia!' the Leader screamed. The pictures were from the files: Lord and Lady Eversley opening a factory the year before, and Lucy Kahn at the time of her wedding. It went on to praise Lord Eversley's marksmanship and police efficiency. The *Telegraph* often praised police efficiency, except for the times when it called for the blood of some policeman who had not been efficient enough to suit it. Its own foreign news was a day behind *The Times*; it said that Kursk had changed hands again.

The *Manchester Guardian* also quoted Carmichael extensively. It went so far as to show a picture of him, taken the day before, outside the gates of Farthing. It urged the House not to allow its natural sympathy for the Farthing Set in their misfortunes to overwhelm it in the vote this evening. Carmichael read that twice and thought hard about it, closing the paper without more than glancing at the foreign news headline: 'Hitler's work camps: are they really efficient?'

He went down to breakfast in a thoughtful frame of mind, and found Royston already at the table, reading the *Daily Herald*. 'You're up early,' he said.

'Bloody bird wouldn't shut up,' Royston said. 'I hate the country; you can keep it. Will we get back up to London today, sir?'

'I should think so,' Carmichael said. 'What news?'

'Lord Eversley shot a Bolshevik, nation rejoices. And the police want to hear about anyone who saw a man on a motorcycle,' Royston summarized.

'How about the foreign news?' Carmichael sat down and rang for his breakfast.

'Foreign news?' Royston squinted at him suspiciously. 'The Emperor of Japan is to visit President Lindbergh in San Francisco to discuss closer economic ties between the Asian Co-Prosperity Sphere and the USA. Oh, and Kursk changed hands again.'

'You've restored my faith in the papers, sergeant,' Carmichael said, as the landlady brought his breakfast. 'I was beginning to think that the foreign news had no overlap whatsoever.'

'Why did you want to know?' Royston poked gingerly at a sausage.

'I wondered if this business, that looks at first blush as if it relates to British politics, might possibly relate more to politics in some other country, such as Soviet Russia, or possibly Nazi Germany. This theory would seem to be disproved, at least if one relies on the great British newspapers to tell you anything.'

'Anything interesting in the other papers?'

'The *Telegraph* urges the country and the Tories to stand firm behind the Farthing Set, while the *Manchester Guardian* wants them not to be swayed by natural emotion into giving the Farthing Set too much power.'

'They've got too much bloody power already,' Royston grumbled, mopping up his egg yolk with his toast.

For the second day running, there was a fat envelope waiting for Carmichael at Farthing. 'Check into the billiards thing,' he said to Royston. 'Do it yourself, don't let Yately do it, if Yately even bothers to show his face here this morning. Find out who remembers Normanby and Thirkie playing billiards, and what time it was.'

He opened the envelope. Before he could do more than glance at the top report, on Bolshevik activity, the telephone rang.

'Call from London for Inspector Carmichael, police priority,' the operator sang. Carmichael waited with the big clumsy receiver tucked between his ear and his shoulder, reading the report, a pen in his hand for taking notes. It seemed that Soviet, Bolshevik, Communist, and Trotskyist activity had been rather low of late, according to police sources, and there had been no rumors of planned assassinations or attacks.

'Is that you, Carmichael?' a voice barked in his ear.

'Yes, sir,' Carmichael said, putting down the report, his heart sinking. Chief Inspector Penn-Barkis would telephone himself only with bad news, or if he meant to interfere.

'I've had calls from very high places about your keeping everyone penned up down at Farthing. I didn't give in to them, I said you could keep them there until ten this morning, but after that, anyone you don't arrest is free to

205

go. And better not be too enthusiastic about arrests, considering who these people are. There's nothing more to do down there — come back to London.'

'Yes, sir,' Carmichael said, writing neatly on his notepad: 'There is one law for rich and poor alike, which prevents them equally from stealing bread and sleeping under bridges.'

'They've been told already,' Penn-Barkis said. 'Do any last interviews you need to.'

'Yes, sir,' he repeated, drawing a box around what he had written.

'Come in and see me when you get back to the Yard.'

'Yes, sir,' Carmichael repeated. 'Is that all?'

'No. Sergeant Stebbings wanted a word about the raid last night. I'll put you through to him now.'

'Thank you, sir,' Carmichael said, automatically, drawing curlicues around the box and contemplating the words inside. If he'd told some factory workers or miners suspected of murder to stay at home where he could talk to them, nobody would have raised the slightest murmur.

'Stebbings here,' Stebbings said.

'Yes, Carmichael here, sergeant, what is it? Something on Brown?' He tapped his pen.

'Brown, or Guerin, doesn't have a record here under either name. Nothing known. I've sent you down what we have. We're investigating in Bethnal Green, where it seems someone of that name did live at that address. He lived alone, so there's not much progress as yet.'

206

'Oh well,' Carmichael said, crosshatching the corners of his square.

'What I wanted to say, sir, was we found a link with the other man.'

'Which other man?' Carmichael asked.

'Kahn, sir. We went into his flat last night, tidy search, like you asked for. Nobody would know we'd touched a thing, but we turned it over properly.'

'Yes, yes, but what did you find?' Carmichael dropped his pen and it rolled over the table, sputtering ink.

'Very incriminating letters from a member of an underground Jewish group, urging him to revolutionary action and murder,' Stebbings said, as if he were remarking on the weather. 'They didn't mention this specific case, but they wanted him to find an opportunity to get Sir James Thirkie, Lord Eversley, Lord Timothy Cheriton, and Mr. Normanby together and blow them up.'

'Were they blackmailing letters?' Carmichael asked. 'Did they threaten, or say 'Unless you do this we reveal something about you'? Or were they just encouraging him to do it?'

'The latter,' Stebbings said. 'From the letters we have, it appears he kept refusing, but he continued to correspond with them and to send them money. We only have their half of the correspondence, but there's a constant tone of 'Thanks for the money but it isn't enough, take action against this fascist family you've married into.''

Kahn. He'd been completely wrong. Kahn all

the time. He'd pulled the wool over his eyes properly. Kahn and an underground Jewish group. But Guerin wasn't Jewish, he was a Bolshevik, and the Bolsheviks hated the Jews almost as much as the Nazis did. 'Are they signed?'

'They're signed Chaim, though I don't know if that's how you say it,' Stebbings said, pronouncing the name like *chain* — 'C-H-A-I-M.'

'All of them?' Carmichael rescued the pen and wrote the name down.

'All of them. Same hand, too. No addresses on them, though they are dated.'

'What are the dates?'

'Over the last eight months, which would be since Kahn moved into this flat, on the occasion of his marriage. If there were earlier ones, we didn't find them. The most recent one is dated last Tuesday, May third.'

'On May third they were urging him to blow up the Farthing Set with a bomb,' Carmichael said, smelling his lady-sawn-in-half again. 'And on Saturday night he kills Thirkie, alone, by gas? How often were the letters sent, normally?'

'About once a month, or every six weeks,' Stebbings said.

'Thank you very much, sergeant,' Carmichael said. 'I don't suppose you have any idea who this person is?'

'None, sorry, sir. I checked the name, but we don't have anything, and it's just the one name, don't know if it's a first or a last name.'

'No known Bolshevik connections?'

'No, sir.' Stebbings sounded regretful.

'Does he sound like a Bolshevik, in the letters?'

'Rather the opposite, if anything. He says several times that Stalin's as bad as Hitler. He talks a lot about smuggling people out of the Reich and says that Stalin's copying Hitler and they'll have to smuggle people out of Russia soon too.'

'A Jewish underground group,' Carmichael said. 'Do we know of any?'

'One or two, which we'll check out now,' Stebbings said. 'They mostly want to establish a Jewish state in Palestine.'

'That isn't illegal,' Carmichael objected. 'Perfectly respectable people want to do that. Balfour when he was Prime Minister wanted to.'

'You know more about that than I would, sir,' Stebbings said. 'I was talking about people who go out to Palestine and blow up railway lines or shoot at soldiers, terrorist actions like that.'

'Ah. That's a red herring from the sound of things. What I was wondering from the content as described was whether these letters might have come from the Continent. Are they in envelopes? Did they come from England or across the Channel?'

'No envelopes, so no telling,' Stebbings said. 'The notepaper is cheap, but it doesn't look foreign. You should look at them yourself, sir. Should I send them down?'

'I think I'll be back in London later today — hold on to them for now,' Carmichael said. 'I'll be in touch, sergeant. Thank you again.'

'One more thing,' Stebbings said. 'It turns out

209

he may be a sodomite too, Kahn. There's letters in Mrs. Kahn's possession from her brother, who was in the RAF with Kahn, talking about their undying love, and David and Jonathan, and all manner of Greeks.'

'Probably just boyish stuff and nonsense,' Carmichael said. 'From Mrs. Kahn's brother you say?'

'They're everywhere, sir,' Stebbings said, gloomily.

'Well, this doesn't have any bearing on the present case, being as Mrs. Kahn's brother was killed in 1940,' Carmichael said. 'Put the whole lot on my desk. I'll go through them when I can.'

'See you later, sir,' Stebbings said, and rang off.

Carmichael turned his pen in his hands, then wiped his fingers on his handkerchief. He looked at what he had written, but it didn't apply. Kahn, however Jewish, however queer as a young man, was rich, had been rich before his marriage, he came of a rich banking family. He had a friend who was a Jewish revolutionary, a friend he sent money to, a friend smuggling Jews out of the Reich, a friend who urged him to violent acts. Was that enough to arrest him for the murder of Sir James Thirkie? Surely not. But could he risk letting him loose, when he had letters in his possession urging him to kill a man who had been killed, and at a time when he had the means and the opportunity? If he arrested Kahn, Kahn would hang. He would be convicted in the press before he ever got to

210

trial, and a prosecuting barrister would look at Carmichael's thin thread of evidence and paint it as broad as a highway. Then Kahn would hang, and if he wasn't guilty, the guilty person would be laughing. But Kahn could have done it, have decided not to kill his own relations-by-marriage but satisfy his friend with Thirkie, who had stopped the Jewish war.

He reached out for the bell-pull, to ask Jeffrey to send Kahn in, and hesitated. Not Bolshevik, Stebbings had said, rather the opposite. Guerin/ Brown had that Bolshevik card. If this was a political plot, then it was a Bolshevik one. Guerin/Brown could have been unconnected with the Thirkie murder, but he couldn't quite believe it. Carmichael ground his fists into his eyes, feeling as if he had everything upside-down. He rang the bell, and waited. He read the report on the Bolsheviks. It said nothing about Jews.

Jeffrey knocked. 'You rang, sir?' he asked.

'Please ask Mr. Kahn if he can see me,' Carmichael said. 'And send in some China tea for us both, if it isn't putting too much of a strain on the kitchen at this time of day.'

'Yes, sir,' Jeffrey said. 'Is it true, sir, that everyone is allowed to leave after breakfast? The London servants are all in a flurry about it.'

'Yes, most people will be leaving,' Carmichael said. 'There's no reason to keep everyone here any longer.'

Jeffrey left. Carmichael put down the Bolshevik report — why did they have to have so many antagonistic splinter groups anyway? Most people got on splendidly without any. Underneath it was a brief report on Alan Brown, tenant of 23 Sisal Villas, Bethnal Green. Date of Birth, 6 February 1925. Unemployed. Last place of employment: Mottrams. Position: fitter. Reason for leaving employment: dismissed 3 January 1949, accused of trying to start a union. Not known to the police.

So he'd been out of work since January, and he sounded like a red, all right, trying to start a union. But if his real name wasn't known to the police either, why was he living under the name of Brown? Faked identity cards didn't come cheap.

Lizzie brought tea, and Carmichael poured a cup for himself. Then Jeffrey tapped on the door again, and ushered in Kahn. He was wearing a light gray traveling suit and carrying a slate gray coat.

'My wife and I are ready to leave,' Kahn said.

'Sit down, and have a cup of tea,' Carmichael said, pouring a cup and pushing it across the desk. He waited until Kahn was sitting. 'Who's Chaim?' he asked.

Kahn betrayed absolutely nothing. The cup did not tremble in the saucer. 'I have no idea what you're talking about,' he said.

Carmichael took the pad where he had written it down, noticed in time what was written above it, turned to a clean page and wrote it down again. He handed it to Kahn. This time there was a reaction — he saw him flinch a little, and his teaspoon tinkled.

'Chaim,' he read, pronouncing it more like

'Kiy-am.' He looked up from the paper, distress visible. 'Where did you find this name?'

'Who is it?' Carmichael insisted.

'He is a friend of mine, a hot-headed Jewish friend,' he said, setting his cup down on the desk. 'You've found his letters? You've searched my flat?'

Carmichael said nothing for a moment. It wasn't the answer he was expecting. He had expected more absolute denial, which would have been very hard to deal with. 'What's his full name?' he asked.

Kahn opened his mouth, then closed it again. 'I don't have to speak to you, Inspector, and I certainly don't have to betray my friends to you when that would mean betraying them to the Gestapo and having them end up in a worse place than you could ever imagine.'

'I've seen the reports on the work camps,' Carmichael said.

'The press know nothing — ' Kahn began dismissively.

'I've seen the real reports,' Carmichael interrupted. 'Your friend Chaim gets people out of them?'

Kahn stared at him for a moment, then spoke. 'Yes. When he can. More often he helps people escape before they get to them — false papers so they can live as Aryans, passports or visas so they can get out.'

'And you give him money, to help him with this?'

Kahn nodded. 'Not very much money, not enough, but how can I refuse?'

213

'The Gestapo are always telling us that our rich Jews are financing the escape of their Jews,' Carmichael said.

Kahn laughed without mirth. 'I hope you deny it.'

'I always have so far,' Carmichael said, evenly.

'I don't have to say anything without a lawyer present,' Kahn said, immediately defensive. 'When it's a matter of helping you catch a murderer, a murderer I know nothing about, then I will help you as much as I can, even though I see suspicion falling falsely on me simply because I'm Jewish. But when it comes to this kind of thing, you can't make me talk.'

'We can go that route if you like, Mr. Kahn, but I have to tell you that if you make such a request, I'll be forced to arrest you, and once the machinery of arrests begins to grind, you might find yourself very rapidly on the gallows for the murder of Sir James Thirkie. I don't want that, because I'm by no means sure you did it, but from the evidence we have against you it would be possible to make a very good case.'

Kahn picked up his tea and took a sip, and then another. 'What do you want to know?' he asked.

'As well as helping European Jews escape the Reich, Chaim urged you to revolutionary actions in this country?' Carmichael asked, quite gently.

'You have searched my flat,' Kahn said, putting his tea down again. 'Very well. Yes. Yes he did. He was always coming up with some scheme. He thought that since my marriage brought me into contact with people he called

British fascists, I should take some violent action against them.'

'And what did you think?'

'That he was talking nonsense, of course!' Kahn said, vehemently. 'The Farthing Set aren't fascists; there are no fascists in Britain. I hoped that Lord Eversley and his friends might learn from this connection that British Jews are much like other British people, and perhaps agree to allowing more European Jews into the country, or into other parts of the Empire. If I'd killed them, even one of the out-and-out anti-Semites, I'd have made everyone hate the Jews. Britain might have become as bad as Germany. It was madness. It could only make things worse here, to no purpose.'

'And is that what you said to Chaim?'

'Of course it is, over and over again. Every time he wrote I'd send him back a long letter explaining all this business. He didn't understand the British situation. He saw that things here aren't perfect, and thought half a loaf was the same as no bread, which is arrant nonsense. My father manages to get a number of visas every year, entirely legally, by money and influence, not very many, true, but for each individual life saved it makes all the difference in the world. We can't help European Jewry by using the methods of fascism. It's much more likely that we can change public opinion and policy, slowly.'

'And is the hope of being in a better position to do that why you married Mrs. Kahn?' Carmichael asked.

Kahn looked at him as if he were a worm. 'In your world, do people marry for political reasons like that?' he asked. 'I married Lucy because we love each other.'

'As you loved her brother?'

'You really are despicable,' Kahn said.

'I'm sorry,' Carmichael said, sincerely. 'Let's leave all of that on one side. These political views you just expressed, are they the views you expressed to Chaim?'

'Over and over again,' Kahn repeated.

'But we don't have your letters,' Carmichael pointed out. 'And you continued to send money.'

'He's doing good work in Europe,' Kahn protested. 'He didn't understand the British situation, but I approved of what he was doing there. Last year he managed to get a hundred people out of a death camp at Stavrapol, in the Reichskomissariat of Ukraine, and right across Europe to Portugal and then to Brazil.'

'How do you know Chaim?' Carmichael asked. 'Where did you meet?'

'We were at school together.' Surprisingly, Kahn blushed. 'I was educated abroad,' he said, airily. 'Between 1929 and 1937 I was at a private school in St. Tropez called Aquitaine College. It was run along the lines of a British public school, and education was in English, but it was in the South of France.'

'Why was that?' Carmichael asked, making a note. Chaim was a sufficiently unusual name that it would be unlikely to be too hard to trace him from a clue like that.

'It's difficult for Jewish boys to have public

216

school educations in England,' Kahn admitted. 'There are quotas. Aquitaine College was an attempt to provide an English kind of education, in pleasant surroundings.'

'Were many of the pupils Jewish?' Carmichael asked.

'Practically all of them,' Kahn admitted. 'Not all of them were English, however.'

'So Chaim is an old friend. You argue like old friends. He suggests you do ridiculous things, you tell him he's full of nonsense, but you send him money to help him do things you do approve of.'

'He's never been an adult in a country that was free,' Kahn explained. 'He doesn't understand England, because all he knew of it was at school, and at school in France. If England were the way the Continent is, then he'd be right. Killing Hitler, if it were possible to get close enough to him, would be a duty, and might even make a difference. He thinks killing my father-in-law would be the same thing, because he doesn't understand the situation.'

'Is he a Communist?' Carmichael asked, slipping the question in idly.

'Good gracious no!' Kahn looked astonished. 'He hates Stalin almost as much as he hates Hitler.'

Carmichael picked up his tea, which was almost cold, and drained it in one draught. He looked at Kahn, and decided to take the risk. 'I'm not going to arrest you, Mr. Kahn,' he said. 'But I am going to have to ask you to do me an immense favor, because otherwise I will have to arrest you. Promise me you'll stay here, in Farthing, and consider yourself under house arrest. I don't think I could persuade my superiors, in the circumstances, to let you loose in London. But if you stay here, in your parents-in-law's house for a few days, while I complete my investigations, then I think I can assure you that if you've been telling the truth you can go free.'

'This is intolerable!' Kahn said. 'We're ready to leave. Lucy hates it here. Lord and Lady Eversley are leaving. We can't stay here alone.'

'I think Mrs. Kahn will understand if you explain it to her,' Carmichael said. 'Especially if you explain the alternative. British justice grinds exceedingly fine, and when it gets grist, it assumes it is there to be ground down. You had the opportunity to kill Sir James Thirkie, and those letters could be used to prove you had a motive. In a few days, we'll have the real culprit.'

'Are you threatening me?' Kahn was white with anger.

'Far from it, Mr. Kahn. I'm trying to make you understand your position. I believe in at least the strong probability of your innocence. Do me the courtesy of believing in my good faith.'

# 19

I almost cried when David told me we had to stay. He was furious. He gets white around the lips when he's really angry, and he was like that now. He paced around the bedroom fuming, and at the same time throwing off his London clothes, because he couldn't feel comfortable wearing town clothes in the country. 'He doesn't even think I did it!' he said. 'He just thinks there's too much evidence to let me free, just because I'm a Jew.'

'What evidence?' I asked.

'My friend Chaim, who I've told you about, wrote to me that he thought I should make a bomb and blow up the Farthing Set, to prevent fascism from taking root in England. I told him it was nonsense, that we could never have fascism here because people were in essence too decent. But just having a letter like that in my possession damns me, apparently.'

'How did they know you had a letter like that?' I asked.

'They searched the flat,' he said. 'They must have. It's the only way. They searched the flat because I was Jewish. I'm sure they didn't search Normanby's flat, or your Uncle Dudley's house. And they read your letter from Hugh. The Inspector alluded to it.'

The thought of policemen searching our flat, touching our things, reading our most private letters, examining everything, made me feel rather sick. The year before, Eddie Cheriton had been staying up at Stirling for the shooting, and the house had been burgled. When she described the burglars pawing through her things I felt exactly the same sort of disgust. The burglars left her clothes and things in a terrible mess, apparently, though she didn't lose anything but a gold chain with a cross on it that her godmother had given her at her confirmation. I felt then that if that ever happened to me I'd have to throw away all the clothes that they'd touched. I felt the same now. I even wanted to sell the flat and move somewhere else, somewhere undefiled.

'What a violation,' I said, and I saw at once that David felt the same sort of horror.

'It's nothing to what Jews have to go through on the Continent,' he said. 'Nothing at all, you know that.'

'But that doesn't make it acceptable,' I said at once. 'The standard is not to be better than the worst thing available. It's not much of a thing to be able to say it's better than the deal Hitler gives the Jews!'

David came over and hugged me then, which was a comfort to me and I think to him as well.

'A few days in Farthing on our own won't be too bad,' I said. 'Mummy and Daddy will be in London, and so will half the staff. It's years since I've been down here on my own.'

'The servants will resent us,' David said. 'They probably long for their freedom in the quiet times.'

'The servants will make a big fuss of us, if my

experience is anything to go by,' I said. 'Their lives usually alternate between frantic panic, rushing about when everyone's here, and boredom when nobody is. Abby and I stayed here for a month on our own once when I had chicken pox, and everyone was lovely to me.'

'As soon as I'm properly dressed, we should go and say goodbye to your parents before they leave,' David said. He always stuck to the rules in matters like that.

'Inspector Carmichael will have told them we're staying,' I said. 'Or if he has any sense, he'll have told Sukey and let her tell Mummy.'

'Why would that be better?' David asked, frowning. He was halfway into a pair of proper country trousers, linen ones with a crease.

'Because it's Sukey who would have to do any organization necessary, not that there'd be much, beyond telling Mrs. Smollett to feed us. And Sukey can always tell Mummy things in a way that doesn't make her angry, even if she doesn't agree.'

'I've never really understood Miss Dorset's status,' David said.

'Well her title is housekeeper-companion, and she counts as one of the family because she's a distant relation of Mummy's. Her father was a second cousin or something, and a clergyman, and poor as a church mouse, of course, though if he'd lived he might have been a bishop I suppose. Anyway, he didn't, he was killed — in the Boer War, I think, or it might have been the Spanish Armada.' I waved my hand vaguely to indicate that it was a long time ago and I couldn't be expected to remember what war it was. David almost smiled. 'Anyway, Sukey's mother was left with a baby, so Grandfather Dorset naturally took her in, and just as naturally put her to work. Sukey was brought up with Mummy, she's a few years older than she is, and Mummy brought her with her when she married. Also,' I added, remembering that it was all right to talk to David about this sort of thing now, 'they're lovers, of course, in a Macedonian way.'

'Your mother and Sukey Dorset?' David asked, in a very surprised tone. He was adjusting his tie and he made an awful pig's ear of it because what I said made him pull just when he shouldn't.

'Hugh caught them in bed once, and I've seen them kissing myself,' I said.

'And does Lord Eversley know?'

'Daddy doesn't interfere with Mummy very much. But it isn't Bognor, I mean adultery — I'm sorry, darling; I don't mean to be putting in my own silly words all the time except where there aren't any proper words. It isn't adultery because Daddy does know even if he shuts his eyes to it. Hugh thought maybe Mummy made it a condition when they got married, that she could bring Sukey.' In fact, Hugh and I had never considered it Bognor because it had been going on for longer than we'd been alive and we'd always just accepted it as part of how the world was. I'd never really thought it through. 'I suppose Daddy could insist on getting rid of her if he really didn't like it, though I don't know what Mummy would do, maybe put poison in his coffee.'

And that was just the wrong thing to say, because just when I'd got David calmed down I reminded him of murder and he tensed up again, worse than ever. He finished messing about with his tie. 'Let's go down and make sure they understand the situation, and say goodbye to them,' he said.

We went down to the drawing room. We walked in on a blazing row. Mummy was sitting in her chair. She glared at me as we opened the door. Daddy, his arm still in a sling, was standing by the fireplace. Mark was sitting on the sofa, and Angela was standing by the window.

'I don't want to go to Campion,' Angela was saying. 'I want to go to London to sort myself out, and then up to Thirkie. Baby should be born at Thirkie.'

'It'll be some months yet,' Daddy said, reasonably. 'Old Lady Thirkie wants to see you; you can comfort each other. It's a very long way to Thirkie. You could take the train to Campion, changing at Newport, and be there by tea time.'

'James's mother hates me, she always has,' Angela said. 'I could take the train to London, though it's absurd that the police have impounded the car. James didn't die in the car, after all, he died in the dressing room.'

'It would be best for everyone if you went to Campion for a few days,' Mark said, in a very reasonable tone. 'Only a day or so. Then you could go to London and get ready to go up to

223

Thirkie for the funeral.'

'I don't see any reason why I should go and humor that terrible old lady,' Angela said. She looked like a two-year-old about to have a tantrum.

'I think you'll find it best,' Mark said, in a very significant way, though what he was saying was anything but significant.

'It'll look good with the press too,' Daddy said.

All this time we'd been hesitating in the doorway and Mummy had been glaring at us, but hadn't said a word.

'I didn't agree to all this just so I could be bullied by all of you!' Angela said.

'Either come in or go away again, Lucy,' Mummy said. Angela gave a kind of gasp when she turned and saw us. 'Angela, you're doing little enough and for all the benefit you're getting. I doubt a few days at Campion will kill you.'

'Oh!' Angela shouted, and stormed out, pushing past us.

David gave me a 'What was all that about?' look, to which I just shrugged my incomprehension.

'I suppose you've heard that we're staying on for a few days,' I said, going in and sitting down on the sofa against the wall. David followed me and sat down next to me.

'Yes, Inspector Carmichael was kind enough to inform me,' Mummy said, not unthawing at all. 'In the war I believe there were several requisitions of private houses by government ministries. I shall think of this like that.'

'Oh for goodness sake, Mummy!' I began, but David cut me off.

'I'm terribly sorry to inconvenience you in this way, Lady Eversley. It's a matter entirely out of my control, and I wouldn't have imposed on you like this for the world.'

Mummy inclined her head a little. She always approves of good manners, from anyone.

'Of course you can't help it,' Daddy said. 'And you're welcome to stay here for as long as suits you. Lucy knows her way about. Ride, if you like, or borrow a gun any time you want to.'

'That's very kind of you, sir,' David said, stiffly.

Mark got up then. 'If you'll excuse me, Lady Eversley, I should see if Daphne's ready to go. Eddie's driving us to the station, and we wouldn't want to keep her waiting. I do hope you have a nice stay at Farthing, Lucy, Mr. Kahn.' He nodded to us. 'I'll see you two in London.' He bowed over Mummy's hand, as if they didn't see each other practically every day.

'Is everyone off?' Daddy asked.

'Tibs and Dudley are coming with us in the car,' Mummy said. 'The Francises and the Manninghams have left. That's everyone.'

'Sukey coming with us?' Daddy asked.

'She's driving down separately in my car with Jackson, once he comes back from taking the servants to the station.'

'You mean we're going all the way to London in the chuffer?' Daddy asked in dismay. The chuffer was the Rolls, a splendidly grand car that Daddy hardly ever used because he didn't think

225

it had enough room for his legs.

'You'll just have to put up with it. If we're taking Tibs and Dudley, we ought to take them in style.'

'I'd give odds they'd rather go in comfort,' Daddy grumbled. He turned to us. 'How's your little Hillman for leg room? Fit in it all right?'

'I find it very comfortable,' David said. 'There's plenty of room in the front, but as we always drive it ourselves, I'm not so sure about the back.'

'Probably better driving yourself than keeping chauffeurs eating their heads off about the place,' Daddy said. 'Bad as horses. How many servants do you get by with?'

'Just three,' David said. 'A cook, a housemaid, and a kitchenmaid. We send all our clothes out to laundries, as you can in London.'

'You dress yourselves?' Daddy asked, clearly marveling at the concept.

'I suppose you find it very difficult to keep servants,' Mummy put in, looking pityingly at us.

The annoying thing about that is that it was true. Ordinary Jewish families, like David's family, don't have any trouble. They hire Jewish servants. One of the best ways of getting Jews out of Europe actually is to bring them in as servants. I know a professor of physics who was smuggled into England as a valet. He went on to work in physics, obviously, but plenty of people who had their own small businesses in Germany and France are only too happy to work in service in England, at least for a few years. Our own

226

Mrs. Smollett is an example. I know for a fact she wasn't a cook in Poland, and she didn't live in a ghetto either; she owned her own restaurant on one of the most stylish streets in Warsaw.

David and I, however, didn't have it so easy. The advantage to Jewish servants of being in a Jewish household was that the food would be right, and they'd be able to keep the Sabbath — which means doing nothing at all between sunset on Friday until sunset on Saturday. We didn't keep the Sabbath — David didn't even before he met me — though we often had a pleasant quiet sort of day on Saturday, just lazing around at home reading and making love. We also didn't keep the dietary laws, though I wouldn't have minded and I sometimes had the feeling David wanted to. His breaking them was a deliberate taboo-breaking thing for him. He ate pork because he wanted to be seen as English, not because he wanted to eat it. I resented it when people served it to him specially. He never talked about it, except once, when he said how he wished that people would read the rest of the things Jews aren't supposed to eat and take to serving us buttered lobsters or shrimp on toast.

We had very good servants now, who understood us, and we were happy with them, but in our first few weeks of marriage there'd hardly been a week in which someone hadn't given notice because we were either too Jewish for them, or not Jewish enough.

'Yes, servants these days are terrible, especially

in London,' David said, in almost Mummy's own tone. 'They hear they can get more working in a factory, or a shop, and they're off. There's so little old-fashioned loyalty about. We've had to find servants from the country and train them ourselves, except for our cook, who's a Frenchwoman and simply devoted to us.'

Mummy absolutely lapped this up, but I had to look away, because if I'd caught David's eye I'd have started to laugh. I'd never seen him do this kind of imitation in front of someone before, though he did it often enough when we were alone, or with friends who'd appreciate the joke.

'Shall I have Youd bring the car around?' Daddy asked.

'Well I'm certainly ready,' Mummy said, getting up out of her chair. 'I'll leave the house to the barbarians — do try not to break anything, Lucy dear.'

I hadn't broken anything important since I was ten years old when I broke the ear off the bust of Hadrian in the library, but that had been an occasion when I'd been left in the house without Mummy. I smiled as sweetly as I could.

'Thank you again for letting us use the house in your absence,' David said.

'It's a pity there was all this unpleasantness during your visit,' Daddy said, shaking hands with David. 'You'll have to come down again in the autumn when we can get a bit of partridge shooting in. You'd enjoy that.'

'Certainly, sir. Thank you.'

By the autumn, I thought, kissing Daddy and pressing cheeks with Mummy, even if we did come down for a few days, I'd be halfway through the pregnancy. He or she would be born at the end of January or the beginning of February, at lambing time, born with the snowdrops at the very beginning of spring.

# 20

Mrs. Normanby came into the room jerkily, like a puppet, Carmichael thought, or a piece of badly spliced film. Nevertheless, she looked much better than she had the last time he had spoken to her.

'I can't imagine I'll be any use to you, Inspector,' she said. She was wearing a plum red suit with a dark blue blouse. Her dark hair, previously disordered, was neatly brushed into its fashionable shingle. She was smartly made up, but Carmichael, who had lipstick on his mind, noticed that the shade of lipstick she wore was too light for her suit. The dark Dior shade he'd seen in her sister's room would have been just right.

'I'm just making some inquiries,' he said. 'Do you and your husband share a bedroom, Mrs. Normanby?'

She looked startled. 'That's a very personal question, Inspector.'

'Nevertheless, I'd like you to answer it, Mrs. Normanby. Policemen are unshockable, you know, like doctors.' He smiled at her. She returned his gaze without changing her expression at all.

'We don't share a bedroom at home,' she said, after a moment. 'Here, we have connecting rooms.'

That was exactly what Carmichael had

expected to hear. He couldn't, even under policeman's privilege, ask her what had possessed a smart woman like herself to tie herself for life to a bastard like Normanby.

'So, do you know what time your husband got up on Sunday? It might be relevant, because of the time he found the body.'

'Oh, I see,' she said. She fiddled with the clasp of her handbag, then looked out of the window at the hydrangea. 'Yes, Mark got up at about eight-thirty. He came into my room as I was dressing, to borrow a comb. We talked for a little while, then he said he'd meet me at breakfast, he wanted to check that James was — ' She bit her lip as her voice wavered. Had there been the slightest hesitation before the word 'comb'? Carmichael rather thought there was.

'He told you he was going to wake Sir James, yes, I understand,' Carmichael said. Either she was lying, or Normanby had really done what he said he had done.

'Yes,' she said, looking back at Carmichael, blinking away tears.

'Were you very fond of Sir James,' Carmichael asked, gently.

'Yes, very,' she said. 'He was a lovely man, very honest and decent, the best brother-in-law any woman could hope to have.' She had regained her equilibrium by the end of the sentence. 'I'll miss him,' she added.

'The whole country will miss him,' Carmichael said.

She nodded, again close to tears.

'You wouldn't know what time your husband went to bed the night before?' he asked.

'No,' she said. 'No, I don't know when Mark came up.'

'And what time did you go to bed yourself?'

She hesitated. 'I was playing cards with Kitty Manningham and Eddie Cheriton and Lily Palgrave. I went up when Lily and Oswald left, just before midnight I think.'

'Had you seen Sir James that evening?'

She started and almost dropped her handbag. 'At dinner,' she said after a moment. 'I don't think I saw him anywhere later.'

She hadn't been one of those who went to the billiard room, then.

'Thank you for talking to me and clearing that up, Mrs. Normanby,' he said, standing to show her out. 'Have a good trip back to London. Are you driving?'

'No, we're going on the ten-thirty from Farthing Junction,' she said.

There was a knock on the door, and it opened to reveal Normanby. 'There you are, Daphne,' he said. 'Have you finished with her, Inspector? We've a train to catch.'

No, Carmichael thought, seeing them together, they wouldn't share a bedroom, those two. It must be a white marriage, probably always and certainly for years. They looked as if they were on better speaking terms in public than in private.

'I've finished with Mrs. Normanby — she's been very helpful,' he said, and was not surprised to see a brief frown pass over Normanby's face.

No, he wouldn't want his wife talking to the police. But was it just his sexual habits, or was it something more?

'Goodbye, then, Inspector,' Normanby said. 'Come on, Daphne, Eddie's running us to the station, we don't want to keep her waiting.' He took her arm, and his grip seemed to Carmichael to be tighter than was necessary.

'Goodbye, have a good trip back to London,' Carmichael said, and closed the door behind them.

There was nothing more to do here; he might as well get ready to go himself. He gathered together all the papers from the desk, sorted them into a neat pile, and slid it into his case. He crumpled up the sheet with his doodle on it and dropped it into the wastepaper basket. Then, on second thought, he leaned down to pick it out again. He was just retrieving it when Royston came in.

'Nobody,' he said, with an air of satisfaction.

'Nobody?' Carmichael asked blankly, then catching the sergeant's meaning again, significantly: 'Nobody?'

'Absolutely nobody. I asked everyone, starting with the most likely, Lord Timothy and Mr. Francis and Mr. Kahn, and working my way through. It seems Lord Timothy and Mr. Kahn had a game last night, and Mr. Normanby and Lord Timothy had a game afterwards, but apart from that nobody will admit to having been near the billiard room all weekend.'

'Mrs. Normanby hadn't been there either,'

Carmichael said. 'So Normanby's lying.' Carmichael pushed his scrumpled doodle into his trouser pocket.

'Lying or mistaken,' Royston said, with the air of one bending over backwards to be fair. 'Or he could be telling the truth that they played billiards and lying about other people coming in, or lying about the billiards but telling the truth about being together.'

'We can't trust that one A.M. time any longer,' Carmichael said. 'The doctor's report said he'd have put the time of death as earlier, without that, perhaps eleven. We need to check where everyone was at eleven.'

'But they're all leaving, sir,' Royston pointed out. 'Most of them have left already. Besides, eleven was before Hatchard locked the door, and while there were still other guests in the house. Anyone could have done it.'

'Anyone leaving could have noticed his car, with him in it,' Carmichael said. 'If it was here. It might have been somewhere else, and then brought back. Did we check it for fingerprints?'

'None, not even Thirkie's or Lady Thirkie's. It had been wiped clean.' Royston sighed. 'Fingerprints aren't what they used to be before people got used to them. Now, we might as well not bother doing them; if there's anyone up to anything suspicious, they'll have wiped it.'

'Cheer up, sergeant, it does prove someone was up to something suspicious in the car,' Carmichael said.

'That's true,' Royston said. 'It could still be

cover up after a suicide though, the way we were saying last night.'

'Do they have a chauffeur?' Carmichael asked.

Royston frowned. 'Apparently they do, or rather, one who doubled as chauffeur and valet for Sir James, but they didn't bring him down with them. They usually do. Lord Eversley's valet had to dress Sir James, and didn't think much of it.'

'How very peculiar,' Carmichael said. 'I wonder if that might be proof for the suicide theory, because if he'd been thinking about killing himself in the car he might not have wanted someone here whose job it was to look after the car. Also, Normanby knew Sir James didn't have his valet here. That was his excuse for going in to wake him.'

'The valet who wasn't there, like the dog that didn't bark in the night,' Royston said.

'Penn-Barkis will sack you if he catches you quoting Sherlock Holmes, sergeant,' Carmichael said. 'What do you mean?'

'Just that there are any number of interpretations for his absence, if you see what I mean,' Royston said.

'You can go around to Thirkie's house in London and speak to him tomorrow,' Carmichael said. 'Find out from him why he wasn't taken, what was said to him, and how unusual it was.'

'Yes, sir,' Royston said, making a note.

'And while you've got your notebook out, did we ever find out when this party was arranged? Jeffrey told us it happened in a

235

hurry and that wasn't usual, but I don't remember any more about it.'

'Confirmed by all the servants,' Royston said, without looking. 'Lady Eversley said she'd decided to have the party on the spur of the moment because the weather was too good for London. Spur of the moment seems to have been the Tuesday before, the third, sir.'

'What else happened on the third?' Carmichael asked.

Royston looked blank.

'Kahn received a letter from an anarchist of the bomb-throwing variety. Anything else?'

'Kursk changed hands again?' Royston ventured. 'I mean, are you still looking for external events?'

'Yes, sergeant. Do you have any?'

'They decided to have this vote, the one they're holding tonight, the confidence vote in Mr. Eden, which the papers seem to think will very likely give us a new Prime Minister, though not a General Election.'

'And you think that might have prompted Lady Eversley to hold a houseparty?'

'Gather the faithful and feed them crumpets, that kind of thing,' Royston said.

It fit, it made sense. Carmichael sighed. 'Come on, sergeant, we've been given our marching orders. Let's hie us to the metropolis where information can be gathered, via the Station Hotel where our bags can be gathered, and possibly a spot of lunch.'

On the way back through the seemingly endless countryside, Carmichael tried to consider what it was he found so oppressive about it. Was it the lushness of the greens? Was it the size and age of the trees? Was it the hedgerows that prevented you from ever getting a long view? Or was it the pure contrast with the stark landscape of the Lancashire moors, where the land stretched out before you, sloping up to the mountains and down to the sea?

He let Royston drive and tried not to think about the case or the countryside. The car purred along past majestic trees, thick hedgerows of hazel and thorn, white with may-blossom and heavy with its scent. After half an hour or so, Royston interrupted his thoughts.

'Is there any special reason why they called us back to London now, sir?' he asked.

'Lord Eversley and his friends were tired of waiting at Farthing,' Carmichael said. 'And Penn-Barkis seems quite sure the Bolsheviks did it.'

'But they really could have,' Royston said.

'Not without inside help,' Carmichael said. 'We established that.'

'But that was before the billiards, sir,' Royston insisted.

'It was, too, you're absolutely right, sergeant,' Carmichael said, chastened. 'So now it could have happened anytime — I don't suppose we asked when people saw him last before Normanby?'

'No, sir.'

'No, because we're as bad as Yately with his 'Mr. Normanby wouldn't do it, he's an MP,''

Carmichael said, mocking Yately's accent viciously. 'Why the devil would a fellow like that lie?'

'To shield someone?' Royston ventured. 'But if so, who?'

'Or to get something, but if so, what?' Carmichael could feel the crumpled ball of paper in his trousers pocket. There is one law for rich and poor alike . . .

'Or to cover something up,' Royston went on. 'Again, what?'

'The Bolsheviks could have done the whole thing,' Carmichael said. 'Killed him, around eleven, gone straight into the house in the confusion of the big party, arranged him in his dressing room, and walked out again.'

'Carrying a dead body up two flights of stairs in the middle of a party?'

'They could have gone up the back stairs, the servants' stairs.' Carmichael knew he was reaching. 'No, just as likely if not more likely that the servants would see them. Unless they had help from the servants, which puts as back where we were before.'

'Say he killed himself or the Bolsheviks killed him and made it look like suicide, at eleven, and Normanby found the body shortly after,' Royston said. 'He could have waited until the house was quiet and then carried him in and arranged him.'

'But they were friends, allies, brothers-in-law,' Carmichael protested. 'What had Normanby to gain from the masquerade?'

'Maybe it's not that. Maybe he'd have lost

from him being found dead in the car, and the masquerade wasn't to scare anyone but to get sympathy, for Thirkie, for the Farthing Set, for Normanby himself. He could then make sure to find the body himself later.'

'Much better to leave it to someone else to find,' Carmichael said. 'But maybe he wouldn't have thought of that. That makes sense — that's the first explanation that does. If Thirkie had committed suicide, or if it appeared he had, there would have been investigations and rumors, and maybe the Farthing Set wouldn't do too well out of the vote tonight. And that would go double if it was suicide and if there was a note saying 'Normanby made me do it' or anything like that.'

'Normanby drove me to it,' Royston suggested. 'Car, drive, oh never mind.'

'I don't suppose Normanby did drive him to it, but just the suicide would work that way.' Carmichael stared out of the car. They were leaving the country at last, and entering a small town. The road would run through civilization now until it came to London. A cloud passed over the sun.

'And the Bolsheviks could have managed that part of it, if it wasn't suicide.'

'No, we mustn't forget the Bolsheviks.'

'Or anyone else for that matter,' added Royston. 'Anyone could have killed him, or it could have been suicide, and Normanby arranged the body with the star, which he probably picked up in France as a souvenir, and Thirkie's own dagger.'

'Lipstick,' Carmichael said.

Royston drove on in silence. A heavier cloud was covering the sun now, and showing no signs of passing.

'Have I foiled you, sergeant?' Carmichael asked after a moment.

'It was definitely stolen on Friday, when all the suspects were in the house,' Royston said. 'Maybe Normanby stole it for some other reason and used it because he had it to hand.'

'If Normanby wants lipstick he can steal his wife's, which would be much better quality than Woolworth's Carmine,' Carmichael said. 'Leaving aside entirely the question of why a respectable male member of Parliament might want lipstick at all.'

'Maybe he wanted cheap lipstick,' Royston said. 'Remember that man with the stockings? He only stole nylons — silk was no good to him. Maybe it's like that.'

'I think the resemblance this theory has to a nylon is that it's getting a little stretched,' Carmichael said. They drove on. As they came to the outskirts of London proper, the skies opened and Royston was obliged to put on his windscreen wipers.

'We had beautiful weather all the time we were in the country,' Carmichael couldn't resist saying.

'Just as well. It doesn't really matter if it rains in town,' replied Royston, irrepressibly.

# 21

I could see the moment we were on our own in the house how uncomfortable it was likely to be. The servants wouldn't mind, but David was sure they would. We'd be tiptoeing around the place afraid to do anything or cause any trouble, and with nothing to do ourselves. So I scuppered that right away. As soon as Hatchard and all the other grand servants had gone off to the train I rang for Jeffrey. We were still sitting in the drawing room, David rather sunk in gloom beside me.

'Mrs. Smollett wanted to know if you and Mr. Kahn would be wanting lunch, madam,' Jeffrey said, before I could say anything.

'We'll be wanting something,' I said, 'but I don't think it will be a formal lunch. What we'd like would be sandwiches — is there any of that salmon left? And we'd like it in the garden.' David looked at me and made a tiny noise of protest. I put my hand on his but went sailing on. 'Also, please tell her we don't want dinner, not a huge family dinner with courses. We appreciate the difficulty we're putting her to, and what we'd really like today is a nursery tea.'

David laughed, and Jeffrey smiled. 'Really, madam?' Jeffrey asked.

'Yes, really, a nursery tea with bread and butter and boiled eggs and cold meat, and perhaps a kipper, and cake.' Hugh and I used to call nursery teas 'broken meats,' which was a term he'd found in some story, because the meat would be the end of what had been served for some other meal, and the cakes were never whole. 'And we'll want something like that every day we're here — sandwiches or a light snack at lunchtime, and a nursery tea with perhaps one hot dish, in the early evening. We won't eat in the dining room, either, so you can close it up as you normally would. We'll take all our meals in the breakfast room.'

'Very good, madam,' Jeffrey said, and he was grinning quite broadly now.

'It'll be less trouble for you and much more what Mr. David and I enjoy,' I said.

'It'll be just like when you were here with Miss Abbott after you'd been ill,' Jeffrey said. 'Do you ever hear from Miss Abbott now, madam?'

'Yes, I do. She's given up governessing. She's married and she helps her husband to run a school,' I said.

'I'm very glad she's happy, miss — madam, I mean.' Jeffrey caught his slip at once. 'I'll tell Mrs. Smollett and Mrs. Simons what you've said, and perhaps you could have a word with Mrs. Simons tomorrow morning before she goes in to Winchester to do the marketing.'

It was on the tip of my tongue to say I'd go in with her. Market day in Winchester had been a Wednesday as long as I could remember, and going along with Sukey, or Abby, or Mrs. Collins, the housekeeper we had before Mrs. Simons, had been one of the pleasures of my early life. Winchester has very narrow medieval streets for the most part, except down by the

Cathedral Close where they're all splendidly eighteenth century. The market stalls make the streets even narrower. They all have striped awnings and are manned by cheerful country people. The wares vary tremendously — vegetables and fruit, fish, meat, cloth, hardwares, all in enormous quantities and piled up in heaps. A stall that's absolutely all gleaming red apples might be next to one that's all shears and tape and little screws. Anything you can buy anywhere, you can buy in Winchester market. There's a man there who carves. He used to be a shepherd, and he carved his own crock so well that the other shepherds asked him to carve ones for them, and then people seeing them asked him to carve other things, and now he's employed full time making beautiful carvings, and he sits there behind the stall with his big white beard tucked into his belt and his knife in one hand and the wood in the other. He just keeps on carving away while his wife sells the spoons and sticks and children's toys he's turning out. But fortunately, I managed to catch the train that time, and not say it. Because what David had agreed with Inspector Carmichael was house arrest, and going in to Winchester market would be breaking it just as much as going home would be.

'I'll speak to her in the morning,' I said.

'Would you like tea with your sandwiches?' Jeffrey asked. 'Or there's a bottle of Montracher that was opened this morning for Lord Manningham to take his tablets. He has to take them in Montrachet, doctor's orders, he says.

243

But there's only one glass gone out of it, and it seems a shame to waste it.'

'You could drink it yourself, Jeffrey,' I said.

'Montrachet? Filthy stuff,' he said.

David laughed. 'You need to educate your palate, Jeffrey,' he said.

'Yes, sir,' Jeffrey said. 'Shall I bring it out with the sandwiches, then?'

'You may as well,' I said.

He went out, smiling, and when I turned to David he was smiling too. This was just what I'd hoped for in suggesting a nursery tea, to make David understand that for years my relationship with the older servants at Farthing was one of conspiracy — a conspiracy in which they and I were on the same side, and Mummy and Daddy were on the other. I wanted to establish to them that David was firmly on my side, and to David that the servants understood.

It's a funny thing, really, having servants. They're employees, they're paid to serve you, to live in your house and take care of you — picking up your mess, cooking your meals. It can't possibly be an equal relationship, and it's not surprising that some servants come to absolutely despise their employers, and others come to be terribly snobbish about the most absurd things. I once heard Uncle Dudley's valet telling another valet that he wouldn't dream of lowering himself to work for anyone less than a Marquis, now that he'd worked for a Duke. I'm quite sure he meant it, that he'd have happily accepted a job with a Prince for less pay than he got from Uncle Dudley, but never one from

Daddy, for more pay, because Daddy is only a Viscount. Yet what does it matter, really? His employer's rank wouldn't objectively make the slightest bit of difference to the man, whereas the things that would matter, how much he was paid, how comfortable the situation was, whether his employer was a nice person, wouldn't count with him.

Abby taught me long ago to see servants as people. She was in an ambiguous position herself, as a governess, not quite a servant, but never a member of the family either. She'd been governess at several houses, and at some had a terrible time, even being raped by the elder brother of her charges once, when the little girls were in the next room and she could not cry out. She taught me not to take servants for granted, to see that we live very intimately with them and that they know our secrets, that we cannot purchase loyalty with pay. She said servants sometimes took out their resentment on people like her, in-between people, giving her bad service, not cleaning her shoes or returning her laundry, refusing to answer her bell. She made me see how privileged I was, and how I might unthinkingly make a servant's day worse, simply because I was bored or lazy. It's a commonplace that old servants become almost family, and that well-treated servants will stay with you, but it's also true in a way that the commonplace doesn't touch. Abby was my governess between the ages of six and thirteen, and she looked after me in the holidays until I was seventeen. She taught me to appreciate poetry and do simple arithmetic, but her accomplishments didn't extend much beyond that — I found out when I went to school that my French was the worst they'd ever heard. But she loved me, she taught me right from wrong, she taught me how to live, and she was far more of a mother to me than Mummy ever was.

David and I went out into the garden. The whole estate is garden in one way, but what we call 'the garden' was a little sunken garden at the back of the house. There are wooden chairs and tables out there, and we keep cushions for the chairs inside so they don't get wet. We sat out there in the sunshine, though there were clouds coming in from the north and I could tell the bright weather wasn't going to last. We ate our salmon sandwiches and finished up the Montrachet and sat and read our books until the clouds came over quite heavily, when we went in to the library, taking our cushions in with us.

I don't know if it was the Montrachet, or the disappointment, or the baby starting to change my body, but I felt quite tired, although it was hardly two o'clock. I kicked my shoes off and put my feet up on the leather couch in the library and settled down to read *The Treasure Seekers* for about the thirtieth time. David sat on the chair where Mummy had been sitting the other day, under Portia, and took up *Three Men in a Boat*, which he said he'd never read and always meant to. Before long he was completely engrossed.

I felt like dozing off, and yet I didn't. I just lay there, half-reading the very familiar episodes, and looking over at David now and again, feeling quite content really, because I didn't mind being at Farthing at all now. It was Mummy who made me feel claustrophobic.

I started thinking about the murder, and about the Bolshevik, and what could really have happened, and about Inspector Carmichael thinking he'd been led by the nose. I was sort of facing up to things I'd only thought about before in between thinking of other things and wanting to get away. Someone had killed Sir James. Someone had shot at me and Daddy and Daddy had killed him.

I thought about the murder of Sir James. Daphne had found him, and gone into a state of shock; then she'd got Mark to lie and say he'd found him. Daphne couldn't have killed him, she loved him. She was probably the only one who did, if it was true what Eddie said about Angela's baby not being Sir James's. Could Angela have killed him? She certainly had a motive. She could do what she liked now — even if Mummy and Mark were trying to bully her. What had Mummy said to her, doing little enough for all the benefit you're getting. What benefit? But Angela was too silly and feminine to have stabbed Sir James, too irresolute to have carried through a course of action like that, and much too silly to have thought of trying to frame it as a political assassination.

Wondering who else benefited, I could see why Inspector Carmichael wanted us to stay here. I could see his case against David very clearly. It frightened me. The only thing that would really clear David would be finding the real murderer.

I don't suppose you've ever considered what it would mean to know that someone close to you had done something unspeakable — and by that I don't mean shooting a fox or putting lemonade into a single malt, the way Daddy would. I knew David hadn't done it, but just for a moment I considered it as if he had. He'd have had to have got out of bed without my noticing it. He'd have had to have made certain preparations in advance without my knowing, getting the star and so forth, and probably getting a dagger as well, as I'd never seen him with one. He had a revolver, an ordinary military revolver, which he kept at the bottom of his underwear drawer. So he'd have had to have prepared, and then got out of bed and got the things, and gone down the hall to Sir James's room — it was between our room and the bathroom, nothing would have been easier — and gone in and stabbed him in his sleep. Then he'd have to have washed off any blood that got onto him — Daphne had said there was blood all over the body — and come back into bed with me.

I couldn't imagine it. I could imagine him killing someone, even killing Sir James, but that wouldn't have been the way he did it. Of course, he had killed people, lots of people, during the war, but they'd all been Luftwaffe pilots.

Just then David chuckled at something in the book and looked up and saw me looking at him. He read a passage out to me, it was the bit about the tin opener, and as he read I knew it was absurd to think he could have done it. If he'd

248

decided to assassinate Sir James for the Jewish cause, though how it could advance it one jot was beyond my understanding, David would have at the very least woken him and shot him, and probably taken him out somewhere a long way from the house. He wouldn't have left his body there for Angela or Daphne to walk in and find. David's a very thoughtful person. He'd never have done it that way. To do that he'd have to be someone else, someone entirely different. Maybe Inspector Carmichael could picture that different David, but he didn't live with the real David as I did.

So it definitely wasn't David, which would have been a load off my mind, except that if it wasn't David it had to be Mummy. I'd known that for days really, if I'd been prepared to face up to it, ever since Inspector Carmichael had said he felt led by the nose. Mummy had the resolution, and the planning. She might not have been up to it physically, but as usual she wouldn't have had any difficulty finding someone else to do it for her. Her motive was the only difficulty. Sir James was an ally. She'd undoubtedly have ditched him without a qualm, but why would she need to kill him? But given that she had a reason, if Mummy had done it, she would have had someone else do the actual stabbing. Daddy? Mark Normanby? And could Angela have known about it and could her widowhood be the benefit?

Frankly, I didn't feel any happier at the thought of her doing it than I did at the thought of David. They hang people for murder, and while I didn't exactly like Mummy, she was my mother after all. Though do they hang Viscountesses? Worse than that, if she'd done it she'd have been much too clever for them ever to catch her. There would be no possibility of them hanging her. She'd have defense in depth.

'Do you think Mummy knew, and invited us down so you'd be a suspect?' I had asked. And David had replied in a tone of humoring my fancies: 'That would mean she knew Sir James was going to be murdered.'

She'd have arranged a scapegoat, and that scapegoat could perfectly well be David, because she didn't like him, and she didn't care a scrap about me. We'd been lucky so far because Inspector Carmichael wasn't stupid, but we couldn't count on our luck lasting.

I started to make a plan then as I lay on the sofa, half a plan. I expect it looked to David as if I was falling asleep. What we could do, where we could go, what we should take, if it came to it. Who would help us, who we could really trust. Every so often I'd look over at him as he sat there smiling over the book. He was a man, and he'd fought in battle, and nearly died — he had medals to prove it though he never wore them or used the letters he could put after his name. And he was a Jew, one of the most persecuted people in Europe, and he knew more about what went on in the Reich than I did, and what I knew was quite nightmarish enough. Yet I felt he was innocent in a way I was not, that I knew more about evil than he ever could, because he had parents who loved him and wanted the best for him while I had grown up with Mummy.

# 22

It was half past four when they got to the Yard. London looked dirty and wet and run-down. Even the trees, which had leafed out in their absence, seemed thin and shabby compared to the lush spreading trees of the country. Black taxicabs dodged in and out of traffic, sending up sprays of water that drenched the pedestrians, scurrying in their drab raincoats and black umbrellas towards red buses or the beckoning mouths of the Underground. Royston drove Carmichael down the Strand, around half the crescent of the Aldwych and up the Kingsway, the dreariest street in London. He pulled up smartly by the No Parking sign in front of the new Scotland Yard building, which had been built at the end of High Holborn when the old 'New Scotland Yard' building had been put out of action in the Blitz. They just called it the Yard, as usual. Carmichael had never known the old building, so he generally ignored the complaints of old-timers for whom the new one would never be a replacement. Today, in the rain, the building, halfway between Palladian and deco, and lacking the virtues of either, looked particularly dreary. He could understand the superstition that had grown up that made it bad luck to walk in its shadow. Respectable lawyers from Lincoln's Inn and Gray's Inn crossed the road and then crossed back again later rather

251

than pass too close to the portals.

'Park and come to my office,' Carmichael said to Royston, ducking out of the car and preparing to dash up the stairs past the basrelief abstract sphinxes that flanked them.

The bobby on duty opened the door for Carmichael with a lackluster salute. Stebbings was, as usual, at his glassed-in desk in the central portico.

'Back at last,' he greeted Carmichael when he put his head around the door to say hello.

'Any news of my villain?' Carmichael asked, going completely inside the glass box. Stebbings's desk was neatly organized, with papers in tidy piles and alphabetized pigeonholes. There was a wireless set and four telephones, three standard black and one a daring cream.

'Which villain?' Stebbings asked.

'Brown. I can't imagine there being any more news of Kahn at present. I left him safely tucked in at Farthing.'

Stebbings put his hand in his G pigeonhole, but did not draw out the paper. 'Report here from the Garda, saying nothing known. In private they say the same thing. Michael Patrick Guerin could be anybody or nobody, all three names are common enough, but they don't have any records on any specific fellow. Jenkinson, who always deals with them since that business with De Valera's dog, says he's sure they'd have told him at the very least that they weren't going to tell him anything to pass on to his English masters, if that was the way of it.'

'I didn't think he was one of theirs,'

Carmichael said. 'There was something about him. Liverpool Irish is my guess. Any joy from Runcorn?'

Stebbings drew a sheet out of his *B* hole and read from it. 'Chap of the name Alan Brown — sounds like a pseudonym, doesn't it — born in Runcorn on the date specified, educated at Runcorn Boys Elementary School, left in 1936 — what a wonderful year to enter the workforce at the age of eleven I don't think — no police record, whereabouts unknown.'

'If you were a fitter of the name of Brown, why would you make up a name like Guerin?'

'A nom-de-guerre?' Stebbings suggested, and almost smiled. 'Maybe his Bolshevik pals said he needed a nom-de-guerre and as a workingman without much French and with friends among the Liverpool Irish even if he wasn't one himself, Guerin came straight to mind.'

'It's as good an explanation as anything I can think of,' Carmichael said.

'We've been through his house top to bottom, and found nothing of the slightest interest to anyone.' He put the paper back in under *B*. 'There are copies on your desk if you want the details.'

'Have you traced the girl? I sent you the picture.'

'No joy with the girl yet. We've been showing it around Bethnal Green but not a nibble. Probably not important. No luck tracing any of Brown's Bolshevik connections yet, either. We've rounded up a lot of Bolshies and fellow travelers, which is Simpson's department. He's pulling

253

them in and booking them all as accessories to this. He's quite grateful to you for giving him an excuse to bring them in — he knew who they were all right, some of them outright publish Bolshie articles in the papers, but they're very canny about keeping their feet on the right side of the law. Catch one of them on something that looks like spying or treachery, then they'll be splitting hairs and calling for their lawyers. The law's too soft on them. It's not like we'd be able to do that in Red Russia, not while preaching bloody revolution and going around shooting people.'

'Any of them admit to knowing Brown?' Carmichael asked.

'Not a one of them, not under either name. That's what you'd expect them to say, of course.' Stebbings sounded mildly regretful.

'Of course,' Carmichael said. He couldn't find it in his heart to be very sorry for Communists, even if they weren't connected with Guerin/ Brown.

'Chief Inspector Penn-Barkis wants to see you. I think he's hoping for a final report.'

'This afternoon?' Carmichael rolled his eyes. 'He's got a hope. I want to sniff around myself after Brown and see what I can find.'

'Tell the Chief,' Stebbings said.

'Thanks for the tip on Normanby, by the way,' Carmichael said. 'He's a nasty piece of work. He's definitely been telling us lies, too, only I can't work out why. He can't have done it — or rather, he probably could, technically, but he's got no percentage. The dead man was his friend.'

254

'*Evening Standard* is tipping him to be Prime Minister tonight. Should have done him for gross indecency when we had the chance, dirty bugger,' Stebbings said, in his usual flat tone. 'No justice, is there?'

'None,' Carmichael agreed. 'Well, I'd better push off and see the Chief.'

Royston was in his office when Carmichael pushed the door open. 'I'm off to see Chief Inspector Penn-Barkis,' he said. 'Did you park the car all right?'

'No problem. Got it into the lot — Inspector Blayne was just coming out as I got there.'

'That was a piece of luck.' Carmichael put down his case on his chair. His desk was covered with toppling piles of paper. He scanned the piles for anything recent and on a second try pulled out the report on Brown's lodgings. 'Read through this and get familiar with it. We'll be doing some scouting around after Brown.'

'You still want me to check into Thirkie's valet?' Royston asked.

'Yes,' Carmichael said. 'Tomorrow will do for that.' He hesitated. 'This case is like a big ball of string, with ends sticking out all over. I get the feeling that if we pull on the right one, it'll all come loose at once. Brown's a good place to start pulling, because Brown's the one we know is a villain and a murderer. But the chauffeur, valet, whatever he is, he's definitely another loose end.'

'Yes, sir,' Royston said.

Carmichael bent to check his hair in the mirror on the back of the door, put there so he could see behind suspects he might be interviewing. He walked down the hall and pressed the button for the lift. Penn-Barkis's office was at the very top of the building. The lift came and took Carmichael up, his stomach following just a little later.

Penn-Barkis's office was said to have one of the best views in London, looking south over Lincoln's Inn Fields past the original Old Curiosity Shop towards Fleet Street. Today the windows were clouded with condensation and running with rain. Penn-Barkis himself was sitting comfortably in an armchair, smoking a cigar. He was not an impressive-looking man, being bald, slightly tubby, and with heavy white eyebrows, but he succeeded in intimidating all his subordinates. He was said, in whispers, to have an excessively domineering wife, but it may have been wishful thinking from people who wanted to believe that there was someone who could put the Chief Inspector in his place. In his presence, Carmichael tried hard to modulate all his vowels and sound as Southern as he could, because Penn-Barkis had once said he had Lancashire on his breath the way another man might have whisky on it.

'Ah, Carmichael,' he said. 'Take a seat. Have you finished all that Thirkie nonsense?'

'Nonsense, sir?' Carmichael sat in the other armchair and waved away a cigar.

'Members of Parliament and Bolsheviks and Jews, all waiting around for you to finish talking to them — it sounds like nonsense to me,' Penn-Barkis said. 'But now you've evidence that the Jew and the Bolshie did him in between them, and we can close the case?'

'No, sir,' Carmichael said. Penn-Barkis's eyebrows went up. Carmichael took a deep breath. 'The case on the Bolshie's clear enough, he was standing there with a rifle in his hand, a .22, but a real rifle, good enough to kill someone. He shot at Lord Eversley and Mrs. Kahn, wounding both of them. But as for his involvement with the Thirkie murder, it's impossible that he should have done it. He couldn't have got into the house. Thirkie was gassed in his car, sir, and then his body was taken into the house, which must have needed help from inside at the very least. There he was arranged in his bed as if he'd been stabbed, with lipstick over his chest to simulate either blood or the red breast of the Farthing robin, and a Jewish star attached by a dagger.'

'Why go to all that trouble? Why not just stab him in the first place?' Penn-Barkis asked.

'Possibly to intimidate Thirkie's friends, or possibly to implicate the Jews in the murder, sir,' Carmichael said. 'Or it's possible that there were two parts to the business — one party who killed him, and another who arranged his body later. It's even possible the death was suicide.'

'Why would a man like Thirkie kill himself? He had everything to live for. If the vote tonight goes the way it's looking, he'd have been Home Secretary.'

'Yes, sir.' Carmichael thought about the vote. 'Maybe someone else wanted the job.'

'Do you have any evidence of that?'

257

Penn-Barkis sounded incredulous.

'No, sir,' Carmichael said. 'I do know that Mr. Normanby lied to us about the time he last saw the dead man alive, and I don't know what purpose he had for lying, but that's all.'

'Probably something perfectly rational.' Penn-Barkis puffed at his cigar and sent out a cloud of smoke. 'Or he might have been mistaken. Did you ask him?'

'There's no possibility he could have been mistaken, sir. But as you say, he could have been lying for some reason unrelated to the murder, and I didn't like to press him too hard, as he's a member of Parliament and also as he had no reason to kill Thirkie.'

'I thought you implied he wanted his job.'

'Mr. Normanby was tipped to be Chancellor, and now he seems to be tipped to be Prime Minister. Thirkie would have been junior to him in any case, sir.' Carmichael frowned.

'And what about this Kahn, the Jew?' Penn-Barkis asked. 'Have you arrested him?'

'No, sir. He had no reason to do it, and the crudity of the star rather points away from an intelligent man like Kahn than towards him. He's also a rich man and a banker. The only real evidence against him are some letters in his possession from a man called Chaim, a Jewish revolutionary, not a Bolshevik, an anti-Bolshevik, calling on him, as recently as last Tuesday, to blow up the whole Farthing Set. I prefer not to arrest him without a closer link, but he remains under house arrest at Farthing.'

'So what do you want to do?' Penn-Barkis put

down his cigar. 'I can't have this dragging on too long. The politicians are at my heels as it is.'

'Yes, sir,' Carmichael said, wishing there was no such thing as politics and that he'd never heard the word. 'I want to keep Royston, and I want to dig a little more into Brown, the gunman, his background, his friends, to see if I can find anything that leads me anywhere.'

'You can have until the end of the week,' Penn-Barkis said, looking at his watch. 'It's a quarter to six now, and it's Tuesday. That gives you two whole days, but that's all.'

Carmichael stood. 'Yes, sir.'

'On Friday morning, we're announcing the whole thing, that someone's in custody, or that Brown acted alone, and everything has to be tied up by then.'

'Yes, sir,' Carmichael said, because he could say nothing else. The crumpled paper pressed through the lining of his trousers pocket.

Penn-Barkis picked up his cigar again.

'I'll get on with it then, sir,' Carmichael said.

Back in his own office, Royston looked up inquiringly. 'Have a bad time, sir?' he asked, sympathetically.

'We have until Thursday night to wrap this case up, sergeant,' Carmichael said. 'Friday morning, Penn-Barkis will be announcing that it's all settled.'

'Ah, and I was hoping I might get down to the George for a pint this evening,' Royston said. 'I expect you would have been glad for a quiet night in too, sir. We'd better get down to Bethnal Green, though, but at least we'll sleep in our own

259

beds — that's a comfort.'

That was more of a comfort than Royston imagined, Carmichael thought. He picked up his case. 'Where the devil is the photograph?' he asked. He cast about on the desk unsuccessfully. Royston sat quietly, and Carmichael appreciated the lack of reproof in his silence. At last he found it, in an envelope. 'Leigh on Sea,' he read again on the back. 'We may have to go down there, but I hope not.'

'Southend, isn't it?' Royston asked.

'The posh end of Southend,' Carmichael agreed. 'All benches and pensioners and fading gentility.'

'Not much for a Bolshie,' Royston said. 'Shall I bring the car round? It's still raining stair-rods.'

'Yes, bring it round,' Carmichael said. 'I'll come and wait in the portico.'

Stebbings was talking into his cream telephone as Carmichael passed. He signaled for him to wait. After a moment he put the telephone down and snapped on the wireless. It gave a hum and then the drone of the BBC announcer came up. The six o'clock news, of course. 'After the confidence vote this evening in the House of Commons, it appears that Mr. Mark Normanby will be the next Prime Minister . . . '

Stebbings snapped it off again. 'Told you he'd get in, the sodomite,' he said. 'Though it'll be good for us, of course. Apart from when it comes to himself, he's very strong on law and order.'

'Gah,' Carmichael said, and stepped out once more into the driving rain.

# 23

I came back to my senses a little later, when I remembered about the Bolshevik. That Bolshevik was real; Inspector Carmichael had told me about him. Besides, he had shot at me, or at Daddy, and Daddy had killed him. Mummy would never get anyone to shoot Daddy — Mummy needs Daddy too much. Daddy gives Mummy her own position. Besides, she'd never make an alliance with the Bolsheviks either. She hates the Reds like poison, not just Russia but Reds in this country as well, the trade unionists and people like Bevan. She wouldn't have anything to do with them, which meant I must have been wrong, paranoid perhaps. Maybe pregnancy makes you paranoid, I thought. Besides, there wasn't any reason for her to kill Sir James.

Then we listened to the six o'clock news, in the library. The BBC announcer told us the result of the vote, Mark to be Prime Minister, and his new cabinet to be announced soon. Then Mark himself came on, his voice thin and distorted by the wireless. 'Some anarchists and Bolsheviks and Jews have this week attacked those of us who have sometimes been called the Farthing Set,' he said. 'As usual, these people were cowardly and attacked people when they can't hit back. They managed to murder Sir James Thirkie, architect of the Peace with

261

Honour, perhaps the best man in England, and one of my greatest friends. They killed him in his bed and attached a Jewish star to his chest as a calling card. But they could not subdue the Farthing Set, or frighten us, or keep us from power. Even as he lay dead, Sir James did not make the symbol they wanted, of a helpless dead man slain by a cowardly Jew. His chest was stained red with his own blood, red, like a robin's breast, like the Farthing robin that symbolizes our part of the Conservative Party. Sir James is murdered, but the rest of us live on. Lord Eversley managed to kill one attacker, a card-carrying Bolshevik, who sniped at him from cover. We will take extreme measures against these cowardly terrorists, who attack not just us, but England in us, and our conception of the way the country can go forward and be a better place.' I stared at the set. 'That was the Prime Minister,' the BBC announcer concluded. 'Meanwhile, in San Francisco, President Lindbergh has announced closer ties — '

David snapped the wireless off. 'I wish he hadn't added Jews to his list,' he said. 'Still, I suppose there is that star.'

'The sooner Inspector Carmichael finds the real murderer the happier I'll be,' I said. Then I saw why Mummy might have killed Sir James, if it wasn't for the Bolsheviks. She could have killed him precisely to sway public opinion towards the Farthing Set, to make the sympathy vote go in their direction, to make Mark become Prime Minister. I wondered about the 'extreme measures' he wanted to take, and shivered.

262

Lizzie knocked on the library door. 'Tea is served in the breakfast room,' she said.

Mrs. Smollett turned up trumps with that nursery tea; it was everything I could have hoped for, and the very antithesis of the terrible artificial Frenchified meals in six courses we'd been eating since we arrived. In addition to all the things I'd asked for, there was half a heavy dark fruit cake, the brandied kind. I don't know where she can have magicked it up from — it isn't the sort of thing people can keep lying around. When we'd been eating for a few minutes, Lizzie opened the door and Mrs. Smollett herself came in with a tray containing a huge plate of hot Polish pancakes, and a little red earthenware pot, like a jam dish only more curved, full of caviar, and another matching little dish of cream and chives. She gave us a smile as big as Trafalgar Square as she set the tray down. She's a big woman, not fat at all, but big, with coarse gray hair scraped up under a cap, and of course she wore a big apron, like any cook. She wouldn't normally come out of the kitchen, and if we'd been eating in the dining room rather than the breakfast room I'm sure she wouldn't have come even now. She'd come for the perfectly sensible reason that she'd made the pancakes specially as a treat for us and she wanted to see our reaction.

'You really are spoiling us, Mrs. Smollett,' I said. 'You shouldn't have gone to all this trouble.' Though even as I said it I was reaching for one and helping myself from the little red pots.

'I don't mind how much trouble to go to cooking for those I know will enjoy it,' she said, in her funny English that was still accented after all this time.

I couldn't answer because I had my mouth full, and it was exquisite, the hot pancake and the cold cream and the caviar simply exploding on my tongue.

'We certainly do appreciate it,' David said. He was being polite and finishing up the bite of roast beef and bread and butter he had left on his plate before taking a pancake.

'Mmmmmmmmmm!' I said, incoherently but emphatically.

Mrs. Smollett laughed. 'I was sure you would like.'

'Doesn't Daddy count the jars of caviar?' I asked, finishing my mouthful. I knew he counted the wine and the spirits.

'That is Mrs. Simons's affair. When the family are in residence I use what ingredients I like, just the same as Mrs. Richardson does.'

'Mrs. Richardson could never have given us anything half as delicious,' I said. 'Do take one while they're hot, David darling.'

'I intend to have my fair share, not just one,' David said, jealously.

I laughed. 'Mrs. Smollett,' I said, taking another (they're tiny things, Polish pancakes, in case you've never been fortunate enough to have them, only about two inches across), 'if you ever feel you're ready to leave Farthing, you know we'd be only too happy to give you a home, and employment, and all your heart desires, if you'd

264

only cook these pancakes for us once in a while.'

'If ever I leave Farthing, which is my second home, it will be when I've saved enough to open once more my own restaurant, in London as it used to be in Warsaw,' she said.

'You used to have your own restaurant, and you know how to run it yourself?' David asked, his head coming up like a dog scenting a rabbit. 'How much do you have saved?'

Before I knew it, she and David were deep into the financial details of what it would take, and he'd as good as promised to set her up!

'Sit down,' he said, and she was so bemused she sat down with us, still in her cap and apron.

'Have a pancake,' I offered, selflessly. 'Or perhaps one of these lovely scones?'

'No, no, I couldn't,' she said.

'You'll have to come into the bank and fill out forms,' David said. David hadn't stopped eating, he was simply steamrollering through the pancakes. 'But from what you tell me, I don't think we'd hesitate for an instant. It would be my decision, and I'd be all for it, except for a slight ethical qualm about sitting here eating their caviar and tempting you to leave Lord and Lady Eversley. Are you sure you won't have some yourself, it's extremely good.'

'I am on three months' notice, which I could at any time give,' Mrs. Smollett said, shaking her head at me as I offered her the pancakes again. 'It would take that long at least to find a suitable place and make it ready. But I think perhaps when I fill in the forms you would find I was not a suitable person. I am not British born, and I am a Jew, and a woman.'

'My bank makes a speciality of lending to Jews and women,' David said. 'That will be something that counts for you, rather than against you. We lend small amounts, and to a banker what you're talking about is a small amount, though it may seem large to you. We lose some money, but we do very well in general. In addition to loans, we invest in businesses that do well for us, when they want to expand, and I predict that in future that might come to be the main part of our business.'

'And for how long have you done this?' Mrs. Smollett asked, her dark eyes wide.

David hesitated, a pancake halfway to his mouth. 'As a separate bank of my own, only this year. But it has been my division of my father's business since the war — we just split it off that way recently.'

'Your father subsidizes you?'

'My father is a very rich man; he can afford to do it,' David said. 'He began by subsidizing me completely, and not really believing in me. I saw it during the war, looking at the way society interlocks at the bottom, talking to the other pilots. I saw how wealth could be expanded from the bottom up, rather than the top down. My father and uncles took a lot of persuading, but now they admit that I'm right and this method can actually make money. Take your restaurant. You're right: no conventional bank would lend you money, a woman, a Jew, an immigrant, a servant. You could show them what you'd saved in twelve years, you could cook them pancakes, which really are excellent beyond words — ' He reached for the last one, which was his by strict count so I let him have it. I was stuffed full anyway. I cut myself just the tiniest sliver of the fruitcake.

'But they'd take no notice, because they want to invest in the railways and big factories, steelworks, shipworks, or maybe — if they are a little more visionary — in some big picture like the industrialization of India. They're not interested in a little Polish restaurant in London. You're too small for them, and too insecure. But I don't see a little restaurant; I see a successful business that will employ, what did you say, ten or twelve people, besides yourself. It will take a dozen people who are presently unemployed, or barely employed, who are a burden to the country, or who are working in menial positions, and give them jobs with hope.'

Mrs. Smollett nodded. 'Twelve people, waiters and dishwashers and assistant cooks and cleaners. That's what it took in Warsaw.' I nibbled my fruitcake and poured myself another cup of tea. I always loved hearing David talk about his work, and it was quite fascinating to almost see him doing it.

David finished his pancake, and went on, quite quietly but utterly sincere: 'And perhaps, as well as employing twelve people and making a profit for you, and for us, it will also help in a small way with the position of the Jews. Maybe the Londoner, instead of saying from ignorance that the Jews are greedy and cowardly, push to the front of queues, take seats on buses, will say on reflection that they are not so bad; Mrs. Smollett cooks pancakes to make the heart glad, and David Kahn lends money to poor people to start businesses, and he fought all through the Battle of Britain.'

Mrs. Smollett shook her head. 'They will never say that.'

'Why not?' David frowned. Behaving as well as possible to be a good counter-example to people's beliefs about the Jews was one of the things he believed in most dearly. I put my hand on his and squeezed gently, but he didn't look at me and hardly seemed to notice.

'My restaurant, my old restaurant in Warsaw, the Nazis — ,' Mrs. Smollett said, then faltered, and began again. 'When the Nazis came, my customers did not say, 'Oh, do not persecute the Jews because Mrs. Szmolokiewitsz makes lovely pancakes and Mr. Szmolokiewitsz has willingly accepted his draft call into our army and their son Yusef is a doctor and their young daughter Marya is at the conservatoire learning to play the piano.' They said, 'Oh, the Nazis are right, the Jews are greedy and treacherous and we have always hated them.' When they smashed the window of my restaurant, it was not the Germans who did it, it was the Poles. And one of them who was in the front with stones in his hand was a customer, who I had served my special dumpling soup only the week before, and given his little son a candle on his crème brulée because it was his birthday. But now his face was screwed up with hate and he would have smashed me as well as the window if I had not run.'

'Where are your family now?' I asked.

Mrs. Smollett turned to me as if she'd forgotten I was there. 'Dead,' she said. 'My husband was killed in the fighting. He died in September 1939, honorably, defending his country. Marya was shot by a Heinkel as we escaped across France. The road was blocked with refugees and they wanted it for their tanks, so they flew over and shot at us, just to clear the way. I flung myself in a ditch, but Marya fell, shot through the head. I stayed in the ditch and watched the tanks passing over her body. Then after that I got up and took the money she was carrying from her shoe, and kept walking. Yusef died in 1946 in a camp called Treblinka. I heard from somebody who managed to escape, who knew him there. He came to find me. Yusef, he said, was able to help many people before he died, because he was a doctor. Without medicines or instruments, without even bandages, at night after working all day in a factory on slave rations, still my son was a doctor, and I can always be proud of that.'

She had tears streaming down her face. I got up and put my arms around her, unable to see so much sheer misery without trying to help, however inadequate such a thing was. She shrugged me off angrily and turned to David. 'You think what you do can make a difference to whether that happens here,' she said. 'You think we Jews in Poland, in Germany, in Hungary, we did something wrong, something to deserve what

269

happened to us. No. It doesn't make any difference. It wasn't our fault. It isn't something it's at all possible to control.'

'But England is different,' David said. 'You've been safe here for ten years. We fought against Hitler, and we'd fight again if there was any threat of him coming here.'

'They didn't fight him in Europe,' she said. 'Besides, you still don't understand that it wasn't Hitler who broke my window. It wasn't one mad German — it was the hate that everyone has inside them against the Jews. I used to think just the same as you do. I thought so until I was forty years old. You've just been lucky so far, that's all.'

'I've been very lucky, I know that,' David said. 'But come and see me in London about the money for your restaurant.'

Then Mrs. Smollett got up, and went back to the kitchen.

'She's lost sight of hope,' David said. 'Not surprising, considering what happened to her family, to lose every one of them like that. But she's wrong about England. People care about liberty and justice, and there's resentment, but not that buried hatred. That kind of thing would never happen here.'

'I wonder what drastic measures Mark has in mind?' I said, before I could catch the words back.

# 24

The gutters of Bethnal Green ran with rain. There were few people about, and most of those looked as if they wanted to be home as soon as they could. It was still daylight, but the heavy clouds made it almost dusk already.

'Where will we find people who know Brown, sergeant?' Carmichael asked.

'In the pubs, of course, sir,' Royston said. 'It's about the only place we're likely to find anyone on a night like this.'

'We could try temperance meetings, or bible readings,' Carmichael suggested.

Royston looked at him in horror for a moment, then began to laugh.

They hit gold on their third attempt. The Queen's Head knew nothing of Brown, and the White Horse could tell them only that he was an unemployed fitter from Sisal Street, which they knew already. But at the Three Feathers, a most superior establishment owned by Bass, which sported polished horse-brasses on all vertical surfaces and rejoiced in a public, a lounge bar, and a snug, the landlord knew Brown and was prepared to talk to them. The pub had only just opened for the evening. The landlord, a beefy man with a wispy moustache, left a barmaid in charge of the other bars and led them into the snug.

'Liked a scrap,' the landlord said, handing

them each a free pint of bitter, the policeman's prerogative in any poor London area. 'He wasn't above letting someone pay him for it neither.'

'You mean he was a hired bullyboy?' Royston asked. Carmichael sipped his beer and found it indifferent.

'Not exactly that. Not full time, like, or with a gang.' The landlord leaned across the bar and lowered his voice, though the only other person in the snug this early was an ancient man nodding over his pint in the corner. 'Brown wasn't a Londoner,' he confided.

'We believe he was from Runcorn,' Royston said.

'Some such heathenish place,' the landlord agreed. Carmichael buried a smile in his pint. Southerners! 'Anyway, he wasn't a Londoner, and he wasn't in any gangs or anything like that. I wouldn't have let him drink in here if he was,' he said, with an air of assumed virtue.

'But if you wanted someone beaten up . . . ,' Royston suggested.

'Maybe. In a small way, from time to time.' The landlord looked from one to the other of them. 'I don't know nothing definite, and he always behaved himself in here, but that was the tone of what I heard. Not like a bullyboy, more like if there was a scrap going, Brown would stand up with you for a couple of quid.'

'Did he have a lot of friends?' Royston asked.

'No. He kept to himself, mostly. He'd come in here with a group from work, but nobody really close. Most of the Mottrams fitters drink in here. Then when he was laid off, he'd come in and see who was here, on a Friday or a Saturday, drinking one half-pint over the whole evening unless someone stood him a round.'

'Laid off?' Royston asked.

'Don't say you don't know about that?' The landlord looked quite excited. 'Laid off from Mottrams, he was, right after Christmas, because he tried to organize a union among the fitters and boilermakers. Big fuss there was about it at the time. He was quite a hero.'

'Red, was he?' Royston asked, with a casual ease Carmichael admired.

'Not really.' The landlord frowned. 'We get them in here, of course, the Reds: the Labour lot, and the Union lot, and the Commies, and the Trots. They all hate each other worse than poison. They sit in groups in the public, ignoring each other. Some landlords would see them off, but I don't mind them. They're mostly quiet, and they hold their drink. If there's any trouble, say one of them were to get drunk, the rest of them take care of it. But I never seen Brown with any of them, except the Union crowd right after he was laid off. I don't think he was organized, like. In fact, I think Brown wanted to better himself. He wanted more out of life than to be a fitter. Maybe that's why he wanted a union, so he could work in it. He used to read, you know, when he was working, always a book in his pocket.'

'Do you know what books?' Carmichael asked.

The landlord looked at him as if he had taken leave of his senses. 'What books?' he echoed. 'Just books . . . small ones, mostly,' he added, as

273

if that might help. It amazed Carmichael that there could be men in the world for whom the distinguishing characteristic of a book was its size, or possibly its color. The landlord was by no means stupid. Indeed, he was far more observant than most; he'd have made a good policeman. He had probably left school at eleven or twelve and sunk his talents into managing this little business for a big brewery, his intellectual horizons ending at the far side of the bar.

'Did he have a girl?' Royston asked.

The landlord turned back to him with an air of relief. 'No. Or at least, if he did he never brought her in here. And he could have. We're smart, as you can tell — we have lots of ladies coming in the lounge bar, especially at the weekends. You can't pick and choose your customers in this trade, at least; you can turn people away, but I don't do it unless I've a reason. Brown was someone I wasn't sure about, because of what I told you. If I'd seen him with a nice girl I'd have felt happier — that would have gone with the books and the bettering himself. Or if I'd seen him with the other kind of girl, that would have meant something too. But I never did, and from time to time I'd hear that he'd been in a scrap, and I'd prick my ears up, because if I ever heard anything for sure that made my mind up he was a nasty customer I'd have banned him.'

'Not queer, was he?' Royston asked, cocking an eyebrow.

'Certainly not!' The landlord looked affronted. 'I don't allow any of that sort in my bar.'

274

'How about guns?' Carmichael asked. 'Ever hear that he might do anything with guns?'

'No.' The landlord looked almost frightened. 'What's he done, shot someone? I'll ban him now. I'll never let him show his face in here again.'

'He shot at someone, and they shot back and killed him, so you'll have no need to ban him,' Carmichael said.

'So he was caught up with gangs after all?' The landlord stared at him in consternation.

'No, you weren't wrong in your guess; it doesn't look anything like gangs at all. It seems he was a rum fish altogether.' Carmichael finished his pint and looked at Royston, who drained what was left of his in one draught. 'I think we can move on, sergeant,' he went on. 'Landlord, you've been very helpful and it's much appreciated.'

'Any time I can do anything for the police, only too happy,' he said.

Back in the car, Carmichael shook his head. 'He could have hung out with other Reds elsewhere,' he said. 'They all hate each other. His group might have met anywhere.'

'Or the ones who go in the pubs and talk Red are the ones who only talk, and the ones who take action stay quiet about it,' Royston said.

'I wish we could find the girl.' Carmichael patted his case where her picture was. 'I'm surprised by all that, him liking a scrap and the books. I wonder what they were? It seems as if we're no closer to untying our ball of string, sergeant; it only gets more knotted however we try.'

'Should we check the other pubs now, sir?'

'Yes . . . no.' Carmichael frowned at the rain-streaked windscreen. 'Let's get a bite to eat and then check out Thirkie's chauffeur, and then let's come back and check the other pubs.'

'Probably a good idea,' Royston said. 'Though we can kill two birds with the first part. The Black Swan down the road serves food.'

The Black Swan knew nothing of Brown, but served an adequate steak and kidney pie with a half of stout for Carmichael, and a greasy gammon and chips, with another pint of bitter, for Royston.

Thirkie House was just off Sloane Street, within walking distance of Harrods and Harvey Nichols and the Knightsbridge tube station. Its eighteenth-century elegance looked dark and forbidding in the rain. A footman answered Royston's authoritative knock.

'There's nobody here,' he said, reluctantly letting them into the front hall after they had revealed their identity. Carmichael looked around with appreciation. The original Georgian plaster moldings were very fine, and the hall table, with barley-sugar legs, was one of the best he'd ever seen. A silver card salver sat on it, empty. 'Lady Thirkie has gone down to Campion Hall.'

'We want to talk to Sir James's valet, or chauffeur, or whatever he is,' Royston said. 'I assume he's here?'

'Whatever he is,' the footman sneered, with

the aura of one whose position has been clearly defined for centuries. 'Marston, his name is, and he isn't here either.'

'Where is he?' Carmichael asked, before Royston could open his mouth.

'Gone down to Campion too. Lady Thirkie rang up this morning from Farthing and said for him to take the car down there to meet her, to drive her up to Thirkie tomorrow or the next day. He set off right away, but it's a long drive, and in all this awful rain, I don't expect he's there yet.' The footman didn't look at all sorry for his fellow's labor.

'Where is Campion?' Royston asked.

'It's in Monmouthshire,' Carmichael said, remembering the will.

'Almost to Wales, I've heard, though I haven't been there myself. Old Lady Thirkie lives there, Sir James's mother,' the footman said.

'Lady Thirkie went there by train from Farthing, I take it,' Carmichael said. 'Why does she want to drive from there to Yorkshire? The train would be much quicker and more comfortable, surely?'

'And if she did want to drive, why would she want the two-seater?' the footman asked. 'Sir James hardly cold yet, either, shocking I call it.'

'Are you suggesting Lady Thirkie and Marston are conducting an improper relationship?' Carmichael asked, delicately.

The footman laughed. 'You could put it like that,' he said. 'Disgusting, isn't it?'

'Did Sir James know?' Carmichael asked.

'He left Marston here when they went down

to Farthing, didn't he? That looks like knowing to me, or something like it. But I don't know. He didn't dismiss him, just said he wouldn't be needing him and left him here.'

'Was Marston here all the time they were away?' Carmichael asked.

'Oh yes, and grumbling every minute of it,' the footman said. 'Couldn't go and didn't want to stay and never happy, not even now she's sent for him.'

There was nothing more to be got out of him. When they were safely back in the car and headed in the direction of Bethnal Green, Royston ventured, 'Another knot, sir?'

'If it's true and he knew, it's a very good motive for her to kill him,' Carmichael said.

'And Brown and the Bolsheviks?'

'Opportunistic sniping in the open season,' Carmichael suggested.

'Could she have got his body back up to the bedroom? He was quite big and she's quite small.' Royston frowned. 'I don't think she could have done it alone. And you checked whether Marston could have gone down to help her.'

'He could have. It's only a two-hour drive, and he had a car. He could have left London after sour grapes in there went to bed, got there at eleven-thirty or midnight . . . ' Carmichael trailed off. 'It's possible, but it's very elaborate, and it would have had to have been planned in advance. I want to talk to Marston, and I want to talk to Lady Thirkie again.'

'Should we go to Campion?' Royston asked, expressionlessly.

'Not tonight, sergeant. We want to chase Brown a little more tonight, and we want to sleep in our own beds. Maybe tomorrow.'

'Yes, sir,' Royston said, pulling up in front of the Old Red Lion. That pub, where Carmichael telephoned Jack to say he would be home late that evening, knew nothing of Brown. Nor did the Admiral Benbow or the Stonewell Tavern produce any significant results. They had seen Brown for an occasional pint, but it seemed that he was a regular only at the Three Feathers.

At nine o'clock, when the pubs were starting to get rowdy and Royston, having downed seven pints of best bitter, was starting to get rather the worse for wear, they tried the Bonnie Prince Charlie, where the landlord admitted Brown used to drink sometimes when he was in work, denied that he had any connection with the Reds, but recognized the picture. 'Oh yes, that's his bird. Lives at Southend or somewhere. He showed me that snap once.'

'We're going to Southend tomorrow, sergeant,' Carmichael said, as they went out into the night. It was truly dark now, and the rain was beginning to ease off. 'We may be going to Campion afterwards, but we are definitely going to Southend first.'

'Nearer than Wales, Southend,' Royston said.

'I'll drive you home, sergeant,' Carmichael said.

'That's not right, sir,' Royston said, as Carmichael rolled him into the passenger seat. 'That's against nature. World turned upside down. That's another pub name, pub out by

279

Greenwich, isn't it?'

'Somewhere like that,' Carmichael said.

'We've been in a lot of pubs, but not that one. No reason to think Brown drank at that one. Or Guerin. Or Thirkie. Or Lady Thirkie. Or Kahn . . . ,' he trailed down.

Carmichael threaded his way through the dark and ancient streets of London, almost bare of traffic now except buses and taxicabs. He found the attention he had to give to driving soothing. Light from streetlamps and the flashing Belisha beacons at zebra crossings reflected from black puddles of standing water. It was late, and soon he would be home.

He pulled up in front of Royston's house. 'Can you get from here to the Yard in the morning?' he asked, taking Royston's bags out of the boot, where they had sat since Farthing Junction.

'Yes, sir,' Royston said. 'Done it often. Got to see about the bird in Southend tomorrow.'

'I'll drive myself home. I'll see you at the Yard first thing,' Carmichael said. He knocked on Royston's front door.

It was opened by a little girl of about eight who, with her long pale hair and sharp features, bore a strong resemblance to the way Carmichael had always pictured J.M. Barrie's Wendy. 'My Mum's not — ' she began, then recognized them. 'Dad!' she said. 'Uncle Carmichael! Where have you been? Why didn't you say you were coming back? Have you brought me anything?'

'Your Dad's ready for bed, Elvira,' Carmichael

said. 'And we haven't brought you anything. You know we never bring you anything until we finish the case.'

'Rules, Ellie,' Royston said. 'You know the rules.'

'I know them,' she said, but her face fell. 'When you catch the villains.'

'That's right. But take this to be going on with, and make sure your Dad gets a good night's sleep. I need him bright and early in the morning to help me catch villains,' Carmichael said, and handed her half a crown.

'Good night, sir,' Royston said.

'Come on, Dad,' Elvira said, opening the door wide and helping him up the step.

Carmichael waved and drove off into the night, going forward happily towards his own home, his own bed, and Jack waiting in it.

# 25

What 'drastic measures' meant, according to *The Times* the next morning, was that they were taking on powers the next thing to dictatorial, in the name of protecting themselves and the country from the Jewish Bolshevik Menace. *The Times* rather approved of it, from the tone of their editorial. I wanted to scream, or strangle someone, preferably Mummy. I'd got up early, before David, and gone down to get the paper before he could see it. I took it into the library and curled up on the sofa to read it.

I was so horrified by the whole thing that I read *The Times* all through, as if knowing everything would change the import. I read all the boring details, and even skimmed the foreign news. (It seemed the Indians were still agitating for Dominion status, and Kursk had changed hands again. I'm not sure where Kursk is, but it seems to change hands every thirty minutes on the dot.)

Mark was Prime Minister, and all the ministries were therefore his gift. There had been what they call a reshuffle, meaning that all the Cabinet posts were redistributed. Daddy was Chancellor of the Exchequer, which, strictly speaking, he shouldn't have been. He was a Viscount, so he sat in the Lords, and according to the ancient and unwritten British constitution, the Chancellor was supposed to be an elected member and sit in the Commons. I knew this from hearing people grumbling about it for years. It didn't make any sense, as such, but it was supposed to be more democratic for the highest ministers of state to be elected. Mark, according to *The Times*, had decided this was only a custom and one that should be relaxed. *The Times*, in its typical ponderous way, said it would be wrong for the Prime Minister to create peerages and grant them to unelected men he wanted to appoint to office, but that it was equally unfair to keep an able man, meaning Daddy, from high office because of an accident of high birth.

Tibs had the Home Office, and Richard Francis had the Foreign Office. Richard and Clarinda had been there at Farthing all weekend, and I don't think I've mentioned them once. That's probably because they were so absolutely boring. I don't believe they said a word or uttered an opinion or even dropped a fork the entire time they were at Farthing, any of the times. They are a totally gray couple, complete nonentities. Uncle Dud was given the War Office. Eden, who had been Prime Minister before the party vote, was given the Ministry of Education, which was Sir James's old job. Hamilton, who everyone had expected to be Prime Minister this time, had the Colonies. Churchill had apparently been offered and turned down Commerce, and it was being taken by Sir Thomas Manningham. So on all down the line, the plums for the Farthing people, and the others either in the wilderness or given the unimportant hard work. That nice Kim Philby who had played croquet with me the weekend before my wedding, was made junior minister at the Foreign Office.

You could say that this was what Eden had done to them, and that this was what Parliamentary democracy was about, and I expect people all through the country were saying that. All the same, I was surprised to see Mark behave so unchivalrously. But none of that was really a problem, it was all backscratching business as usual. Once the Parliamentary Party had chosen Mark, he had the right to appoint who he wanted to the Cabinet.

The bad things were all announced in the speech he'd made in the Commons after he'd made the 'desperate measures' speech on the radio. The identity cards we had all carried ever since the war were to be tightened up, to prevent forgery, and they would carry photographs, which would help the police, and more information, such as religion. Apparently a young Labour hothead called Michael Foot had leapt up at this and said it amounted to persecution of Jews and Catholics, which Mark had answered by sneering that nobody was talking about making anyone wear yellow stars, it was equitable, we would all have our religion marked on our cards. *The Times* seemed very concerned about what atheists would put, though I didn't see why 'atheist' couldn't just go on the card. I immediately thought that it's what I'd suggest David say he was — after all, he was racially Jewish, but hardly religious.

Next came Mark's policy on foreign nationals in Britain, who were causing dissent, unemployment, and trouble. Unless they could find three British sponsors, they were to be repatriated to their original homes. *The Times* thought this was quite generous, as it was to be at Britain's expense. I wonder if they would have thought so if they'd heard about Mrs. Smollett's original home the way I had the night before.

The Communist Party, along with its newspapers, was to be outright banned. The Labour Party was to be checked by MI5 for secret Communist 'sleepers' that might have infiltrated their ranks. The line taken was that the innocent had nothing to fear. Nobody protested in Parliament at this, probably because they were all too afraid, or maybe somebody sat on Bevan and Foot. Even worse, if you believe anything could be worse, instead of being subject to party votes or votes of confidence, Parliament was to be set on a new footing with a regular general election once every four years, as in America. *The Times* wasted much ink in praise of this, and only at the end mentioned that the first such election would, of course, be in four years time, giving Mark what amounted to practically a dictatorship for those years.

'They elected you leader of the Conservative Party, which made you Prime Minister — they didn't nominate you for God,' I said, bitterly, aloud. Nobody heard me except the white cat, who was curled up on the rug in a patch of sunshine. She looked at me inquiringly. The sympathy vote, Daddy had said. The British care about liberty and justice, David had said, and all the time in London this was being put before the House, who had raised only quibbles. 'Reichstag fire,' I said.

David came in. 'I wondered where you were,' he said. 'Who were you talking to?'

'The cat,' I said.

The cat rolled over, purring, showing her belly.

'She's disgusted by politics,' I explained.

'Any politics in particular?' David asked, warily.

'British politics this morning, and you might as well see for yourself how bloody it is,' I said, handing him the paper.

While he read it I went over to the window and stared out. It was another lovely day — the sky was that beautiful shade of blue it gets when the rain has washed out all the dust. The huge old ash tree on the edge of the lawn seemed to be reaching heavenwards in coils. The wood looked infinitely inviting. It's coppiced, of course, oak and hazel, so it's easy to walk in even off the path, and wonderfully shady. You have to stick to the path if you're riding, as Daddy and I had done the other day. I could just catch a glimpse of the blue of the lake, reflecting the sky. Would Mummy have allied with a Bolshevik? Could she possibly?

'When I came in, you were saying 'Reichstag fire,'' David said, after a while, throwing down *The Times*.

'Murdering Sir James,' I said. 'Having that

286

Bolshevik shoot at us. It gives them an excuse for all this.'

'It's funny, I was just thinking that Chaim's going to say he was right,' David said. He put his arms around me and rested his chin on the top of my head, and we just stood there like that for a little bit, taking comfort.

'If we had to live in another country, where would you want to go?' I asked after a while.

David stiffened, I felt him, every muscle instantly tensed. 'Leave England?' he said, with such pain in his voice that I turned around and hugged him fiercely.

'It won't come to that,' he said after a moment. 'If we had to go, well, one of the Dominions — New Zealand, or Canada perhaps.'

'You wouldn't want to go to Palestine?' I asked.

'No, nor Brazil either, so don't be absurd,' he said.

After breakfast, at which we didn't talk about politics, David went off to telephone his father and I went to talk to Mrs. Simons about the marketing. There wasn't really anything to say, except that we didn't know how long we'd be here. I was hoping to ask her to pick up some talcum powder for me in the chemist by the butcher's, because I'd only brought a little travel bottle and I was getting rather low.

I found her in her pantry, which was a tiny sitting room really, down by the kitchens. I didn't know her; she was new. Her predecessor, Mrs. Collins, had retired at Christmas. Daddy'd given her a pension and she'd gone to live with her married sister in Harrogate. They'd found Mrs. Simons somehow, not promoted her, so I'd never seen her before. I'd heard Mummy boasting how efficient she was, that was all.

She was sitting at a little desk, an escritoire really. It used to be Sukey's before Mummy spilled indelible ink down it. She had lists on the drop-down shelf part, lined up very neatly, as if she were ready for Waterloo. She was about forty, I suppose, with very crisp pepper-and-salt hair shaped almost like a battle-helmet.

'Good morning, Mrs. Simons,' I said.

'Good morning, Mrs. Kahn,' she replied, frosty and thin-lipped.

'As you know, Mr. Kahn and I will be staying for a few days, and we aren't sure how long,' I said, as pleasantly as I could. 'I'm sorry to put you to this inconvenience. Jeffrey thought I should speak to you about what might be necessary.'

'Yes,' she said. 'In future, should anything of this nature happen, I'd prefer to be told directly, rather than through the servants. And I've already had occasion to reprimand Mrs. Smollett for extravagance.'

My first impulse was to apologize and appease her, but hard on its heels followed my second impulse, which was to put my chin up and tell her to go to hell. I had to defend Mrs. Smollett in any case. 'I believe it's up to Mrs. Smollett what to serve when the family are in residence, as it would be to Mrs. Richardson,' I said, very evenly.

'But the family are not in residence,' Mrs. Simons said, with a smile that would have curdled milk. 'You've married out of this family and you can't expect to keep the privileges that came with being born into it now that you're married to a Jewboy.'

I wasn't quite sure what to say. It was true in one way, and I didn't expect to keep the privileges — Daddy had talked to me very plainly about that. On the other hand, I don't think staying in my parents' house in their absence was all that much of a privilege. On the other other hand, or should I start counting by feet at that point, I was conscious that we were in the wrong. Mrs. Smollett probably shouldn't have given us the caviar. On the last foot, she'd insulted me directly with the last word. If it had been 'Jew,' that would have been all right, but 'Jewboy' was out and out insulting. I just stood there with my mouth open.

Before I could make up my mind to say anything at all, Mrs. Simons went on. 'As I understand the situation, you are not really even guests in the house. Mr. Kahn has been forced to stay here by the police as a kind of arrest. In the circumstances, I think my duty is rather to prevent his escape than to make him excessively comfortable.'

'Mrs. Simons,' I said, my voice shaking. 'I don't know what you imagine you can achieve by talking to me this way, but I think I am still sufficiently a daughter of this house that I could prevail upon my parents to have you sacked.'

'I doubt Lady Eversley would let me go at

*your* behest,' she said, openly sneering now. 'She has often spoken of you in my presence.'

Yes, I bet she had too. I could just imagine what she had said. I thought of her remark about the Jews in front of Hatchard on Sunday morning. 'Nevertheless, Mrs. Simons, I'd thank you to remain polite,' I said, holding on to my composure with both hands, and probably both feet too.

'Well then, Mrs. Kahn, do you have any special requirements while I am doing the marketing in Winchester? I'm not accustomed to providing for Jewboys, so please do inform me.'

I wanted to ask for roast duck and buttered lobster and perhaps some special wax polish for David's tail, but I thought better of it. 'I simply came down to let you know you should be aware that the household will contain two more people for the next few days and to take that into account while in Winchester,' I said, as icily as I could manage. I wasn't going to ask her for talcum powder — she'd probably buy itching powder instead.

I swept out of her little room then, thinking the most uncharitable thoughts, such as being glad she had an ink-stained old escritoire while at home I had a gorgeous old Arts and Crafts writing desk, and that she was ugly and nobody had ever loved her. I wished she'd be hit by a bus in Winchester, or struck by lightning on the way. I was shaking a bit, and almost crying, but I didn't want to see David and have to explain to him what it was about. He'd be either in Daddy's little office (the one where Inspector

Carmichael had been working) or, if he'd finished on the phone, in the library, so I went out into the garden and pretended to admire the lilies of the valley and harebells and primulas while I got control of myself.

The funny thing was that normally insults like 'Jewboy' and so on didn't upset me at all. They usually made me laugh. It took me a little while out in the garden on my own to work out what the difference was. It was power. Mrs. Simons had, or felt she had, power over us. She said her duty was to keep David here. She acted like a jailer. She took the petty little power she had of knowing Mummy didn't like me and used it to humiliate me. I thought of how she'd said she'd prefer to be told directly, rather than informed by a servant, when she was a servant herself. Probably she'd had to put up with a lot of slights and insults and unthinking cruelty; probably she had to put up with it regularly from Mummy. I'd gone out of my way to make the servants' lives easier. I always went out of my way to consider them as people, I had for years. But considering them as people only went so far; it was perfectly possible to dislike people as people. I didn't like how quickly I'd resorted to threatening to sack her, but at the same time I was quite sure Daddy would back me up in it. I wondered how she behaved to Mrs. Smollett, who had no redress at all. That made me think about the people with the stones in their hands smashing the windows of her restaurant. Mrs. Simons would have had stones in her hands. She already had them in her mind.

I heard the sound of the station wagon puttering down the drive, and knew she'd gone off to Winchester. The very air seemed relieved to have her gone, almost as if she'd been a thunderstorm, or, for that matter, Mummy. I paced about the garden for a while, getting calm, and after a while David saw me through the library window and came out to join me.

# 26

The only new thing on Carmichael's desk at the Yard in the morning was a note about Captain Oliver Thirkie, the heir to the Thirkie baronetcy, should Angela's baby prove to be a girl. He was ten years older than Sir James, had two sons, one at Winchester and the other at Oxford, and was serving with the Army in India. He clearly had nothing to do with anything, just another loose end that led nowhere. Carmichael tossed the report onto a pile. One of these days he really should sort out the desk, he thought.

Royston came in, looking not the least the worse for his indulgence the night before. 'Taking the car to Southend, sir?' he asked.

'Yes, I think so,' Carmichael said. 'We could go on the train, it's probably quicker, but we may want to go straight on to Campion Hall without bothering to come back here.'

'Yes, sir.'

They exchanged nods with Stebbings on their way out. 'Seen the papers this morning, sir?' Royston asked, as he slid automatically into the driver's seat.

'No, I didn't feel like facing the news,' Carmichael said. He had lingered in bed, and got up in time to gulp a cup of tea and a biscuit. 'Anything relevant to the case?'

'Oh no, nothing like that. It's just that they're going to introduce new ID cards with pictures on them, like passports I suppose. That'll make this sort of thing easier, and a lot of other things too. If Brown had one of those, we'd know who he was for sure.'

'Any paper we can put out, some villain will find a way around it,' Carmichael said, pessimistically. 'And you know what they say about making things foolproof — do that, and God will come up with a better fool.'

Once they were out of central London, they drove quite fast. They were going almost due east most of the way and had the sun in their eyes, but most of the traffic was going in the other direction, into London. It was built up almost all the way, towns and suburbs, odd patches of fields, but no deep country such as they had been in at Farthing. The roads were good and they reached Leigh before ten, and stopped for a late extra breakfast at a little transport café next to a run-down secondhand bookshop on the high promenade. The Channel lay, chilly and rumpled, far below them — the high promenade ran along the edge of a steep slope leading down to the water. After a greasy but satisfying breakfast, which they justified by saying that now they would need no lunch, they walked along the upper promenade. 'We'll try the photographer first,' Carmichael said. The proprietor of the café had displayed no knowledge of the girl in the picture.

There were benches every few yards on the side of the road that faced the sea view. The other side rejoiced in a little parade of shops. There were very few people about, as May was too early for Leigh to be enjoying the height of its 'season.' The photographer had a sign in the window saying that he would be open from eleven until four. Without discussion, the men continued to walk on past it, downhill, towards the lower promenade, and eventually, Southend and the actual sea.

A little way down the road was a tea shop of enviable gentility, painted with pastel flowers and patronized by a group of elderly ladies whose hair was rinsed a delicate powder blue.

'Let's try in there,' Royston said, indicating it.

'You can't want more tea already, sergeant,' Carmichael said. 'And if you did, that wouldn't be the place to get it.' He pushed open the door, making a set of chimes jangle. A middle-aged waitress came bustling up from the back, clearly astonished to see two relatively young men in her domain.

She squinted at the picture and thought there was something perhaps vaguely familiar about it. Carmichael was used to this reaction; he smiled and praised her. He tried it on the customers next, and got a bite at once.

'That's Agnes Timms. She works at Chicks,' the first blue-haired lady said.

'Where is Chicks?' Royston asked, eagerly.

'Mrs. O'Sullivan meant to say Colette's Chic Hair Salon,' another blue-haired lady interrupted. 'And it's just up the promenade, not a quarter of a mile.' She indicated the direction in which they had just come.

Colette's Chic Hair Salon lay just beyond the secondhand bookshop, and their car. Inside it was an old lady under a heavy hair-drying machine, a middle-aged lady seated at the cash register, and the young lady of the photograph, looking so exactly the way she did in the picture Carmichael had studied for so long that he almost wanted to poke her to be sure she was real. She was pretty as only girls of her class could be pretty, with a brief bloom that was destined to fade too quickly.

'Miss Timms?' Royston asked. 'We're police. We want to talk to you for a moment.'

'I'm working,' she said, indicating the woman under the device, and giving a desperate look to the woman on the cash register.

'I'll take care of it, Aggie,' the other woman said, her face registering stern disapproval.

'Come outside, if you would, Miss Timms,' Carmichael said. It would clearly be hopeless trying to talk in the shop, where there was no privacy at all.

'Shall we sit on a bench?' Royston suggested. They crossed the road and sat down, Agnes Timms between the two men.

'I haven't done anything wrong,' she said, as so many people did. A little breeze played with a strand of her light hair; she pushed it back impatiently.

'Do you know a man called Alan Brown?' Carmichael asked.

She didn't try to deny it. 'He was my fiancé,' she said.

'Do you know what has happened to him, Miss Timms?' he asked.

'It was in the paper,' she said, and tears came

to her eyes. 'I knew something had happened when he didn't ring me Sunday night like he said, and then on Monday it was in the paper. It had all gone wrong, and they'd killed him.'

'What had all gone wrong?' Royston pounced on that.

'His joke. But you can't make me give evidence against him; he was my fiancé.'

'That's only wives,' Royston said. 'Besides, if you were engaged, where's your ring?'

'Colette won't let me wear it at work, because of catching on hair,' she said, prosaically, and reached under the neck of her dress to show them the tiniest gold hoop with a pitifully small chip of rhinestone. 'There. See. Now that's all I'm saying.'

'Anything you know could be of inestimable value to us,' Carmichael said.

She put her chin up. 'Why should I care? Alan's dead, and now I'll never get married or have children, or lead any sort of life. I'll carry on being a spinster in a hair salon until I die.'

'You might be able to save the life of an innocent man if you can tell us what Alan's joke was and why he was playing it,' Carmichael said.

She looked at him indecisively for a long moment. Carmichael held his breath. 'All right,' she said, in a very small voice. 'It can't matter at all now anyway.' Tears started to run down her face, and Carmichael, breathing again, handed her his handkerchief.

'When did you last see him?' Royston asked.

'Saturday,' she said, and blew her nose on Carmichael's handkerchief. 'He came down on

Saturday. I have a half-day, and since he was laid off from Mottrams it makes no difference to him. Usually he stays for Sunday as well, but not this week. He told me he had work to do on Sunday. I last saw him Saturday evening, about seven, when he set off back to London.'

'On the train?' Royston asked.

'No, on his motorbike,' she said, and began to weep seriously. 'I'm sorry,' she said, between sobs. 'It's just thinking of him on that bike, in all weathers, with his black coat flapping like an old crow, and I'll never see him again, never speak to him, never tease him about it.'

They sat for a moment and let her weep. Royston raised an eyebrow at Carmichael, who shook his head. After a while, Carmichael asked, 'Did Alan tell you where he was going on Sunday?'

'Not exactly.' She blew her nose again and got control of herself. 'He told me he was doing a job, and it would be enough money that we could get married, and we'd be able to get a house and he could get a job as a fitter somewhere they didn't know his reputation.'

'What reputation would that be?' Royston asked.

'He tried to organize a union at Mottrams,' she said. Good, Carmichael thought, she's decided to tell us the truth. 'He thought it would be better for everyone. They sacked him right away. The whole thing was crazy, I knew it was.'

'Was he a bit of a Red, then?' Carmichael asked.

'Not really,' she said.

'Come now, he must have been a bit of a Red if he wanted to start a union.'

'You'd think so, wouldn't you, but actually it was me who voted Labour and him who voted Tory. He wanted a union for better conditions, that's all, and I don't care if you believe me.'

'Would it surprise you if I told you he was a Communist?' Carmichael asked.

'It would do a lot more than surprise me,' she said. 'But I think I can tell you about that. The job he was supposed to be doing on Sunday was to frighten someone, as a joke. He'd been given a rifle, not a real one, a rook-rifle, but it looked like a real one. He'd also been given a card, a Communist card, with someone's name on it, some Irish name, Patrick Somebody Something. He showed it to me. He was supposed to go to a certain place, and hide his bike where he could run back to it easily, wait until he saw this person coming, then shoot past him a couple of times, drop the rifle and the Communist card, and run back to the bike.'

Carmichael and Royston exchanged a glance of bemusement.

'But poor Alan wasn't quick enough, and Lord Eversley shot him instead,' she finished.

'Who told him to do this?' Carmichael asked.

'Lady Thirkie,' she said. 'And she did more than tell him, she paid him fifty pounds, which I've got. Alan left it with me, all but a fiver, which he kept to buy petrol and stay the night. You won't take it from me, will you? Only it's enough to start a new salon of my own.'

'We'll need to see the numbers of the notes,

299

but we won't take the money,' Carmichael said. 'In fact, if you give me the money, I'll replace it with other money that you can spend, because that cash belongs in evidence, but that's no reason you should be deprived of it.'

Royston gave him a jaundiced look. 'Are you sure it was Lady Thirkie?' he asked the girl.

'Of course. He told me. Besides, I used to work for her. I was her lady's maid, before she got married. When she got married, I left her and came down here and got this job. But it was through me that she knew Alan. He said she went to see him, and said she'd heard he enjoyed a bit of fighting from time to time and might take money for it, which is true. It wasn't very genteel of him, and I'd spoken to him about it ever so many times, but it's how he was. He didn't want to do this, because shooting at someone with a rook-rifle is different from putting your fists up, but she told him it was a joke, and besides, he'd been out of work for months, and the money was so good.'

'You'd swear to this in court?' Royston asked.

'Would I have to?' She looked frightened.

'Alan's dead, but think of saving an innocent man's life,' Carmichael said.

'Then I would, I suppose,' she said.

There wasn't much more to be got out of her. After taking down details of where she could be found, they walked her back to the salon.

Back in the car, on their way out of Leigh, Carmichael was the first to break the silence. 'Angela Thirkie,' he said. 'I didn't think she had

300

the brains. In fact, I wondered if she was a nutter.'

'Maybe the valet has the brains. He must have had the brawn, that's for sure,' Royston said.

'Well, that about ties that one up, sergeant,' Carmichael said.

'He must have been an awfully bad shot,' Royston said. 'Brown. He hit both of them.'

'Did you ever know a fitter who could shoot?' Carmichael asked, rhetorically. 'She probably didn't check that. She wanted someone who'd do the job.'

'Why didn't she get him to shoot Thirkie then?'

'He'd probably have had scruples about actually shooting someone. This was a joke, remember.' Carmichael hesitated. 'Though the way she killed Thirkie remains very peculiar.'

'Maybe she still liked him in a kind of way and wanted him to die peacefully. It's a peaceful thing, gas. We thought it might have been suicide, remember.'

'I remember,' Carmichael said. 'It's all so unnecessarily complicated. Why would she want Brown to shoot at Lord Eversley anyway?'

'Divert attention,' Royston suggested. 'Get out the sympathy vote?'

'Angela Thirkie doesn't care about the sympathy vote,' Carmichael said. 'Not about any vote, once Thirkie's dead, unless someone voted in a Bolshevik government who'd take her money away.'

'Maybe she was in league with the others,' Royston said. 'We'll never pin it on them unless she confesses though, not now.'

'Well, we'll do what we can to make her confess, or turn King's evidence,' Carmichael said. 'We might not get a conviction, her word against his, but we could probably end Normanby's career if we could put him in the dock.'

'You don't like him, sir, do you?' Royston asked.

'I don't like anyone who thinks other people are only there to be manipulated,' Carmichael said.

'Well, we've got enough to take Lady Thirkie to trial anyway,' Royston said, trying to cheer him up. 'And we can be pretty sure Kahn didn't do it, so that Mrs. Kahn you like will be able to go where she wants to again.'

'Yes, sergeant,' Carmichael said.

When they got back to the Yard, there was nowhere to park. 'Stay in the car, Royston,' Carmichael said. 'We're heading off down to Campion Hall as soon as I've picked up a couple of warrants.'

Stebbings signaled to Carmichael as he came through the door, and put down a telephone. 'I've wrapped it up,' Carmichael said.

'That's good,' Stebbings said. 'Because there's another piece of evidence just come in from Blayne that seems to make it indisputable.'

'What's that?' Carmichael asked eagerly.

'The star. Remember the star?'

'Of course I remember it; I saw it pinned to Thirkie's chest. What about it?' Carmichael was impatient.

'Bought in France by an Englishman without coupons, a month ago, as a souvenir, the

302

shopkeeper took his name and address.'

'Yes, yes, who was it?'

Stebbings shook his head slowly. 'You'll work your way to apoplexy if you keep getting as excited as this about cases. It was Kahn, of course, David Kahn, and he gave his own London address.'

'No!' It couldn't be true.

'Absolutely verifiably true. Sound as the Bank of England.'

'Kahn hasn't been in France.'

'Not that he told us about, no. Maybe he was helping his friend Chaim with a little smuggling over there. We know they get across the Channel somehow.'

'Not and give their names to the Nazi authorities,' Carmichael protested. 'Besides, anyone could give his name.'

'Now you're stretching a little, aren't you?' Stebbings said. 'It's the link we wanted; now we'll pull him in. The warrant's being made out now — do you want to take it down yourself?'

'Lady Thirkie did it,' Carmichael said. 'Agnes Timms, Brown's girlfriend, knew all about it and is willing to give evidence.'

'She's probably romancing,' Stebbings said. 'Or maybe they were in league. Bring him in anyway. We can ask him about her.'

'I'll take the warrant down,' Carmichael said. 'Send it to my office when it's ready. Royston's waiting in the car.'

He went into his office and sat down. He rested his elbows on the desk, pushing over piles of papers and causing a minor landslide. Kahn couldn't have done it. He had no reason to. He hadn't been in France. He wouldn't have been in alliance with Lady Thirkie. It didn't make any sense. If he'd done it, it would have been clean and simple and he'd have been miles away with a reliable alibi.

There had been times in his career when Carmichael had been uncertain of the arrests he'd made. There was even one man who had been hanged when Carmichael hadn't been sure, not absolutely sure. He still woke in the night sometimes from dreams of that case. But he'd never before been asked to arrest someone he knew was innocent, and risk passing up on the real culprits. 'We'll never pin it on them . . . not now,' Royston's remembered voice echoed in his ears.

He put his hand on the telephone. He had broken the law before — the police often had to, to do their jobs. Those times he'd always been on the right side of it, the side the lawgivers and the law enforcers would approve. This time — but why, in the end, was he a policeman? Not just to keep himself in teapots and fine linen handkerchiefs. He loved his job, loved finding out what had happened and seeing people who had thought they could make a mockery of the law punished. There had always been one law for the rich and another for the poor, but this was taking things too far. He picked up the receiver. 'I'd like to put a call through to Farthing House in Hampshire,' he said. 'It's on the Winchester exchange, and the number is 252. Police priority.'

304

# 27

It was a tiny bit chilly, and we wanted to eat lunch outside again, so I was going upstairs for a cardigan when I heard the telephone bell. Normally, Jeffrey would have answered it and called me, but as it was, I picked up the extension in the hall.

'Could I speak to Mr. Kahn?' Inspector Carmichael asked. I'd have known his voice anywhere, even on a bad line, it was so distinctive.

'This is Lucy Kahn speaking, Inspector,' I said. 'I'll just fetch David now.'

'That's all right, I can talk to you just as well, Mrs. Kahn,' he said. 'Tell me, did Mr. Kahn go to the Continent at all this year?'

'No,' I said. 'He'd be mad to go. You know he's Jewish. David hasn't been to the Continent since before the war.'

'And if he had gone, even briefly, you'd know about it?'

'Yes!' I was annoyed. 'This is nonsense, Inspector.'

He pressed on regardless. 'Has he gone on any business trips at all since you've been married?'

'No. He's a banker, he works out of an office in London, he doesn't need to make business trips. No, hang on,' I said, remembering. 'He went up to Edinburgh once to inspect a shoe

305

shop that wanted to expand, and I went with him and we stayed in a tiny little hotel just below the mountain.'

'Apart from that, he hasn't been out of London at all, to your knowledge?'

'Not for more than a few hours, or a weekend staying with friends — both of us, that is. What's all this about?'

'There's some evidence come to light that strongly implicates Mr. Kahn in the purchase of the star that was found pinned to Sir James Thirkie's chest,' Inspector Carmichael said. 'It was purchased in France a month ago.'

'But — ' I started indignantly.

'A warrant is being made out for his arrest for murder,' the Inspector went on. 'I shall be leaving Scotland Yard as soon as it is drawn up, which I expect to be at any moment now, and coming down to Farthing to deliver it. Do you understand?'

'Yes, Inspector,' I said, and I did, because this was a very important piece of the whole kaleidoscope whirl of jigsaw I'd been putting together. It made everything definite. Someone, whether it was Mummy or whoever, had deliberately implicated David.

'Please make sure you remain in the house until I arrive. That's very important, Mrs. Kahn. Do you understand? Stay there until I arrive to arrest Mr. Kahn and take him back to London. Do you understand?'

'I understand perfectly, Inspector,' I said. 'Thank you so very much. Goodbye.'

'Goodbye, Mrs. Kahn,' he said, and I put the

receiver down and just stood there for a moment.

The day before, in the library, after lunch, I'd made a plan. I heard the sound of wheels on the gravel. That would be Mrs. Simons coming back. I continued upstairs as if on my original errand. As soon as I was in my bedroom, I slipped off my skirt and pulled on a pair of slacks. My blouse was all right, so I left that. Instead of my cardigan I put on my old stained lilac jacket, and I also picked up my big clasp bag. I put my wallet, my hairbrush, and my jewel case into it. I went down one flight of stairs and without hesitating went into Mummy's room and slid her country jewel case, her gold brush and comb and mirror, her crucifix, and the tiny china bowl that's the second piece Josiah Wedgwood ever made, into my bag with my own things. I didn't think at all while I was doing this. I just did it automatically as if I did it every day. I pushed a silk scarf in on top to stop things rattling and to protect the Wedgwood bowl. I closed my bag and went down.

I was almost at the bottom before I remembered my cheek. It didn't hurt at all now, but the marks were still very visible. I went back up and took my make-up bag, which fortunately fit into the pocket of my jacket, because the bag was full. I stuffed a brassiere and two pairs of knickers into the other pocket.

I went down, and out to the garden. David smiled at me as he saw me coming across the lawn. Lunch, sandwiches again, and a tray of tea, was waiting on the table.

307

It takes two hours to drive from London to Farthing, perhaps a little more from Scotland Yard, and perhaps he'd do his best to drive slowly and give us a little extra time. I couldn't count on that. The clock in the village was just striking a quarter to one. It was excruciating to have to sit down.

'Lizzie's brought lunch,' he said.

'Inspector Carmichael has called,' I said. 'He's coming to arrest you. Somebody has faked some evidence of you buying the star in France earlier this year.'

David went terribly pale; then the color all came back into his face with a rush. I could practically see him grabbing for his stiff upper lip. 'Oh my darling,' he said. 'I'm so sorry to have brought this on you.'

'We have to run,' I said. 'We can't stay here. They'll hang you. They might have anyway, but this looks like solid evidence. You and I know that it's faked, but a jury wouldn't.'

'We have to run,' he said. 'Where could we go?'

I took a sandwich and bit into it. Egg mayonnaise and lots of cress, on Mrs. Smollett's homemade granary bread, and absolutely delicious.

'We can't take the car, because there's a policeman on the gate, still, and besides, Mrs. Simons will see and try to stop us,' I said. 'Maybe some of the other servants would, too. But we can say we want to ride around the woods, and get horses,' I said. 'Then we ride to Farthing Junction. It's hardly five miles.'

'They'll be looking for us in London,' David said. He was white and tense and looked like a boy expecting a beating. 'When Carmichael arrives and we're gone, they'll speak to the police in London and they'll meet us on the platform in Waterloo.'

'Trains run both ways,' I said. 'In the other direction, they go to Southampton and then on to Portsmouth. You could buy tickets to London, and I could buy them to Southampton. Do eat something, David. Then we could change in Southampton and go down into the West Country. Or we could buy new tickets on the train and go to Portsmouth.'

'What could we do in Portsmouth? Oh — Abby,' he said. He was very quick, as always.

'Abby loves me and trusts me. She'd take us in, and we could stay there either until they catch the real criminal, or until you can contact Chaim or somebody and we can get out of the country.'

'If I run, it looks as if I'm guilty,' David said. 'They'll stop looking for anyone else — they'll just hunt for me.'

'If you're in prison they'll make you confess,' I said. 'They can make people confess to anything. They have techniques they got from the Germans, Daddy says. If you run, at least you'll be alive. I'll have you, and our baby will have its father.'

I hadn't mentioned the baby before. I wasn't sure. I knew, but I wasn't sure, if you understand the difference. I wouldn't be sure for weeks. David looked stricken, and just sat there, not eating or doing anything. I shoved the rest of my

309

sandwich into my mouth and I got up. I went into the drawing room through the French windows and rang the bell. Lizzie came almost at once. 'Tell Harry to get Manzikert and Clontarf saddled up,' I told her. 'We've decided to go riding straight after lunch.'

'Yes, madam,' she said.

I went back out to David. 'We have to go,' I said.

'You should never have married me,' he said.

'I love you, silly,' I said. 'And it's more the other way around, if it comes to that — it's my relations who are trying to frame you, not yours me.'

'You think it's your relations?' he asked.

'I think it's Mummy,' I said. 'Now eat. Goodness knows when we'll get the chance again. We need to give Harry ten minutes to get the horses ready.'

David bit into a sandwich as if he thought it would choke him. 'My clothes,' he said.

'We can't wear riding clothes, because we'd look fools on the train. I'm all right in these slacks. You'll be all right too, but you need a jacket, and you may have things upstairs that you need. I put this jacket on because it's old, and hanging in the closet, and if the police have been through our bags, they won't have it listed. There's a leather jacket in the closet too. It's huge. If it fits you, you might want to wear it.'

'All right,' he said, expressionlessly.

'It was Hugh's,' I said, trying to buck him up a bit, and besides it was perfectly true.

'How Hugh would have loathed this!' he burst out.

I nodded, and then I didn't feel organized and excited the way I had. I just wanted to bawl. David finished his sandwich, very resolutely, and went into the house to change and get hold of whatever he wanted to get hold of. I sat stuffing the rest of the sandwiches, partly because I was ravenous, and partly because I didn't want anybody to be suspicious. Poor Mrs. Smollett would have started preparing her nursery tea for us already, but we'd never eat it. By teatime we might be in Portsmouth.

David came back, with the jacket casually over his arm, folded so the inside showed and the outside didn't, so it could have been anything. I'd never have thought of that in a week. He put his arm in mine as we walked down to the stables. We couldn't take any clothes, or anything. It was all very well for that day, but I could see us as very shabby fugitives in no time.

Harry had the horses ready. Manny was delighted to see me. David and Clonnie looked at each other much more suspiciously. David didn't really care about horses and riding, though he never let on, because it was one of the things he thought of as English. If he'd gone to school in England he wouldn't have felt that way. Being Jewish in an English public school is like having a stammer or a limp; it's a social handicap you can live down with time and personality. He'd have been more naturally English — and after all, he was English, he was born here. It was the French school trying so

311

hard that made him feel so very passionately attached to things most people don't give two hoots about.

We mounted up, and Harry offered David a gun, exactly the way he'd offered Daddy one on Sunday.

'No,' David said, very definitely.

'There's nothing worth shooting,' I said.

'No, you're right, there really isn't,' David said. 'Nothing.'

We waved at Harry as we rode off. We went up to the woods, and without hesitating at all I led the way through the forbidden gate, onto Adams's land, along past the hedge where the Bolshevik must have been hiding on Sunday, and down to the road. From there it would have been simpler to just ride on to Farthing Junction, but I'd developed a dread of meeting Inspector Carmichael and Sergeant Royston on their way here, so I cut across country on bridleways, which was nicer for the horses anyway.

When we'd got nearly to the station, I realized the big weakness in my plan. 'What should we do with the horses?' David asked.

We couldn't leave them at the station. We also couldn't leave them running loose. It took ages, and we missed a London train, which we didn't want anyway, before we found a field with good grazing and reasonable hedges, where they could stay safely until someone found them. I took off their gear and left it under the hedge.

We saw a few people as we were riding along, but those on horses just said 'Good afternoon,' and rode on, and those on foot, farm laborers

312

mostly, just touched their caps. Fortunately, only one person came along as we were putting the horses in the fields, and I knew him, he was an absolute village idiot from Farthing Green. I told him we were going to London, and he made riding motions.

We went to the station separately. I bought a first-class day-return ticket to Winchester. I'd decided that was more plausible than Southampton. 'Yes, Miss Lucy,' the stationmaster said. 'Have a nice afternoon now.'

Then David came in and bought a second-class single to London. He wasn't recognized, as far as he could tell.

There's only one platform at Farthing Junction, fortunately, or this plan might not have worked. We both stood on it, and when the two o'clock slow train to Portsmouth via Southampton came puffing in, we both got onto it. I went straight into the first-class bathroom and made up my face. If I absolutely caked myself with powder, which meant doing my mouth and eyes as well, because otherwise I looked a fright, I could cover up the cut. I had some stuff in a little bottle which was meant to be dabbed onto the bags under your eyes, and I used that quite lavishly and then powdered on top. I looked like someone with rather bad taste, but there are more of them around than there are women with cuts across their cheeks. I had to do my eyes three times, because the train would go round a bend just as I was getting my mascara on.

I came out at last and joined David in second class. When the conductor came around, we both bought singles to Portsmouth from Weston Colley, which was the next station back towards London, before Farthing Junction. This was my idea, because although it cost us more money, it could make us safer. Even apart from his knowing me, the stationmaster at Farthing Junction would be bound to remember us, or anyone who bought a ticket. So few people got on the train there that he'd probably remember every one of them, for a day or two at least. But the conductor was a busy man, who sold a lot of tickets to a lot of people. If we seemed ordinary he probably wouldn't remember us at all after half an hour. He'd still have the stubs of the tickets, but by the time the police came to look at them, if they weren't from Farthing Junction, they might not work out that they were ours.

The conductor didn't appear to pay the slightest attention to us, which was good. Until we were past Winchester I was nervous, because I was half afraid I'd see someone I knew, but I didn't. In Winchester a woman got on with a basket of ducklings, which she must have bought at the market. Lots of other people got on, but all of them strangers. I was wishing I'd brought a book or even a newspaper, because we had nothing to do but fret. We couldn't talk, not properly, because we weren't alone and I might have mentioned something I shouldn't.

Most of the people got out at little halts, including the woman with the ducklings. More people got on — it was quite crowded by the time we came into Southampton. The train waits there for ten minutes, so I got out and rang Abby

314

from the coin box on the platform. David stood with his foot in the door of the train, ready to hold it for me if it tried to start. I went into the red box with my two pennies ready and somehow I managed to press Button A and Button B and put my coins in in the right order.

'Talbot's Academy for Young Ladies,' someone answered the telephone.

'Could I speak to Mrs. Talbot, please?' I asked.

'Certainly, who's calling?' the voice inquired.

I didn't want to give my name, just in case. 'This is Phillipa Potts,' I said, making it up as I went.

She went away and fetched Abby. 'Mrs. Talbot here,' she said.

'Oh Abby,' I said. 'It's me. I'm in terrible trouble. Can you hide me for a day or two?'

'Have you run away from your husband, Lucy?' she asked.

'No, he's with me — we've run away together. It's terribly serious trouble, Dachau-level trouble. I'll tell you when I see you. But can we come?'

The train started raising steam then, and nearly everyone was on. I don't know what I'd have done if she'd said no, but I knew she wouldn't. When she'd been my governess we'd often talked about the Jews in the Reich and what happened when you had to run. Dachau-level trouble would make her realize how serious things were.

'Yes, of course, though I don't know how well I can hide you, child,' she said. 'We'll talk about it when you get here.'

'I'm in Southampton, and I'm getting on the train right now,' I said, because David was beckoning to me. I practically flung the receiver down. I dashed back to the train, only to find that it was a false alarm and the train waited another few minutes getting up steam and procrastinating before it finally chugged out for Portsmouth.

# 28

Carmichael persuaded Royston, without much difficulty, to stop at a country pub just outside Alton for a late lunch. The landlady was profusely apologetic that she couldn't give them anything but bread and cheese. The bread was homemade and there were three kinds of cheese: one sharp cheddar, one Stilton, and one new soft cheese, almost as mild as butter. She also gave them the best beer they'd had all week, and they told her so.

'You could taste the hops in that,' Royston said. 'Wouldn't mind stopping there again, sir,' he added, as they set off once more.

'If we have to come this way again, sergeant,' Carmichael said. He hoped and believed they would never have to, at least not to Farthing. The road unwound before them like a reel to a fish, and Royston followed it mile after mile, dodging villages, spinneys, fields, coming closer and closer to Farthing, where Carmichael had no wish to be. He hoped Mrs. Kahn had understood. She wasn't such a fool as she seemed, he thought, despite the hand clapped to the mouth and the awkward little laughs.

'I'd never have imagined Kahn and Lady Thirkie being in conspiracy together,' Royston said, as the road became the green lanes of the Farthings.

'Maybe she killed him and left him in the car

317

and Kahn found him and arranged him,' Carmichael suggested. It was the only scenario that fit, and he could have believed it if not for the star. If Kahn had bought a star, he would not have given his name and address. If Kahn had been mad enough to go into Nazi France in the first place, he thought, though he must speak French as he was educated there. He had friends there. Mrs. Kahn might not have known. But he wasn't a fool. Even if he hadn't been planning this, if he'd been there for some other reason and wanted a star, he wouldn't have given his own name.

'But if she meant it to look like suicide, why would she arrange for Brown to shoot at Lord Eversley the day after?' Royston asked.

Carmichael shrugged. 'Maybe it *was* suicide; maybe she meant to send Thirkie riding and had told Brown to kill him, and the joke bit was just what he told Agnes Timms so she would respect him.'

'I think she was telling the truth,' Royston said.

'I'm sure she was, but he could have lied to her,' Carmichael said. 'That's actually the simplest hypothesis so far. Thirkie finds out about his wife's adultery, and she arranges to kill him. He kills himself before she can. Kahn finds his body and arranges it so as to make the murder look political. Brown shoots at the wrong person. I don't suppose he'd have known Thirkie. Even if his girlfriend worked for Lady Thirkie before they married, he'd have just been going for a man on a horse.'

'With a .22?' Royston pointed out. 'And Kahn's motive is still very puzzling.'

'He saw a man he hated dead and decided to humiliate him in death,' Carmichael suggested, not believing it even as he said it.

Royston frowned. They came into Clock Farthing as the clock was striking a quarter past four. 'But he must have known he was bound to be suspected.'

'Playing practical jokes with corpses is wasting police time, but it isn't a hanging offense.'

'But getting involved at all made him suspected of murder,' Royston objected.

The bobby on the gate recognized the car and flagged them down. Royston pulled up. 'What's up, constable?'

'Mr. and Mrs. Kahn went riding after lunch and haven't come back,' he said. 'The housekeeper sent a servant down to tell me. The stablemaster and some of the other servants are checking the woods in case of an accident, and I told them to telephone to Winchester for more police.'

Carmichael couldn't simulate surprise, or any of the emotions he knew he would be expected to feel at the news. It was the most he could do to keep relief off his face.

Royston, on the other hand, was genuinely astonished. 'Run!' he said. 'But why would they have run? Well blow me down! I'd have laid odds he didn't do it, despite the warrant and the evidence.'

'Running means guilt, does it, sergeant?' Carmichael asked.

'What else could it mean, sir?'

'Fear,' Carmichael said.

'That's the same thing,' Royston objected. 'Well, nearly.'

'If they're innocent they've nothing to be afraid of?' Carmichael asked, ironically.

'Yes, that's right,' the bobby put in. 'Just like Mr. Normanby said in his speech on the wireless last night.'

They drove up to the house, and had hardly parked when the housekeeper, Mrs. Simons, came rushing up to them.

'I hear they've run,' Carmichael said, getting out of the car.

'Not only that, but they've stolen several things!' she said. She was pink-faced with excitement, clearly enjoying the drama.

'What's missing, Mrs. Simons?' Royston asked.

'Lady Eversley's jewelry, and her Wedgwood bowl, and her brush and mirror. They must have taken them to sell!'

'Were they very valuable?' Royston asked, getting out his notebook.

'Oh yes, frightfully valuable. The bowl especially. But the jewel case too, more so than usual, because Lady Eversley left the Ringhili diamond in it this time.'

'Good gracious, does Lady Eversley have the Ringhili diamond?' Carmichael asked, genuinely surprised. 'I remember reading about that as a boy.'

Royston looked blank. 'What is it, sir?'

'It's a diamond worth a province — there was

320

an Indian prince, early in the last century, before the Mutiny. The British were going to conquer his kingdom, but he persuaded Sir Charles Cavendish to accept his homage to the Crown instead, in return for this absolutely amazing diamond.' Carmichael's adolescent enthusiasm came back to him. He remembered finding the story in the school library, in a book glorifying the Empire Builders. The book had not altogether approved of Cavendish, but Carmichael's adolescent soul thrilled to the thought of the diamond, although a gift of money would have seemed shameful. 'The diamond was very old even then, and there were stories that had already attached to it as it had passed from hand to hand.'

Mrs. Simons gave him a wintry smile, which reminded him of Lady Eversley. 'Well, Sir Charles Cavendish had a daughter who married Lord Varney, and they had a daughter who married the Duke of Hampshire, and their daughter was Lady Margaret Eversley's mother. She later became Duchess of Dorset, of course, and gave the diamond to her daughter on her marriage. So you see how the diamond has come down from mother to daughter ever since 1835.'

'And now Mrs. Kahn has it,' Carmichael couldn't resist adding. 'What a romantic story.'

Mrs. Simons glared at him.

'What else was in the jewel case?' Royston asked. 'Perhaps we should go inside and you should give me the whole list.'

'After that, check the Kahns' bedroom for what's missing there,' Carmichael said. 'I'd better telephone the Yard.'

'I have spoken to Inspector Yately, and he's on his way here,' Mrs. Simons said, frostily.

'Good,' Carmichael said, and walked away into the house.

No Hatchard was waiting in the hall today. Of course, he would be in London with the family. He was a little surprised not to find Jeffrey there instead. Carmichael went into what he had been thinking of as 'his' study, which seemed very bare and empty now. He pulled the bell cord, and picked up the telephone to place a call to the Yard.

Lizzie arrived while he was still waiting for his call to come through.

'Where's Jeffrey?' he asked.

'Searching the woods in case something's happened to Miss Lucy and Mr. David,' she said. She was twisting her apron in her hands, but stopped when she saw Carmichael looking.

'When did you last see Mr. and Mrs. Kahn?' he asked.

'When I served their lunch,' Lizzie said. 'It wasn't a proper meal, just sandwiches and tea, and they ate it in the garden.'

'What time did you take it out?' he asked.

'Half-past twelve, on the dot, which I could tell because of that confounded clock.'

'Nobody's likely to be confused about the time in this house, anyway,' Carmichael said. Twelve-thirty was also the time he had telephoned. 'Were they both there when you took the sandwiches out?'

'Yes, sir, both sitting peacefully reading,' Lizzie

said, perhaps a trifle too glibly.

'And you didn't see them again?'

'No, sir, when I went to bring the lunch things in again they'd gone, and I said to myself that I hoped they had a nice ride.'

'You knew they'd gone for a ride?' Carmichael asked.

'Oh yes, sir.'

'Had it been planned in advance, or was it a spur of the moment thing?' he asked.

'Oh, planned at breakfast time at least, if not last night,' Lizzie said, not quite looking him in the eye. 'I heard about it at breakfast as quite a settled thing, and I think they may have mentioned it to Mrs. Smollett last night — they were chatting to Mrs. Smollett last night, sir, and when I said to her this morning that they were going to ride she said just yes, as if she knew already.'

Carmichael knew she was lying, but couldn't understand why she thought it better to make him believe that the escape had been planned in advance. 'So you weren't surprised when you saw they'd gone from the garden?' he asked.

'Oh no. If I'd been surprised, if I thought they'd run away or anything, or seen anything suspicious, I'd have gone to tell Mrs. Simons that they were gone so she could tell the police,' Lizzie said, and Carmichael could only secretly applaud. So Mrs. Kahn's friends among the servants had kept the escape quiet as long as they dared. What else might they have been lying about earlier?

'Well it doesn't matter anyway, Lizzie,' he said.

323

The telephone rang as his London call came through, so he dismissed her and she scurried back to the kitchen, no doubt to tell Mrs. Smollett that she'd got away with lying to the Inspector.

There was nothing Carmichael could do to obstruct the hunt. It swung into action as inexorably as a thunderstorm. Before long, there were local policemen scouring the county, Metropolitan police at the Kahns' London residence, his parents' house, and at Waterloo and the other mainline stations, ready to intercept passengers from trains. Yately was on his way to interview the stationmaster at Farthing Junction. Carmichael had given them what time he could to take cover; he could do nothing more for them now.

He interviewed Harry at the stables, whose story agreed with Lizzie's, that the ride had been organized well in advance and had not seemed at all unusual. He said they were dressed for riding, but was very vague as to what exactly they were wearing. Carmichael didn't press him. Mrs. Simons had given a very exact account of what Mrs. Kahn had been wearing in the morning, which he told Royston to pass on to the manhunt unchanged.

'She said she was wearing a pink skirt, and when I checked her things there was a pinkish skirt on the bedroom floor,' Royston objected.

'Never mind,' Carmichael said. 'I think she had two.'

'I don't think so,' Royston said. 'I have Yately's list from when he searched their things, and it

324

only has one pink skirt on it. And there's a pair of beige slacks missing.'

'Let it go through, sergeant,' Carmichael said. 'Are there any jackets missing?'

'Not as far as I can tell,' Royston said. 'Mrs. Kahn was wearing a cream silk blouse — that isn't here, so she's still wearing it. Some of her underwear is also missing, unless it's being laundered. Mr. Kahn doesn't seem to have taken a jacket, though he has a light sweater.'

'They'll be cold come evening,' Carmichael said. 'And they'll have trouble booking into a hotel without luggage.'

'Yes, sir,' Royston said. 'Though if they've gone to London and they've got money they could buy a suitcase easily enough.'

'The Yard's sending Jenkinson to speak to Lady Eversley to see if she knows of any friends who might shelter them,' Carmichael said. 'You give Mrs. Simons's description to Yately to give to the Winchester police. Say she might also have slacks if you like.'

'Yes, sir,' Royston said, his face unreadable. 'Sir — how do you think they knew to run? We didn't know we were coming down until just before we left, we were still on the trail of Lady Thirkie. Nobody knew last night, when they were making plans to go.'

Lizzie's story had cleared him as well as herself, Carmichael realized, with a lifting of the spirits.

'Perhaps someone told Lord Eversley about the star last night or this morning, and he got in touch with them,' Carmichael said.

Royston went off to speak to Yately, shaking his head.

Yately came in before Carmichael had time to do anything. 'I need to use the telephone for the description,' he said. Carmichael pushed the instrument towards him, and listened while he gave it. Mrs. Kahn was described as wearing a pink skirt and cream blouse, or possibly slacks, carrying a large cream purse, with a recent wound on her cheek. Mr. Kahn was apparently wearing a brown jacket, perhaps leather.

'They were definitely at the station,' Yately said when he'd finished. 'We've found the horses in a field near there. He bought a ticket for London and she bought one for Winchester. The station-master knew her, but not him — Jewish-looking fellow in a brown jacket, he said. He didn't see what train they went on; he wasn't looking out at the platform.'

'Kahn didn't have a brown jacket,' Carmichael said.

'He must have picked it up somewhere. Cunning they are, Jews, especially about clothes. Well, we'll be able to have a crackdown on them now — some of the lads are quite cock-a-hoop about it.'

Carmichael didn't ask where, in the verdant but essentially empty countryside between Clock Farthing and Farthing Junction, Kahn might have found a brown jacket growing on a bush. 'Where could they get to, in the Southampton direction?' he asked instead. 'We've got plenty of men in London on the lookout already.'

'I've alerted the local forces across the whole

West of England,' Yately said. 'If they'd changed at Southampton they could have gone anywhere, on the Salisbury line, or on to Portsmouth, even back to Aylesbury and into London that way. You should have someone watching Paddington as well as Waterloo.'

'We have men at all the mainline London stations,' Carmichael assured him. 'We've also sent out an alert to garages who hire cars to be aware of the possibility they might try to take one. That's nationwide.'

'The description will go out on the BBC tonight,' Yately said. 'Wherever they're hiding, they won't be able to lie low for long, and then we'll have them.'

'Sergeant Royston and I are going back to London tonight,' Carmichael said. 'I don't see that there's much we can do from here that you can't do yourself, though we'll stay in close touch.'

'Yes, sir,' Yately said. 'I'll be sure to keep the Yard informed of anything that comes up here.'

The phone rang. 'That'll be my call to the Yard now. I'll let them know how we're getting on. Then I'll collect Royston and leave.'

Yately gave a wave that was half a salute, and left the office. Carmichael picked up the phone, and in moments he was connected with Sergeant Stebbings.

'Not much progress,' he said, and outlined what Yately had found at the railway station and all that had been done. 'With Kahn, it's just a case of waiting until they get unlucky or we get lucky, and we'll pick him up. Tomorrow I want to go down to Campion and speak to Lady Thirkie.'

'The Chief wants this wrapped up quickly,' Stebbings reminded him. 'Come into the Yard in the morning and we'll see what needs doing. No use chasing hares into thickets when it's obvious we've got our man.'

'There's much more solid evidence against Lady Thirkie than against Kahn,' Carmichael protested.

'Ah, but he's run, which is a sure sign he did it,' Stebbings said, comfortably. 'I'll see you in here in the morning then.'

# 29

Abby met us in Portsmouth station. She was wearing a coat, quite naturally, because it had started to rain as we'd been crawling around the south coast, and she had a carpetbag with her. Apart from that she was just Abby, the same as always, with a little more gray in her hair. When she saw us she hugged me, and then David, which was wonderful of her because she'd only met him once before, when she'd come up to London for the day and we'd all had lunch. She hadn't been at the wedding because Mummy had control of the guest list, and she naturally regarded Abby as no more than an ex-servant.

'There are police by the station entrance,' she whispered into my ear as she hugged me. 'I don't know if they're looking for you. Come into the buffet and have a cup of tea. We can go out when the London train comes in, if they think you're coming from Southampton.'

I think she said the same to David. He took her carpetbag, quite naturally, and we all went into the buffet. It's a poky little place, but they gave us stewed tea and that rather nasty fruitcake that the railways always seem to serve.

The buffet was L-shaped, and we went into the part of the L away from the counter.

Abby opened up her bag as we sat down, and took out of it an off-white raincoat and a black macintosh. 'I hope this coat fits you,' she said,

329

giving it to me. 'The mac will have to be for you, David, because I didn't have anything else that might be a man's to hand, and I didn't want to take anything Mr. Talbot would miss.'

'You're amazing,' I said.

'I hope very much that I'm overreacting,' she said. 'We shouldn't talk about it here, in case. Put your purse inside my carpetbag. I think the best thing is if you carry it, David, as if you've just arrived from London and Lucy and I have come to meet you.'

David took off the jacket and we put that into the carpetbag too. Then he pulled the mac on and looked quite different, much less respectable, as if he might be some kind of insurance agent or a man who kept a bicycle shop. The white coat was too big for me, but I belted it tightly.

'You shouldn't have put yourself into trouble for us,' David said.

'I thought they might know your clothes, and they might be looking for a man and a woman together or separately, but not for an older woman as well,' Abby said.

'If they ask, I'll be your daughter and David my husband,' I said.

The London train came in then, wheezing its way onto the platform like an old man with asthma. None of us had touched a drop of the tea or a bite of the wretched fruitcake. We all stood and went out onto the platform, waited until the doors opened and people were rushing out, and rushed out with them. We were soon out onto The Hard, the Portsmouth seafront by the docks, where Nelson's *Victory* is, and the huge bay that is always full of Navy ships painted battleship gray. There were two young policemen, fresh-faced and with a country look to them, standing at the station entrance. They were scanning the crowd but they took no notice of us, whether because they weren't yet looking for us or because there were three of us I don't know. The train had taken what felt like hours to get to Portsmouth, though nothing like as long as it would have taken to get to London, but I had absolutely no idea how long it would take the police to start seriously looking for us.

'We can't go home just yet, unfortunately,' Abby said, leading the way down the harbor, away from the docks. 'I don't know if you know, David, but my husband and I run a day school. The girls go home at five, and after that we can smuggle you in. What a pity it's summer and light so late!'

'What time is it?' I asked.

'It's a quarter past three,' Abby said. 'I think the best thing to do would be to have tea in one of the hotels. Again, nobody will be looking for the three of us. It's possible that later they'll start to check your friends, but I doubt they'd do it yet.'

David was looking at Abby with undisguised admiration. 'Have you ever been a spy?' he asked.

Abby laughed. 'Hasn't Lucy told you?' she asked.

David looked at me. 'Told me what?'

I looked at Abby. 'You told me not to tell

331

anyone!' I protested. I looked around. There was nobody on the seafront in the rain but us and a few black-backed herring gulls, skimming along the rails like figure skaters. 'Abby's one of the stations for getting people out of the Reich,' I said.

'I can't believe you didn't tell me!' David said. 'I told you about Chaim!'

'And I'd have told you if I'd been doing anything. I wasn't. It's just Abby.'

'You helped with money from time to time,' Abby said.

'Who do you work with?' David asked.

'Children, mostly,' Abby said. 'That means people who have just been discovered to be Jewish, or people from newly conquered parts of the Reich. I hide them at the school, where one child more or less doesn't cause much comment. Then we send them to Canada, or Brazil. Sometimes it's easier to get papers for one, sometimes for the other. But doing any of this at all makes you think about security. I'm not in the danger the stations in France and Germany are. But I'd be in trouble if I got caught, and I'd stop being able to help people.'

'Are you Jewish?' David asked.

'I'm a Quaker,' Abby said. 'Now, here we are — the Queen Anne's Head is a very superior sort of hotel to take tea.'

The hotel was very grand, in a faded way. It had dusty potted palms and Edwardian gilded scrollwork chairs. It had a huge white piano. It looked as if it had been designed before the Great War for good times that had never come. It should have been inhabited by men in spats and women with enormous ostrich feathers reaching up from their hair. A faded waiter came out of some recess and looked at us as if we were rather poor replacements for the ghosts of grandeur that haunted the place.

'Tea,' Abby said, crisply. 'Earl Grey tea for three, and your afternoon tea.'

'Yes, Mrs. Talbot,' the waiter said.

'They know you?' I asked, as we sat down among the fronds.

'I take tea here regularly with parents of pupils, and prospective pupils,' she said. 'He'll take you for some of those. He's also extremely unlikely to come back after he's brought our tea. I rather like the place, I know it's dowdy, but it's dowdy in such a grand way you feel honored to be allowed to see it. So much of Portsmouth is pure eighteenth-century squalor. Now, make yourselves comfortable, because we need to stay at least an hour.'

We took off our coats, though I kept on my jacket. The waiter came back with a big silver tray, which he put down on the table. There was a huge teapot and everything you need for a really good cup of tea, and a plate of little cucumber sandwiches cut into triangles with the crusts cut off, and two plates of buns. 'The amazing thing is that it's no more expensive than the Kardomah café,' Abby said. 'I don't know why more people don't come in here.' The waiter left, smiling a secret smile, as if he knew why people didn't come in, but he would never tell.

'Now, tell me why you're here,' Abby said,

pouring the tea. 'I assume it has to do with the murder of Sir James Thirkie? You didn't kill him, did you?'

'Of course not,' I said.

David looked rather awed at the matter-of-fact way she was taking it. 'Would you be sitting here eating buns with us if we had?' he asked.

'I'm sure Lucy wouldn't kill anyone without a very good reason,' she said. She handed David his tea. 'And although I don't know you very well, I'm prepared to trust her judgment, at any rate for the time being. So, you didn't kill him?' She handed me my tea, just as I like it, delicate and exquisitely perfumed.

'I didn't kill him,' David said. 'I had nothing to do with it. I was asleep in bed and knew nothing about it until the next morning. But it seems that someone has been going out of their way to make it look as if I did it.'

'Jews and Bolsheviks. Did you see the papers this morning?' Abby asked.

'We did,' I said. 'It's awful.'

'It's a terrible attack on liberty,' Abby said, and took a bun. 'So, why did you run?'

'Somebody warned us that the police were coming to arrest David, with new trumped-up evidence,' I said. There was no point telling Abby who it was.

She nodded. 'Do you know who actually killed him?' she asked, practical as ever.

'I have ideas,' I said. 'But not real proof, not police-station proof.'

'And without that their frame against David is likely to hold?' she asked.

'Who do you think did it?' David asked me.

'Mummy,' I said. 'At least, not just Mummy. Mummy and Angela and Mark and maybe Daddy.'

'Reichstag fire,' Abby said, immediately.

'Exactly,' I said. 'That's what I said this morning when I saw the papers. The only thing that doesn't fit is the Bolshevik. Can you imagine Mummy allying with a Bolshevik, or even speaking to one?'

'Lady Eversley might feel she could touch pitch on this occasion,' Abby said. She took a bite of her bun and cream oozed out. She wiped her mouth with her napkin. 'But why would she want to get rid of Sir James?'

'Reichstag fire,' I said. 'The sympathy vote. I'm not sure how much Daddy knew and when. He knew about it yesterday, I think, but perhaps not on Sunday morning.'

'There's no evidence,' David said. He had taken a cucumber sandwich and was playing with it, opening it and separating out the pieces, but not eating anything. He looked terribly fretful.

'What is the evidence, Lucy?' Abby asked.

'It's all terribly circumstantial and inferential,' I said. 'Things like Mummy being up at six in the morning and on our corridor, where she had no reason to be, and Angela behaving oddly, and the very strange conversation she was having with the others about whether she should go to Campion, where Mark and Mummy were bullying her, and the way Mark was looking at Daphne, and a large dose of *cui bono*, of course.'

'They definitely benefit,' Abby said.

'Oh, and, this is important, Mummy absolutely insisted that we go down this weekend, and there was no real reason. I didn't want to at all but David thought it might be an olive branch so we did.'

'Beware of Greeks bearing olive branches,' Abby said, which made me snort and almost choke on my eclair.

'She wanted to ask me to talk at a subscription dinner in London in June,' David put in. 'I think in all of this you attribute too much to Lady Eversley, Lucy. It's far more likely Mark Normanby is the driving force. He's the one who has really benefited, and also the one who was in France and could have bought the star and given my name.'

'Well, it would have to be a very good case to take to a solicitor if you wanted to argue against them, and it seems you have a very feeble one,' Abby said. 'We're going to have to get you out of the country.'

David gave a little moan. I took his hand. 'We'll be together,' I said.

'Jews are supposed to be wanderers without a home of their own until they regain the Promised Land,' Abby said, in a cheerful bucking-up tone of voice — though it was as bad a thing to say as the worst thing I might have said, because of the way David felt about everything. I squeezed his hand hard.

'I know that's the accepted view, but if that's the case, I must be a very bad Jew,' David said. 'I've always loved England so much.'

'Do you have any money?' Abby asked.

'A few hundred pounds,' David said, which amazed me. I thought if he had twenty-five it would have been a lot. 'Just what I carry around,' he added.

'I have less than ten pounds,' I said. 'But I brought some things we could hock. Mummy's Wedgwood bowl, and her gold mirror and set, and her jewel case. I don't know what's in it — whatever she was leaving in Farthing, I suppose. I have my own jewel case as well.'

'That might not have been a sensible idea,' Abby said. 'That means you have broken the law. Theft isn't murder, but it's still wrong.'

'In a Dachau emergency?' I asked.

Abby sighed. 'No, perhaps not. Might as well have a look at what you've got. Money's going to be necessary.'

'My father would help us,' David said.

I pulled my bag out of the carpetbag and extracted Mummy's jewel case. The case itself looked worth a bob or two, being gold, and although it was monogrammed, it was Mummy's monogram, ME, which anyone might use. I tapped the clasp to open it. Inside, among a cluster of earrings and bracelets and pearls nestled the greatest mother-daughter heirloom of all, the one she had refused to give me on my marriage, the Ringhili diamond.

'Good gracious,' Abby said. 'You'd better put that away.'

I closed the case. 'Well we certainly can't sell that,' I said. 'The rest of it's probably worth another few hundred pounds. The Wedgwood bowl's worth more, but we wouldn't get the full amount for it in a hurry.'

'Can you get in touch with your father?' Abby asked David.

'It'll be dangerous,' David said. 'It'll be easier in a little while when everybody isn't searching for me. They'll probably listen to his phone and read his mail.'

'Chaim,' I suggested.

'Chaim will be back in the Reich by now,' he said. 'He won't be in England again for months. When he is, yes, he can contact my father.'

'Better to think of your father as an ongoing source of funds, then, rather than an immediate one. What you have is enough for the time being. Actually, I could get you to Canada almost immediately. I have some children going tomorrow. You could go as their parents. The papers would cost me five hundred pounds.'

David looked desolate.

'I think it's the best choice at the moment,' I said.

'It may be there will be a lot of others following you,' Abby said. 'This new government — well, that's how Hitler came to power, you know, under democratic forms, but without being elected. I didn't like the tone of any of those changes. Religion to be put on the new picture ID cards. Though I spoke to Rabbi Schwimmer this morning and told him that the Friends Meeting House here will be happy to accept any Jew who visits us once, and thereafter they can quite truthfully say they are Quakers, and we'll support them. Though how long it'll be safe to be a Quaker I don't know.'

She stood and stretched. 'It's half past four. There's an antique shop down the quay that doesn't close until five, where you might try the mirror and a bracelet, Lucy. Then tomorrow you might try to get rid of a little more of it in some of the others, and maybe I could try some in one over in Southsea where they don't know me. You'll be able to sell the rest in Canada.'

'I don't know what I'd do without you, Abby,' I said. 'I don't know what I'd ever have done without you. I don't think I'd have grown up to be a human being without you, and now you're saving my life, or at least David's.'

'I don't know how I can ever thank you,' David said, struggling into that ridiculous mac again.

'No need. What you can't pay back you pay forward,' Abby said. 'Come on now!'

# 30

They made him hang about at the Yard waiting, where he had nothing to do but try to clear his desk, and then they told him he couldn't have Royston.

'You don't need a sergeant for a job like that, sir,' Stebbings said. 'A constable should be quite sufficient. What's more, there's a constable here who was sent up from Winchester yesterday who wants to go back. You can take him.'

'I'm not going to Farthing,' Carmichael growled. 'I'm going in the opposite direction, to Campion in Monmouthshire.' *The Times* lay neatly folded on Stebbings's desk. The headline read 'Kahn did it,' which didn't help Carmichael's temper.

'Well stick him on a train at the end of the day where he can get home,' Stebbings said, unsympathetically. 'Salisbury can't be far out of your way — he can get to Winchester from there. And make sure you're back here this evening. The Chief Inspector wants to see you, and no messing about.'

'I need Royston,' Carmichael protested. 'He knows the case. He understands what's going on.'

'You seem to be treating Royston like your private property since you got onto this job,' Stebbings said. 'He's needed here today. The Yard does have other cases than this one, hard as

340

it might be for you to remember it.'

So Carmichael set off for Campion with Izzard at his side. The day was overcast and gloomy. On the way out of London they passed hoardings for the *Herald*, which screamed 'Kahn runs!' and 'Manhunt!' and for the *Telegraph*, 'Lady Eversley disowns daughter.' Carmichael grunted at them, and Izzard showed no indication of having seen them. The long drive was unenlivened by much conversation. Carmichael had to navigate, the map open on his lap all the way. Izzard had never been so far from home, and said this every time he mistook left for right and took a wrong turning.

Campion Hall turned out to be a miniature castle, built by the Normans to keep down the Welsh, destroyed by Cromwell when the Welsh supported the king against him, then lovingly restored by the Victorians. They had made additions they were sure the medievals would have added if they'd only thought of them, such as pointed turret-tops, Rackhamesque wall paintings, and running water. The only thing they'd missed was a moat, probably because the place was on the side of a hill, nestled among pine trees. It was most picturesque and utterly monstrous.

'What a ghastly thing,' Carmichael said as they parked in front of the scrollwork portcullis.

'What, sir?' Izzard asked.

Carmichael shook his head, yearning for Royston. 'It doesn't matter, constable.' He rang the bell-pull. At the side of the portcullis was an ordinary wooden door, which was opened by an elderly butler.

'I'd like to see Lady Thirkie, please,' Carmichael said, offering his card.

'Follow me,' the man said, after scrutinizing it for a long while.

Carmichael and Izzard followed him down a long passage, decorated with wall paintings illustrating Aesop's fables, and into a large drawing room, the walls painted with trees, but furnished in the prevailing style of about 1880, massive pieces of mahogany furniture upholstered in red velvet and decorated with white lace anti-macassars and doilies.

'Please wait, I'll fetch Lady Thirkie,' the butler said. Carmichael strolled about looking at the walls. The draftsmanship was as exquisite as the taste was terrible. Izzard took up a position resembling parade rest near the doorway, seeming to take no notice of anything.

The woman who came in at last was certainly not Angela Thirkie. She must have been forty years older. She was dressed head to toe in black, like a Victorian widow, or like Queen Victoria herself, whom she somewhat resembled, except for being so much taller.

'My name is Carmichael, of Scotland Yard,' he said, bowing. 'I was hoping to see Lady Thirkie?'

'Yes,' she said. 'I am Lady Letitia Thirkie, and I recognize you from your newspaper photograph, though you're certainly rather more handsome in person. I must say you fellows have taken your time. She's flown the coop.'

'Who has what?' Carmichael was bemused.

342

'Isn't that the expression? I found it in Edgar Wallace. She's left. Gone. She'll be halfway to Thirkie by now.'

'You're the dowager Lady Thirkie?' he asked.

'We both are, now,' she said. 'My daughter-in-law, Angela, has left, I'm sorry to tell you. Do sit down. And you too, sergeant — is it sergeant?'

'Constable Izzard, madam,' Izzard said, without moving a muscle.

'Ah.' Lady Thirkie contemplated Izzard for a moment. 'I wonder if you'd be more comfortable in the kitchen?'

Izzard looked at Carmichael. 'Yes, go on, constable,' Carmichael said.

'They'll give you tea or something while I talk to the Inspector,' Lady Thirkie said. 'It's straight down the corridor and the door on the left.'

'That's this side, Izzard,' Carmichael added.

'Yes, sir; thank you, madam,' Izzard said, and stumped off.

'It must be a sore trial to you to have to deal with such people,' Lady Thirkie said, sympathetically.

'Izzard is on loan,' Carmichael admitted. 'He does have good qualities, but they are not of the conversational kind. My usual assistant, who is both clever and useful to me, is busy today.'

'Yes, you must all be very busy with all this terrible business with Bolsheviks and Jews and anarchists and goodness knows what shooting at people,' Lady Thirkie said. 'But Inspector, whatever else they might have done, shooting at Lord Eversley and so on, they did not murder my son James. My daughter-in-law did that. She

343

as good as admitted it to me, in this very room.'

'I knew it,' Carmichael said, most unprofessionally.

'You'll have a long drive ahead of you. She's going to Thirkie, in North Yorkshire. Her so-called chauffeur came down from London last night to take her. They left immediately after breakfast.'

'What exactly did she say?' Carmichael asked.

'She said I need not worry that James had died painfully, they had taken the utmost care that he had not, by gassing him before he was stabbed. I asked why murderers would take such pains. She was very vague, and said something about Jews too worn out for factory work being gassed on the Continent.'

If they'd found him in the car with the star, they might have thought of that themselves, Carmichael thought. 'He was gassed, and it wasn't painful,' he said. 'The police have been very careful to keep that from everyone, so there's no chance she could have known that innocently.'

'She is not a very clever woman,' Lady Thirkie said. 'Are you aware, Inspector, that she was not my son's first choice? His first wife, Lady Olivia, was a Larkin, you know. And after she was killed, in the Blitz, it was Angela's sister Daphne that James fell in love with. She was married, to that parvenu Normanby as it happens, so James married the sister, who had some resemblance to her, but not, regrettably, in wits. James told me at Christmas that the marriage had been a sad mistake, and that he had little hope of an heir.

He told me he was going to invite his elder cousin Donald Thirkie, at present at Oxford, to visit Thirkie and begin to know it. Donald's father, Oliver, will inherit it now, which he can never have expected.'

'Lady Angela Thirkie is expecting,' Carmichael said.

'Yes, she told me. I am assured by her personal maid that the baby is the chauffeur's. It's a blessing that she'll be hanged before it can be born to taint our name.'

'The baby is innocent, surely,' Carmichael protested.

'Innocent, perhaps, but not my grandson,' Lady Thirkie countered, as if that were guilt enough. 'Let me continue. I was not suspicious at the news of the gas, although it had not been in the newspapers, because, after all, she had been there and I didn't know what you might have told her. I became a little suspicious when she told me she was in the family way — that's another expression I've gleaned from my reading. Another is 'bun in the oven.' But in any case, when she said she had a bun in the oven,' Lady Thirkie repeated the words with loving emphasis, 'I was surprised, but ready to be delighted at the thought of the family continuing. I had two sons, Inspector; I went through pregnancy and childbirth twice, and to do that for nothing, no grandchildren, no continuation of the line, is tragic. My elder son, Matthew, was killed in France, you know.'

'I did know,' Carmichael said. 'I'm very sorry — and I'm even more sorry for your recent loss.'

345

'Thank you,' she said, with dignity, and her face crumpled for a moment. 'But do let me go on. If I stop to think about that I shall be undone. At dinner last night, we were naturally talking about James's death, and about the motives of the murderer, or murderers. Angela betrayed the greatest knowledge of these motives. She said they had gassed him because they did not want to hurt him — Bolsheviks and Jews, whose reason for killing him would be that they hated him and hated the Peace he brought to us all! She said they moved him after killing him to show that it was they who had done it — when anyone would want to show the opposite. Even with a political assassination of that nature, they would want to distance themselves to the extent of not incriminating themselves. Kahn was right in the house. We talked about Kahn, whose flight was announced on the six o'clock news yesterday. Angela expressed disgust for Mrs. Kahn, who had been Lucy Eversley, and said the Jews deserved everything they got and brought it on themselves. This was not my son's view, Inspector. He did not like the business practices of the Jews, and he disapproved of intermarriage between our people and Jews, but he regarded the excessive hatred of them, which so many people display, as pathological.'

'Is that also your view?' Carmichael asked.

'I don't know that I've ever met a Jew,' she said, after a moment's reflection. 'I live very quietly here and rarely go out. Perhaps if I did meet one, I would feel this instinctive revulsion some people say they feel. Or perhaps not. I would not have wanted my sons to marry one, but at present I feel very sorry for young Lucy Kahn, and for her husband.'

'So do I,' Carmichael admitted. 'But do go on.'

'Beginning to be suspicious, though without knowledge of her motivation, I started to press Angela on the motivation of the murderers. She began by saying the obvious, that the Jews would hate him because of the Peace, and so on, but then she suggested that some people might want him out of the way because he was such a good man.'

'Noted for his personal integrity,' Carmichael said.

Lady Thirkie raised an eyebrow.

'That's what the Scotland Yard report on him said. That he was noted for his personal integrity.'

Without any fuss at all, Lady Thirkie took a white handkerchief out of her reticule and mopped her eyes. Carmichael could not help contrasting this to Agnes Timms's display on the bench at Leigh the morning before. Yet, different as they were, Agnes Timms and Lady Letitia Thirkie together would hang Angela Thirkie, and perhaps Normanby too.

'I had seen as much in the papers,' she said. 'But it seems especially significant and creditable that it would be noted in a police report.'

'I'm sorry I never met him,' Carmichael said.

Lady Thirkie wiped her eyes again. 'It seems to me,' she said, after a moment, 'that this would be the reason for killing him. James would never have gone along with this unconstitutional coup, this nonsense that upstart Normanby has rammed through Parliament on the fear and excitement that murder creates.'

'You don't think Lady Angela Thirkie acted alone, then?'

'She's too much of a fool to do something so complicated on her own,' Lady Thirkie said. 'She might have killed him, but she could never have covered it up. I'm sure Normanby was involved, and that probably means his wife as well, though I'm making an assumption there. Angela several times said things about what Normanby thinks and what Normanby will do, which made me think she was privy to at least some of his plans.'

'You'd be prepared to swear to this in court, Lady Thirkie?' Carmichael asked, as he had asked Agnes Timms the previous morning.

'More than that, I'd be delighted to,' she said. 'We can't let her get away with this. After dinner last night, when she'd announced her intention to go to Thirkie today, I interrogated her maid, and discovered that it was almost common knowledge below stairs that Angela had been having it off with the chauffeur. I'd thought it peculiar when he drove down from London on Tuesday night. That settled her motive for being involved beyond any doubt.'

'Why didn't you contact the police?'

'Inspector Carmichael, I'm disappointed to see you use that ugly Americanism 'contact' as a verb. There are many pithy expressions and neologisms that can improve the language, and there are others that diminish it. In any case, I did not communicate with the police, because I was sure you'd be here without that necessity — as indeed, here you are. I did not imagine that if I could put together a case against Angela and Normanby, you would be far behind me.'

'No, indeed, Lady Thirkie,' he said.

She smiled. 'It's true that the police are wonderful,' she said.

Carmichael was embarrassed. 'I think I'd better go back to the Yard now, and talk to my superiors about our next step. Is Lady Thirkie likely to stay at Thirkie?'

'At least until after the funeral, and she says she'll stay there until the baby's born,' Lady Thirkie said. 'Let me know when you want me to give evidence. I shall enjoy it a great deal. I've never been in a criminal court.'

Carmichael thought he'd enjoy it a great deal, too. He collected Izzard from the kitchen and set off back eastwards. They stopped in a little restaurant in Gloucester for lunch. Carmichael, despairing of Izzard's conversation, read a crumpled copy of *The Times* that the restaurant found for him. 'Kahn did it' had no more power to distress him. Kahn would soon be restored to his bank and his China tea. He had evidence now that would stand up to anything. News of Normanby's reforms were almost irrelevant. Soon, whether or not they could convict him, Normanby would be in the dock beside Angela Thirkie, his political career over and a new government formed. The news that Hitler would be in London for the opening night Covent

Garden production of *Parsifal* interested him but little. He did not care for Wagner. He went on plodding through the paper as he plodded through the uninteresting roast beef and tasteless potatoes the restaurant had brought him. His eye was caught by a tiny headline on an inside page:

## GANGLAND KILLING IN SOUTHEND

Yesterday evening, a member of a Southend gang, believed to have been aiming at a member of a rival gang, accidentally shot and killed a hairdresser's assistant who was passing on the other side of the road. Miss Agnes Timms, 25, of Leigh-on-Sea, was taken to hospital but was pronounced dead on arrival. The killer is unidentified but police hope for an arrest soon.

His beef turned to dry dust in his mouth and he almost choked trying to swallow. They had killed her. Somebody had killed her to shut her up, directly after he had seen her yesterday. It was as if he had killed her himself, because if he hadn't found her and talked to her, she would be alive now, cutting women's hair, dying it blue, planning for her own salon. Forty-five pounds had seemed a fortune to her, and she had probably died with his handkerchief still in her pocket. What's more, half of his evidence was gone. All he had now was Lady Letitia Thirkie. Would they attack her? Would they kill her in the same cavalier fashion once he revealed that she had information? Was he even safe himself?

Might there be a gunman waiting, a tragic accident, a policeman killed in the course of his duty? The man he suspected of killing Thirkie, for the most cold-blooded political reasons, and killing Agnes Timms to stop her telling what she knew, was Prime Minister. Could he go against the Prime Minister?

'Eat up, Izzard,' he said. 'We're going back to Campion Hall, and you are staying there to protect the old lady.'

'From what, sir?' Izzard asked, uninterested in the sudden change of plans.

'Terrorists and assassins,' Carmichael said.

# 31

I sold the mirror and an emerald bracelet, and the nice man gave me fifty pounds, cash, and didn't ask me where I'd got them at all. I suppose he thought I was a thief, and I suppose he was right, because they were in fact Mummy's, not mine. We spent the night in the basement of Abby's school, which was quite comfortable, only rather dark. We didn't see Mr. Talbot at all; Abby said it was safer that way. We did, of necessity, see the children who were also hiding there, three girls and a little boy. I was afraid they'd do something to give us away if the police came, but that was nonsense. Those children had been halfway across Europe undercover; they knew far more about hiding than I did. Even the boy, who was only three, could have given me lessons.

The oldest one was called Tania. She was Russian, or anyway Ukrainian, which isn't quite the same thing. She was ten. Abby had been teaching her English. 'We're going on a boat tomorrow night,' she told me. 'It's to Canada, not America. They don't allow Jewish people into America, not any.'

'We're going to come with you if we can raise enough money,' I said. 'We're going to pretend to be your mother and father.'

'We'll be quiet,' she said. 'I speak the best English, Rivkele speaks it very badly, and Naddy and Paul don't speak it at all. They do speak French though. In some parts of Canada people speak French, Abby says.'

'Naddy and Paul don't sound like Jewish names,' I said.

'They aren't, but they don't know what their real names are,' she informed me. 'They were hidden by French people who gave them those names — then those people were caught, and taken to the camps. We were all at a camp, and we were all going to be gassed, only we were lucky and got away.'

I was astonished at how self-possessed she was, and how calmly she accepted all these horrors. Up until then, sitting there in the basement, it had been exciting, in a way, even when it was terrifying, even when it had been boring, on the train. Selling the things had been rather fun. I hadn't really felt what poor David had been feeling all this time, the absolute loss of our old life, our home, everything. It suddenly occurred to me to wonder what I was going to do in Canada, how I would live when the money from selling the things was gone. Would I have to sell the Ringhili diamond? No, I assured myself, that was sacrosanct, however poor we were. I would pass that on to my daughter when she married, whoever she married, whether or not I disapproved. I didn't know if the baby I was carrying would be a son or a daughter, but I felt sure that one day I would have both.

David guessed somehow that I was feeling miserable. He came and sat by me, with his arm around me. We told stories to the children, and where they didn't understand we put in words in other languages. David and Tania and Rivkele knew some Hebrew, and I knew some French, though my French still wasn't very good, even after school and Switzerland and all the trips buying clothes in Paris and everything. They laughed at me, even Paul, and it did them good to laugh. David said we'd have to play games that taught them English, and started a singing game that they all loved. I could see that he was going to be a wonderful father. Eventually little Paul went to sleep on David's shoulder, and he carried him off to bed. We sent the others to bed too. Abby had set up four cots in one of the rooms for them. They were used to sleeping together, Tania said, though they had done it in some funny places. Counting off the funny places, which were enough to make my blood run cold, they fell asleep.

Abby came down and sat with us for a while and told us how to get in touch with her. We arranged for her to get in touch with David's parents after a few months, by going to see David's father at work as if she wanted a loan. We thought that would be safe enough. I kept feeling surges of something between excitement and fear — we're really going, we're really leaving the country, police and people are really searching for us. Our descriptions had been broadcast on the BBC. Yet we kept sitting there, drinking tea and chatting as if nothing was happening.

'How do you get the children?' I asked.

'There's a guard at one of the camps who

rescues as many as he can of the condemned,' she said. 'It's almost always children because the others wouldn't make it. Children are very resilient, I find, though sometimes the experience makes them resentful and angry. These four are good children. You'll find them a good readymade family.'

I blinked, but David said, in the half-dark, 'I think we already have.'

'They have tickets for a boat leaving Southampton tomorrow, calling at Halifax and then New York. People will be watching the boats, but they'll be looking for a couple, not a big family. You're a plausible family, at least, color-wise. I sometimes get gypsies, very dark, and once a Negro girl whose mother had been a nightclub singer in Paris, before. These four are all Jewish.'

'I'm amazed that Jews in Europe are still having children,' I said, unthinkingly.

'What, when you're having a baby yourself?' Abby asked. I'd told her earlier, and she'd congratulated me. 'People have babies whenever they have hope, and while hope is thin in Europe, it isn't quite dead. The new children are coming from newly conquered areas, like the Ukraine, and countries voluntarily submitting to the rules of the Reich, like Bulgaria and Romania, whose Jews felt safe until recently, in the same way that British Jews thought they were safe.'

I went cold all over at the thought of those things happening in Britain, happening to people I knew. I could see that they would though

355

— the process was almost inevitable from the moment Mummy killed Sir James. Maybe they would send the Jews off to Hitler's camps, or maybe they would form camps of their own, because it wouldn't only be the Jews, any more than it was in the Reich; it was also anybody who disagreed with the way things were organized. The Jews were just the easy way to get started.

'Tania said Naddy and Paul don't know their real names,' I said.

'They don't know their real names or who their parents were, or even if they're really Jewish, and they never will now that the people who were sheltering them have been taken to the camps. Naddy was only four, and Paul was a babe in arms. It'll be your responsibility to let them know who they are now, because they'll never know who they once were.'

'Are you asking us to take on those four in the long term?' I asked.

'Yes. Normally, they'd have gone to a Friends orphanage in Halifax, where we'd have tried to find homes for them. But I'm getting the papers changed to say you're all a family, emigrating. It's cover for you and for them, but it does mean you'll have to take care of them.'

'Of course we will,' David said, without hesitation, sounding better than he had for days. 'We'll be glad to. And if there's anything more we can do later, when we're established, we'll do that too, of course.'

I thought about having four ready-made children, immediately, and I tried to feel cheerful about it, but I couldn't help feeling that it would be a bit of a burden with no nursemaid or governess or anything.

The next morning, Abby sold the jewel case and the hairbrush in Southsea, for a hundred and ten pounds, and I sold another bracelet and a whole mess of earrings in two different shops in Portsmouth, for eighty pounds. I put a shawl over my head, partly to look like a poorer kind of woman, but also to disguise the wound a bit. Even with make-up it was visible if you looked closely.

That gave us enough money for the papers, though Abby said time would be tight and we might have to take the next boat, a week later. I bought a few things, chocolate for the children, and drawing books, and crayons, and things to read to them, and books for David and me. I bought myself *War and Peace* because it was so long and because I'd never read it, and I bought David the new book from the man who wrote that animal book that was so popular a few years before, some kind of scientifiction thing called *Nineteen-Seventy-Four.* He always loved Wells and Verne, and I thought something like that would take his mind off things. Abby bought us some clothes — I didn't dare buy them myself because clothes shops seemed like the kind of place they might be looking for us, though much more likely in London than Portsmouth.

Then I did something terribly risky. I took a pile of pennies and went into a phone box and rang Daddy. I rang him at work, not at the House, and not at home either where I'd have had to speak to servants and possibly Mummy. I

357

knew now that Mummy would do whatever she could to track us down and hurt us. But to speak to Daddy in the office I only had to dial direct, which was all right, because I knew the codes, and then go through one secretary. I knew what to say, which was that I was Mark Normanby's new secretary and could she put me through. I was through to him in half a minute.

'Hello, Daddy?' I said.

'Luce! Bunny, where are you?'

'I'm in a call box,' I said. 'I'm safe. What I want to know is, how could you go along with this?'

'It rather ran away with me,' he said. 'You know how these things do. Come home, Bunny, I'll see you won't be hurt.'

'But David will,' I said. 'You just went along with it? You mean you knew it was happening?'

'Vaguely,' he said. 'Your mother did mention something about it. I knew that chap was going to shoot at me, but he was supposed to miss, dammit, he wasn't supposed to hit you. I'm sorry about that.'

'She mentioned something about murdering a friend of yours and framing my husband?' I asked.

'She didn't say anything about that,' he assured me. 'It was just supposed to be Jews and terrorists generally. I didn't even know you'd been invited until I saw you at dinner on Friday.'

'Daddy, I don't know how much of this is Mark and how much is Mummy, but now that it's started it'll keep going like a snowball rolling downhill until there's no liberty and nothing left,

358

as bad as the Bolsheviks, worse, as bad as the Reich. You think you're in control, and you can be now; you can stop it if you speak out, now, but soon it'll be too late, you'll be afraid as well. Stop it now, Daddy. Go on the radio and tell everybody what's been done. You didn't want to kill Sir James, and surely you don't want to live in a country where that's the way to power?'

'But Luce, you're being absurd,' he said. 'It's nothing like the Bolsheviks. It's people like us who keep the Bolsheviks out, to stop the little people crawling upwards hand over hand, dragging us all down by the coattails. I didn't disapprove of your marriage, although your mother did. I wanted you to be happy. Come back. I'll do what I can for Kahn.'

'Congratulations on being Chancellor,' I said. 'I don't expect I'll see you again, or speak to you, but I wanted to say goodbye.'

'Where are you?' he asked. The pips were going, and I didn't want another three minutes. The last I heard was his voice saying plaintively, 'Luce? Bunny?'

I wasn't his Bunny, or anybody's Bunny. I hadn't been for years, really, but it was only then that I noticed, and felt different. Daddy could just drift into murder and fascism, but I refused that entirely, for myself and for the future. It was the way I'd thought before, about living in a tiny flower garden in the midst of fields of manure. I couldn't close my eyes to the fact that keeping the flower garden meant pushing other people off into the manure. Daddy might mean what he said about doing something to help David, though I didn't think he'd really be able to do it, but even if he could it wasn't enough if other people like David who didn't have pull were being pushed off. That's why the law has to be impartial and has to be fair, and that's what Abby explained to me from the time I was old enough to think about these things at all. I wish Daddy had had someone like Abby to explain it to him. I wish everyone had, or if they had, that they'd paid attention.

In the afternoon, Abby came down to say our tickets and papers had come through, and that we were sailing from Southampton on the evening tide. She also said the railways were being watched very carefully, so we'd have to take a risk, both on the train and on the boat. She said our descriptions and photos were all over the papers, and all over the wireless as well, and everyone seemed sure David had done it, even the *Manchester Guardian,* which was usually Abby's byword for liberality and giving the benefit of the doubt.

We looked at our papers and practiced our new names. Then Abby made up my face very carefully. My scrape was the thing that was hardest to disguise. She lent me a hat that shaded my face to some extent, but I was still afraid someone would see it. She came down with us to the station.

The children were excited. They wanted to go on the train. David had been telling them about trains and drawing trains for them. They were really a wonderful distraction for David, just what he needed. They'd been in the boat before, so the ship all the way to Canada didn't seem as exciting as the one-hour train trip. Abby bought the tickets, and waved us off. There were more police, but they hardly glanced at us. I carried Paul and kept my face down over him. I thought I'd do the same going onto the boat.

I hugged Abby goodbye fiercely. I wished so much that she were coming with us, though I knew she couldn't and she was doing more good where she was. We piled into a compartment, which we had all to ourselves, and settled down. We waved as long as we could see Abby standing on the platform. I didn't know if I'd ever see her again.

The children soon got tired of the train. We passed the first part of the journey playing noughts and crosses and drawing stories. The older ones liked me to draw something for them to color, so I did that too, though I wasn't very good. I could manage women in long dresses, and cats — Abby taught me a very good way of drawing a cat, all in one line. It wasn't very natural, but you could tell what it was. They thought it was wonderful. I started to feel that I might be able to deal with being a mother after all.

'Where will we live in Canada?' Tania asked as we jolted out of one of the little stations.

'We'll land in Halifax,' David said. 'That's a big port, bigger than Portsmouth, I think, as big as Southampton. It'll be exciting. We'll see flying boats and ships there. Then after Halifax I think we'll go on the train, a long long way, all day on

361

the train, inland, through Nova Scotia and New Brunswick.'

'Are those countries?' Tania asked. She was opposite me. Paul was next to me — he'd fallen asleep and was leaning against me, rather heavily. You wouldn't think a three-year-old could be so heavy.

'No, they're parts of Canada. Provinces,' David said.

'You must have been frightfully good at geography,' I said, enviously.

He laughed. 'I've just looked at maps,' he said. 'You need to get good at maps to be a pilot.'

'Are you a pilot?' Rivkele asked. 'A flyer of aeroplanes?'

'Yes, or at least, I was,' David said. 'I think I will be again, now. It'll be different from being a banker, but you can't be a banker without capital. Maybe later I'll have capital again, and I can go back to banking. We'll see. But for now, I think we'll go to Montreal. That's in Quebec, the part of Canada where people speak French. They don't mind Jews so much there — at least, that's what I've heard. In the war, I had a friend in the squadron who was Quebecois, and that's what he told me. We'll find somewhere to live, and you can go to school and grow up, and our new baby will be born, and things will be all right.'

I believed it, when he said it, sitting in the train, bucketing onwards through the quiet green countryside, not knowing if we'd ever get to Canada or even whether we'd get safely on the boat. It was still quite likely that the police would catch us and hang David and repatriate the children to the death camps and probably lock me up in a madhouse. But we were going on in hope, to a new life, new names, new possibilities. Things would be very different.

I sat there, David against my side and Paul heavy on my other side, and thought back over the last week — it was less than a week, from Saturday afternoon when David had come in furious at Angela Thirkie mistaking him for the waiter, until Thursday afternoon when we sat in the train going to a new life. I decided there and then to write all this down. To have a record of it, to publish it if possible, if there is some press somewhere in some country that isn't afraid of the consequences of ceasing to appease these people, and maybe one day even in England. Maybe one day we'll go home, when England is truly free again, and not just giving lip service to freedom while sinking deeper and deeper into oppression.

'I love you,' I said. 'Are you frightened?'

'I'm terrified, but I love you too,' David said, and kind of nuzzled against my neck in that lovely way he has.

Then the train pulled in to Southampton station.

# 32

Everything made sense; all the inconsistencies and implausibilities that had plagued Carmichael were gone. If he hadn't been so afraid, he'd have been ready to sing. He made it to London, to the Yard. There was nowhere to park. He had to leave the car on a newfangled American meter in Lincoln's Inn Fields and walk the rest of the way, fearing snipers, fearing immediate and sudden death as he had not since the end of the war. They had killed Agnes Timms, and he knew more than she knew.

Inside the Yard, Stebbings was sitting as usual in his cubicle. He beckoned to Carmichael. 'The Chief wants to see you immediately you come in,' he said. His tone was even, as always, but Carmichael thought he seemed somehow less friendly than usual.

'He doesn't want me to write up my report first?'

'Immediately,' Stebbings said, shortly. He had it written down on a notepad in front of him, Carmichael noticed. 'Carmichael: immediately.' His name was underlined.

Carmichael went to the lift preparing arguments to use to his Chief. He was within his deadline. He had wrapped the case up. They could take it to the Director of Public Prosecutions as it was. Agnes Timms's murder was one more piece of evidence, and he and

364

Royston had both heard what she had to say and could testify to it. He was elevated, again leaving his stomach behind as he rose, and at last stepped out into the Chief Inspector's office.

The view was splendid. Clouds were streaming south across London, and he had a bird's-eye view.

Penn-Barkis was sitting at his desk, fingers pressed together. 'I take it you've finished with the Thirkie case?' he asked.

'Yes, sir,' Carmichael said, sitting in the chair in front of the desk that Penn-Barkis indicated. If he could not see the view, at least he wouldn't be distracted by it. 'Let me explain it to you.'

On the long drive back, Carmichael had put it all together and now he could lay out a clear picture of the Thirkie murder that made sense. He spoke without any interruptions at all. Penn-Barkis sat still with steepled fingers, listening intently.

'It was a political assassination, though not in the way we thought. Mark Normanby wanted to get rid of Thirkie in a way that gave him a chance to capitalize on his death to take power. Angela Thirkie agreed to help with this, because she wanted her husband out of the way. They either waited until she was pregnant or moved their plans forward because she was pregnant. The timing of the houseparty had been planned to coincide with the vote, either because Lady Eversley was a conspirator or because Normanby had put pressure on her. The Kahns were invited along to be scapegoats and set the country against the Jews.' Kahn was probably the only

Jew Normanby knew well enough to persuade to come to visit.

'Ahead of time, Normanby impersonated Kahn in France in order to get hold of the star. Kahn wouldn't have given his own name and address; someone wanting to implicate him certainly would. We know Normanby has been in France this year.' And we know Kahn hasn't, and couldn't have been, if we believe Mrs. Kahn, but Penn-Barkis probably wouldn't accept that.

'Also before they went to Farthing, Angela Thirkie paid Brown to play the trick on Lord Eversley on the Sunday. Lord Eversley may or may not have known about it. Brown was paid to play his 'joke' and set them against the Bolsheviks. If Brown had been told to shoot to miss, it might explain why he didn't do better against a shotgun. On the other hand, that might just be his relative inexperience with his rifle. She also made sure Thirkie brought his dagger with him, and got hold of the lipstick. She may have got her maid to steal it. Her maid seems fairly easy to intimidate; we could almost certainly get more information from her, and probably from the chauffeur as well. She's having an affair with the chauffeur, and it seems likely the baby is his.' Talking to Angela Thirkie's servants would be the next thing. He'd have to go up to Yorkshire. It was a pity he hadn't caught her at Campion, but talking to the old lady had been quite sufficiently informative.

'On the night of the murder, Saturday sixth May, Angela Thirkie somehow persuaded Thirkie to sit in the car — I don't know how.' He couldn't imagine her doing the dance of the seven veils in the headlights, or Thirkie sitting still for it. It might have been earlier, when it was still light and she might have asked him to pose for a photograph in the car. How long exactly did the poisoning take?

'If she hadn't persuaded him, then Normanby must have threatened him into it, making it technically suicide, but isn't driving someone to suicide an offense?' It should be. Penn-Barkis didn't answer, just kept on looking at him most disconcertingly. Carmichael had seen him like this before at the end of a case. He just kept on.

'Most likely, Normanby threatened to reveal something he knew — probably not Angela's adultery; it must have been some other hold he had over Thirkie, something Thirkie had done that he himself considered shameful. Possibly it was a sexual passage between the two of them, or perhaps something political. In any case, Thirkie died painlessly in the car. After death they took him upstairs and arranged him so as to frame Kahn. Maybe Normanby did this alone, because Angela Thirkie displayed signs of shock on hearing where her husband's body had been found.' That had thrown him off, and made him think about two sets of murderers for too long.

Penn-Barkis listened in silence, his eyes fixed on Carmichael's face. 'Normanby lied about playing billiards with Thirkie, probably to conceal the time of death, which was earlier than we initially thought. He also arranged to find the body himself.'

Penn-Barkis laid his hands flat on the desk and

drew a deep breath. 'Have you finished?'

'Yes, sir. I can tell you where I have my evidence from, if you like.'

'That's not necessary. I'll take it on trust that it's all verified and that you have witnesses or material evidence. You're sure, quite sure, that what you've said is the case?' Penn-Barkis stared at Carmichael without blinking.

'Yes, sir,' Carmichael said, feeling as if he had run ten miles.

'Your policeman's itch to find out exactly what happened, which was plaguing you so badly when we last spoke, is entirely satisfied?'

'Yes, sir,' Carmichael repeated.

'Then forget all this,' Penn-Barkis said. 'Put it out of your mind. It may well be what happened, and it's certainly an explanation that covers everything, but the important thing to remember is that Kahn did it.'

'But sir!' Carmichael almost jumped up out of his seat.

'When I was a boy, I was told that only little goats butt,' Penn-Barkis said, with a thin smile. 'Kahn did it, and the reason Kahn did it is because Mr. Normanby is our Prime Minister and thinking these things against him almost amounts to treason.'

'Scotland Yard is above politics, and the courts are above politics, and the law — '

'Nothing is above politics, Carmichael,' Penn-Barkis said. 'I'm so sorry to disillusion you, at your age.'

'The law — '

'But you're not above breaking the law

yourself when it suits you, are you?' Penn-Barkis asked, gently. 'You made a telephone call from your desk here to Farthing yesterday at twelve-thirty. What was the purpose of that call?'

Carmichael blushed hotly. 'I rang to tell Mrs. Kahn there was new evidence and to expect me,' he admitted. 'I didn't tell her to run.'

'I've heard what you both said, and I think a court would agree that you came sufficiently close to make no difference,' Penn-Barkis said. 'We record all police priority calls, as a matter of course. Didn't you know? We don't want that privilege being abused. But it isn't only that. You told Royston to allow a false description to go to the press.'

Carmichael could say nothing. He couldn't believe Royston had betrayed him, but he must have.

'Oh yes, Royston told me,' Penn-Barkis went on. 'He believes you've been led astray by being a little in love with the Kahn woman, but I know better, of course. It's not likely that you'd be in love with any woman, is it Carmichael? We know about your relationship with your . . . servant. 'Long-term companion' is what they say in the obituaries, isn't it, about relationships of that nature, when the participants are of the same class.' Jack. They knew about Jack. Carmichael shut his eyes for a moment. This meant ruin. Why was death so much easier to face than ruin?

'If you were prosecuted you would both receive a prison sentence, and a rather harsh one.' Penn-Barkis steepled his fingers again. 'I suppose it's possible that if it were to become a criminal matter you might not be convicted — such cases are notoriously hard to prosecute when nobody complains and there isn't any public indecency. Proof is challenging, and the courts do insist on it. But even if you were to be acquitted, you could hardly continue to live together. Also the general knowledge, or even suspicion, of your proclivities would severely inhibit your career, not to mention your esteem in the eyes of your colleagues. I imagine Sergeant Royston for instance would be rather less eager to work with you if he knew. Sergeant Stebbings too would be disgusted, but then he holds an old-fashioned prejudice against people like you.'

Did Stebbings know already? It was general belief at the Yard that Stebbings knew everything anybody knew. He could imagine the look in Royston's eyes, the turning away, classing him with those who molest children, with Normanby and the traffic of Charing Cross Underground.

Penn-Barkis was waiting. 'Well, Carmichael? You hold the law so high that nobody can break it with impunity except you?'

'No, sir,' Carmichael said, woodenly.

'But you agree you have broken the law when it suited you?'

'Yes, sir,' Carmichael said.

'Then I'm sure you'll agree that Kahn did it,' Penn-Barkis said.

The devil's bargain was laid out plainly. Carmichael could tell him to go back to hell and take the consequences, but it wouldn't achieve anything. Without Penn-Barkis, without the apparatus of the law, he was nothing, could achieve nothing to bring Normanby to justice. One man alone could not put the Prime Minister in the dock, even for murder. If he held by the truth he would gain nothing but the satisfaction of knowing himself right. It would be a cold comfort when it was all he had to face the future, when he went to prison for abusing his police privilege or for homosexuality. On the other hand, he could damn himself and live his life, keeping quiet, doing what good he could. On the one hand, Kahn and prison (and justice, he added); on the other, himself, Jack, and his career. It was no choice, but if it was no choice, why was his tongue like lead in his mouth?

'Yes, sir,' he said, too quietly.

'Eh?'

'Yes, sir,' he repeated.

'Very good. We need men like you in the Force,' Penn-Barkis said. 'Men who won't rest until a case is solved, but who can let it go if that's what's necessary.'

'What about old Lady Thirkie, sir?' Carmichael asked.

Penn-Barkis frowned at him. 'That really isn't your business. However, if she's prepared to keep quiet about what she imagines she knows, Izzard will very likely foil a Jewish-terrorist plot to blow her little castle up tonight.'

'Thank you for telling me, sir,' Carmichael said. He didn't know whether he hoped she would keep quiet as he had when faced with the same choice, or whether she would hold on to her integrity and be blown sky high. He remembered the way she had wept for her son,

371

and expected the latter. He thought of warning her, but he could not. He had given her Izzard. Now she was his first betrayal. How long before they sent *him* off to blow up brave old ladies?

Penn-Barkis looked at his watch. 'My goodness, it's almost six o'clock. Do you have dinner plans, Carmichael?'

'Yes, sir,' Carmichael lied once more. The thought of eating with the Chief, of breaking bread with him over their devil's bargain made him feel sick.

'Well I mustn't keep you from them then,' Penn-Barkis said. He stood up and put out his hand. Carmichael shook it, automatically, by reflex, not even thinking what he had done until it was over. Then he went down in the elevator, went to the bathroom, and stood there shaking. He did not actually throw up. He drank a little water.

Nobody would kill him. Killing him would raise questions and coercing him was so much easier. Killing him made him a corpse beyond questioning; coercing him gave them a tool, a useful tool to their hand. He remembered a few years ago talking to colleagues in the Milice and the Gestapo over a case of an international smuggling gang, and finding them nice chaps. He had wondered how they could live with themselves and do some of the things they were expected to do. Now he knew. Lady Thirkie. Agnes Timms. He dashed water on his face and looked at himself in the mirror. Same old Carmichael, same nice bland English face, no outward changes.

He walked out of the Yard. Stebbings was talking on one of his black telephones. He gave him a nod and a wave as he went by.

Carmichael wanted to go home; he wanted terribly to go home and see Jack, and close the door and shut the world away and find, within his own small space, what security and comfort he could. But there was something he needed to do first.

He walked, leaving the car on the meter. Let the police move it and see it was one of their own. Let Scotland Yard and the Mets argue over it. Now the case was over it wasn't assigned to him any longer. He could still have used it; he didn't want to.

Walking relieved some of his energy. Up Southampton Row, past Russell Square, and Tavistock Square, up through Bloomsbury, passing shops pulling down their shutters for the night, and streetwalkers just beginning their working hours. Several of them solicited him. He looked at their overpainted faces and tightly pulled shirts in revulsion. Even for those who were attracted to women, what a parody of femininity they were. Some of them were very young, and he knew that almost none of them had a choice about their profession. He pitied them, even when they abused him for ignoring them. He passed houses that had once been grand and were now almost abandoned to many tenants or none. The rich had moved on to other parts of London, or to the country, like crabs that leave their shells behind to be inhabited by other fish. A light rain began to fall as he reached

King's Cross station; he turned up his collar against it. It should have been dark, he thought, or it should have been raining the way it had been the night he and Royston had gone to Bethnal Green.

A church clock struck seven as he came into Camden Town. There was a rhyme about the church bells of London, but he didn't think Camden Town came into it, unless St. Martins might be there. He thought it was more probably the inappropriately named St. Martins in the Fields down by Fleet Street. After all these years in London, he still didn't really know it. He made his way through the side streets where children were chalking on the pavement and chasing after each other. He thought about Lancashire where he and his brother had played on the moor, damming streams and intimidating sheep. London wasn't good for children. But Lancashire wouldn't be any safer, nowhere would, safety was now in compromise, doing what he was told, making sure he was on the right side not of the law, or of justice, but of expediency.

He knocked on the door. It was a small door, belonging to a small house that belonged to a landlord. Who knew what pressures had been put on Royston, economic and otherwise? It was Elvira who opened the door, as usual. 'Who's there?' he heard Royston calling from inside.

'Hello, Elvira,' he said.

'Hello, Uncle Carmichael,' she said, then called, 'It's Uncle Carmichael!'

Royston came to the door and stood behind

the child. 'I'm sorry,' he said.

Carmichael ignored him. 'It's you I've come to see,' he said to Elvira. 'The case is over.'

'So you're going to give me a present?' she asked, wriggling with excitement.

'The Chief asked me directly,' Royston went on.

'If I hadn't done it, you wouldn't have had anything to tell them,' Carmichael said, without looking up at him. He fished in his pocket. 'Here, Elvira, do you know what this is?' He tossed it to her. The coin flashed as it caught the light, first the King's head and then the perky robin, as she caught it.

She examined it for a moment. 'It's a farthing,' she said, in deep disappointment. It was the shiny new farthing he had picked up from beside Brown's body.

'Do you know what it's worth?' Carmichael asked.

'Four-farthings-make-a-penny,' she recited, in the singsong tone of a nursery rhyme. 'A quarter of a penny.'

'And what can you buy for a farthing?' Carmichael asked.

'I really didn't mean to — ' Royston said.

'Not very much,' Elvira said.

'Whatever you meant, you heard what Agnes Timms said, sergeant,' Carmichael said, over her head to Royston. 'You knew Kahn was innocent as well as I did.'

'What did you find out today?' Royston asked.

Carmichael looked at him for the first time, and saw only the same honest Sergeant Royston

375

he had always known. He sighed. 'I found out that Kahn did it, whatever the evidence looks like and however much of it I had. I found out that I'm the kind of person who can compromise and keep on going. And last, but definitely not least, I found out that a farthing doesn't buy very much.'

'Sir — ' Royston protested.

'Here, Elvira,' he said, and slipped her a pound note. 'You'll find that buys a little more. Good night, sergeant.'

Carmichael waved once to the child and walked away up the dirty London street.

## HA'PENNY

### Jo Walton

In a world where England has agreed a peace with Nazi Germany, one small change can carry a huge cost . . . Following the Farthing Peace, England appears to have all but completed an inexorable descent into a fascist dictatorship. However, when a bomb explodes in a London suburb, resistance seems to be underway. The brilliant but tormented Inspector Carmichael of Scotland Yard is assigned to the case and uncovers a conspiracy of peers and communists to murder the prime minister and his ally, Adolf Hitler . . .

# A CHRISTMAS HOMECOMING

## Anne Perry

1897. Caroline Fielding and her husband Joshua, a noted actor and director of plays, agree to perform an amateur dramatisation of *Dracula* over the Christmas period in exchange for the financial backing of Charles Netheridge, their new benefactor. As Joshua's company assembles at Netheridge's house in atmospheric Whitby and begins its preparations, a stranger with an intimate knowledge of the novel arrives, asking for shelter from the growing snow storms outside. And as the players learn more about one another and intriguing secrets begin to emerge, the dark nightmares of *Dracula* are played out off stage as well as on. Who exactly has Netheridge invited into his home? And when one person's life is taken, can the culprit be found before the snow melts?

# THE BEDLAM DETECTIVE

## Stephen Gallagher

From a basement office in London, Sebastian Becker investigates wealthy eccentrics whose dubious mental health may render them unable to manage their own affairs. His interview with rich landowner Sir Owain Lancaster, whose sanity has been in question since a disastrous scientific adventure in the Amazon killed his family and colleagues, coincides with the disappearance of two young local girls. When the children are found slain, Lancaster claims that the same dark forces that devastated his family have followed him home. Sebastian Becker's search for answers brings him face to face with madmen and monsters, both imagined and real; confronting immense danger in his hunt for the truth, he explores murder, tragedy, and the tempestuous depths of his own mind.